CHAMPIONS OF ELONIA BOOK 1

# DIVIDE AND CONQUER

## CARMEN FOX

PRAISE FOR DIVIDE AND CONQUER

*"Urban Fantasy doesn't get better than DIVIDE & CONQUER. Action, excitement, and 2 kick-ass heroines to root for fill this rich, complex and dynamic world. Carmen Fox does not disappoint!"* ~ National & USA Today Bestselling author Anna J Stewart

*"This is a wonderful beginning to a new series."* ~ Paranormal Romance Guild

*"Fox does a wonderful job of capturing every gritty detail, and writing from a point that gets you amped up for these awesome characters."* ~ Thatentertains

*"I give this a 4.5 fang review."* ~ Paranormal Romance and Authors That Rock

*"This is a must-read book whether you like urban fantasy or not, and if you aren't sure about fantasy in general, it's likely that Fox will change your mind."* ~ Red City Review

*"If you're looking for an action-packed read with multifaceted, courageous characters and a little bit of romance, this is the book for you."* ~ Authors To Watch

*"Carmen Fox is the author to watch. Her debut novel DIVIDE AND CONQUER is a smart, exciting book with twists and turns that will keep your interest piqued."* ~Julie LaVoie, YA Author

*For Nana*
*WYWH*

# CHAPTER ONE



*"You never get a second chance to make a first impression. Not if they go down with the first punch."*

I'd barged right into a trap.

The whirling vortex of the Gate propelled me from sunny Elonia into an inky Seattle suburb. I skidded and found my footing in a puddle the size of Lake Devron. Heavy raindrops dripped into my eyes and pelted my leather jacket when a familiar prickle on my skin commanded my attention. Ripples of magic fired through the air from between two buildings across the road.

I'd have preferred to enter the city during the day, but travel between the realms was unpredictable. Channeling the vortex to open in Seattle rather than at any of the other natural destinations like, say, Alaska, took a great deal of skill as it was. At least the late hour meant the street was devoid of people. All the easier to spot the solid shapes shifting in the night.

Seven fuzzy blobs equaled seven Shades. Men or women, I couldn't tell. But no doubt each one eager to blast me into the afterlife. How had they known I'd be here?

The Gate whooshed shut, cutting off my retreat. Time to pull up my big girl panties. Not like I had a choice anyway.

Running into the Shades, the enemies of my people, had been a foregone conclusion. They had scouts all over the country, but I hadn't expected their company so soon. And yet these shapes, although blanketed in darkness, didn't seem like ordinary scouts. More like a welcome party.

Yet that was impossible. There was no way the Shades knew I was coming, because we'd taken great pains to keep the purpose of my mission a tight secret. Only a handful of people knew I was to take Lea, the "lost Elonian," from her world into mine. Still, whatever the Shades' plan demanded, whatever schemes their tiny brains concocted—as long as I was the Royal Champion of Elonia, leader of our army, it would be my duty, and indeed pleasure, to deny them success.

Their scurried movements told me something had them on edge. The night had obscured the Gate's mouth, but the vortex's roar could have alerted them. Shades were dangerous, conniving and downright evil, but not deaf.

The pungent aroma of salt water and garlic clams turned my already tense stomach. I skulked along the wall of a toy store. Maybe my hunched form would be more difficult to spot.

The Shades spread out and prowled vaguely toward me.

"There she is." The tallest of them jabbed a finger in my direction.

Poof went my plan to sneak away unseen. I picked up the pace. Unlike our magically challenged Kindred cousins asleep in their homes around us, Shades didn't rely on guns. They got their message across using their magic and brawn. As their nickname suggested, they drew strength from the darkness, which meant right now, the odds were against me.

Just the way I liked it.

As welcome as the workout might be, my mission came first.

If I got injured or killed, Lea would remain defenseless. She didn't know her powers yet, had no inkling of the future a prophecy had mapped out for her, or that without her and me, Elonia would fall. Soon. According to our sources among the Shades, their war preparations were running at full power once again.

Mission before fun. Always.

My quick three-sixties were fruitless, not to mention risky on the wet ground. I'd visited Seattle many times, but my boilerplate surroundings could be located anywhere. Three lanes stretched into the distance. Well-kept sidewalks ran along them, dotted by yellowing trees. But no alleys or side streets to offer a quick getaway.

The Shades weaved through a small cluster of parked cars and hustled into formation. The narrow brims on their distinct helmets shielded them against the rain. I had no time to envy them their protection because the burning stench of singed rubber signaled their trademark attack move: manipulating the shadows into a thick, billowing fog. In one surge, a dark plume trapped me in its choking stink, hampering my visibility.

I backtracked, still caught between my duty to stay alive long enough to find Lea and my desire to stand up to them like a woman. Through the dense cloud, two Shades raised their hands high. Their powers focused at their fingers into a shock of shimmering blackness. They jerked down their arms, and magic slammed into the ground. The earth shuddered and reformed in a tidal wave of broken concrete, charging toward me.

Car and house alarms erupted, kicking me into action. I broke into a sprint and followed the overhead cables that traced my only visible escape route. Curtains twitched in the homes on either side of me. A handful of nosy Kindreds opened their doors. Although the fog blocked their sight, it cloaked neither the noise nor the tremors that shook the land.

The seven Shades stuck to my combat boots like bloodhounds tracking the whiff of sausages. Who knew they could run that fast? I injected more speed into my strides. A bolt of energy soared above and struck the road in front of me. A hole opened up and widened into a pit, and from the moist earth rose the odor of rotting vegetation. I dipped low, pumped my arms, and exploded into the air. Knees tucked into my chest, I leaned forward and somersaulted across the void.

My feet skidded on the wet asphalt. *Slice it!* I teetered. Caught myself. Salvos of rocks and tarmac chipped away at my heels, cracking through the silence like gunshots. If the Shades dug that deep into their trove of tricks, they must be pissed.

Was it too early to activate my own brand of magic? Elonians relied not on darkness but the light for power, and without the sun to refuel me, the effort might consume my reserves too quickly. But there was safe, and then there was alive. Should my venture pay off, I'd be able to shake the Shades once and for all.

I squeezed a muscle at the base of my skull to tap into my powers, and a sizzle poured from that spot into my blood, heightening my senses. Just as easily, the incantation to call on the forces of nature flowed from memory.

In a flash, my nerve endings fired, and my power well connected to the elements. The air's molecules bounced off my skin like living, breathing entities. Focusing on the grassy edge between road and sidewalk, I wove the atmosphere into a thin mass dense enough to bear my weight. A parked car served as my springboard, and I catapulted off its hood toward the sky. An airstream caught me eight feet off the ground and cradled me in solid, invisible wings.

Now that I was airborne, the Shades would have their work cut out.

With my boots clamped tight by the thin sheet of atmosphere, I flew past lampposts and trees. The rain whipped my face and the wind tangled my hair, while the urge to laugh rose inside my chest. Despite my yearning for a quieter life, the thrill of the chase still quickened my pulse.

Up here, my visibility improved. In the distance, the night's black gave way to a navy blue, but the sky's transformation wasn't as fast as I'd hoped. I needed another edge over my clingy entourage. Find a place to slow them, or maybe lose them altogether. Shifting my weight, I turned right, away from the city lights.

The Shades' swells of magic echoed below me then ceased. No point in checking if they'd fallen back. My luck didn't swing that way. No, they'd probably decide to wait me out. Smart move, too. The lack of energy-giving sunlight would force me back to the ground. Already I felt the drain in my feet and hands.

My brother, the king, had warned me overconfidence was going to kill me one day. If he were here now, he'd shake his head at my miscalculation. Any fool knew not much of the early rising sun would reach between the houses. Slice it and double slice it. I'd hate to prove him right.

One last assignment, he'd said, and he'd release me from my oath. All I needed to do to earn my leave was return Lea to our fold, so she and I could stop the Shades from seizing power. Simple, right?

Maybe, selfishly, I was hoping she could take over from me one day, become the next champion. The job demanded the focus of someone less jaded, someone who actually craved the responsibility and the sacrifice it entailed.

But predictably, the Shades had nothing better to do than

thwart my plans. If they could kill me now, they would. If they discovered who I was after and why, Lea too would be dead. She was our ace, our secret weapon, and our last hope in averting disaster.

Did the Shades ever stop and think about *their* orders? About how this fragile peace between our nations could be a stepping stone to something wonderful, something lasting, rather than a brief recess to consider new strategies for maiming and butchering innocents?

To Balor with the Shades. I wouldn't botch my mission this close to the goal line.

Scraping the bottom of my energy reserves, I rose higher, up, up, up, until I hit my power's ceiling.

The alley a few yards to my left would make a perfect bottleneck. To conserve energy, I dropped height. Flying a few feet above the ground, I ducked scraggy branches and rocketed into the narrow path between two buildings.

The scaffold came out of nowhere. Tubes and boards spanned almost the entire width of the alley. Ladders and ropes blocked the spaces between them. A lump hurtled up my throat, halting my breath. Was I going to fit through the slim opening? In hindsight, the blueberry muffin I'd eaten before my departure might have been a mistake.

My focus narrowed on the passage separating the metal structure from the unconnected house wall. I commanded the air under my soles to steer me into the gap.

The wind swerved.

I didn't.

My body folded around one of the bars, like a towel slung over a clothesline. The collision drove the breath from my lungs. I slipped off the scaffold and smacked into the mud-covered ground. Even though my hard-wearing leathers protected my legs and elbows from the sharp stones, they didn't pad me against the impact itself. My head banged against my flat hand, the force jangling my brain. I spat out a few hairs that had found their way into my mouth, despite my tight ponytail.

One of the Shades yelled, probably a cry of victory.

Not if I could help it.

I clamped my teeth shut against the throbbing pain, scrambled up, and beat feet. By the end of the alley, the Shades had closed the distance to twenty yards. I was done playing the prey. Done running for my life. The role of predator suited me better. I backed against a lamppost and reached for my thirty-five-inch martial arts stick, a hanbo that had saved my butt more times than I cared to remember. Its magic coating had helped it survive the fall and made it more than a match for the Shades' knives.

"You've already lost." A Shade built like a rhino approached, his blade raised. "But death doesn't have to be painful."

*Suck it, slimeball.* "Why don't you bring your shady friends over here and meet my buddy, Mister Hanbo?" I adjusted my grip. "Don't be shy. He's real friendly."

The Shade lunged and jabbed his knife forward.

I grinned. A tap from my stick against his arm paralyzed his limb. He dropped his weapon and stepped back.

I kicked the second attacker in the stomach and nailed the third in the face with my elbow. Blood shot out of number three's nose and covered his brown leather tunic in red. Numbers four to seven gaped at the mess and backed off.

"Told ya." I twirled and whacked my hanbo against Three's jugular, sending him back a few feet.

But their blades kept coming. Twice they caught my sleeves, and without my leather uniform, either of those hits could have spelled my end. A film of sweat reduced the friction between my stick and my hand, weakening my grip. With the lamppost behind me, I swiped the hanbo at their legs, used my free arm to land blows to their faces where I could.

Seven against one had sounded like fun, but the reality was less amusing. Still, I kept up, parried their attacks, but my labored breathing told its own story. I was nearing the limits of my ability.

There! The skin on my neck twitched—and dawn arrived at last. I breathed in the sun's beams. Wrapped them around me. And made myself invisible.

I zoomed off at top speed. After this cranky welcome, I was done with this city. Just one thing to do now. Bag Lea and get her butt to Elonia, whether she wanted to or not.

# CHAPTER TWO



*LEA*

*"I'm not a nerd. At best I'll admit to being socially challenged."*

Monday morning, attired in my new business suit, I parked in front of the building that housed one of the largest scientific translation companies this side of the Atlantic. My first 'grown-up' job.

My cell phone jingled. "Hello?"

"Hi, Peanut. It's Mom."

"Hey, Mom. Have to keep this short. Isn't it the middle of the night in Germany?"

"Yes. I was about to go to bed when I heard about the earthquake in Seattle. Are you all right?"

The nice woman on the local morning news had mentioned *a seismic event*, but her reassuring smile had downplayed the severity, if my mother was right.

"Yeah, I'm fine. I didn't feel a thing." I adjusted my rear-view mirror and twirled my long hair to give its natural waves extra bounce today.

"Really?" The line crackled. "...road caved in. It sounded serious."

My gaze fell on the strip of neat grass that framed the

parking lot. An uneven row of bushes shielded it against the noise of traffic from the adjacent street.

"The earthquake was on the other side of town. Must have slept right through it." I gathered my bag and stepped out of the car.

My three-hour board game session had run late last night, but pre-work jitters gave me no choice. Nothing staved off stress like immersing myself brain-deep in strategic battles. The King's Armory, my go-to form of entertainment, also happened to be the only cooperative game I knew that could be played by just one person.

"Can I call you back tonight?" I locked the door with my key fob. "I need to go."

"Hang on. I wanted to wish you luck. And if the job doesn't work out—"

"Mom!" I'd have stomped my foot if she could have seen me. "Stop it."

"All I'm saying is that DESY's got a few exciting projects in the pipeline." Her voice vibrated with enthusiasm. "You could live with us and re-apply to university next year."

Typical Mom. Since Dad's cancer had come back, she'd been super clingy, and she knew how to tempt me. DESY, the German electron synchrotron, was high on my list of ideal employers.

"No more university." I snorted. "And not that I don't appreciate the nepotism, but moving back in with my folks at twenty-four is the ultimate admission of defeat."

"Very well," Mom said. "I only wanted to mention it in case you change your mind."

"How's Dad?"

"He's been asleep for a while now, but I'll let him know you asked." Her cheery voice totally failed the honesty test. "So, when do you start?"

"Now."

"In that case, I'd better let you go then. Knock 'em dead, kid."

Knocking them dead was part of my plan.

What my mother didn't understand was that I didn't pick scientific translations as my job on a whim. Mastering the intricacies of patent writing would make me hugely desirable to the DESYs of this world.

CERN, inventor of the touchscreen and, oh yeah, the fraking World Wide Web, had recently discovered an interest in filing patents, while MIT had been generating hard income from their patent portfolios for years. In any case, learning about intellectual property rights while coming into contact with the latest technology before it hit the market should give me an edge over other applicants. After all, every scientist worth his salt coveted positions at the world's leading research institutions.

Of course, every scientist worth his salt also had a PhD.

Okay, my plan wasn't perfect. If my parents had had it their way, I'd have slugged away at Caltech for another three or four years to get my doctorate, but I'd already missed out on so many things.

It took dedication, stubbornness and sacrifice, but I graduated in the top ten percentile, even though I was far from the smartest person there. Every single one of those wonderful people I met, the incredible professors with careers as illustrious as my parents', they were the real deal.

I lifted my chin, smoothed my suit, and opened the building's frosted glass doors. The polished floor exuded a biting smell of lemon, while far too bright, artificial light blasted onto my dark navy suit, making tiny particles on my sleeves flicker and flash. I gave the lady behind the desk my name and my most dazzling smile. She pointed at the seats and punched a phone number from a list of names. I sat and clamped my hands between my knees.

A few minutes later, a woman with sleek, long, strawberry-blond hair and perfect makeup approached. Her skirt was too short to be professional, although short enough to be *professional*.

"Hi, I'm Vicky." She shook my hand. "You're Lea?"

I nodded. Her open and friendly manner helped unknot my shoulders. How would she have reacted if she'd bumped into the nerd me down the street, dressed in my customary sloganed hoodie and worn sneakers? Good thing the fabric of my blouse was thick enough to hide all evidence of my lucky bra, a gray, shapeless construct that barely kept my breasts in check.

"You met Sasha, our personnel director, at the interview, right? Sasha asked me to show you around." She gestured toward the elevator. "Have you done any technical translations before?"

The door closed, and a motor began to whirr, pulling us upward. In the tight space, the sweet floral notes of Vicky's perfume spread into every corner.

"Not really." My tongue felt thick and lazy. I mentally kicked myself. Couldn't I come up with something more engaging? "But after living in German for a few years, my German's decent."

"You're from Pasadena, though, right?"

"No, I was born in Seattle, finished high school in Germany, studied in Germany and then Pasadena, and am now back in Seattle." I shrugged. "My parents moved a lot."

"How interesting." Vicky turned toward the mirror that made up one wall of the elevator and brushed a finger over one plucked eyebrow. "Military family?"

"No, they're scientists."

"Pasadena. That's Caltech, right? That's a good school."

Yes, and Voldemort was a little bit grumpy. Caltech was an extraordinary place, but also extraordinarily difficult. Many of my fellow students—just as smart as the rest of us—dropped out, and I didn't come out the other side unscathed either. Now, I was burned out. Done with learning. Done with missing out on life.

"Has Seattle changed since you were a kid?" she asked.

"Utterly and completely." I laughed. "The scruffy, rocky Seattle I remember from my childhood isn't the Seattle I see today. Streets that used to be deserted are teeming with life; tower blocks are taller than the eyes can see. Then those weird spheres… Total transformation."

My cheerful tone obscured a sense of melancholy, though, because, underneath the city's glitz and glamour, the drabness of poverty and a rising homeless population battled the bright graffiti of street artists struggling to make a living.

Vicky gave an indeterminate hum, either unimpressed or that much into her eyebrow. The elevator jerked, and the doors opened.

I followed my guide down a corridor, inspired by her poise. How much training went into her polished gait? Or did it come naturally? Such grace was out of reach for me, but at least I hadn't said anything too idiotic. So far.

Vicky's thorough orientation spun my head. Within an hour I knew when to go to lunch and where to find the washrooms. She made sure I could recite the basic regulations, explained potluck lunches, and helped me with insurance forms.

Finally, she herded me out of the conference room and past a series of offices. "The earthquake was scary. Some doomsday experts are already predicting many more on their way. Maybe you're used to them, having lived in California." She turned her head toward me. Her long hair whipped around, only to land in a perfect split over her shoulders, as if she'd intended it that way all along. "Maybe Mother Nature thought a quake or two would help you feel at home."

I grinned. "Mother Nature should have sent the sun."

"Amen to that." We stopped at a cookie-cutter office with a set of shelves, a desk with a computer, and a chair. "This one's yours."

My stenciled name in the glass pane next to the door made my heart swell. Definitely a step up from the nametag I got to wear at Starbucks.

She gestured. "It's not a large space, but feel free to make it your own."

"Thanks." The bare walls did cry out for a personal touch, but my poster of *Farscape's* Crichton in all his leather-clad glory would remain in its box at home. A landscape calendar would convey a more professional impression.

"If there are any problems, pop in to see me. I live two doors down that way." She pointed to the wall on her left. "How about at noon we lunch at the coffee shop around the corner, and I can give you the inside scoop on this place?"

I'd eaten, scarfed and inhaled food before, but I'd never *lunched.* "Sure. I'd like that."

"See you then." She left and closed the door behind her.

My computer account details were printed on a memo for my eyes only, and my new corporate life was but a password away. Instead, I sat on the chair and played with the hydraulics, lifting up and down. The soccer-ball-sized tangle in my stomach crushed my diaphragm. What the frak was I doing here? The Lea Danielses of this world shouldn't work Jane Average jobs.

But losing heart now was counterproductive. My plan was rock solid. Once I'd found a good research position without my parents' input and without a PhD, I'd work my way up and finally shine. Until then, I'd make the best of my new freedom.

After all, work only accounted for eight hours in the day. Add to that eight hours for sleep, and I'd have another eight for fun and adventure.

I hadn't been admitted to Caltech for being a dummy.

My cell phone beeped. I opened the text, and my heart gave a jig.

*"Feel like getting a drink next Thursday?"* Kieran's message read. *"How about the Orchid Lounge after work? Around six?"*

My heart instantly went into overdrive.

In preparation for my new job, I'd embarked on a weekend shopping spree, which left me more muddled than after watching an episode of Westworld. Did a coordinated blue suit look better than a casual combo of a white top with black slacks? Would a red jacket be too aggressive, or a gray blouse too mousy? The woman in the store wasn't blessed with patience, and I left dejected and without having taxed my credit card.

The board games café I'd passed earlier was already bursting with people, so I headed to a coffee shop instead. At first, Kieran was merely a guy who took the chair on the other side of my table, but within minutes, we got talking.

"I'm not up-to-date with women's fashion, so take my advice with a grain of salt," he said. "But the women in my office keep it casual-professional. Black pants and a white blouse. Muted colors, you know. Sometimes they spice it up with a colorful bag or a scarf. Does that help?"

It did. Thanks to him, I was now the proud owner of a long, stylish coat, several outfits suitable for work, and a bag large enough to make Mary Poppins jealous.

After I bought him a second cup of coffee as a thank you, I promised to message him so he'd know how his sartorial recommendations went down.

I hadn't expected him to contact *me*, though. It would be nice to get out of the house for once, hang out with someone—or was he asking me on a date? Unlikely. Sure, Kieran was awesome, but I hadn't gotten romantic vibes from him. He'd neither flirted with me nor touched me as if by accident. Our conversation hadn't produced butterflies in my belly either.

I jutted my chin forward and typed. *"I'd love to get a drink."*

After all, the whole raison d'être of my plan was to create new experiences, meet people and make connections.

Twenty seconds later, my cell pinged again. *"See you there."* Accompanied by a smiley.

A sizzle curled around my heart and gave it an encouraging squeeze. Letting out a happy sigh, I reclined in my chair and intertwined my hands behind my head. With step one of my plan taking shape, all systems were go.

# CHAPTER THREE



*"Let's save time and just assume I've already beaten you to a pulp.
Now, what can you tell me about your king's plans?"*

I frowned at the cell phone's small screen. How I hated that little gizmo. My brother's intense love for Kindred technology had filtered into our entire culture, from Elonian-made soap operas on TV down to disposable diapers. The perks of being king, I supposed.

My trust in Kindred technology died the day a television set slipped from my hands. The discharge of sparks could have sent the fairies into hiding. Just because phone signals traveled across the Divide didn't mean we had to use the slicing things.

*"Move northwest from your current position."*

Goody. *Another* possible location. Did the king ever get as sick of directing me to new spots in the city as I was of visiting them? Why would an Elonian choose to live in Seattle anyway? Lea might not know of her heritage, but surely she had to crave the light the way the rest of us did. I glanced around the university district to get my bearing. Even here, car fumes and grime filled every corner, making my stomach roil.

Without divination and prophecies, I wouldn't be in this

crummy situation. Despite being only twenty-nine years old, I'd be long retired, planting flowers in my garden and tending my chickens. Still, when the king challenged me to a side bet, I put my money on the oracles to track down Lea before Googlebook or any of his other Interwebsites did. Sadly, the oracles weren't on a clock. That, or they were having a bad month, because each of their recommendations to the king was a bust. The lost Elonian remained as elusive as the alchemists' recipes for turning sand into gold.

Silly me. Here I'd thought finding her would be the *easy* stage of my mission. Stopping the Shade king's grab for total dominion was supposed to be the tough part.

But I had faith. Sooner or later, the oracles *had* to get the location right. Through skill, luck, or by process of elimination.

With my invisibility shield wrapped around me, I followed the king's directions and headed northwest to my new hot zone, an area roughly two square miles in size. A building at the far end of the street overlooked its neighbors and made the perfect base camp. Once perched on the sloping rooftop, I pulled in my knees and tilted my face up. My invisibility shield fell, and the world around me exploded in a cacophony of bright colors. Briny air filled my lungs and cleared away the car fumes that had built up in them over the days. Ray by ray, the sunlight replenished my power well.

Saturated with energy, I tasked the air with its challenge. To search for one name among the thousands of voices. As I'd done from various spots all over the city, I whispered the word into the sky, mindful to enunciate. "Lee-ah." Then I shut my eyes and listened.

A flutter to my right broke my concentration. The flap of a seagull's wing? Or an early sign of danger? Stealth was second nature in my job, but being tall occasionally caused me to stick out. My gaze scooted to the rooftops of the adjacent buildings.

I squinted and expelled a long puff of air. A plastic bag. Nothing.

Warriors walked a fine line between watchfulness and paranoia. For now, my common sense insisted I was safe. Between dawn and dusk, most Shades caught up on their sleep. Only their scouts braved the sunlight, and a single scout posed no challenge to me.

I rolled my shoulders to release the stiffness and focused again. A moment later, the wind offered a promising wisp of conversation from maybe a mile away.

"Morning, Lea," a man said, his tone rough and deep. "Don't fall in, girl."

"You're funny, Earl."

I perked up. The name Lea wasn't a rare one, so I checked the vicinity of the man's voice for an Elonian's magical signature. The gust of air I'd sent out for this purpose returned with the telltale flutter against my skin. Only a strong presence of magic at the other end had this effect on the atmosphere.

Instantly, my diaphragm expanded. On my command, the wind locked on the voices' place of origin.

I scrambled across the roof and leaped off the eaves into the air. In a fraction of a second, a cloud formed in my mind. I tied my magic around the image. Made the connection. The cloud contracted into a solid patch, the size of a large frying pan. The wind cushion slowed my fall until my feet touched the ground. A flick of my wrist released another burst of energy, and the atmosphere behind me solidified to nudge me forward. Bearing left, I came to a wide road, six lanes separated by a median strip. On the opposite side, a path led me into a park.

Finally, the first step of my mission, to find the lost Elonian, was nearly over. The prophecy gave no time frame, but with the Shades preparing for war, haste trumped caution.

I inhaled the clean and fresh air. An unsullied spot like this was a rarity in the city. The wall of air pushed me toward the owner of the voice that had uttered Lea's name. He was a short black man in his fifties with white tufts of hair sticking out underneath a jaunty fedora. He strolled along the wide path, cooing at pigeons between sips from his cardboard coffee cup.

He looked up, lifted his hat and gave a nod.

I shot him a grin and broke into a light sprint.

Early morning dew clung to the lawn. The soft ground padded my steps, without being so muddy I'd slip. I blew into my hands to warm them and glanced around for a sign of Lea. On either side of me stretched wide expanses of lawn, sparsely punctuated by yellow and red leaves. Through the row of trees ahead, the dark water of a lake glistened like ice-tipped fur. A figure, dressed in running pants and a navy down jacket, jogged alongside the lake, her strides determined rather than graceful.

Lea. Her luster—the glowing, all-body aura that marked her as an Elonian—danced around her shape in pulsing waves.

I picked up speed and circled around the asphalt trail to where the tightly woven branches of bushes and trees would obstruct me from her view. Here, I sat on the hard ground and waited, like an ordinary Kindred in need of a helping hand. After all, this was what Kindreds did best—rely on others rather than grit their teeth and make it on their own.

The bright light of Lea's luster entered my field of vision first. Seconds later, Lea herself jogged into sight. I gripped my calf as if in pain.

Her eyes widened, and she came to a halt, puffing hard for air. "Are you all right?"

She'd scraped her hair back into a ponytail of auburn curls. Sweat plastered loose wisps around her ears to her skin. Although she was shorter and curvier than most Elonians, she appeared to be healthy enough. Or tried to be.

I scrunched up my face and pointed at my calf. "Not really. I hurt my leg."

"Oh." She scanned the park.

The girl needed a push. Good thing I'd practiced the right facial expression to evoke empathy and the correct tone to sound meek.

I looked up at her from under my eyelids and lowered my voice. "Could you help me up?"

She approached and held out an arm. Her gaze caught on something over my shoulder. "What's that? A stick?"

My bad. If I'd concealed my weapon with a stronger spell, I wouldn't have to improvise. "It's a hanbo. I was on my way to martial arts practice."

She heaved me up with both hands.

I stood on my left foot and tested my 'injured' calf. "Ouch."

"Doesn't sound good."

"It probably needs ice." I added a grunt for emphasis.

"Rice," she said.

I interrupted my acting performance to frown at her. "Not rice. Ice."

"Rest, ice, compression, elevation." She counted on her fingers. "RICE. I saw it on TV."

What a strange girl. Influenced by years of working in solitude, I'd made no secret of my distaste about collaborating with another person, but she was something else entirely.

"I'd give it a try, but I'm not sure I'll make it home." My voice contained just the right amount of sheepishness for my purpose. "Not on this leg."

Once again, a stark frown clouded her face. "Should I call an ambulance? I have a phone." She held up the small purse dangling from her wrist.

"I don't have insurance." I tried to look contrite.

"Well, do you want me to call *anyone*?"

"Not really. I'm new to the city, and I haven't met anyone yet."

Lea nodded. "It takes a while, doesn't it? I've lived here for about a month now and still have the same problem. Hey, if you can make it back to my place, I'll give you a ride home. It's not far." She pointed to her left.

"That would be great. Thank you."

"Okay, then, it's a date. Um, that would be weird. Definitely not a date." Her expression flickered from pained to confused before she gave an almost imperceptible shrug. "Here, let me help you." She slung my arm around her neck.

I limped alongside her and suppressed my unease at the closeness as well as my smugness at how smoothly events had unfolded. At the same time, an uncomfortable truth began to dawn on me. Lea might be Elonian, but she'd been raised as an emotion-riddled Kindred. To gain her trust might require an excursion into the unknown. Slice it. No one had prepared me for sharing my feelings with a stranger.

Lea's body radiated heat against my side, giving off a citrusy note, probably from her deodorant, with a dollop of perspiration. The slight pong reassured me. To take on the Shades, she had to be ready to get stuck in, work hard, and run like her life depended on it, not jog on dainty feet because it was fashionable.

"I'm Lea, by the way," she said.

"Nieve."

She led me out the park, along an uneven sidewalk, past homes constructed from the same blueprint. "So, Nieve's a pretty name."

"My mother felt the same way."

She chuckled. "What do you do, job-wise?"

This girl was a talker. Once again, I dipped into my chest of prepared answers. "I'm a coach."

"Like, for sports?"

"Yes. All-body fitness and martial arts."

"Cool. I'm a translator, at least until I find a job in research." Her hand dug into my waist, half carrying, half dragging me.

We stopped at a two-story brick house with an attached garage. On the gravel driveway, a burnt-orange car reflected the sun's beams into a cloudless sky.

Cars and I didn't mix. The first time I entered this realm, I was on a training mission with the king. One of these four-wheeled contraptions proved too tempting for him to resist, and we learned the painful way driving wasn't a skill one picked up from watching Kindred television. Another reason to state my business pronto, before Lea turned the car ride she'd offered into a hellish reality.

She marched us up the walkway. Sweat glistened on her forehead, yet her grasp of me hadn't weakened.

"This is it. I'll get the car keys." Her glance bounced between her front door and me. She jutted her chin. "Maybe you should come in and rest for a minute."

Any other day in the future, this trusting naivety of hers might get her killed. Right now, her invitation saved me from having to spin more of my made-up story. Surrounded by her own walls, she'd be more inclined to listen without freaking out.

I hoped.

The house smelled of fresh paint and solvent. We followed the cream-colored corridor into a living room, furnished in blacks, reds, and oranges. In a large cage between a TV and a cardboard box labeled 'stuff,' a guinea pig nibbled on its greens.

"His name's Feynman. I call him Feynie for short." Lea snorted. "Now that I think of it, it sounds like a combo of fanny and heinie, huh?" She cracked a crooked smile.

Not sure what reaction she'd been hoping to elicit, I kept my face blank. "Could I get a glass of water?"

"Sure. Or I can make us a cup of coffee. You could probably do with a caffeine hit, right?"

I hated coffee. "Sounds great."

She towed me into the sleek kitchen. White cabinets and a white tile floor softened the harsh angles of the black countertops, and a white plastic sheet spanned the table. A Dali-esque melting clock ticked persistently, an unnerving reminder of my tight schedule. After depositing me on a black and chrome chair, she passed me a bag of peas from her freezer. I crunched the contents in my hand, letting the cold bite into my skin. She lifted my foot onto another chair, careful not to hurt me.

Maybe my deception took things too far. The last thing I wanted was to start our relationship with broken trust. Turning two people into partners-in-war wasn't easy under the best circumstances. The burden of fusing us together would be mine. And while she was the one who was ignorant of the situation, I'd been wading in unknown waters for weeks myself. Who was this Lea? How would she—and I—avert Elonia's destruction?

Lea picked up a coffee pot and opened the faucet. "When did you move to Seattle?"

Water poured noisily into the pot.

"I… Oh, slice it." Given the stakes, I'd had no choice but to lie to her, but it was time to repair the damage.

"Slice what?" she asked.

"No, it means 'to hell with it.'"

"To hell with what? I don't…" Lea turned off the faucet. "Maybe you didn't catch that. I asked when you moved to Seattle?"

"I didn't." I pressed my two rows of teeth together and sucked in air. "I haven't been entirely honest. I went to the park specifically to find you."

Lea's eyes widened. "What?"

"I'm here because…" I tugged on my earlobe. "Elonia needs your help."

"Who's Elonia?"

"Not a person. It's a place." A deep breath. "A world where magic exists."

Her shoulders tensed. "Magic? You mean David Blaine style?"

"No. Like flying. Invisibility. A feeling you get when your body connects to the elements, and the power to shape this feeling into something useful." I gave a nod. "Real magic."

"Real…" Her gaze darted through the kitchen, no doubt considering her fight-or-flight options. "Real magic? Like, elemental magic? Bone magic? Voodoo?"

I kept my face blank. "We just call it 'magic.'"

"Lame." She raised her brows. Tiny grooves appeared on her forehead. "Your ankle's not injured, is it?"

"A necessary lie." I shrugged off my jacket and exposed the tiny tattoo in the shape of a chandelier on my shoulder. "Look. You have one just like it, right?"

Her hand came to rest on her collarbone. Even though she didn't look in the least reassured, a hint of uncertainty crept into her expression. "Yes. No. I mean…"

I zipped up my jacket and made myself small in the chair. Anything to appear more harmless than I was. "My world is home to two nations: the Shades and the Elonians. I…" I patted my chest. "…am Elonian. So are you."

Lea stared as if I'd spoken a subdialect of the Old Language. "Uh huh." Her fingers slid over the countertop and curled around a knife.

"I'm serious. Hang on to the silverware if you like, but it's important you listen. I'm what's called the royal champion.

See?" I gripped my necklace's champion pendant bearing the same chandelier-type symbol and lifted it for her to see.

She blinked but didn't lean forward to take a closer look. Instead, she hugged the knife to her chest, the blunt side facing in my direction. If she couldn't even correctly hold a weapon, what chance did she have of helping me save Elonia?

"Your realm and ours are kept apart by a spell that's called the Divide." I let go of my pendant and anchored my feet around the chair's legs. "The Shade king, Galleo, wants to destroy the Divide and conquer your world. If our information is correct, we don't have much time before he strikes."

"What's that got to do with me?"

"Your birth mother was renowned for being an extremely skilled fighter." I peered up to check her reaction. "You do know you were adopted, right?"

Her eyelids fluttered.

Slice it. Maybe I should have eased her into that revelation.

"Yeah." She inhaled sharply. "I know."

"Good. We hope you have inherited her abilities."

Why else would the prophecy have singled her out? If I, the royal champion, wasn't enough to wreck the Shades' plans, my partner would have to be one hell of a warrior in her own right.

Lea shook her head, a choppy motion as if she couldn't control it. "Come on. Magic? Am I supposed to believe all that?"

"What if I proved magic is real?" I pushed back the chair.

She jumped.

"I'm not going to hurt you." Keeping my hands in plain sight, I inched around the table where I had more space.

Doe-eyed, she tracked my movements but didn't speak.

I concentrated on the molecules around me. The use of air magic indoors wasn't without its problems, but I still built an air sheet that would hold my weight. I stepped onto it and rose until my hands touched the ceiling.

"How are you doing that?" Her tone was breathy. For the first time since she'd picked up the knife, her arm dropped.

"Air magic is inherent to Elonians." I lowered myself onto the floor. "Including you. It's one of the things I want to teach you."

A crack of a smile appeared on her face. "Are you saying I can do that too?"

"Yes." I sat back on the chair. "But I'm not done. Your life is in danger. The Shades may be aware of your existence. That means they'll hunt you. And try to kill you."

"Kill me?" Lea's face transitioned from pale to ashen. "Why? And who are the Shades?"

"I told you. The Shade King wants to seize control of your world. If he thinks you're going to stop him, his people will come looking for you. I assume you see now why I can't take no for an answer."

She raised the knife back to her chest again. "Well, even if any of this were true—which I'm not saying it is—I'm certain you have the wrong person. I've never fought anyone." Her eyes were dinner-plate wide, her skin and lips white. "Let's pretend you never came here. And as long as you won't tell the Shade king you found me, I'll be fine. Right?"

Her demand would have carried more punch if, instead of using her free hand, she'd used the knife to gesture. "Lea, listen."

"No, you listen. I'll call the police." The pitch of her voice fell. "I'll do it." She took a step toward the living room.

I shot up from my chair and blocked her way. "Haven't you been paying attention? I'll give you three, maybe four days before the Shades find you. Their scouts are everywhere. Pushing me away isn't going to make you any safer. Quite the opposite."

Her frame shrunk, and her lips quivered. "No, I don't believe you."

This tactic was getting me nowhere. As vital as it was to get Lea to Elonia, to get her safe, I wasn't without a heart either. A world-changing surprise might take a few hours to digest. If I watched over her, I could buy her a day to recover. "Okay, I'll go. I'll go."

She mumbled something unintelligible.

"Here." I scribbled my phone number on the small blackboard attached to her wall. "For when you change your mind." Putting on a relaxed smile, I marched toward the door.

She followed at what she probably thought was a safe distance.

At the end of the hall, I lingered. "The longer you refuse to accept your part in this, the more likely it is the Shades will find you. Whatever you do, don't go out at night."

I stepped into the cold. The door slammed shut behind me.

# CHAPTER FOUR



*"I don't suffer from insanity. Or so the Martian overlords that live in
my underwear drawer assure me."*

After my encounter with Nieve, it had taken a full
breakfast and latte at Coffee Diem to stop me from
acting like a hysteric hummingbird. The delicious
cinnamon scents of chai, mixed with the bitter notes of coffee,
acted like a comforting blanket. My mental cool-down didn't
come too soon. If I'd driven my car this morning, a pileup
would have been inevitable.

Why had I invited Nieve into my house? Who cared if she
was one of the prettiest women I'd ever met? She was also one
of the nuttiest. I should have twigged from the moment I
noticed the stick on her back. Hell, I was all for making friends,
but sanity was such a low bar to set, I never expected I'd meet
someone who couldn't clear it.

She'd sounded American, although her accent was hard to
place. As to her appearance—who the hell had white eyelashes?
She looked like she'd just stepped out of a blizzard. Either she
was from one of the Southern states, or her white-blond hair
and Beyoncé-inspired tan were the results of time-consuming

beauty treatments. Weird, because from the way she acted and spoke, she hadn't struck me as an overpreened doll.

I ripped open the building's glass doors, which earned me a warning glance from Ms. Beeblebrox, as I'd named the receptionist in my head. Efficient like a person with three arms, two heads that saw every transgression, and an ego the size of Mount Fuji.

I rushed into my office and placed my bag on my desk.

Vicky caught the door before it fell shut.

"You're late." She squeezed between the two shelving units and propped herself against the whitewashed wall. "Are you all right?"

I shrugged off my jacket. "Car trouble. I had to cab it." My lie sounded thin and tinny in the small room. I slumped into my chair and booted up the computer.

"I hate when that happens. Any plans for the weekend?" She gave me one of those exaggerated winks that could squeeze the juice from lemons. "We could hit the town again on Saturday if you want. See if we can expand your circle of friends."

"That would be great." I busied myself arranging my stapler, hand cream, and stress ball in a neat line. "By the way, I'm meeting a friend tonight."

"Good for you. Anyone I know?"

Despite her model-perfect looks and professional attire, I had Vicky pegged as the office gossip from day one. Owing to her incisive questions, and aided by my pathological need to overshare, it had taken her less than a week to wheedle my entire personal history out of me. She'd still invited me to meet up with her and her friends.

"No one we work with." I smiled. "Just a guy I met. I never thought he'd get in touch."

"I wouldn't give a stranger my real number. You never know

what weirdos are out there. But when you're single, you don't have a choice, do you?"

"Oh, it's not a date." My computer pinged, preventing me from arguing the point.

"Guess that's my cue," she said. "Besides, the project manager's already on my case. That's the thing about this place. Someone's always hassling you." She breezed out of my office.

The door clicked shut behind her, and I caught her casual goodbye wave through the glass panel. At least she hadn't suggested to make me over again. Sure, finding a guy to date would be neat, but these things had to be approached scientifically. Besides, today I welcomed normal company. Chatting about stuff other than magic and Shades on a rampage was so underrated.

I checked the time. After nine o'clock. Vicky wasn't the only one with a full workload. My next translation lay topmost in my in-tray. With a quiet sigh, I gave the title a read.

But Nieve's obnoxious blue eyes didn't leave me alone. They'd looked so sincere when she spun her crackpot tale. Her words had connected to a secret hunger in me. True, I was long past the age where I believed I'd be plucked from obscurity to fulfill a great destiny and save the world, but it would be nice if something I did mattered.

I rubbed my temples. It would, if I exercised patience and followed the plan. Right now, I was a scientist whose only experience with fighting was watching Bruce Lee marathons. Five years down the line, though, I'd be smashing particles into each other and finding new ones in the process.

For the twentieth time today, I thrust Nieve out of my mind.

Like the terminator, she kept coming back.

# CHAPTER FIVE



*"The difference between what we call destiny and plain misfortune isn't always clear. Let's just say, if other people laugh at you, Lady Luck wasn't on your side."*

Disaster struck around nightfall.

After our unsuccessful first meet, I trailed Lea to work. On a roof on the other side of the street, I sat watch, invisible.

She emerged from the building at five thirty in the evening. The sun no longer cast shadows on the ground, and the temperatures had dropped. Lea wore a denim jacket over a white shirt, with black slacks that brushed the ground. She hopped into a cab that drove not to her house, but into the city. Stupid girl. Hadn't she paid any attention to my warnings?

Riding the thermals ten feet off the ground, I followed her past large department stores and small boutiques. With every yard, the buildings grew shinier, more impressive.

The taxi stopped on the other side of town. Lea popped into a store that hadn't yet closed for the day. I remained outside and studied the Kindreds rushing to and fro. As soon as my mission was over, my life would be more than just the mindless buzzing of worker bees like these. Maybe I'd buy a house, become an artist, and take up gardening.

Even though the king's promise kept me going for now, retirement couldn't come soon enough. Once Lea had honed her skills, and once we'd fulfilled our part in the prophecy to save Elonia, I'd be of no more use to my country anyway. Maybe my subsiding hunger for battle was the reason the prophecy had decided I needed help in the first place.

Lea came out of the shop.

Still invisible, I peeled off the wall and stayed behind her, zigzagging my way through the passers-by.

From further up the street, thick dark shadows rolled toward us like a bank of fog. My pulse picked up. Within moments, the cloud fell over my shoulders and crept into my nose and ears. I'd done battle in this fog many times, knew its noxious piss-and-skunk smell and its sticky, oily feel as certainly as I knew the taste and texture of ripe strawberries. These were the shadows conjured by Shades to conceal themselves and their prey from curious eyes. Just as they'd done when they'd welcomed me to Seattle.

The *how* was a more difficult question. Daylight still clung to some corners of the sky, but the Shades' greatest powers lay dormant until dark. At least I'd *thought* they did.

Was this an ambush meant for me, or was this confirmation that the Shade king knew about Lea and her importance to us?

Up and down the street, Kindreds stopped and gave each other reassuring smiles or conjectured about a fire in the neighborhood, probably triggered by the fog's peculiar smoky tang. Others picked up their pace, a hand in front of their mouths to prevent the dense mist from entering their airways.

A bald man slipped in behind Lea, his broad back blocking my view. A group of teenagers crowded around him. Guided solely by Lea's seven-foot white-yellow luster, I elbowed my way through the thinning crowd. Only one thing mattered. I mustn't lose her.

The fog tightened and extinguished her glow.

*Screw my cover.*

"Lea!" I hopped and threw myself forward. My hanbo caught on a woman's handbag, interrupting my advance. I tore myself free, forced a mother and child apart, and forged ahead.

But Lea's figure didn't re-emerge.

Blanking out the tightening of my stomach, I searched for her bouncy curls or her denim jacket, even rose into the air for a bird's eye outlook, but failed to locate her through the haze. Visibility was too bad. If I couldn't see my own feet, how was I supposed to spot her?

Above me, the darkness swallowed the last rays of the sun. Night fell early today, and with it, my ability to maintain invisibility shrunk.

Chances were, I'd misread the situation. If the Shades had singled out Lea or me as dangerous, why wouldn't they wait the ten minutes until nightfall, when they were at peak power?

More likely, the Shade who'd produced the fog was a scout prowling the city. He'd spotted Lea's luster, thought she was a random Elonian in the Kindred world, and decided to play a trick on her. Scare her. Let her know he knew she was there.

Maybe my disaster could become a blessing. Scouts were low-level warriors and easy to overpower. If I stopped this one from reporting Lea's whereabouts to his friends, she'd be safe, and I'd get a chance to interrogate him. If luck was on my side, he'd divulge the Shades' true plans.

I called on the wind to pinpoint the magic's source. The atmosphere around me thickened then disintegrated, with tendrils of clear air shooting out through the fog. My search didn't last long. A single flutter, indicative of a single, magical presence, came from an alley across the street.

My fighting stick was the only offensive weapon I possessed, but, one-on-one, it was all I needed. I positioned myself at the entrance of the fog-filled path and drew my hanbo. "Come out, Shade."

A shuffling noise. "So you can kill me?" His tone was an odd mix of mockery and tension.

Deep inside the alley, the fog pooled and added cover for the coward who hid in its depth. The urine smell coming at me from the sides stopped me from edging further in. For now.

Spine straight, shoulders back, I built myself up to block his path from the alley to the main road. "You've violated our treaty and spun your shadows around an Elonian."

"Your treaty doesn't concern me, Spark."

My stomach roiled at the familiarity in his tone. My skin itched just from having to be near the enemy. More than that, I hated the word 'spark.' Elonians drew energy from light, which had earned us the moniker, but 'spark' implied something fleeting, something the Shades would eventually outlive.

"As part of the truce between our countries, King Galleo has declared that none of his shall harm an Elonian." I craned my neck, but the Shade continued to elude me. "Do you wish to dishonor your king's promise?"

A muffled laugh chased goosebumps down my back. Not evil as such, more a sound of resignation. "My king's promise is not my concern either. Let's not mention the fact that I didn't harm her. In any case, I believe the treaty doesn't apply to the Kindred realm."

At least I had confirmation. The fog show he'd put on had been meant for Lea. "Give me your word that you will not bother her or me again, and I will spare you."

"A generous offer." He gave a loud sigh. "I will consider your proposition."

The fog dissipated into the night air, save for his small

pocket at the back of the alley. I exhaled, but my stomach refused to settle.

"It wasn't a proposition, but a demand." I pitched my tone at the right level of authority.

"How about we talk for a while first?" The Shade coughed. "Exchange information?"

Lea might be on her way home now, safe and sound. Besides, the opportunist in me sensed this guy was worth investigating. He might have vital intelligence. "What information might you have that would interest me?"

"Oh, maybe proof that not every Spark is as loyal to your crown as you think."

His accusation punched me in the gut. "You lie."

"Suit yourself. But how do you suppose I knew about Lea?"

The Shade knew her name. That alone lent credence to his claim. My whole mission was suddenly in jeopardy, not to mention Lea's safety. How much did he know? More importantly, how much did the Shade king know? There was no way to tell. If there was a traitor in our midst, they could have shared all our secrets.

I took another daring step into the alley. "Assuming I believe you, what do you want in return?"

"I want to know more about the Elonian I let go, of course."

Did a shadow just move or had I imagined it? I clattered my hanbo against a building's wall, past a trashcan, my stomach revolting from the alley's stink. "What do *you* know about her?"

"She's important, and definitely more than she seems."

The racket I'd made didn't flush him out of hiding. Damn him. "*More* in what way?"

"She's special. Almost unique. The same could be said about you, Nieve."

"You seem well informed for a scout."

There was that quiet chuckle again. "I do, don't I?"

I relaxed my grip on the hanbo without relaxing my guard. "What's your name, Shade?"

"Yeah, that's a question I'd rather not answer."

I bit my lip. He was playing a game, and I didn't know the rules. "Tell me this, then. Why did you let her go? You could have called your friends and waylaid her in the dark."

"Seattle is a small place. She's unaware of her situation and shows a tremendous lack of caution." The confidence in his tone grew. "Finding her isn't hard. *You're* the elusive one. Talking to you is a great honor."

Flattery rolled off my back like my enemy's blood. "I'm not all that interesting."

"Come now, Nieve. We both know that's a lie. Look at yourself. You're strong."

I frowned. A sizeable bounty on my head was nothing new. "I'm tough to kill."

"I didn't mean that. For all the death you've seen and caused, you're out here, still doing your country's bidding." He gave a short laugh. "War eats your soul, and you've seen more than most. How you're not lying under a bed, curled up, and shaking, is remarkable. A sign of true strength."

I lifted my head and swallowed hard. The voice didn't belong to a Scout, but to a warrior. "You shouldn't jump to conclusions."

In this dirty alley so far from any battlefield, I might have run into my first Shade with a conscience. A Shade who didn't glorify murder. Maybe a Shade who'd suffered the same nightmares.

I advanced, despite the stink, despite the darkness. "Did you fight? Did you—"

"Kill?" For a second, only his breathing sounded. "Of course I did. They say it gets easier, you know. That killing gets easier. The first lie of war."

Was his face showing sorrow? Were his fists clenched like mine? "The first lie of many."

"Then you know. I thought you might." A clank came from his location, as if he'd struck something metal. "Maybe we're alike, you and I."

I glanced over my shoulder to ensure we were still alone. Out on the main road, people strolled as if the fog had never happened.

But the fog did happen. Because the guy I was talking to was a Shade. Fog was their weapon. Deceit their trade. And this conversation was probably just a distraction, or an attempt to mess with my head. A sophisticated tactic for a Shade, and highly effective.

"You and I, alike?" I scoffed. "Hardly. You Shades have more in common with traitorous gargoyles than with those of us who still honor the ways of the Old Ones."

He fell silent. My comment must have hit a nerve.

The insult had been a mistake. His words had pulled me out of kilter, and I'd lashed out when I should have kept him talking. Any information could help me discover what the Shades planned to do with Lea. Kill her to ensure she didn't side with us? Lure her to their cause instead? This man might have the answers.

This man, who was bold enough to deny his king's authority.

"Are you still there?" I checked the area, even dared take a few more steps into the darkness.

"You should go." He sounded hurried. "My kinsmen are on their way, and they aren't as friendly as me."

I sent the wind and almost immediately received confirmation. Seven sources of magic headed our way.

Why didn't he want me dead or captured? He knew my reputation, sure, but Shades typically didn't shirk battle. Then again, there was nothing typical about *this* Shade.

"Will we continue this conversation?" I holstered my hanbo. "I still have questions."

He laughed. "You're lucky to have cajoled more information out of me than I out of you, but yes, one day soon we'll meet again. Until then, take care of yourself."

I backed out of the alley, without the haste I should have shown. This Shade, whoever he was, was supposed to be a monster, but he'd sounded like a soldier. Tired. Disillusioned. Had all that been an act? If so, he deserved a trophy.

Once back on the street, I glanced up the road to where I'd last seen Lea. If the Shades were on to her and to our plan, she was out of time. I lowered my head and rushed away from the stranger who'd given me so much food for thought.

# CHAPTER SIX



*"Dating in the twenty-first century is less about buying flowers and more about hoping your Internet connection doesn't let you down."*

By the time I'd extricated myself from work, it was too late to stop off at home to pick up my car. Besides, driving would only interfere with my plan of drinking wine-flavored courage. Since neither my prim, professional blouse nor my denim jacket screamed *woman about town*, I undid the top two buttons and swapped my librarian pink lipstick for a vixen red I picked up on the way. With any luck, no one would notice the extra pounds my new jogging regime had so far failed to shift.

Against all odds, I got to the Orchid Lounge at six sharp. An upbeat tune blasted from the speakers, and although the air-conditioning blew a soft breeze through its vents, I was warm enough to take off my jacket and showcase the V of my top. The typical bar smell, like rum mixed with musky aftershave, spun my head. I zigzagged around occupied chairs and black tables, squinting against the bright spotlights recessed into the wooden floor.

Kieran stood by the mirror-framed bar. His brown hair was

just a shade darker than mine, and he'd let it grow into a day-old beard. Despite the facial hair, he wasn't edgy enough and too pretty for me to be attracted, but the woman three seats down from him didn't share my opinion. She eyed him as if each bat of her lids removed another of his items of clothing. The poor guy was oblivious.

As I approached, he glanced up from his phone. His chin lifted, his posture straightened, and finally he slid his cell into his pocket. His admirer misunderstood and gifted me a toxic stare.

"Hi." I smiled at him, letting my vixen red lips rile her that little bit more.

"I'm so glad you came." He held out both hands and planted a kiss on my cheek.

With his palm pressed against my back, he guided me to my seat. An intimate gesture for a non-date. Hell, why did social situations not come with labels attached?

"I can't stay long, unfortunately." I climbed onto the tall stool with what little elegance its smooth, frictionless surface allowed and placed my large handbag on my lap. "Maybe an hour?"

A total lie, but until I was certain of his intentions, a fail-safe was the smart play. The question was, would Vicky applaud my caution or chastise me for it tomorrow?

"Okay. No problem." Once he'd ordered a chardonnay for me, he turned on his chair with a roguish look. "How was work?"

If he'd been after more than company, he'd have shown disappointment, for sure. Instead, his relaxed posture and casual tone hinted at a purely platonic meaning.

I picked up the glass, relying on the fruity dryness for a clever answer. "Let's..." *Voice too rough. Cough and try again.* "Let's say my day's improving." A solid start to the friendly banter. I scored my forward opening with an eight out of ten. "How about you? You said you were in advertising, right?"

"Yeah. I gotta say, my day wasn't any better. First thing in the morning, they roped me into a long meeting to brainstorm innovative ways to market cars." He stuck out his tongue as if to get rid of a bothersome taste. "I should have skipped it. Ruffled some feathers. It's not a good idea to be irreplaceable, you know."

"Isn't it?"

"Think about it. If you can't be replaced, you'll never get promoted."

I chuckled. "I wouldn't risk my job on the off-chance of a promotion in a backward-thinking scheme, but I like the way your brain works."

A tinge of red flecked his cheeks, and he scratched a faded scar that was hiding near the base of his neck. "You enjoy your work then?"

My shoulders dropped as I briefly shifted my gaze to the back of the room, where framed retro posters added to the Orchard Lounge's sophisticated atmosphere. "It's okay."

"Just okay?" His eyebrows shot up. "You said you went to Caltech, right? That's a good university. You studied..."

"Physics. Well, first, I studied Math in Germany. Following my parents' urging, I then applied to Caltech to get my Bachelors in Physics, to tread in their footsteps, as it were."

"Tough gig?"

"Yeah, and not just in terms of the work. As relaxed an environment as Caltech is, it isn't what you'd call a social hub, and coming in as an older student didn't help me integrate with the younger ones either."

"Yes, you're positively geriatric." He have a half=grin. "Anyway. With such a background, you could have picked any job you liked."

"Ah, you're confusing knowledge with job skills. I have none, but I do have a plan."

"Okay." He gestured with his drink for encouragement. "I'm all ears."

I took another sip of my wine. "I'm going to work as a translator for a year, during which I learn about the patent process while keeping abreast of scientific developments and gaining a better insight into related fields."

"Let's call that phase one." He gave an encouraging nod. "What's phase two?"

"Armed with my new experiences and skills, I apply for research positions at the best places. From the Large Hadron Collider in Switzerland to the Jet Propulsion Lab in Pasadena."

"I see you're aiming high."

I crossed my legs at my ankles and sighed. "Maybe I'm aiming *too* high. I got a good degree, excellent references. But I'm not an idiot. Of course, a PhD would make one of those jobs a slam dunk. It's just, I'm tired of giving life a miss, you know?"

He placed a comforting hand on my arm. "I didn't say you're aiming *too* high. It's a good plan."

I shook my head and laughed. "Maybe we shouldn't call it a plan. Sounds too grand for the series of hopes and dreams I've attached to it."

"Nah, I get it. I do. Since I was little, my father had my future written in stone, and nothing was going to derail it. Girlfriends, socializing, hell, just catching a movie once in a while, that was for other people."

"What did your father want you to become?"

"He hoped for a career in the military." He waved me off then picked up his drink and took a deep swig. "Does that sound remotely like something I'd want to do?"

"Instead you chose advertising."

"It's creative, it pays enough, and most of all, it makes my father mad as hell."

I wagged my finger. "You rebel."

"Are you saying your parents are okay with your plan?"

"Stop calling it a plan." I gave him a shove. "And no, they're not okay. But they're my parents and they have to be supportive, so they pretend they're happy with my decision."

"But you know better."

I dropped my gaze. "I know better."

Mom had been vocal about her opinion in the past. Dad less so. He said he wanted nothing more than see me settled, with a great job and a vow of celibacy. Life kept knocking him down, and each time it was getting harder for him to get up, and if extending my studies made any difference, then I wouldn't hesitate. But a PhD had little healing power—the wrong kind of doctor.

"Hey." Kieran gave my leg a light kick.

I lifted my face and grinned. "Sorry. I space sometimes."

"That's okay." He raised his glass. "Here's to rebels."

I picked up mine, and we clinked them together. "To rebels."

Kieran emptied his glass then hit me with a calculating look. "So why move to Seattle?"

I placed my forearm on the counter and brushed its smooth surface with my fingers. "A number of things. Mainly, I needed a change of scenery. Plus, the company I work for has a stellar reputation in its field."

Contrary to my words, it was the city itself that had called me back. Despite its shortcomings and intense transformation, Seattle had retained the weirdness and charm that I remembered. Its heart beat strong, and, going by the political art and messages of hope I'd seen posted across the streets, I didn't doubt it would continue to do so for many more decades.

"Why study science, though?" Kieran leaned forward.

I turned my head toward my drink to hide my faint smile. This was beginning to feel like a proper conversation between lifelong friends. Who knew hanging out could be so stress-free?

"I want to contribute." I lowered my voice. "Be useful."

"Win a Nobel Prize?" A thin curtain of brown hair fell over his eyes, without obscuring the devil-may-care twinkle.

"Sure. That would be great." I returned a grin. "I'll settle for seeing my name in science journals, though. And you?"

"Honestly?" He leaned back and scratched his scar again. "I'm not sure what I want from life."

"That's okay, too. Take your time. Just make sure it's something that fulfills you. Something you want to get out of bed for."

"Usually the only thing that makes me want to get up is a full bladder, but I suspect there's no career in that." He laughed and checked the clock on his phone. "I guess it's time to go. Did you drive?"

"No." Putting a time limit on tonight had been such a mistake. My life of new adventures and great experiences was off to a slow start.

"I'll give you a ride then." Kieran grabbed his coat. "Come on."

The woman who'd earlier cast her keen eye over Kieran once again shot me a slightly threatening glance. If she'd been paying attention, she'd have noticed the lack of heat between us.

We stepped out of the bar and into a rainy night. Kieran folded his collar up to over his ears. I produced a mini-umbrella from my bag and held it up to keep both of us dry. Ish.

"My car's parked down that way," he said. "It's not far."

The area was well lit, although unpopulated. A multitude of tinny tunes vented from open windows, adding a sway to my gait.

"Did you see the way that woman stared at you?" I pointed

my thumb over my shoulder while side-stepping a puddle. "Not sure about man-eater, but yeah, she was hungry for you."

"Of course I noticed her. She was a bit obvious, wasn't she? Tight dress, perfect make-up, and sitting alone in a bar."

I grimaced. Since when did I judge another person by their style? "Probably a great personality, though."

He nudged my shoulder mid-walk. "Aww, that's sweet. You could be right, of course. Maybe I should go back and ask for her number."

"Really?" I stopped and looked up at him in the glow from a boutique, heat rising in my cheeks. "If she's your type, you should. I didn't mean to make fun of her."

"No, just kidding. She's not my type." The amusement had fled his voice. "I gotta admit, I have no idea what my type is. I always figured I'd know when I meet her."

It would have been nice to hear I was somebody's type, but I'd be lying if I said I wasn't relieved. If I'd trusted my gut in the first place, we'd still be sitting in the bar, talking and laughing.

"I feel the same." I resumed walking. "It's like—"

A shadow flitted between two cars. Or had it? I swiveled my head, turning left, right, nearly doing a one-eighty, like Chucky come alive. Nothing stood out. Nothing screamed *danger*.

Kieran glanced over his shoulder. "It's like what?"

Darkness had never bothered me before. The thousand shades of gray that make a street appear like an old-fashioned photograph held no nightmares for me. After all, it was nothing but the absence of light. People didn't get more violent, and monsters didn't suddenly rise from the shadows. But common sense was in scarce supply tonight, and I blamed the crazy chick in her come-whip-me leather outfit. Nieve had definitely left me with a deep-seated sense of paranoia.

I exhaled evenly to quell the swirl in my belly. "It's like I've been so engrossed in my studies, I'm only now discovering the world, and not at the speed I'd envisaged."

"Not living life to the full yet?" He laughed.

Another movement distracted me. Something about this part of town was off. The glass fronts of the cafés and small boutiques reflected misty outlines of moving ghosts, even though the street was empty. The air shifted, transforming my body into a walking goosebump.

"I've been out once with a friend from work, but other than that… Don't tell anyone, but in my spare time, I've been playing multi-player computer games." I gripped the umbrella handle with all my might.

"While we're sharing secrets, I prefer staying at home, too, but sometimes, you just need to get out and—"

"—talk to a human being rather than your guinea pig?"

"Random, but…"

Within the space of a few seconds, a dark mist rose up around us. A similar fog had confused the locals only a couple of hours earlier. *Ugh.* The same burnt-rubber stink. Most likely, the wind had blown smoke from a nearby fire into town and now herded the plumes through the streets. The perfect setting for a horror film.

"Crap." Kieran's pressed tone didn't allay my worry as he steered me to a silver convertible. "This is my car. Come on. Hop in."

He unlocked the car with a beep and a flash and hurried to the driver's side. A hollow clunk punched through the night. My heart jumped into my mouth.

I shook out the umbrella and opened the door.

A figure grabbed me and lifted me onto their shoulder. My forehead struck the side of the car, and a sharp pain needled through my brain.

I sucked in air and blinked against the jackhammer

pounding inside my skull. When had the world started revolving about me? I kicked out, rolled off the shoulder, and fell onto the wet ground.

A hot trail of pain shot through my hip.

Dragging my bag behind me, I scrambled around the car on all fours, where another figure pressed against the door to prevent Kieran from leaving his vehicle.

Strong hands grabbed me by the shoulders and flipped me onto my back. A man, dressed in a medieval-style leather tunic, crouched and straddled me, pushing the cell phone in my pocket into my flesh. The crown of his head was covered by a silver…helmet?

My pulse rattled my veins like the 4:13 from King Street Station. "Get off me, you freak."

Water ran into my collar, down my blouse and bra, while the constant rain drenched me from above, weighing down my body. I was weaker than my attacker, but surely I could outsmart him?

The man laughed. "Stop struggling."

"I said, get off!" I yanked on his unusual headgear, and the strap beneath his chin tore.

His eyes narrowed, and he slapped me.

The impact left my head ringing. My vision blurred, and it didn't help that the fog was by now dense enough to block even the car from sight. No one was going to come to our aid. Whatever these freaks had planned—steal our money, take our lives—they would probably get away with it unnoticed.

My attacker's thin lips pulled into a smug grin, but worst of all were his eyes. Bulging, they seemed to have too much white and too little blue, with a large black center.

"Please don't hurt me," I whispered. "My wallet's in my bag."

He leaned in, his breath stale. "I don't want your money,

little Spark. Just come with me, don't make a scene, and you'll be all right. Agreed?"

So the guy could kill me in the comfort of his own backyard? Christ, this wasn't happening. Rule number one: never allow yourself to be taken to a secondary location. Every woman this side of the #metoo movement knew that. How had this night deteriorated into a nightmare? Maybe I should shout for help, although that might provoke him into finishing me off right now.

"Help!" I shouted and felt utterly naked doing it. "Somebody? Help!"

He pressed his palm against my mouth.

I aimed for his chin but spun the helmet off his head instead and whacked it in his face. The force sent his headgear—my one weapon—rolling onto the street.

He gave out a braying yowl then got hold of my arms.

"You shouldn't have done that." His rough tone injected a chill into my spine.

"I'm sorry." My words were so quiet, I wasn't even sure he'd heard them.

"A hand, Marcello?" he shouted to his friend while keeping my arms trapped. "She's scrappier than expected."

My fingers went numb with cold. This wasn't a random attack. They'd targeted me.

Was Nieve's story true? *No, no, no, no, no. No way. Nuh-uh.* If these time travelers from ancient Rome were the Shades she'd warned me about, she'd be around here. She'd have followed me, protected me. Right?

"Marcello?" he called out again, hardly ruffled by my kicks and desperate contortions.

The more I fought, the less room for movement his iron grip allowed. A dark pressure swelled from somewhere, nowhere, and settled over my lungs like a concrete wall. I couldn't die.

Who was going to take care of Feynie? Hell, how would my parents cope with the news?

My mom had already buried her father this year, and my father's illness had taken its toll, too. The loss of her only child would thrust her over the brink.

My attacker shot to his feet, yanked by Kieran, whose grimace had turned his kind face into something scary. He pulled the Roman wannabe toward his mouth and whispered in his ears.

The guy's eyes widened, his mouth slacked open. Finally, he nodded, slowly at first, then faster as if eager to please Kieran, or at least quell my friend's anger.

I struggled to my feet and took two steps back. How was I still alive? Despite the nausea, despite my bleeding head wound, despite my shaking legs, I'd survived.

A small voice in my head screeched at me to run and hide, but I wouldn't leave Kieran. That wasn't what friends did.

Kieran gradually put distance between my attacker and himself. "Now, run."

The guy waited for Kieran's fist to let go off his jacket, then took off as if the devil himself was after him.

"What did you say to him?" I asked while kneading warmth back into my fingers.

"I told him what I'd do to him if he hurt you. His courage wasn't that great after that. Idiots."

"And the other one?"

"The same. A themed office party gone crazy, I assume. You know, silly costumes, alcohol, a pretty girl. You read it in the papers all the time. Still, quite brazen."

"I guess." A reasonable explanation for anyone who hadn't heard of Nieve and her Fables of Doom. "Thank you. You know, for..." I tipped my head in the vague direction of the scene of the fight. "…that. For helping me, I mean." My cheeks flushed with heat, and I dropped my gaze.

"You're welcome." Gradually, the seriousness fled his face and the smile returned. "Now, let's get you home."

"I'm soaked, and I'm dirty."

"You're alive and unhurt. That's more important." This time he opened the car door for me.

In a surprising betrayal of my feminist convictions, I thanked him.

I leaned slightly forward so as not to schmutz up his seat. "I'll sleep with the lights on tonight, that much is certain."

He peeled away from the curb. "I feel like curling up in bed myself."

"Ha. Ha." I shot him a thin smile. "You were totally in control."

"I faked it." He shrugged. "Sometimes that's all you've got, you know. I smelled the alcohol on their breath and knew that, with the right push, they'd do a runner."

I gave him a sideways glance. Maybe his theory was right. It certainly sounded plausible enough. Our attackers had left after a stern talking-to by Kieran. Hardly the action of the crazy killers Nieve had talked about.

The radio station's DJ played a soft pop tune that, under different circumstances, would have had a soothing effect.

"So, all in all, quite a night, huh?" I asked.

"Memorable." Three syllables. One tone.

I produced a nervous giggle. I wanted to say more, talk about everything that happened, tell him about Nieve and Shades. If we were truly friends, he wouldn't laugh at me. Except, I hardly knew him. Maybe one or two months down the line, we'd cross barriers, spill secrets, but we weren't there yet. Instead, I wedged my still shaking hands between my thighs and stared out the window, only interrupting my silence to give directions.

He pulled into my street. Most windows were still lit, and their soft, warm light thawed the icy sheet of unease that covered my heart. I pointed to my left for him to stop.

He turned in his seat. "I'm sorry the evening ended like this. I will make it up to you."

"It's not your fault." I glanced into the street, where my neighbor's cat was prowling for feline company, then back at him, with a brave smile on my face.

He blinked twice, the second one dragged. "Get some rest. I'm off to befriend a whiskey bottle myself. Call you tomorrow?"

"Okay. Sure. And again, thanks." I quickly left the car and headed inside, where I double-locked the door.

Safe in my living room, my hand lingered over the phone. How could I possibly explain today's events to my mom? She'd insist on boarding the next flight to America. Instead, I discarded my dirty clothes and slipped into my PJs.

I'd always figured I'd be braver in an attack. Fiercer, more dominant, more kick-ass. But once again reality had pulled me back to a cold, hard Earth.

With Feynman on my lap, I spent the next couple of hours munching cookie dough ice cream in front of the TV. Something about Walt Disney's *Mary Poppins* usually calmed my nerves and convinced me the world was a better place than it actually was.

For the first time, it didn't work.

# CHAPTER SEVEN



*"Accepting magic is real is only a small step toward understanding the universe. To me, the greatest mystery is how they make those red and green pieces of candy that crackle on your tongue."*

For two hours I combed the city looking for Lea, but not even the wind could track her location. Either no one mentioned her name, or she was outside the range of my powers.

Slice it. I headed to the hotel I'd booked as a safe haven at night, even though events hadn't allowed me much sleep. Every corner held potential danger, and I went to great lengths to circumvent suspicious-looking shadows. All efforts to sneak into the Kindred world to recover the lost Elonian had been in vain. We had a traitor in our midst. The nauseating words spun inside me, bouncing off my stomach and lungs when where I really needed them was in my brain, sitting still long enough to be made sense of. The Shade's knowledge of Lea's existence was proof that he'd spoken the truth, but why would anyone betray our country?

I opened the hotel door with a thump, slid my hanbo out of its holster, and dropped onto the springy mattress of the king-sized bed. Speculating as to the identity of the Shade collaborator would do no good without evidence. Rooting out a traitor, getting Lea, training her... If all the work landed on my shoulders anyway, why did we involve the Council in our plans to begin with? I was a one-woman army under a battalion of leaders. The total opposite of efficient.

I closed my eyes for a second. My body demanded rest, but with time pressing against me, sleep would have to wait once again. I sat up and called my brother for an update.

"Was it a scout who conjured the fog?" His tone barely restrained his displeasure.

"The city's brimming with them, but no, I don't think so."

"But you made sure he didn't follow her." It wasn't a question.

I rolled my hands into fists, a sign of irritation I allowed myself only because he couldn't see me. "Of that I'm certain."

"That's something. Did you—"

The line went dead.

Slicing time shifts. The first time we got disconnected on one of my trips to the Kindred world, I'd feared the worst and sped home to check on Tristan's wellbeing. My near-blind panic, however, hadn't been necessary. Several days had passed in Elonia by the time I got back, and my brother had already forgotten our interrupted conversation.

I got up off the bed and pushed the button on my display again.

After twenty seconds, my brother finally answered. "How long are you going to be? I'm getting impatient."

The time jumps and lags across the Divide could be disorienting. Still, over the years I'd come to accept them, the way I'd come to accept microwave popcorn, battery-operated flashlights and other technologies. I wasn't a fan, but in what I could only call a huge oversight, the Old Ones hadn't put me in charge of the world.

"Soon," I said. "Do you remember what we were talking about when we got cut off?"

"Maybe. In any case, I've sent you a file with everything we've learned about the lost Elonian. Did you read it?"

"We just hung up, so no. What does it say?"

He mumbled something, punctuated by a grunt, then took a deep breath. "Now that we know where Lea lives, we've been able to learn about her. For one, she's a scientist, which means she will react well to logic."

"Not that I've noticed." I smoothed the bedsheet and then took a seat in a narrow leather chair in the corner of the room.

"Her parents live in a different country, and her father suffers from cancer, a serious disease the Kindreds haven't eradicated yet."

"I know what cancer is." History had been a passion of mine when I was a child, before killing and the constant threat of death replaced my other hobbies.

"She's twenty-four years old. Hang on." The rustle of paper sounded at the other end of the line. "She listens to pop music, enjoys action films, and spends a lot of time playing computer games."

"Do I need to know all that? I don't want to date her."

"It seems you've forgotten who you're talking to." His commanding tone refreshed my memory at once. "If you don't need my help, then go to her house and do your job. Now."

"I will, but you should know it's night here."

His silence hit me worse than any insult he could have lobbed at me.

"*Royal champions don't fear the darkness,*" he used to shout at a sweat-soaked me during my workouts. "*Royal champions don't fear anything.*" He'd been right, of course, but did he even see a sister when he thought of me, or had I become nothing but a fixture, a tool to help him do his job?

"Very well." I got up from the chair, relying on my aching legs to get me through the rest of the night. "I'll go."

"Good. Our sources tell me the Shades have completed their war talks and are beginning to move their forces, so no more delays. We need her, Nieve. You should have brought her home already."

"It's not for lack of trying." I told him how my plan, successful at first, had shattered. Who could have known convincing Lea of her heritage would prove harder than getting a six-year-old to eat his vegetables?

"Maybe my promise to release you from royal duty has gone to your head? Your approach was too heavy-handed from the start." Tristan's voice nearly buckled under his frustration, but he wouldn't be king if he didn't know how to rein in his temper. "How do you expect deception to pave the way for her cooperation? Only patience will gain her trust."

Where had all that advice been when we'd planned my mission?

I ripped my spare top from its hanger and stuffed it into my pocket. "I was more concerned with her safety. I didn't have time to stroke her ego."

"Clearly it would have been better if you *had* taken the time. Mend the holes now and earn her trust. Need I remind you of the stakes?"

He didn't, and with the clock ticking, I'd run out of excuses. No matter how dark and how rainy the streets were, no matter how unyielding and difficult Lea was, I had my marching orders.

The Shade's accusation would have to wait, too. Without proof, the king would not easily be convinced of treachery by one of our own, and the mere suggestion would make him lose the rest of his temper.

He hung up.

In some ways, he had a point, of course. I'd royally screwed up the Lea-situation. The whole thing had been one hiccup after another.

I picked up my hanbo and placed my Champion's necklace around my neck. The medallion weighed heavier today than it had when my brother first handed it to me a decade ago. Maybe it had absorbed all the blood I'd spilled in its name.

More likely, the weight difference was the result of an overactive imagination.

After a final check to ensure I'd left nothing behind, I exited the pre-paid room, this time for good.

The wind whipped my face, tautening my skin. A construction site to my right threw up scents of earth and metal. I averted my head and winced. The tension sat deep in my muscles, and not even vigorous rubbing got rid of the hard knot in my neck. What if talking to the Shade earlier had been another mistake? He could have been a distraction that allowed his friends to pick Lea up without my interference.

At her driveway, a sliver of light fell through a gap between the blinds and the frame, and I inched closer without making a sound. Either Lea was back home—or the Shades had found her and set a trap for me.

Inside the room, a lampshade on a night table emitted a glow onto a lumpy blanket. Dark hair spilled out one end, framed by the light of Lea's luster. The pressure pounding inside my muscles subsided. She was safe.

I knocked on her door.

She left me waiting a good while before popping her head out.

"You again?" She scowled. "Do you know what the time is? I need sleep. It's been a rough evening."

"What happened?"

"A friend and I were attacked."

I leaned forward, eyeing the scratch on her head. "By whom?"

"Two guys in helmets. Drunks on their way back from a costume party."

"Brown…" I inhaled sharply. "Brown leather uniforms?" My low voice betrayed none of the nerve-rattling going on inside me.

Lea's short frame tensed. "Yeah. How do you know?"

"Shades." Slice it. They'd found her.

My carefully crafted script, the rehearsed facial expressions, the entire strategy I'd devised to bring her to safety, they'd all failed. *I* had failed.

Maybe the guy from the alley *had* distracted me, and I'd fallen for his act like a boot warrior, a rookie too green to tell mud from horse excrement. Unless the Shades had already known where she lived? No, she wouldn't have been slumbering innocently in her bed if they had.

I sharpened my voice. "How did you escape?"

"My friend talked to them."

I squinted. "She what?"

"*He* told them to scram. Threatened them, and off they went." She shrugged, although her rigid face belied her indifference. "In the end, it wasn't a big deal."

Not Shades, then. Thank the Old Ones. According to a well-known Elonian saying, the only way to curb a Shade's urge to fight was to kill him. A threat would have no effect, no matter how menacing the tone.

"I'm sorry I wasn't there to help." I opened my eyes wide to convey sincerity and softened my tone. "But I'm here now. Please let me in."

"Now? It's after eleven." She rubbed an eye. "Come back in the morning."

She closed the door and replaced the security chain.

This girl was testing my patience. Yet patience was what the king had demanded of me.

I withdrew my hanbo and used the enchanted tip to unlock the door and sear through the chain. Tristan might insist I take baby steps with her, but he'd said nothing about being careful with her property. I entered her gently lit room and tapped the light switch with my hanbo. The ceiling lights came on.

Lea's head whipped up. One, two, three seconds of shock, then she scrambled back against the headboard. "Christ."

I approached her bed, kicking a T-shirt and jeans from my path. "Hello again."

Her bedroom was a jumble of colors. The rusty-orange walls were bare, the closet and dresser drawers stuffed to bursting, with sleeves and bra straps hanging out. A boxy looking games station sat on a dresser with cartridges scattered around it. A broken perfume bottle lay abandoned on a shelf, giving off a penetrating citrus smell. Had she seriously just moved into this house?

"How did you get in?" She lifted a quivering hand to her nose. "Are you crazy?"

Her gaze flitted around the room, likely looking for a weapon. A good trait in a warrior. That instinct might one day save her life. However, her composure under stress needed serious work.

I wetted my lips. "We hadn't finished our conversation. Has tonight's attack convinced you that you're not safe?"

"Maybe. I don't know. If those two were Shades, they aren't as scary as you made them sound."

"Maybe they were, maybe they weren't. The point is that if you'd been alone tonight, you could have sustained more than a scratch." I raised my gaze to her forehead. "What do I have to do for you to take me seriously?"

"Nothing." She tugged the purple blanket to her chin. "But feel free to show me more magic. You can borrow Feynie. He's the closest thing I have to a rabbit."

A grumble vibrated deep in my throat. Old Ones, send patience. Or a knife, because this girl was asking to be cut down. "Rising into the air, or flying, isn't a magic trick."

"Yeah, sure it isn't."

"You want more proof? Watch this." I dropped my magical defenses, allowing my luster to envelop me in its powerful light.

"Holy crap." Lea jumped out of her bed and squeezed against the far wall of the room.

Finally, a reaction.

"It's called luster." I twirled to prove I wasn't hiding a flashlight behind my back. "It's a by-product of an Elonian's affinity with light. Anyone sensitive to magic can see it unless I suppress it."

In my mind, rows of thick bricks piled one on top of another around me, extinguishing my luster.

"A-are you an angel?" Her airless voice barely traveled the distance between us.

I tipped back my head and laughed. "Definitely not."

She unglued herself from the wall and took a few steps toward her bed. "You said I'm an Elonian. Why don't I shine?"

"You can't see your own luster, but it's there. Without the training to suppress it, you're a living flame to the Shades. It's how they'll identify you. You know, before they kill you."

Lea twirled hair around her finger and stuck the ends into her mouth. While her teeth were gnawing on them, her focus went distant, no longer in this world. Something I'd said must have triggered a switch in her brain. Not a day too soon.

I trotted to the corner by the window and picked a collection of stuffed animals off the armchair. From the deep V between Lea's brows, it was clear her thought processes weren't going anywhere fast. Once the toys occupied the windowsill, neatly arranged by height, I sat.

With her dark lashes, a tiny nose and a sprinkling of freckles, she looked so young and unworldly. Long-buried memories ripped through my chest. For the first time, a heavy load pressed onto my diaphragm, making me feel like I was an evil monster come to chop up her innocence like next week's firewood.

Even though she was still a total stranger, her pale, elfin face stirred in me a glimmer of recognition, of familiarity even. My childhood friend Belinda had had a similar innocence about her. She'd chew the end of her pen for hours while pondering her words. Her poems were meant to bring joy to a war-torn land. Instead, they burned with her when King Galleo's men invaded her village.

Just one of many reasons I'd happily accepted my promotion to the position of Royal Champion of Elonia. The Shades had to die. Under Galleo's rule, there were no innocents.

My opinion hadn't changed over the last decade. What had changed was my belief that they had to die at my hand. Belinda's loss fueled my war fever for the first few years, drove me from battle to battle, but at some point, the wide eyes and silent pleas of the fallen began crowding out my righteousness. I'd started to feel…something. Not empathy, surely, but whatever it was, it kept me up at night more and more. Even now, during our fragile peace, sleep was a luxury.

Lea would not share Belinda's fate. I'd see to that with all the vengeance I could salvage. More than that, this girl would help me save Elonia and maybe even put a stop to Galleo once and for all. His death would be the perfect retirement gift. By the end of the training, Lea would be able to take on a whole battalion of the bastards by herself, maybe succeed me to become the new royal champion, and under her, Elonia would know a new kind of peace. A lasting one.

Lea scratched her leg with her other foot and mumbled something under her breath. I squinted at her short stature and took a sobering breath. Maybe my ambitions for her were too lofty. From what I'd witnessed so far, it would be a miracle if I could get her to hold a knife the right way up.

Getting her ready was going to be tough. Probably the greatest challenge of my career. Fulfilling the prophecy would be easy by comparison.

The armchair under me creaked as I shifted once again.

Lea dropped her hair and skewered me with a shrewd look. "Okay. Say I believe you. It doesn't change anything."

Her commanding tone would have had a better effect if she hadn't grabbed a sweater from her bed's wooden post and clutched it to her chest.

"You believe me?" I straightened. "Finally. Can we—"

"Are you listening?" She gesticulated, and her sweater slipped from her fingers, soared across the room, and landed near a cemetery for discarded clothes. "Even if everything you say is true, I don't want any part of this. I'm building a new life. One that is going to be this close to perfect." She showed her index finger and thumb separated by a narrow gap. "You're not taking that away from me."

"But if you believe me, you understand the stakes for my world, don't you?" I tightened my arms around my torso. "The Shades will find you wherever you go. Every minute you resist me eats into valuable training time. To remind you, it's not only my home but the Kindred realm, your world, that's at risk."

She shook her head. "Not happening. Have your people tell the bad guys I'm not involved. I'm Switzerland. Completely neutral."

"It doesn't work like that."

"It has to. You don't get it. For the first time, in like, forever, I'm making friends." She crossed her arms, her glance utterly defiant. "Go find someone else."

Under normal circumstances, a woman wearing pink pajamas covered in tiny blue boxes begged not to be taken seriously, but her cheerless face sapped the humor from my bones.

"This is your destiny." I kept my tone laid back but emphatic, concealing any sign of the lit fuse inside. "If you have even an ounce of your mother's skill, you and I together will be an incredible force. Besides, the king insists I escort you to Elonia. I make it a rule not to disappoint him."

She sat, shaking her head, picking at a loose thread on her blanket. "Not my problem."

Surprise, my brother's new brainwave about using the tiptoe approach wasn't having the desired effect either.

What if I ignored his instructions and followed my instincts? Knock her out, take her home against her will, and deal with her emotions later? But nothing was going to jeopardize my bargain with the king. He'd reminded me how easy it would be for him to rescind his offer. My freedom was worth more than the short-term satisfaction I'd get from clobbering her over the head.

Luckily, I had one arrow left in my quiver. "Your father is sick, isn't he? Cancer?"

"How do you know that?" At once, her voice lost its defiance.

"That doesn't matter. What does is that Elonians have a cure for this disease. Warriors are forbidden from sharing our secrets with anyone, but once you begin your training as one of us, you'd be able to heal your father."

Instead of an elated smile, she gave me a death stare. "You're blackmailing me with my dad's life?"

"No, I'm not." I raised my hands to ward off the accusation. "That wasn't what I meant at all."

As I repeated my words in my head, a chill rose in me. The way I'd phrased my suggestions made me sound like a monster.

I shook my head. "I meant—"

"Just go." Her index finger shot up and pointed at the window. "Go and don't come back."

"I wasn't blackmailing you, I promise." I gave a genuine smile, which I knew from experience would look false on me. "If I could, I'd give you the cure, honest. Slice it, if I were allowed, I'd administer it to all Kindreds. But our laws are very, very strict. Only warriors may use our magic, and only to benefit the country or their immediate family. A perk of the job, if you will."

"That's stupid. Are you saying I have to give up my life to save my dad's?"

Put like that, the deal I'd proposed sounded even worse. The king shouldn't have sent me to fetch her. A diplomat could have cut through her objections without making it worse. Maybe killing was all I was good for, after all.

"I'll give you time to think about it." I trotted as far as the doorframe and stopped on the threshold. "Meanwhile, please be careful and, by the Old Ones, don't go out in the dark again."

I left her room and skulked out of her house, bathed in yet another failure.

# CHAPTER EIGHT

*LEA*

*"Reality is merely a hunch I have when I'm sober. After half a bottle of whiskey, all bets are off."*

Kieran had texted me first thing in the morning, and, in desperate need of a diversion, I'd agreed to meet him. He picked me up from home at eight on the dot.

I climbed into the passenger seat of his car and fastened the seat belt across me and the big bag I'd come to love. "Where are we going? You didn't say."

The rain had stopped, at least for now. The sun had made a brief appearance in the morning, but by lunchtime, it had gone back into hiding. With the darkness setting in earlier every day and Nieve ratcheting up the cray, I was in danger of falling back onto old habits of playing board games with myself, but I'd be damned if I sat at home on a Friday evening because of one deranged woman's determination to freak me out.

Kieran turned his headlights on and set off down the road. "I'm going to prove to you that you can have fun in Seattle without being accosted by unhinged people."

If only he knew how commonplace those seemed to be.

I leaned forward into his field of view so he didn't miss my exaggerated frown. "Color me intrigued and slightly skeptical."

"No, really. It took serious planning, of course, but I predict a violence-free evening."

"We'll see." I forced myself to relax into the seat.

By all accounts, Kieran had reason to be optimistic. He'd fended off the oddly dressed men without a punch being exchanged. That meant, despite Nieve's claims, all the signs were of a random attack, not of a targeted strike by a couple of supervillains.

What I found hard to shake, though, was the conviction in her voice, especially when she indicated she had the power to heal Dad. I'd do anything—absolutely *anything*—to get my hand on a cure, even if that meant ditching my job and joining a karate-obsessed commune, but her talk about destiny and fighting Shades and training was cuckoo, and wishful thinking didn't change that.

"You're enjoying Seattle?" Kieran asked as he gently braked for a red light.

"I guess. It's weird. The lights of Seattle should bring back memories of my childhood, but we moved so much, I grew up everywhere. All the places blur into one after a while. But yeah, I like it."

Weirdness excepted.

Maybe Nieve had a mental problem. Never mind the fact that she'd spun such a wild story, she'd also done intensive research to discover facts of my life I didn't share with just anyone. Not even Vicky knew about my father's cancer. Worse, if Nieve's determination seemed intrusive now, by next week, talking to me might no longer satisfy her stalker urges. People like that could get dangerous. Was it time to get the cops involved?

"That's the place." Kieran pointed at a backlit sign that read

SFORNO. From the outside, the Italian restaurant appeared warm and welcoming.

"Looks nice."

"The food's fantastic." He parked in the small, well-lit parking lot.

Security cameras pointed every which way. Good to know. We got out and entered an establishment with crisp, white tablecloths, old-fashioned music, and the right amount of busy. The clientele consisted of hand-holding couples, young families, and what I assumed were colleagues kicking back after a day's work.

After we'd placed our orders, Kieran rested his elbows on the table and inspected my forehead, which was virtually healed now. "Is it still hurting?"

"Not really."

"Glad you're okay." His voice held an edge I couldn't place.

"Really? That's all the compassion I get for my ordeal?" I pressed my back into the padded backrest and squinted with one eye. "When I said I'm okay, I meant relatively speaking."

He relaxed his expression and grinned. "You win. Relative to what are you okay?"

"Never mind me." I gave a quick shake of my head. "I'm yanking your chain. Seriously, I'm good. The weekend's here, and that alone is cause for a celebration."

"That's all right for some. I, on the other hand, have to go back in tomorrow." He scratched the faded scar on his neck.

"That sucks."

"Let's not talk about work. Agreed?"

"Agreed." I hooked my feet around my chair's legs. "Let's talk about that scar."

"Oh, this?" He pointed.

The waiter served up steaming plates of food. Kieran waited

for the man to leave, then picked up his fork and knife. "Is my scar doing it for you? Because I hear they're sexy."

He shifted his head to show it off. The light from the two flickering red candles on our table reflected off a thin silver chain peeking out of his shirt and caught his scar in its shine.

"Jeez, put it away." I chuckled. "They're not that sexy. Part of a rough-and-tumble youth, or another office party gone awry?"

He shook his hair away from his eyes. "My father made sure my brothers and I are prepared for everything. We practiced hand-to-hand combat, fencing and shooting, and what my brothers call girly stuff, like music, painting, that sort of thing. That scar came from combat, not painting, by the way."

"Any favorites?"

"Sailing, I suppose. If someone gave me a million bucks, that's what I'd do. I'd sail the world." He rotated his glass between his fingers. "Lea. There's something important I need to tell you."

I tipped my fork at him. "Shoot."

"Right. You know how change can be a good thing?"

I arched my eyebrows. "Yes. Sure."

After all, that was what my life was all about. Change for the better.

"Some people sail through their existence without hitting any rough seas," he said. "That's okay for the most part, but it lacks adventure. You almost hope for a giant wave or, I don't know, pirates, right?"

"Pirates?" I smirked. None of his words made a lick of sense, but I was willing to hear him out. "Sure, swashbuckling pirates would certainly be a change from the norm."

His lip twitched, and he glanced down at the table. "I'm talking about things that make life worth living. Only, we're often too scared to take risks, or to accept change. And I don't want to scare you." He gave a nervous chuckle.

A movement to my right caught my eye. I squinted out the large window spanning the width of the building. It was hard to distinguish shapes out there, and the longer I looked, the less I made out.

"…not alone." Kieran pushed his plate away and placed his folded hands on the table. "Are you listening? This is important."

"What?" Despite the warm atmosphere and the great company, I was still tense. "Not alone. Got it." I softened my expression, hoping I didn't look like a startled bunny. "Go on."

"As I was saying. You and I, we're alike." He chuckled. "God, it's not easy finding the right words."

I nodded, but my gaze was once again drawn to the outside. A truck drove by, casting a shadow over the area, which lay empty except for a couple walking arm-in-arm. I turned back to Kieran. His lips pressed together so hard they'd gone pale.

Had I missed the moment where he'd bared his soul? The moment we could have gone from "someone I knew" to "friend"?

"Sorry." I scrunched up my face and groaned. "I thought I saw something, and my mind immediately flipped back to yesterday."

"No big deal." He leaned back and crossed his hands behind his head. "I get it. But I promised a violent-free night, remember?"

The tinkle of a wind-chime fluttered through the air, drawing curious glances from two kids at the table next to ours.

"That's me. Sorry." Kieran shifted aside to pull his phone from his pocket and checked his display. A frown ran across his forehead. He pressed the screen. "Never mind. As I was saying."

His cell jingled again.

"Bad breakup?" I grinned.

He opened his mouth as if to say something, then closed it and stared at the small screen again. "No."

"Everything okay?" I speared two pasta pieces onto my fork and grinned. "Relatively speaking?"

"What?" He glanced at me, and his expression hovered between confusion and concern. "It's my brother. He said something's wrong with my father."

The smile fled my lips in an instant. "Did he say what it is?"

"I don't even know why he's texting. My father and I haven't talked in a while. We fell out over…" Kieran leaned his head to the side and gave me the strangest look as if he expected me to finish his sentence or know about his family's issues. "It doesn't matter why."

"If you need to go, you should go."

"I told you, it's complicated."

I glanced listlessly at the tomato-stained plate before me. "I don't know what happened with your dad, but sometimes, family politics don't matter. You just got to be there."

He studied me again and finally nodded. "You're right. I'm sorry about this."

"There's nothing to be sorry about." Even if, what promised to be a fun-filled Friday, was turning into another day with Feynie and me vegging out at home.

"I'll make it up to you."

I mustered a smile. "Go. See your dad. I'll get the bill."

He rose and pushed his cell back into his pocket. "I couldn't—"

"Seriously, I've got this." I dialed up the smile to high-volume. "I'm a big girl. Go."

He glanced at the waiter, then back to me and gave me a thumbs-up. "You're the best. I'll call you, okay?"

"Sure." I knew he would. Something told me he needed a friend as much as I. "Be careful out there."

He rushed out of the restaurant, leaving me to the pitying glances of my fellow diners. One of the pitfalls of befriending guys was that everyone assumed we were a couple. My best friend growing up had been a boy. We'd play detective, organize snail races, practice circus performances week after week after week. Back then, no one batted an eyelid about the two of us. Being a grown-up sucked the innocence out of everything.

I finished my pasta and called a ride via my app. As soon as my request was accepted, I waved for the check.

"Everything to your satisfaction?" the waiter asked in an accent that sounded more French than Italian, but no less sexy for it.

"Absolutely." I gave him a generous tip and a beaming smile, maybe to convince him that Kieran's departure hadn't spoiled my evening.

He helped me into my jacket, and I left the restaurant. The distinct petrol-laced aroma of impending rain permeated the air. Petrichor this scent was called, according to my Word of the Day calendar. My gaze shifted from one end of the street to the other, on the lookout for suspicious-looking helmets. Or innocent-looking helmets. I was in no mood to discriminate.

The area appeared helmet-free.

Of course it was. Nieve-induced paranoia had struck again.

I checked my cell's display and, at long last, the app informed me my driver was nearly here. That gave me no more than a few seconds to get my shit together.

Just as I wiped the first raindrops from my face, a car slowed in front of me. The number plate matched the one on my display. The moment I got in, I buried my head in my phone to stave off any conversation.

The car jerked into motion, and the heavens opened.

# CHAPTER NINE



*"Death is inevitable. Bummer, I know. But as to the nature of your demise, I take requests."*

At seven o'clock, I tightened my collar to prevent the raindrops from rolling in and down my back, and set off in a brisk walk toward Lea's house, using the illuminated Space Needle for orientation. She'd had long enough to mull over my proposal, which happened to be the same amount of time I was prepared to grant her before resorting to kidnapping. I breathed calming breaths. Everything would work out. I'd make my brother proud.

Here and there, mid-range vehicles pulled into their owners' driveways, red and yellow leaves sticking to car roofs and windows. Their exhaust fumes lingered, then dissipated moments after the garage doors fell shut.

About five minutes from Lea's home, the rain stopped, and visibility improved. I took that as a good omen. Two vehicles drove past me, the light cones from their headlamps leading the way. An unnaturally bright glow filled the first car, strong enough that the glare should have prevented the driver from navigating the street.

Unless the light was invisible to him, like it would be if it were caused by the luster of an Elonian.

Further down the street, the car came to a sudden stop, forcing the trailing driver to slam the brakes. A woman exited the vehicle. Her luster reflected off the wet ground and bounced up into the dim evening sky to create a beautiful white halo around her. The car drove off, leaving the figure, hands on her waist and gaze focused in my direction, behind.

Hadn't I warned Lea of the dangers that waited in the dark? I'd thought we'd made progress. Her stance was that of an infuriated Valkyrie, which was ridiculous seeing how I was the one who deserved to be annoyed.

The doors of the other car opened, and three figures stepped out. My breath rippled in my throat. Brown leather tunics over brown leather pants. Steel helmets.

*No, no, no.* Shades. This wasn't supposed to happen. Wouldn't anything go right for me?

I concentrated on slowing my pulse and calculated the odds.

Even if I was prepared to draw from my reserves, wind magic and the ability to fly offered no advantage. How close to Lea would I get before the Shades spotted me in the air? Besides, a premature charge might force them to kill her on the spot. Pity the mysterious Shade hadn't provided more information about their intentions when it came to the lost Elonian.

The three Shades ahead of me only had eyes for Lea. None of them had turned to see what had caught her attention in the first place. Using a line of trees for cover, I crept closer, careful not to scrape the ground with my soles.

Lea's gaze locked on the Shades, and she backed away.

The spindliest of the Shades stood to his full height and placed his arms behind his back. "In the name of the king, we command you to surrender."

What a pompous idiot.

Lea spun to run away but slipped on the wet asphalt. *Slice it.* She wasn't cut out for this stuff. Another Shade, more fat than muscle on his stocky frame, caught her by the sleeve. She yanked free and darted down the road. He chased after her, strands of curly hair flopping from under his helmet, and caught her by her collar.

No way would she be able to get herself out of this situation. Best I could hope for was that she wouldn't get in my way.

I passed another two trees and crouched, close to where a female Shade kneeled. The woman looked younger than me, but I'd never make the mistake of equating age with experience. Her hands hovered inches from the ground. Ashen magic spewed from her fingers and spilled into the earth. A deep rumble came from below.

Lea screamed.

My heart lurched, but my time hadn't come yet.

The asphalt beneath Lea parted, and her feet disappeared from view. The street gave one more roar and then closed around her ankles. She was trapped.

"We got her," the thin man yelled. "Call up the shadows, fast!"

The triumph in his voice was hardly warranted. He'd caught what was basically a helpless kitten—not exactly big game by anyone's standard. But we'd see soon enough how he coped when he came face to face with a lion.

The female Shade lifted her hands high. The shadows separated from the road surface and rose like mist, then coalesced into a heavy fog that cloaked the street. The smell of burning hair and the taste of something rotting in my mouth accompanied the cloud.

Even though it was harder to make out details, the murky air provided a great deal more cover than the trees and cars did.

"Why are you doing this?" Lea grabbed one of her pant legs,

her foot still stuck in the earth. She lost her balance and tipped over onto the ground, landing on her butt. "Guys. We can talk about this." Her voice trembled.

If she started to sob, I might not even bother taking her to Elonia after all. What good was a crybaby when facing down whatever horrors the Shades had planned? At least, she wasn't calling out for me. That showed a degree of intelligence at least. Maybe even a certain level of trust in my abilities.

The Shades huddled together and appeared to be discussing the situation.

I set my jaw and got moving again. Poor visibility enabled me to edge closer, but not close enough to catch the clipped fragments of their conversation.

The Shades dispersed and crowded toward Lea. Her luster reflected off a metal body cuff in the female Shade's hand.

No more than thirty feet from the nearest Shade, I crouched behind a pickup parked downwind from them and tapped my hanbo against my palm, anxious to show my opponents what I thought of their cowardly trap for an untrained Elonian.

The bulkier Shade ventured within Lea's range.

She yanked herself upright and swung her arm. "Let me go."

Her blow landed under his jaw, where his double chin absorbed the force. "You'll pay for that, you witch."

He circled her and grasped her shoulders from behind.

She squealed and twisted her body, arms flailing.

I allowed myself a grim smile. She did have pluck, I had to give her that.

He caught her hands and pinned them behind her. Even though she'd lost mobility, her face remained hard and determined.

Adrenaline prickled in my veins, needling me into abandoning my caution, but I held steady. Her feet were still stuck, and Elonian magic wouldn't free her.

In a minute or two, the tables would turn. In preparation, I numbered my enemies: One, Two, Three—the order in which I'd take them down.

"Hold her still." Number Two, the female Shade, squeezed the steel body cuff over Lea's shoulders. It clicked shut and jammed her arms against her sides.

The Shades' fog was dissipating fast, and I didn't dare move for fear of giving my location away. Still, my hanbo felt light in my hand, eager for a game of Whack-a-Shade.

"What do you want with me anyway?" Lea raised her voice, calling to the darkness—to me. "Help!"

If she carried on like that, Kindreds would soon take an interest. Nothing ever good came from Kindreds meddling in Elonian affairs.

Shade Two secured Lea's knees with another body cuff. She was entirely at their mercy.

"Ready?" Shade Three, the skinny one, asked.

Shade One, who strutted like he was the man in charge, gripped the cuffs with both hands to test the metal's strength. He nodded, and Shade Two waved at the ground. The earth trembled, and the dirt rose under Lea's feet, lifting her to street level until she was no longer trapped.

I skimmed one last look at the misty scene. The entire chessboard imprinted on my brain, with my staff's targets highlighted. My legs snapped straight, and I bulleted around the pickup. Mid sprint, I jabbed my hanbo's tip into the nearest Shade's jugular. A gurgle escaped his fleshy throat, and he dropped like a cartoon anvil. His limbs flopped to his side as if the fall had disintegrated his bones.

Shade One down.

"It's her!" Shade Three called out.

He covered Lea with his body, while Shade Two approached me, pointing her hand toward the asphalt separating us. The street exploded into pieces of rock. The pressure wave reached me before the noise, driving my lungs hard against my spine. Large stones charged through the air in a scatter too wide for me to duck. Instead, I raised my arm and ordered the wind to deflect the missiles.

The rocks parted, and most zoomed past me without making contact. Two projectiles stayed on course, though. I somersaulted out of their path, swinging my hanbo at Shade Two's legs on my way up.

"Wha— ?" The woman collapsed in a heap, clutching her calves.

I whacked the base of my stick into the side of her skull. The hanbo's crack tore through the night, answered by a car's honking horn in the distance. Her arms rotated like windmill blades. She tipped over and stayed down, out for the count.

Almost immediately, the remaining fog dissipated. Hanbo raised, I advanced on the last Shade, spindly Number Three. He spun on the spot and grabbed Lea's body cuff, dragging her in front of him as a shield. Whatever his thoughts on killing her had been before, he now seemed willing to sacrifice her.

"Hey." In the distance, a Kindred waved.

Fun time was over. Even if the man's curiosity didn't push him toward us, there was a chance he'd call the police.

Restrained by the cuffs, Lea made to hop away, but she tripped and fell. Her head slammed against the ground. "Shit," she half whispered, half coughed.

The Shade reached for her.

She flipped away from his grasp and rolled toward the station wagon the Shades had driven up in.

Rather than crawl after her, he drew a silver knife from his holster. Magic heated its long blade to a red glow. "Only you and me, Spark. More fun that way anyway."

I twirled my hanbo to find the best grip and leveled its tip toward my opponent. "Do you know who I am?"

The Shade licked his lips. "Nieve, I assume. Soon to be *ex-royal champion*."

I stepped forward. "Tough talk. Many Shades know my name. Few have seen my face and survived." My mocking tone was more than mere bravado. Verbal peacocking before the enemy was an essential pre-battle strategy. A single provocative word might tempt him into making the first move and opening himself up.

With snake-like speed, he faked left and stabbed to his right.

I deflected the blow and swung my knee at his legs. Straight into his thigh.

He grunted and jumped back.

I pressed my advantage and closed the distance.

To, fro, right, left—our steps resembled a studied choreography. A dance around the abandoned car in the middle of a middle-class neighborhood. But quickly, groans of exertion punctuated the sounds of steel against reinforced wood, his groans louder than mine.

He peered at my feet.

Not the subtlest move, considering Shades loved digging holes with their powers.

I shaped the atmosphere into a thin cushion and waited for the inevitable next step.

He gestured with his free hand, and as predicted, the asphalt beneath me parted.

I smoothly hopped onto the sheet of air and skated to the right, escaping not merely the hollow underneath, but also the thrust of his knife. "You got to do better than that."

His eyes narrowed. "I will."

I zipped around to land beside him and whispered in his ear. "I don't think so."

He was quick to raise his arm for a powerful blow with his elbow, but I brushed him aside with my hanbo.

He was so near to my face, I heard his rasping breath. Saw the shivering hairs in his nose. Felt the heat radiating off his body.

He came at me again.

I countered his attack with a left fist to his chin.

He stumbled and retreated. Somewhere along the way, he'd dropped his helmet. Wet hair stuck to his forehead like mud. Shadows lined his eyes, his shoulders sagged. But his spirit wasn't broken yet.

"Tired, Spark?" he asked with a hopeful lilt.

I gave him a mocking smile and coated my heart in a layer of ice. Then I reached back. Faked to the side. And plunged the sharpened end of my stick into his chest.

The Shade screamed. Blood spilled onto his boots and inked into a puddle. He tumbled to the ground, dropping his knife. The asphalt parted, and the Earth took his body.

Nothing was left for his mother to mourn. No body, not even his weapon. How long would his children wait for his return before realizing he was gone? I took a deep breath and swept my doubts away. Such was the nature of war. One side lived. The other side...didn't.

I threw a quick glance in the direction where I'd last seen Lea. The darkness had swallowed her form. Whether she'd watched the fight or not, by now she should have a good idea Shades were neither a fantasy I'd concocted nor were they inclined to leave her alone.

I killed the female attacker without ceremony. No point coddling Lea. Better to illustrate the realities of battle right now. What was a little PTSD between friends?

I trotted over to the remaining Shade sprawled on the ground and stabbed him through the heart. Once I'd holstered my hanbo, I sprinted to the car under which Lea had disappeared. The Earth trembled as it claimed the last body.

"Come on." I squatted beside the station wagon to grab her arm and helped her up. The tension in my chest unwound. She'd only received a single new scrape on her forehead. Thank the Old Ones.

"Shades, right?" Lea sounded weary, battle-worn.

"Shades." I unhooked the cuff around her knees and yanked her up from the ground.

"Are they dead?" Her gaze lingered on the mounds of dirt where the asphalt had split. The deep gashes were closing already. Soon the street would look as it had before.

"They're gone." I wiped blood spatter off my hand with my sleeve. "The Shades are of the Earth. It's where they return upon their deaths."

"You had to kill them?" The tremble in her voice was hardly noticeable.

"Yes."

"Why weren't they using guns or crossbows? They'd be more effective than knives."

"Since I can manipulate the wind, arrows are useless against my kind. *Our* kind, I mean. And guns are noisy, plus they have a tendency to react to magic."

"Why? How?"

"Something to do with the energy and the heat of the bullet. I don't know." I flung my arms to the side to indicate I was done answering questions. "You should ask the king. He's into that sort of thing."

"Are you hurt?" She jerked her chin toward my arm where the leather was ripped.

"I'm good. Come on, let's get you safe. The police are probably on their way."

She squinted at the remaining body cuff that bound her

arms to her torso "Walking would be easier without this thing on."

"Most likely, yes."

"Can't you take it off?"

I fixed her with a warning glare before unclipping the lock. "There."

The metal cuff clanged to the ground. She rubbed her sides, then bent over to pick up the bag she'd dropped.

"Now, come on." I dragged her to the street corner.

"What a crappy night." She shook loose. "I only told the driver to stop because I saw you." She peered down at her dirt-stained clothes. "Jeez, look at my jacket. It's all wet now. If this week continues like this, I'll have nothing left to wear."

Was this girl for real? "Forget the jacket, Lea. We're out of time. Your training has to start at once."

"Hang on. I'm grateful for your help, truly. But I can't just up and leave."

Sirens blared in the distance. I nudged her around the corner, out of the line of sight to the incoming police cars.

"You have no choice." I dropped my voice to a near whisper. "As long as you remain untrained, this world is a death trap. Your luster is too bright."

Her face scrunched so her features pointed toward her nose. "What about work? My family? My guinea pig?" She caught a second wind and folded her arms. "I'm an American. You can't make decisions for me. I have rights."

"I wish I could spare you the burden of your heritage, but I can't." I placed a hand on her shoulder. "Let me break it down for you. Stay, and you die. Come with me, and you live. It's that simple."

"But I have a plan." Her cheeks sunk, and she uncrossed her arms. "Can I at least call a friend to have her take care of Feynman?"

I checked the neighborhood. "Be quick."

She turned her back to me to speak into her phone. When she was done, I motioned for her to get going. Mumbling, she dragged herself past me. Better curb my triumphant swagger next to her stiff, wet-pants gait. Until I had her safely before my king, I wouldn't let her out of my sight again.

But I didn't crowd her. The slightest wrong move might send her back home to her beloved guinea pig.

She turned. "Do you really have something that can cure my dad?"

"Yes, we do."

She nodded and now walked alongside me.

Ten minutes to a safe area where I could open a Gate, unobserved by Kindreds. So for about six-hundred seconds, I dissected every movement ahead for new Shade activity. Nothing was going to harm her, not while she was with me. She was entitled to my protection, like any Elonian. The protection of the royal champion.

Whether she wanted it or not.

# CHAPTER TEN



*LEA*

*"What do you mean, I don't have a license to kill? Would you at least consider giving me a learner's permit?"*

My trip through the Gate proved to be the single most terrifying moment of my life. From the outside, the opening looked pretty, like a whirling kaleidoscope of blues and soft grays. A bit like the event horizon of the Stargate in the TV series. But once I stepped inside, a gale wind bitch-slapped me from one side to the other, while my guts got turned upside down. At least twice I bargained away my soul to get out alive. With a deft kick in the butt, the Gate deposited us onto a narrow trail winding its way through dense undergrowth. I tested the solid ground underneath me then straightened my hair and my clothes.

An impossibly bright sun shone through the foliage, stinging my eyes at first, and the climate was mild, if not all that warm. I wasn't a nature person and my experience with forests was limited, but so far, everything on this side of the Gate looked as it did on the other side.

As pointless as it was, I kept an eye out for anything that might spark recognition that this was indeed my home world. A natural landmark or at least a sense of déjà vu. But it was maybe unsurprising that I should have no memories of Elonia. I entered the foster system as a baby, when my brain was more occupied with sleeping, eating, and pooping than with keeping a record of my origins.

So why did I feel as if I'd lost something precious? Some integral piece that defined who I was deep down?

My disappointment waned when we climbed a hill leading out of the woods and I got my first taste of the mighty sandstone castle. It was too perfectly preserved to be a relic of a long-ago, long-forgotten era. Four large towers with toothed crowns at the top reached into the sky, one at each corner of the building. Only the unusually shaped windows that dotted the castle's facade didn't mesh with the medieval architecture.

"Your windows are triangular." I squinted to check I wasn't seeing things that weren't there.

The Gate had done excellent work at drying my clothes, but it had also blown dust and dirt into my eyes.

Nieve half turned but continued along the path without slowing her pace. "There is no reason for windows to be wide at the top. Unless you're a giant, of course."

"Wow. I can't believe I've never thought of that myself. How logical." My reply was only partly sarcastic. If I'd been an architect I might have been able to speak with authority as to the benefits of rectangular windows, but I knew when to keep my mouth shut. Mostly.

The hill dipped into a broad moat. A weathered bridge spanned across it, though instead of water, grass and weeds now covered its depth. Outside the massive oak doors, four men and two women stood sentinel, stiff as rods. Their hands rested on the ends of wide swords held tip-down in front of them. Where I'd half expected knights dressed in metal armor and chainmail, these guards shared Nieve's affinity for shiny leather.

Uncertain how to act, I gave them a shy smile.

No reaction.

Nieve marched through the open doors without acknowledging the guards, and I chased after her.

The sandy stone that made up the castle walls exuded a dusty, almost earthen odor, one I hadn't encountered since a class trip to Hamburg's St. Michael's church many years ago. Maybe that was what history smelled like. The bare walls and large stone tiles echoed our steps and the generous proportions of the corridors allowed us to walk side by side.

I stopped by a window displaying a stunning view of a lush, leafy forest. "It's beautiful here."

Nieve joined me, her face solemn. "It is." For a moment, her gaze lingered on the green canopy below. "Come on. The king is waiting."

Excited voices sounded from up ahead. Roughly forty or fifty men, women and children dressed in ordinary clothes like jeans or slacks had congregated at the entrance into a large room.

"It's her," one of them muttered.

Nieve let her celebrity status roll off her back, but this level of attention was new to me. Maybe, one day, my fellow scientists would clap at one of my discoveries, but of course, people like me weren't meant to be famous. *Scientists worked hard, and they did so for work's sake, not for praise.* If I heard it once, I heard it a thousand times. Despite being accomplished in their respective fields, my parents were modest about their achievements. My attempt to bypass the doctorate offended their core values. Taking the "easy way," they said, would be a decision I'd come to regret.

Had Nieve grafted for this adulation, or was it given to her on account of being a royal champion, whatever that entailed?

"Don't dally," she said, navigating through the gathering into a cathedral-like hall. Tapestries adorned the walls, and sparkling chandeliers dangled from a ceiling that was so high up I nearly tipped backward trying to take in its magnificent fresco of half-naked people with beards and wispy hair.

I could easily imagine the table we passed being covered by oval plates with large roasted birds and other delicacies, while knights ate and passed pitchers of mead.

Nieve climbed a dais with a gilded throne, backed by a blue curtain, and pushed against a door leading into a smaller and less grandiose space.

My feet shuffled across the smooth stone floor and came to a stop in front of a dark metal throne, the only item of furniture. Didn't these people own normal chairs?

I coughed, and the booming echo made me flinch.

Nieve positioned herself to my left with her hands behind her back, ready to take orders. Of course she had every reason to be calm.

This was her home. I was the stranger.

"Why am I here again?" I asked, my voice rough.

"To survive and help save our kingdom."

I twisted to face her and leaned in. "Sure. You said that. And I'm all for saving myself and others. Noble goal, really. But what can I possibly do that an entire kingdom can't?"

"That's what we're going to find out." Nieve's gaze was glued to the wall opposite her. The perfect soldier.

"That makes sense, but... If I went home, would anyone notice?"

"What about the Shades?"

"So some crazy dudes are trying to kill me. No big deal. The Seattle police force seems capable and well-armed. I like that in cops."

"Sh-sh."

Steps approached, and the door at the far end of the room

swung open. I curled up my hands and shoved them inside my sleeves to conceal their shaking.

Even though I resolved not to let anyone see me nervous, my usual hang-ups about speaking to authority reemerged. After all, there was hardly a greater authority figure than a bona fide king.

I leaned even closer to Nieve. "Do I curtsey or something?" My whispers sounded loud in the bare room. "And what do I call him? Your highness? King what's-his-name? Your majesty?"

"King what's-his-name?" The deep, graveled voice teased the sensitive nape of my neck.

A walking triangle of a man, broad shoulders and a narrow waist, swaggered into the room. My breath caught in my throat. Like Nieve, the man wore leather. Unlike Nieve, he rocked the leather. Rocked it enough to drive a blush into my cheeks.

A long sword hung from a belt around his middle. Fine gold stitching in the shape of birds in flight decorated the right shoulder of his jacket. With easy grace he installed himself on the iron throne.

Nieve bowed her head.

*So, this was the king.* Time to delete any silliness from my brain and crack open a bottle of suave and sophisticated conversation.

For a long while he studied me, his eyes, midnight blue and razor sharp. His gaze journeyed from my legs up to my face as if soaking in every angle and curve of my body. No man had ever looked at me like this. Ripples of heat flushed through me, but I bore his scrutiny with a steady gaze.

Occasionally he rubbed his chin, tilted his head, or combed his fingers through his short, light-blond hair. With each passing second, though, his eyes narrowed by another fraction of a millimeter, his features darkened by another microshade.

As did my mood. Maybe I wasn't Miss America, but the

doubt in his expression made me feel like I should be sitting at the ugly table.

"Welcome to Elonia, Lea. It's an honor to meet you. I'm King Tristan." He tapped the throne's arm. "To answer your question, the correct way to address me is *my lord* or *my king*." The over-enunciation of each word reeked of condescension.

Despite my better angels screaming to leave it be, my bruised ego forced a superior smile onto my lips. "But strictly speaking, you're not *my* king, are you?" I countered his squint with a slow shrug. "Just saying."

"You're the lost Elonian. A child of the light. That makes me your lord and king."

"I don't—"

A tiny movement of his mouth quashed my rebellion. He was a king, for crying out loud. His army probably stood waiting outside to waterboard me simply for looking at him funny.

I forced a deep breath. "Okay, I'm the lost Elonian. So now what?"

His jaw tensed. "Nieve hasn't told you?"

"The details are still hazy." I flicked back my hair. A flirty gesture that made me want to kick myself. "I get that the Shades want to destroy the barrier between this world and mine. But I don't know why."

He settled deeper into his chair as if preparing for a long conversation. "To conquer the Kindred world. And Elonia."

"And they have the hates for me because you've convinced them that I want to stop them, right? Thanks for that, by the way. Can't we reason with them?"

He raised an eyebrow. "Sure. By all means. Let's invite them over for dinner."

His sarcasm rolled over me like porcupine needles. "I meant, aren't kings supposed to use diplomacy to resolve these kinds of border issues?"

The king leaned forward. "Shades cannot be reasoned with. But you will be safe here. I give you my word."

He might have intended to provide comfort, but mostly he sounded annoyed.

I pushed my toe into a crack between the marble slabs. "Why do they think, and do you think, that I can make any difference? Just because my mother knew how to fight?"

"We'll discuss this later." King Tristan tapped his armrest again, a deep scowl on his face. "Nieve, please take our guest to the weapons chamber. I want you to get started right away."

"Yes, my lord." Nieve gave me a gentle prod, circled around me, and marched off.

Dazed, I followed. This was it? We hadn't talked details yet. My dad's health depended on me hammering out favorable terms of this—hell, did we even have a contract? I whisked around, just as the king disappeared behind the door.

Guess I'd have to give him a wigging next time.

Lea and I reentered the hall, and the crowd spilled from the corridor into the room.

"Welcome home, Lea." An old woman grinned at me through perfect teeth.

Me? Why were they greeting me?

Maybe motivated by the woman's courage, the others reached out with their arms. "Welcome, welcome."

For a second, their words sounded muffled. I shook my head, unable to decide how I should feel about this reception. The situation was too crazy for words. They didn't even know me. My face burned with embarrassment, worsened when they sidled up to me so close I was in danger of running out of air.

Nieve used her arms and elbows to clear a path. "Let us pass."

I stuck close to her six.

Some people touched me. A few even touched me inappropriately, although the mass of heads and limbs meant the groping could just as easily have been accidental. I used my bag as armor and grabbed Nieve's arm for fear of being squeezed to death by sheer goodwill.

"Here," a small voice said. "For you."

I came to a halt and glanced down. A girl with pigtails, cute as a button, handed me a single yellow flower.

Just like that, my confusion was forgotten. The heat spreading inside my chest loosened the big, fat knot that had roiled my stomach since the Shades first attacked me. I was the lost Elonian, the king had said. As much as these people's attention turned my muscles to goo, clearly, I meant something to them. They were *my* people.

I beamed at the little girl and took her offering. "What's your name?"

"Gerdeling."

Still swimming in the crowd's kindness, I couldn't even make myself laugh at her name. "Thank you, Gerdeling."

"Enough." Nieve's tone carried a level of authority she couldn't have topped if she'd drawn her stick. "Let's go." She took my sleeve and charged through the hall with me in tow.

"Wow." I stumbled after her. "You guys know how to make a girl feel special."

She shooed three teenagers out of her way. "Go home. The show's over."

One by one, the good people of Elonia backed away and we made it back into the wide corridor.

My hand grazed atop the potted plants that, together with a series of identical ebony doors, broke up the yellow-gray of the stone walls. We turned a corner, and Nieve finally slowed her pace.

"Those guys were seriously jazzed." I fanned the flower in front of my nose, letting the fragrance of patchouli and violets infuse my nerves. "All because of me?"

"They wanted to see what all the fuss is about."

"There's fuss? I mean, they weren't just here to welcome me?"

She scoffed. "They believe you are the one who will deliver us from the machinations of the Shades. That the history books will one day write about you. These people have come to meet their savior."

A chill blew away the cloud on which I'd floated since the enthusiastic welcome. "I'm their savior? Talk about pressure."

"I wouldn't worry. The one opinion that matters is the king's, and he doesn't expect you to perform miracles."

"Phew. Because I parted the Red Sea last week and am completely zapped right now."

She gave me a sideways glance. "We try to shield the outside from the severity of our situation. Unfortunately, restricting the flow of information meant they started making up stories with the snippets they picked up. So please don't panic on account of the fancies of the common people."

"Okay." But the panic had already made itself at home inside my brain.

To anchor myself in the Now rather than the Might-Be, I focused on my surroundings. For a castle, the decor lacked opulence. The large hall would make the perfect place to throw a hell of a victory party after a hard won battle. But the rest of the interior didn't live up to my expectations. Sandy gray bricks, a stone floor, and wooden doors were so blah. Where were the suits of armor, the gilded furniture, the breathtaking murals?

"Our first stop is the weapons chamber," Nieve said. "Every one of us has an affinity with a particular weapon. Mine is the hanbo." She gestured at the stick on her back. "The king prefers his longsword."

A small group of men and women, probably soldiers like Nieve on account of their leather outfits, passed us in the corridor. Strapped to their various body parts were weapons—a sword, a dagger, short or long sticks, even a mace. Like a medieval BDSM club.

But it wasn't the Elonian dress code that made me nervous.

The view through a window turned everything I knew about the world on its head. Out there, Newton's laws of physics took a real beating. A tight formation of several leather-clad men and women floated upright through the air, without a broom or a wing in sight.

*Damn. Real magic.*

Nieve hadn't exaggerated one bit.

I wet my lips and whirled around to Nieve, who was approaching the end of the corridor.

"Did you see?" I lengthened my strides to catch up with her. "They can fly."

"Not long ago, you dismissed my ability to fly as a trick."

"Yeah. It's just so...wow."

"Well put." She headed down a spiral staircase. "Nearly there."

At the bottom, a large, wood-framed painting hung high on the wall. It depicted a man and a woman in old-fashioned clothes, with one child on either side. All four were blond, a trait shared by most Elonians, as far as I could tell. My own brown locks set me apart.

"Why am I not blond?" I asked.

"I don't know. Not all Elonians are."

"Is my birth mother?"

"Yes."

I frowned. "So I assume my biological father isn't?"

"I don't know." Nieve sighed loud enough for me to hear. "How about we leave some questions for later? We don't want to run out of conversation, right?"

"How can you not know?" I slowed my steps, my heart galloping in my chest. "My birth parents. Are they here? Can I meet them?"

"The identity of your father is known only to your mother, and sadly she isn't able to tell us."

"Why not?"

Nieve cleared her throat. "Let's say she has mental issues that—"

I tripped over a crack in the ground. "My mother's a nutcase?"

"Unbalanced might be more accurate."

My luck couldn't be that disastrous. I'd never felt the urge to dig up my roots, but I was here. So close. "Can I speak to her?"

Nieve bunched her mouth and placed a hand on my arm. "I wish you could. Even if she were able to comprehend who you are, coming face to face with her daughter might exacerbate her condition. Maybe when she's better."

I didn't buy her excuse. "When will that be?"

"We'll see."

"How long has she been like this?" My voice grew more urgent. "Is that why she gave me up for adoption?"

Nieve pointed at a wooden door at the end of the corridor. "The weapons chamber."

A barely concealed attempt to change the topic, but in the end, I let her have that small victory. "So this is when you'll show me how to kick ass?"

"First you'll pick your weapon, but yes, that's the idea." She blocked my way. "Here's a word of wisdom you'd do well to remember. Being taught the art is a privilege granted to us warriors. Don't abuse it." She swung open the door. "Now, let's get started. Which weapon would you like to try first?"

She shifted and allowed access to a mass murderer's wet dream. Row upon row of weapons of every conceivable size and material lined the walls of an immense room. I stepped inside and twirled, taking in the sheer number of things that could kill me. If it sliced, diced, or pierced, it hung on these walls.

"Let your hand drift over them." Nieve picked up a crossbow and slid her fingers along its length. "One by one. Feel their texture. Their power. If a weapon speaks to you, we'll give it a go. Remember. You've got to carry it for long periods of time, so don't immediately go for the big weapons."

"I hear ya." I walked along the walls, gliding my hand over the weapons the way Nieve had suggested. Her fight against the Shades had been awesome. The speed with which she'd swirled her hanbo alone would drive an opponent dizzy. That said, maybe the arsenal held something less deadly. Like an electroshock weapon that could knock opponents off their feet with less deadly results.

The casual nature in which Nieve had dispatched the Shades hadn't escaped me. Would I ever find myself at the wrong end of her stick? Maybe asking her so many questions wouldn't be good for my health. She said she needed me now, but what would happen when they finally discovered this was all a big mistake? That I wasn't their mythical Wonder Woman by any stretch of the imagination?

"Is anything speaking to you?" She gestured across the room.

I searched the space for a stick like hers, but got distracted by a low buzz from further down the wall. Another step, and the buzz transformed into a melodious hum.

I zeroed in on its source, using my hands to guide me from weapon to weapon. When my fingers touched a steel dagger, a spark zapped from its cold metal onto my arm. I snapped back my hand, but the blade exerted a strange pull like an industrial magnet.

My approach was more cautious the second time around. Once more, a chill transferred from its steel into my flesh, but it was a pleasant chill that filled me with a cold calm. The dagger's smooth texture gave it a light, barely-there feel. I lifted it out of its holder and held it against the light.

"I see you've found something." Nieve stepped closer. "Solid spine. Double-edged. Curved hilt." She reached for my dagger.

I tightened my grip and yanked it away.

"Huh." My sudden possessiveness was odd, especially since I'd been raised to share. "Seems I like this one."

She arched an eyebrow. "Don't you want to look at anything else?"

I shook my head, entranced by the odd vibe humming through me.

"It's one of a kind." She tugged her earlobe. "Warriors in the past have complained because of its unpredictable magic. Maybe we can find something less demanding."

"I want this one." I sounded as tough as a Hell's Angel.

A quirk in Nieve's lips might have foreshadowed a broad grin, but if so, she didn't let it erupt. "Okay. We'll give it a whirl. Who am I to get between a woman and her weapon?"

"What name should I give it?" My dagger's hilt had molded itself to my hand, and I swished it through the air for practice.

"None. It's not a human or a pet. It's a tool."

"It still needs a name. Something fierce. Like Razor. Or Excalibur."

"How about Fallon?" The king, leather clinging to every delicious muscle, joined us in the weapons chamber. Up close, he looked nearer thirty than the thirty-five I'd guessed.

He approached me like a man with a purpose, crowded me

until his spicy, masculine scent filled my head. Then his gaze locked with mine.

"It means *angry beast* in the language of the Old Ones," he said.

My breath stilled. That man should be saying words like 'angry' and 'beast' all day long.

His face was what sculptors would consider perfectly chiseled, with a dimple in his left cheek, and full lips I wanted to sink my teeth into.

As if my obsession with my new weapon wasn't bizarre enough. Hell, I hardly recognized myself in Elonia. This is how Crichton must have felt when he ended up on Moya. Maybe the magical atmosphere had changed my brain chemistry, the way translator microbes did his.

Or was the answer more obvious, and my biological mother's madness was hereditary?

The king turned his back to me to study a sword suspended across two silver hooks. "Fallon also happens to be your weapon's original name."

"Fallon." The name floated over my tongue. "I like it."

He peered at me over his shoulder. "It's rumored to be extremely tough to handle." He held out a hand. "Try something else."

"No, I want this one." I snatched my arms behind my back, hiding the dagger from view.

He turned his full attention to me and a dark shadow fell over his features. "I understand you're not accustomed to addressing royalty, but I will insist on proper respect in my castle."

Heat rose from my neck and pressed against my temples. If arrogance were measured in molecules, his could inflate a hot air balloon. "Listen. I'm sorry you're not happy with how I address you, but you're the one who dragged me into a war I have nothing to do with, and now you want me to beg for the weapon? You're kidding, right?"

His eyes flashed, his mounting intensity charged the air.

"Don't push your luck." His voice sparked against my skin, a potent combo of authority and danger.

He wanted respect? I'd show him respect. I pinned a serene expression to my face. "Oh, may I please use this weapon to defend your precious Divide?"

His benign smile looked thoroughly royal. "Certainly."

Nieve giggled as if he'd said something funny.

"Can we get started?" I jerked my head around and headed out the door, while clutching my dagger close to my chest. "I feel the sudden need to kick ass."

They whispered, followed by a low snort from the king. They shared a familiarity, a certain bond my spidey sense hadn't picked up on before.

I hated being the third wheel, despite all the practice I'd gained over the years.

My mother once lost me in the mall. I was seven. I'd wandered around for hours, even though Mom assured me I'd been gone mere minutes. Until this moment, I'd always assumed I'd never feel that alone again. I was wrong.

# CHAPTER ELEVEN



*"There are two types of Shades—the quick and the dead. Although I haven't yet met one who was quick enough."*

Tall mountain ranges formed the backdrop of our first training session. They framed the Valley of Devron, where Gerrit and the king had instructed me in combat techniques when I was a girl. It was fitting I should bring Lea here for our first session. Maybe the carpet of flowers would settle her mind enough to help her focus.

"Lesson one." Hands clasped behind my back, I paced in front of her. "A dagger's sides are sharp, and the tip is pointed. You must thrust in a straight line."

I slid the training dagger I'd borrowed from the weapons chamber out of its sheath and lifted it above my head.

"If you lock your arm like this, your weapon will move along an arc." Arm extended, I swished the blade through the air. "Not only does this maneuver open you up to attack, you will at best slice into your opponent's skin. But a dagger isn't a kitchen knife, and we don't peel our enemy. We thrust and we kill."

"Kill?" Lea's sandpaper voice broke my concentration. She sat on a fallen tree trunk, knees pulled tight against her chest.

I whipped around. Hadn't we left the stage of her infernal objections in the past? We should have moved on to the eager learning phase by now. "What did you think the dagger's for? Making a sandwich?"

"Well, no. But I don't want to kill anyone."

"This is about defense." I placed my hand against my forehead to block out the sun, careful to point the blade the other way. "Remember, the Shades attacked you. Twice." I held up two fingers of my other hand. "Until we find a way of tickling them into submission, knowing how to take them out with your dagger might save your life."

"You're right." She rubbed her nose and peered up from behind the sleeve of her denim jacket, her eyes large and round.

I loosened the grip around the hilt. "Quite all right." My tone was more muted now, as I didn't want to send her fleeing for cover.

When she dropped her arm to her side, I even added an encouraging nod.

"We're here to learn, so if you have questions, ask away." My stern face ensured she didn't have any. "Now, where were we?" Resuming my original fighting stance, I lifted the dagger beside my head and described a straight line with it. "This is what we're aiming for. Clear?"

"I think so."

A breeze brushed along the tips of the heather covering the ground not far from our location.

Lea shivered and huddled her jacket, stained but no longer wet, tight around her. "Why can't this wait? In my world, it's late in the evening."

"You are safe, but our worlds are not. The Shade king is a cruel man, and soon, he'll move his army across our border."

"But it's not like I'll be at my best tonight." She glanced at the cloudless sky. "Or today."

"I only want to see what I'm going to be working with." Somehow, not a single note of unease had slipped into my tone.

"As long as you know I'm cold, hungry, and confused."

"Understood." I made a mental note to arrange a uniform. The seamstress would have to tailor it from scratch to accommodate Lea's shape, but she was quick with the needle and should have it finished by tomorrow. The durable leather would add an extra layer of protection against both the wind and sharp weapons.

Yet the most effective protection didn't come from the hide of animals, but through pain, sweat, and hard work. Only one training method I knew would keep Lea safe. I'd have to push her beyond her comfort zone.

I gestured for her to get up. "Your turn."

She rose and slid her dagger from its sheath. "Like so?"

She swished her weapon without focus.

I flicked a finger at her. "Try again."

Once more, the blade wiggled before my eyes. *Utterly useless.*

My muscles tensed, yet I kept the strain away from my face. "How about this time you do it the way I showed you?"

Lea pursed her mouth. "I did."

I corrected her position and made her repeat the motion. "How about now?"

For a third time, she looked like she was attacking an inebriated fly.

"Let's try something else." Maybe she needed a moving mark for practice. Good thing I had a Me-shaped target at hand. "Aim for me."

"For you?" She folded her hands under her arms, only to immediately drop them—and her dagger. "Crap, that hurt."

"Well done for attacking yourself." I arched my eyebrows. "Now attack me."

She stuck out her tongue, then picked up her weapon, and slowly straightened. "Fine."

Her stance wasn't terrible. What was missing was her actual movement.

"Don't be shy now." I beckoned with two fingers. "Go on, come at me."

"What if I hurt you?"

"You won't."

She rubbed her palm against her jacket's waistband. "But what if I do?"

"You won't." I stopped her protestations before our verbal exchange deteriorated into a cheap comedy routine. "Slice it, Lea. Will you just go for it?"

The last time my restraint broke like this, the Council had demanded my punishment. Tristan had locked me in the dungeon for an entire day. This time, he'd have been on my side. This woman was impossible to work with.

Lea took one forward step, waited for my nod, and took another. Closed her eyes. Swung the dagger.

I caught her wrist. "Try again. With your eyes open."

"Okay." She repeated her maneuver but stopped her blade five inches away from my arm.

I groaned. "Again."

She thrust, closer this time, and I slipped out of the way. With each attempt, her confidence increased, but her efforts weren't enough. Not nearly enough.

"Faster." I weaved out of her weapon's path. "Come on."

"I'm going as fast as I can."

"Seriously? A three-legged dog would be quicker than you."

She blew a dark strand of hair from her face. "Thanks."

Although her stance and the force with which she propelled her dagger were fine, her hips and feet moved slowly and without coordination. If my taunts didn't cajole her into stepping up her exercise, maybe the problem was her fear of injuring me.

Upon my request, the kitchen staff provided an assortment of fruit: Small yellow grapefruits, slightly larger, purple pomplums, and huge green melons. All in all, roughly fifty spheres, ready and eager to be her victims.

"What's that?" She pointed the tip of her dagger at a pomplum.

"It's a type of plum."

"It's huge."

"Concentrate." I commanded the wind to lift the pomplums high, and set Lea upon her fruity opponents. Soon, she fell into a rhythm that was more *drunken uncle* than *fierce cha-cha-cha*. Sweat dripped down her eyebrows and her nose, and she slipped off her jacket.

Her miniscule improvements didn't chase away my worries. Where did Lea hide those awesome skills that placed her in the prophecy? At the moment, she'd hardly be a threat to butterflies, let alone seasoned Shade warriors.

"Okay." At my command, the produce rearranged itself into a circular formation. "Now let's fight multiple, um, enemies at once."

I let the words of a short incantation flow through my mind. The prickling energy concentrated in my fingertips, and it took a mere flick of my hand to single out a melon. In quick succession, I sent the melon, another melon, and finally a pomplum to attack Lea. The three fruits shot toward her like small, perfectly aimed cannonballs.

Her nose flared and she twitched, rather than ducked, out of the way. "Missed me."

Lea had no reason to feel pride after today's performance, yet she held her nose high, a wide grin on her face.

I subtly signaled a plump grapefruit outside her line of sight. The fruit zoomed in her direction.

Lea spotted it and hopped aside, her stupid grin even wider now.

The grapefruit swerved and collided with a pomplum. The pieces of fruit exploded, and fragrant flesh scattered through the air.

When a particularly large piece landed in Lea's hair, I hummed my satisfaction.

"What the frak?" Covered from head to arms in sticky juices, she spun to glare at me. "You did that on purpose."

"So I did." Another snap of my finger, and a hefty melon slammed into her back.

"Crap." She sprawled to the ground.

I clicked my tongue to express fake disappointment. "How are you going to defeat the Shades if you let yourself get overpowered by a melon?"

"You're a bundle of laughs." Her tone was sarcastic, but her eyes twinkled with newfound vigor. She flung a piece of fruit flesh at me.

I ducked without bothering to conceal a chuckle.

"It wasn't a fair fight." She tested the stickiness of her locks with her fingers. "There's one of me and, like, thirty of them."

"Battle, like life, isn't fair. You can quote me on that. Okay, fun time's over." I motioned for her to get up. "Let's try something else, okay?"

"But I'm covered in goo."

"Deal with it. That could be blood someday. No stopping for a shower in the middle of a battle."

Next, I explained how to stab from the hip, from the side, and from below. More fruit was harmed in the process.

She inched her way toward the correct form, but was still miles away from the destination.

By the Old Ones, what was I going to do? I hadn't expected miracles, but a glimmer of her mother's skill would have settled my nerves.

"Are we done?" Lea's breathing loudly interspersed her words.

I flipped my dagger in the air and caught it by its hilt. "Almost. Let's combine what we've learned." Weapon pointed up, I walked her through two combos aimed at expanding her range of motion.

Her sweat-soaked top clung to her skin. She picked up a bottle of spring water. "If I haven't lost ten pounds by the end of this, I want a refund." She took a huge gulp and placed the bottle back on the ground.

"In battle, the Shades will not grant you any respite. Push past your inner walls."

Her stamina was shot to pieces, and she ran on sheer bullheadedness, but she wasn't giving up.

Instead, she picked up her jacket to mop her brow and soak up the remaining juices from her hair. With a grim face, she thrust her dagger at an overripe grapefruit. "What do the Shades want, exactly? Besides making my life hell."

The grapefruit's shell burst, and its tangy aroma scented the air.

"They are after war." I lowered myself onto the ground and pulled my knees up against my chest. "The Shade king wishes to rule all of us, including your world. We think he's working on bringing down the Divide. The prophecy—"

"There's a prophecy?" Lea ducked one melon and skewered another.

"Don't speak. Fight!" I raised my water bottle to my lips and drank. "Yes, there's a prophecy. It led straight to you."

"Hang on." She stopped moving and glared. "You believe in

that stuff? You upend my life and want to turn me into Karate Kid for a prophecy?"

"Something like that. Anyway, it says you and I will play a crucial role in the fight to save the Divide."

"So, what happens if we lose?" Puffing like a steam train, she dodged a fruit that paid no heed to her need for a break. "What if the Divide, I don't know, breaks or whatever?"

"Stop wasting breath." I pointed at a floating melon that had so far eluded her blade. "If the Divide falls, his army marches, and this land of magic…" I glanced around me. "…my home, will disappear. Elonians and Shades will have to live in the Kindred world."

"Would that be *so* terrible for you? I mean, hello, we have Disney World."

"Of course it's bad. We'd lose our culture, our way of life." I tilted my head. "Besides, Shades and Elonians in one place is never a good idea. Then there's the Kindreds. Once they discover our powers, they will envy and ultimately fear us. Sooner or later the whole thing's going to lead to the master of all wars."

"Oh." Lea ducked a pomplum. "But Seattle's already full of Shades and Elonians. That's what you implied."

"Arm up. The grapefruit could have taken advantage of your carelessness." I picked a blue-petaled flower and twirled it between my fingers. "I would never exaggerate so shamefully. Few Elonians live in your world, and by our estimation, less than a few hundred Shades have crossed the Divide. It's not easy for them to get to the Kindred world. The Gate opens in a few places across your world, but the only access point is here in Elonia."

Lea tripped, but caught herself. Her hair hung limp and wet against her head, but her shaking arm didn't rest. "Then how do they get across? Do you think someone here is helping them?"

"A traitor?" My shoulders fell. We'd assumed the Shades had discovered a way to hijack our Gate. But what if the betrayal the Shade had spoken of in the alley went further than a mere exchange of information?

Was that even possible?

"If that's the case—" She panted. "—don't you have bigger problems than training me? You could shut off the Gate forever, and then you and I could go our separate ways."

"Things aren't that simple." I picked another flower and rolled it in my hand, without taking my eyes off my protégé. "Our world might look medieval to you, but thanks to the king's techno-policies, we have all the modern conveniences. Cell phones, hamburgers, piña colada, you name it. If we cut off supplies, people would be outraged."

Her questions stopped, and her deep puffs for air morphed into a desperate wheezing. And still she didn't give up.

I smiled. If she showed the same stubbornness in a real fight, there was hope yet. "You can stop now."

"If you say so." She bent at the hips, hands against her thighs. She dry-heaved a few times and collapsed onto the ground, her chest working hard to pump oxygen into her lungs.

I pointed to her right. "Three melons have outsmarted you."

"Maybe you should train them instead. Christ, I can no longer lift my arms. See?"

She didn't move a muscle.

I smiled and stretched my legs out in front of me. "Footwork tomorrow, so you'll have the opportunity to rest them."

"All I know is we need to turn me into something fierce soon because I need to get home. If I don't call Mom at least twice a week, she'll be worried."

"You can call her from here."

"Seriously? Phones work across the Divide?"

I shrugged. "Sure."

"Still."

For a while, only the mating calls from distant birds and Lea's heavy breathing wove through the silence.

A few minutes later, she propped herself up onto her arms. "Tell me about my mother."

I snatched a surviving pomplum out of the air and bit into its violet flesh. Chewing time equaled thinking time. "There's not much to tell. Your mother isn't exactly talkative."

"So, I'm here to help you fulfill a crazy prophecy, but can't even meet my bio-mother? What am I getting out of this deal?"

"A cure for your father's disease. But you won't only get to save the parents that raised you, but also all your friends. Isn't all of that worth the inconvenience?"

She made a sobering face and cleared her throat. "Yeah."

"Perspective, Lea. Get some. I'm talking about the fate of our realms."

"I guess. It's just, the concept of saving the worlds is so abstract. Anyway, don't change the subject. What was my bio-mother's job? Do I have sisters or brothers? Aunts and uncles? Grandparents?"

"I believe many of your relatives were killed in the war. As far as I know, you have no sisters or brothers."

"It's not like I ever expected to meet my biological family." Her voice dimmed. "My parents are great. It's just…"

She didn't know that I understood the uncertainty that pressed against her chest until it threatened to suffocate her. That I, too, had experienced the sweeping nausea that accompanied any attempt to imagine my mother's face.

"What about you?" she asked. "Do you have brothers and sisters? A boyfriend? Husband? Anyone?"

"One brother. No boyfriend."

"Why? You're not *that*, um, stiff."

"What a compliment. With your silver tongue, do you turn any heads yourself?" I scoffed.

I wasn't stiff. Then again, from her point of view I had to come across as rigid. She didn't know how much war stole from a warrior. How we clung to rules, commands, anything that gave us certainty.

"Sorry." She laughed. "Anyway. Surely there's a guy out there who likes strong, determined women?"

So far, a guy hadn't. The opposite sex's lack of interest in me was as much down to my status as to my boyish nature. Tristan had treated me like a brother, and I'd fallen into the charade without protest. Besides, I was too tall, too flat, and too capable a warrior to garner the attention of men.

"Unfortunately, a royal champion who can whack hardened warriors to mush isn't every man's wish for a girlfriend." I coughed to remove the bitterness in my throat.

"Pfft." Lea blew a raspberry into the air. "If they aren't man enough to deal with their complexes, they're no good anyway."

A wisp of a smile might have flitted over my face, but I wasn't able to hold it. "Let's not forget we're facing a threat neither world can possibly imagine." I lowered my voice, as was my custom when speaking of our dark future. "Both realms in their current state are at risk of being wiped out. By comparison, dating seems trivial."

"You're too tightly wound." She looked past me. "If you don't believe there's someone who can make you happy, why bother saving the world? I mean, what's your motivation?"

Such insight from Lea's mouth? She wasn't stupid, not by any stretch, but she did a good job underselling herself, playing the clueless girl who lacked substance.

A deep rumble drifted into my ear. I raised my hand to shush her and scanned the area. We were so close to the castle, no

Shade would attack us against home advantage. Or had a wild boar strayed too far out of the woods?

"Oops." Lea patted her stomach. "I'm hungry." Then she burst out laughing.

A growling belly was all it had taken to poke my paranoia once again. I shook my head and laughed. "I thought we were under attack."

She snorted and flailed her hands through the air. "As I said. Tightly wound."

Still chuckling, I got to my feet. "Well, come on then. Let's get you cleaned up and food in your stomach."

She lifted herself up, slow and clumsy, like an old woman. And still she didn't complain.

# CHAPTER TWELVE

*LEA*

*"When picking a personal trainer, go for a pessimist. He won't expect miracles and is just glad he's getting paid."*

The large hall that had previously teemed with people now lay empty.

Nieve led me through the private door into the room behind it with its iron throne, then past an industrial sized kitchen. The servants lined up by the door and locked their sights on me. I averted my eyes. In college, I'd dreamed of leading a linear life holed up in a lab unlocking the secrets of the universe. If I did my job right, the scientific community might one day write about my accomplishments, and I'd work with the biggest names in physics, but in reality, silent acknowledgement of my contributions was my goal. At least that was how I'd been raised.

It wasn't even that I was uncomfortable being the center of attention—although I was—no, it was the fact that I hadn't done anything to earn it that bugged me. All these Elonians knew of me was that I was one of them.

We climbed a carpeted staircase, which opened into an open

plan area, furnished with a music system and two long sofas, both angled at a television set.

Aside from the bare stone walls, this was hardly the magical castle of fairy tales.

Nieve waved at a long passage to our right. "That's the king's bedrooms. Over here…" She pointed to her left. "…are mine."

From all her tough talk I'd assumed she'd be bunking at close quarters with ten burly men who considered her one of the guys. On the other hand, maybe being *royal champion* meant she was some kind of bodyguard. The king had the air of a man who could handle himself, but based on his personality, I didn't doubt he attracted assassins like dark alleys attracted lone women in slasher movies.

"You can stay here." She opened the first door on her left.

It was a small room, furnished for practical use rather than comfort, and scented with laundry detergent. It contained a single bed, a closet, and a massive desk. This was the big welcome for the lost Elonian?

"Reading material." Nieve pointed with her chin. Next to a pad of ruled paper, a stack of books piled high. "The seamstress will see to better fitting clothes later tonight. Breakfast is at eight. The sun doesn't set in Elonia, so you may want to close the blinds before you retire."

"How can the sun not set?"

"It's the way the Old Ones made our land. Our realm is still part of Earth, only different. Torren, the Shades' part of this realm, is always dark. Our part is always light."

Everything in this place was so confusing, from the reason I was brought here to the hundreds of corridors inside the castle. Never in my life would I find my way back. Of course, the concept of "back" had lost all meaning. Where was "back"? Home? I couldn't go home now if I wanted to. Nieve and her king had plans for me, as did those Shades.

Of the two, Nieve seemed the safer option.

She pointed at a door. "You can clean yourself up in there. You'll find soap and shampoo on the shelf, as well as a clean towel and clothes."

"Okay. Thanks."

"I'll see you in the morning." She disappeared behind the door.

And just like that, I was alone.

I emerged from the shower ten minutes later, my hair wet and curly. A honey and lavender aroma trailed my steps. Nieve had left me a pair of jogging pants that, once I'd climbed into them, stretched across my hips, while the legs were too long for me. Her T-shirt fit better. She was no doubt taller than me, but my breasts made up for it in terms of real estate.

A tray of food stood on the desk. Sandwiches, a bowl of pink cream of some kind, a cup of tea. Famished, I scarfed down the food, hardly noticing its taste until I came to the cream dessert. Red wine flavor. I'd had worse, that was for sure.

My large bag that had collected too many receipts over the past few weeks lay on my bed. My only possessions at the moment. If Feynie were here, he might give me a modicum of comfort. At least Vicky had promised to look in on him now and again. After all, I might be here for a week or more, or however long it would take Nieve to realize I wasn't the Bruce Lee of their imagination.

I picked up my phone to check my messages. Kieran had been called away so suddenly and probably wanted to explain. I didn't want to leave him hanging at a time like this. Hopefully, his news hadn't been terrible, and his father was doing okay.

My cell's display showed fifty-one missed calls from my mother.

I stared at the cell in my shaking hand. Had anything happened to Dad? He'd been doing well for the past six months.

Unless, in an effort to protect me from the harsh reality, they'd been sugarcoating the truth.

I checked my messages.

*"I'm getting worried now,"* my mother had written. *"Where are you?"*

Her message before that read, *"This is getting serious. Where are you?"*

And on they went, with decreasing urgency chronologically. Kieran's single message went unread. First I had to deal with my own stuff.

My heart thumping, I pressed the button to call my mother. If my father had taken a turn for the worse, and I remained stuck in Neverland…

"Lea?" Mom answered the phone almost immediately. "I've been so worried. Where have you been?"

"With a friend. What's wrong? Is it Dad?" I closed my eyes because I didn't want to hear her reply. Denial had always been a friend to me.

"What? Dad is fine. We've been worried about *you*."

Dad was fine. *Thank you, thank you, thank you.* "Why are you worried about me? Has there been another earthquake?"

The Shades had seriously shaken up the roads of Seattle. What if they'd caused the quake the night before I started my job? Stranger yet, what if the concept of tectonic plates was a myth, and Shades were responsible for all seismic activity on the planet? I gave a grim smile. Not likely.

"We had a deal." Mom's pressed tone told me her concern was about to be replaced by a tirade of very harsh words. "We haven't heard from you in nearly two weeks. Two weeks, Lea. Can you imagine what it's like for a parent?"

Two weeks? I'd been here a few hours. "Mom, I don't know—"

"Don't play innocent with me, young lady." Her words and

her high pitch combined into a verbal slap. "You weren't at work either. No one has heard from you. I was this close to calling the cops."

"I'm an adult, so the cops wouldn't have—"

My mother's snort interrupted my segue.

"Not the point, I know." I sat at the edge of the bed and took a deep breath. "I got caught up in a bit of an adventure. But I'm good, Mom. Honest."

She left me on tenterhooks for a few seconds. "Seriously, don't do that to me, are we clear?"

"Yes, Mom."

"What's the adventure?"

"Right. The adventure." I frowned. The truth wasn't going to help my cause. "It's a start-up looking into ground-breaking technologies. For example, they're experimenting with the means to enable personal flight." *Ground-breaking* technologies, personal *flight*—I had to be careful not to crack myself up.

"Jetpacks?" Like most physicists, my parents didn't hold much fondness for engineering in their hearts.

"No, more physics-based." I sat up and injected a dose of confidence into my voice. "I wish I could say more about it, but it's all hush-hush."

"Oh. Okay. If you say so."

"It's bringing me face-to-face with patent writing, applying for grants, and other things that will help me get the experience I want." I clenched my fist. Would she buy my bare-faced lie?

"You should have let your old office know," Mom said. "They seemed as confused as I was."

"I did." Now the lies were stacking up. "Word may not have gotten around so fast."

"Okay. Well, how did you come by this new job?" My mother's voice had finally relaxed.

Maybe I was better at deceit than I'd thought. "A chance encounter. I met someone—"

"What's his name?"

Her sudden enthusiasm threw me. Had I become such a loner that my own mother became excited at the prospect of my making friends?

"*Her* name's Nieve." I chuckled. "She's the one who recruited me. Speaking of which, I should go."

After all, I had just about run out of lies to tell her.

"Of course. I forgot it's morning in Seattle." Mom laughed. Not a sign of worry left. "Please don't wait so long until your next call. Agreed?"

"Agreed. And Mom?"

"Hmm?"

"Dad's really okay?"

"He has good days and bad days. At the moment, there are more good days."

I reluctantly said my goodbye and hung up. My mother's hesitant last words and the as yet unexplained time shift made me miss my family even more. If it was morning in Seattle, it was only fair to make another call.

Apologies didn't come easy, but the people at the translation company deserved an explanation for my absence.

"Vicky?"

"Lea. Is that you? Christ, where are you?"

"I'm sorry for leaving like that." I fell back onto the thick, bouncy mattress. "I had personal crap to take care of. Family stuff, you know."

"Yeah, I figured when you asked me to look after your guinea pig. Is everything all right? Your parents have been trying to get hold of you, too."

"There was a mix-up, but it's good now. Only, I won't be able to come back to work for a while."

A brief pause at Vicky's end. "You've been replaced. They couldn't hold the position, and we had no idea when you'd be back. If you'd at least called. But I'm sure they'll let you reapply once your life is back on track."

I hadn't even cared for the job, but the news still hurt. How had I gone from a promising physics graduate to translator to unemployed within the space of a few months? If I'd followed my parents' life map, none of this would have happened. Probably.

I put on a brave voice. "I guess I can't blame them for giving away my job. I hate to ask, but could Feynman stay with you? Everything's kinda topsy-turvy on my end."

"I've already picked him up. But seriously, what's going on? You're all mysterious and—"

"I'll explain when I get back. Thanks."

"Lea, what— ?"

I disconnected the call. The conversation proved predictably awkward, but it was done. Finally.

With my obligations to Vicky discharged, I had one more thing to do. Get a definitive promise that my father was going to be cured *pronto*.

I slipped next door to Nieve's room and knocked. "Nieve, you there?"

No reply.

I slid open the door, but the room was empty. Shoot. Sending out a silent wish not to run into King Snootypants, I tiptoed downstairs.

Nieve's voice sounded from the dining room we'd crossed earlier. "...a group of Shades was already waiting for me. Their sole objective, from what I could make out, was to kill me," she said.

"What are you talking about?" King Snootypants himself asked. "The Shades have neither the ability to predict where a gate might open nor do they have any reason to attack an Elonian in the Kindred world. We have a truce."

I glanced back up the stairs. Eavesdropping wasn't my style, but information so far had been short and sparse. Maybe Nieve and her king would be more forthcoming without me around.

"And yet, there they were." Nieve had the tone of someone who was throwing their arms up from exasperation, but she probably wasn't. She was too reserved for such grand gestures. "Their knives made their intention very clear. At this point it's also worth noting that the reason Lea finally agreed to accompany me was that the Shades had found and attacked her, too."

"Why would they do that? I've heard nothing to indicate they're aware of her or her role in the prophecy."

That darn prophecy again? Maybe the castle wasn't the only thing medieval here. Despite their cell phones and fancy magic, their mindsets seemed to be stuck in the Middle Ages, where superstition still ruled people's daily lives.

"I can answer that, but it's not an answer you want to hear." Nieve sounded grim. "I told you about my encounter with the Shade while I was in Seattle, didn't I?"

"I remember."

"He confirmed not only that his king was aware of Lea and that she was special, but also that the Shades were told by one of our people. We've been betrayed."

"Impossible."

Yet it tied in with what Nieve had said about the gate that she claimed was under Elonian control, but had mysteriously allowed several Shades to pass into my world.

"You're doubting either my word or your ears," she said. "Call your physician if you like, because I speak the truth."

*Boom! Score for my girl Nieve!*

"I wasn't accusing you of lying." The king sounded pissed.

"Did your Shade informer give you the name of this alleged traitor?"

That was it? Where was the demand for respect? The rage at being dissed? I sat on the bottom step and stretched my sore legs out in front of me. Maybe Nieve and the king did have a history. She got away with anything, whereas he'd pounced on me for the tiniest transgression.

"Of course not," Nieve said. "I'll have to investigate this possible breach myself."

"The Council won't be pleased to have a light shone upon their loyalty, and frankly, neither am I."

"That's why your hands mustn't go anywhere near this."

He made a noise, but she cut him off.

"They're used to impertinence from me," she said. "Chances are, they won't even know I'm investigating them."

"Maybe, but if they do find out, I might have to rebuke you in public."

Nieve gave a low chuckle. "That's hardly new."

The king sighed loudly. "It must be done, and done quickly. While you investigate, I'll take over Lea's training."

I snapped my head straight. He what?

"You what?" Nieve clearly shared my horror.

"Should I ask my physician to examine you, too?" The king laughed briefly.

Now he fancied himself a comedian. The only thing missing was the funny.

"Yes, because it sounded as if you said you wished to train Lea." Luckily, Nieve had retained her wits. She'd soon drive the insane thoughts out of his mind.

"I trained you, didn't I?" His tone held no humor now—which was worse. "The Council will welcome my hands-on approach in preparing the lost Elonian, and I will get a first impression of how our prophesied heroine stacks up."

"Fine. By all means, have at it."

*Et tu, Nieve?*

"Just make sure to dial your expectations down," she added, rather hurtfully. "I mean, way down. Dungeon-of-Dubaris down."

I knew my first training session had sucked, but what did they expect? I'd worked a full day, was attacked by Shades who were going to kill me—kill me dead, to be precise—then hailed a hero before being put through my paces at a time when I was usually asleep.

"Lea needs a firm hand to guide her, that's all." The king waved Nieve's objection off with a determined tone. "As for you, you find that leak and plug it."

"You'll have the traitor soon. Trust me."

"Always." Chairs creaked and furniture scraped across the floor. "I just don't know whether to wish you luck or not."

Before anyone could accuse me of listening to a private conversation, I shot back up the stairs. Asking about my dad's cure had to wait another day. For now, my mind was whirling enough as it was.

The king was going to train me. Something told me today's session with Nieve would soon be a memory I'd look back on with fondness.

# CHAPTER THIRTEEN



*"The outcome of a war is never a measure of who was right. It only ever accurately summarizes who's left."*

The morning after my discussion with Tristan, I awoke early with a plan of action. Proving to him that my suspicion concerning an Elonian traitor was justified motivated me, but the idea that someone had betrayed us irked me on many levels. My brother had taken the throne at a difficult time in our country's history and at great personal cost to bring order to the mess left behind by the Mad Queen. Her Councilors beseeched him—then the royal champion—to usurp her and take the throne. Now, one of them had betrayed him.

Digging into the Councilors' actions and whereabouts required a careful plan, or I'd cause Tristan more trouble than necessary. After a quick shower, I installed myself in my desk chair and jotted down a few ideas.

Means, motive, opportunity. A crime movie I once watched on my brother's TV screen had cited these three branches as the foundation of any investigation. But maybe it would be better to first consider my suspect pool as a whole.

Some Councilors had proven great allies in the past, but I'd take nothing and no one for granted.

Of course I'd have to keep an eye on the number of co-investigators I'd employ. No one but me deserved to get into trouble for this, but maybe trouble couldn't be avoided entirely. In a way, it was lucky that my circle of trust was small. In fact, it consisted only of Tristan and me.

More a *line* of trust, really.

If it had been up to me, the Council never would have been involved in our plan from the start, but Tristan relied on them too slicing much. He wasn't born into the crown, and it was no secret the Council's men and women exerted influence on him to do their bidding while they kept their hands clean.

How easy it was to criticize his actions, while the burden of responsibilities ate away at his good humor, not theirs. Many years had come and gone since his coronation, yet his confidence in his abilities—or in his status—hadn't grown. Appointing me as the new royal champion ten years ago marked his first, and only, rebellion. The Council had set their heart on Dachsoon, Regan's nephew, but Tristan needed someone on his side.

That said, our country's laws required I earned my position, so I worked and practiced day and night. My weaknesses with the sword had to be eliminated, my speed increased. One sweaty evening after the other, I edged to the brink of giving up, only to rise again with more determination the next morning. Dachsoon might have been a skilled warrior with more experience, but soon I bested him in almost every discipline.

I poured water from a carafe and took large gulps from the glass. Offering to release me from my obligation posed a huge risk to Tristan's future. Without me, he might have to accept the Council's choice of replacement. Lea, the foretold savior of mythical skill, should have been the one to take over from me.

As an outsider, she would have had no agenda other than doing what was right, and that would have placed her firmly on Tristan's side. Now, after one practice session, my hopes were dashed. Even under Tristan's tutelage, she might never attain the skills she needed to survive the prophecy, let alone to succeed me.

Was I doomed to remain royal champion forever?

In any case, no one suspect had come to the fore. On the face of it, it was none of them, which probably meant it could be any of them.

As for means, I'd have to look into communication. If the traitor met the enemy in person, my best chance of success would involve sending Dian, an impetuous but keen warrior-in-training, to check the stables. Once, she'd been fooling around with one of the grooms, so if anyone would be able to gather information about the comings and goings of the Councilors, it would be her.

I rose and slipped my notebook and pen into the inside pocket of my uniform jacket. A quick peek into Lea's room showed her still asleep. She'd had a long and tiring first day, and I wasn't going to wake her until breakfast time. I ran down the stairs and left the castle by a back door, then along a path thick with bushes and trees. Like all warriors, Dian would have risen several hours before breakfast. Right now, she'd be either studying or working out.

Dian lived with her parents in a training settlement not far from the castle. Approximately forty dark red cottages stood in a grid formation, defining small alleys between them. Many such settlements were dotted around the country, preparing old and new warriors for what was to come. Despite our truce with the Shades, no one doubted peace was only a fleeting state. The Shades' military buildup on our border was proof of that.

I knocked on the door and was immediately granted access

by a woman who was nearly as tall as I was. Dian's mother, red-faced and wide-eyed, described the way into their backyard, where her daughter performed her morning exercise.

Dian's long blond hair was tied into an off-center ponytail, and her strappy gray top had turned almost black from sweat. Her hands behind her head, she lowered herself into a slow squat, with her back facing the door, where I stood.

"Keep your heels down," I said.

Her shoulders tensed, but she did as I asked and completed seven more squats with the correct technique. Then she grabbed a towel from the lush grass and turned to me, wiping her forehead. "What are you doing here?"

I raised my eyebrows.

"Sorry." Her flushed cheeks turned an even deeper scarlet. "I didn't mean it like that. I just didn't expect you."

"I have a job for you. It's urgent and confidential."

"And you came to me?" Her mouth got caught between a smile and a shocked 'oh.'

"I assume that was a rhetorical question, seeing how I'm standing right here." I straightened and linked my hands behind my back. "One of our Councilors has betrayed us, and I need you to help me discover who it was."

While I told her the reason for my suspicions, her lips quivered, but she asked no questions. If there was one person who'd felt the ire of the Council almost as much as me, it was Dian, trouble-maker extraordinaire. If I hadn't plucked her from the detention center, she'd probably still be locked up. Or maybe the reason the Council never took to her was precisely because she enjoyed my favor. Either way, she was the right woman for the job.

"I'll speak to my brother, too." Her tone of voice was all business, only the quick movements of her eyes betrayed her real emotions about the clandestine activities I'd asked of her.

"If they didn't meet in person, they could have spoken on the phone. Dion works for Talk Elonia."

"You understand no one must know about your investigation."

"Of course. Don't worry, my brother won't ask questions."

"Agreed." Cell phones hadn't even featured in my thinking, but not everyone in Elonia shared my aversion to techno gadgets.

"I'll go to the stables straight after training. Thomas, the—"

"You won't be going to training today." I sharpened my voice. "Finding the traitor is our priority."

"Dachsoon is going to write me up." Her body stilled. "I've already earned two strikes this month."

"Then you will endure a third." I gave her an encouraging smile. "You can't tell him why you're absent either."

She sucked in her bottom lip and nodded. "Understood."

The punishment Dachsoon would devise for her would be nothing compared to what would happen if our scheme came to light. Dian was intelligent enough to get that and stubborn enough to not be slowed by the threat of Dachsoon's wrath.

Once I was certain she knew what to do, I set out to investigate the most troubling aspect of the betrayal: motive.

Upon my return to the castle, I knocked on Lea's door.

"Yeah?" she called out, her voice hoarse.

I entered and glanced at the unopened books on her desk. "Good morning. Did the seamstress turn up last night?"

"I don't know. Let me ask the many needle wounds that nearly caused me to bleed to death."

"Funny." I smiled and sat at the side of her bed. "Good news. The king himself wishes to train you from now on."

She shuffled to the back of the headboard and sat straight, her hair mussed and curlier than ever. "He wishes to train me, huh? Wishes? The guy can't stand me. And how is that even good news?"

Lea had a point, but part of being an instructor also required me to motivate and encourage those in my charge. "He's the best fighter I've ever seen. Being trained by him is a great honor."

She rolled her eyes. "Doesn't he have better things to do? Like king stuff? You know, strutting, ordering people around, that kind of thing?"

"He isn't like that. Give him a chance." There was a time when he was a man everyone loved. "Besides, I'll be busy over the next few days."

"Finding the traitor?" Her raised eyebrows showed no sign of uncertainty.

"You eavesdropped?" I rose from the bed and took two steps.

"I accidentally overheard. Big difference. Want to talk about it?"

Once again, she didn't behave the way I thought she would. I'd expected a stomping foot, a few catty comments maybe. Instead, she offered me her ear.

I sat back down. "Okay. I've already asked a young woman I trust to look into cell phone and stable activity, to see who might have sought contact with someone outside of Elonia, but I'm stuck on motive. Why would anyone betray us?"

Lea tugged on her blanket then shrugged. "Talk me through it. Everything. Sometimes, when you explain stuff, you're helping yourself see it from a different angle."

I retrieved my notebook, which still contained too many empty pages, and placed it on my lap.

Lea nudged me with her leg. "Come on. What have you got to lose? Tell me about Elonia and the Council."

"Okay." I pulled my knee onto the bed and placed my

notebook next to me. "Being a monarchy, Elonia's political system is easily understood. The king rules, the Council advises. If a king is as amenable as Tristan, the Council holds tremendous power."

"Amenable?" She coughed in an exaggerated fashion.

"Yes. Now be quiet and listen. Given that the Council is so powerful, what could possibly move them to join forces with the enemy? Bringing down Elonia wouldn't do them any good, not when they'd hand victory to a monster like Galleo, the king of the Shades."

"Has your king pissed them off recently? Like, did he talk to them?"

"Fine. You don't like him. I get it." I raised my hands as the only admonishment. "If all they wanted to do is topple the king, that could be achieved without involving the Shades. A vote of no-confidence, and he'd hand the crown to someone else with a smile. Because whatever you might think of him, he is king out of duty, not for personal gain."

"Okay, okay." She stared ahead, past my shoulder, then refocused on me. "So maybe the king and the monarchy aren't the targets. Think about it. Only you and I have so far been victims of sabotage. Coincidence?"

"I admit, any member of the Council has reason to dislike me. I don't mind disagreeing with them out loud, if I have to."

Lea chuckled. "You, a rebel? Okay, but if that's the case, why act against you now? What's changed?"

"Nothing. Except for you. I was on my way to find you and got attacked. After that failed, they came for you directly."

"Wow." She pulled her blanket higher. "Didn't you say I'd be safe here?"

"Why would anyone sell you out to the Shades? It makes no sense. You're a vital part of the prophecy."

"Sheesh, not that again. What exactly does the prophecy say?"

"You're the lost Elonian." I turned my notebook in my hand, just to feel something cold and real. "You and I are foretold to thwart the Shade king's plans to take over Elonia. Beyond that, Tristan has largely kept quiet on the matter. Maybe that's my fault, but I gave up quizzing him long ago. After all, he's the king, and I just work here."

Lea snorted. "If that were true, he wouldn't have put you in charge of this investigation. What else?"

"That's all I know about what's been foretold. Only the king and his Councilors are privy to the details."

"Well, don't you think it's time for you to take an interest?"

She was right. How could I shine a light on the traitor if I was operating in the dark? If anything could tell me the *when* or the *why* of our role in the coming fight, it would be the oracles' own words.

"Fine. You got me. I'll check out the prophecy, while you be a good girl and meet the king when he's ready."

"And when will that be?"

"Someone will let you know."

"Nieve?"

"Yes?"

"About my father."

"We'll do right by him, don't worry." I patted her leg through the blanket and got up, once again stowing my notebook inside my jacket pocket.

"Nieve?"

I sighed. "Yes?"

"How come my mother thinks I've been away from Seattle for two weeks?"

"Ah, that. Time runs to a different clock in your realm. Sometimes you're ahead, sometimes you're lagging behind."

"That's impossible. Has anyone here even heard of the arrow of time?" She shook out her blanket as if to cool her body.

"Awesome. That would have been good to know before my long absence nearly gave my parents a heart attack."

I grinned. "Well, now you know. Right. I'm off. Seems we both have a busy day ahead."

Without responding to her mumbled objections, I left her room and sprinted down the stairs. My next step was clear, but putting my plan into action wouldn't be easy. Like all historical documents, the prophecy was kept in a large vault, which was heavily guarded.

A few minutes later, I stopped short around the corner from the cast-iron door to the vault. The guards, Kai and Quinton, stood stiffly to either side of the door, exactly the way I'd trained them.

The thing about Kai and Quinton was that both were easily distracted. A butterfly or a squirrel had made them lose focus and fall flat on their butts during flight training more than once. Without a squirrel at hand, I'd have to use magic. I retrieved my notebook and silently tore out a handful of pages, which I crumpled into a ball. With barely a word spoken, I wove the air into a solid net to carry my ball—and smashed the entire thing against the wall around the corner.

Both gave a start and frowned.

The ball whizzed past their ears, down another corridor, bouncing from wall to wall. A loud clang and shatter sounded. One of the ceramic planters must have got in my ball's way.

Kai ran after the zooming sphere, leaving Quinton behind.

Slice it. I pushed more speed into the net of air carrying my ball. Since I had no line of sight, my paper missile would undoubtedly cause more property damage along the way.

"Quin, a hand!" Kai shouted from a good way away now.

At long last, Quinton left his post, too. If my ball did its job, I wouldn't see the guards back here for a good few minutes. Later, I would have to punish them for abandoning their duty, but for now, I thanked the Old Ones for this stroke of luck and pushed open the heavy door.

Rows of shelves crisscrossed the room, roughly the size of the Great Hall. They contained boxes holding documents that archived Elonia's history going back to a time when the Old Ones still walked among us. The ceiling lamps cast a dim light on the thick layers of dust on top of the boxes. To my right, glass domes covered valuable artifacts from our past. Many I didn't even recognize, except for the Mad Queen's bow and quiver, and the ruby-encrusted sword used by Gerrit, Tristan's best friend and former royal champion.

The scroll I was after was laid out in a glass box.

I ran my fingers across the clear lid. What I was about to read didn't just affect Lea's future, but my own.

In stylized calligraphy, black words spilled over a relatively small piece of paper. It spoke of a great change that was to sweep the realms. It would devastate "all that we are and all that we will be."

Only this once I wished the oracles were prone to exaggeration, but I had no reason to doubt them. They had never steered me wrong.

Only the fawn and the snow child would stand against the dark king and his dark prince—Galleo, and his oldest son, no doubt—whose plans would cause great suffering.

Whether I asked for it or not, my role had been destined from birth, when my identity as the snow child was ascertained by a magic not even I was permitted to access. More than once, Tristan had joked the name suited me on account of my fair hair and icy heart.

My training began when I was five, a relentless schedule of school and sparring sessions. Years later, my head start would help me become Tristan's royal champion. One way or another, I was prepared for whatever dark plans were to come my way.

The same couldn't be said about Lea. Discovering that she was the fawn didn't take long either, since all clues led to her mother. Finding her in the Kindred world, however—that had been the tough part.

My shoulders sagged as I leaned over the case and buried my head in my hands. Unfortunately, the prophecy hadn't provided any new insights. When the dark king was planning to make his move remained a mystery, as did Lea's and my exact roles in his scenario. Were we required to infiltrate his ranks and assassinate him? Lead the Elonian army in a last battle against the Shade forces?

I straightened and shot the yellowed piece of paper a disappointed look when one peculiarity caught my eye. Upon my appointment as royal champion, the oracles were required to bestow on me their blessing. The certificate they'd handed me on the big day carried their official stamp, yet it was this stamp that was missing from the scroll.

One of the most important documents in our kingdom, and it wasn't authenticated by the oracles?

I pried open the lid and removed the scroll from its protective environment. Carefully, I turned it over. Above the waxy stamp, it read:

*Lest the Divide be broke and fade into the water of The Vessel of Orrin. On that day, the two children shall unite their powers and battle to preserve the Divide. Yet all shall be lost in the fawn's death.*

My hands tightened around the fragile paper as I re-read the passage. Lea, the fawn, was going to die. How could this be right? I was the one who'd brought her here, promised her safety, and all along, Tristan and the others had known she was a sacrifice in a war that wasn't even hers.

I replaced the scroll and left the vault before Kai or Quinton returned from their hunt.

# CHAPTER FOURTEEN



*"Maybe I do need to adjust my opinion. Doesn't mean I was wrong."*

I quickly closed my mouth, which had fallen open upon closer inspection of the dining room. The wooden cabinet that lined the wall contained many artifacts, from bronze plaques to gold coins, and hand-carved figurines. Some of my board games came with metal miniatures, intricate but nowhere near as exquisite as this collection.

"They're a hobby of mine." The king entered the room and stood behind me, the scent of shower gel strong on his skin. "I paid extortionate bribes to get my hands on this figurine of a horse when it was in Galleo's possession."

I angled my head for a closer look. "It's chipped."

"It's old."

Servants entered with enough food to feed an army, but set only two plates and two bowls on the table.

I shot the king a puzzled glance. "We're having breakfast together? Just the two of us?"

"Feel free to leave if you don't like the company." He turned and sat in the chair at the end of the table.

I took the seat next to him.

On offer were bacon and sausages, a form of fruit, a muddy gooey substance that might have been porridge, and fried and boiled eggs, plus about six different types of bread and bagels. The king spooned brown slop into his bowl and started eating.

I grimaced.

"Stop finding fault with everything." He wagged his spoon at me. "You should be grateful. If nothing else, maybe your days in Elonia will teach you maturity."

"I'm plenty mature." I underlined my statement with a whirl of my fork, one that reminded my sore muscles of the work they'd endured. "I just don't enjoy being treated like a redshirt."

"You're not." The king pushed another glob of slush into his mouth.

I lifted my eyebrows. "Do you even know what a redshirt is?"

"You think we're treating you like an expendable chess piece." He shrugged. "Star Trek. We get Kindred television, you know."

"Oh. Good then." I speared a few slices of bacon onto my fork and transferred them to my plate, where they joined a fried egg and a few pieces of the enigmatic fruit.

He interlaced his fingers and rested his elbows on the table's edge. "Both our homes, the Kindred realm and Elonia, are at risk. Wouldn't you agree you have a duty to prevent their destruction?"

"You talk about my duty but haven't mentioned my rights." I swallowed, then rolled my shoulder to bring relief to my tense neck. "Say what you like about Robespierre, but I'm beginning to understand his extreme dislike of monarchies."

The king's lips tightened briefly. "What rights are you talking about? The right to get killed by Shades?"

"Nieve said anyone in your army will be taught the secret to curing cancer." I listlessly let my fork wander across the plate.

"That's what I want. Teach me to do that, I'll do whatever else you need me to do."

He lowered his spoon and didn't move again until I lifted my head.

While he poured black tea into my cup, his eyes skewered me with superiority. "Your father is sick, I know. And you will discover how to help him as part of your training."

"When?" I gifted my cup with an evil look. The last day I'd started without coffee was a dark twenty-four hours for all who knew me.

"There are no shortcuts to becoming a warrior. You'll be trained in defensive arts, both physical and magical, and if you work hard, I promise I will teach you what you need to know to help your father *and* to protect yourself." He rubbed his eyes and then lowered the pitch of his voice. "I wish this didn't have to fall on you, but this isn't a punishment. It's just the way it has to be."

Maybe what I'd seen in his gaze wasn't superiority but something more humble: sadness. Could a king who could afford everything he desired be sad? Nieve had given me food for thought when she'd described his complicated relationship with his Council. Among them, a traitor. He also had to prepare for a potential war, because—and I only didn't mention it so as to shield him from another harsh truth—I probably wasn't the solution to his problem. My stamina sucked. Jogging a mile was a struggle. Hell, I'd been attacked twice in my life, and both times I'd lost big-time.

But what if the king stopped the training before I got to the bit about saving my dad? What if I let my father down again?

"Do we have a deal?" The king was still staring at me.

I averted my eyes and slowly sipped the hot, bitter tea. "Yes. I'll do what I can."

Because I had no choice. If I wanted to save Dad, I had to

turn myself into a badass like Nieve.

"Did the seamstress visit you last night?" The king asked.

"I remember being jabbed and pricked by a gray-haired woman named Marge with tiny fingers and large pins. That who you're talking about?"

"Good then." He spoke slowly, as if addressing a kid. "And I assume she's already delivered your first uniform?"

"She brought me a pile of leather clothes earlier. My room now smells like Eau De New Car."

"Wear the uniform for our first session. You should get used to its feel from the start."

"Why leather?" I separated a piece of sausage with only my fork, mainly because my biceps hurt too much to pick up a knife, too.

"It's hardy. We also treat it with magic to make it extra tough, yet it remains flexible. The shiny coating helps with optimum reflectivity when manipulating light. Without it, it would be more difficult to make yourself invisible."

I hurried to swallow the last bit of sausage. "Invisible? Cool."

Any attempts at mimicking invisibility I'd read about had involved reflective materials, which could be used to *bend* light rays around a body. Maybe magic did have a basis in physics.

The king had emptied his bowl of mud, and under his careful attention, I shoveled the last pieces of egg into my mouth.

"Good. Now how about you run up and get changed?" He pointed his finger toward the stairs.

I nodded and got up with as much energy as I could muster, but by the time I'd climbed step eight or nine, my pace had slowed. This was going to be another long day.

I slipped into the pants, which were tight but flexible enough to allow for my *knoll*, which is what I called the soft part of my stomach located right under my bellybutton. The uniform even came with a holster so I could carry Fallon, my new—and first ever—dagger, with me. Shiny high boots increased the kink factor. The leather corset-type bralette sat cool against my skin and, unlike a real corset, allowed me to breathe. So far, so sexy. Next, I stuffed myself into the leather jacket.

The zipper ended mid cleavage. Seriously? Was I going to fight the Shades or put on a show for them? I was about to put my T-shirt on beneath it, but stopped. Marge had insisted no fabric should come between leather and a warrior's bare skin.

Since I didn't have a mirror, I dashed into Nieve's room. Yep. As I'd feared. The low V-cut might work for someone as tall and slim as Nieve, but it made me look as endowed as Dolly Parton. I was *not* wearing this jacket.

I rifled through Nieve's closet for alternative clothing, but everything was too long and yet too tight. *Fan-fraking-tastic.* Only one of the tops, black and sack-like, looked about my size. I returned to my room and took off the jacket, which I threw on my bed. Maybe I'd find Marge later and explain my predicament. The black, short-sleeved Tee, on the other hand, flattered my chest without forcing it down anyone's throat.

Of course, the king might not understand my reasoning. He'd given an order, and he seemed to be a guy who expected his command to be followed to the letter. In a brave act of avoidance, I picked up the topmost book from the pile Nieve had left for me, and looked at the title. *Encyclopedia of Magic, Volume 1—Air.* Maybe I had time to read the opening chapter. Anything I'd pick up now could be used to dazzle the king and buy me time to catch up before he kicked me out of Elonia for being useless.

The second chapter got my pulse going, and by the third, I was under the book's spell. The pages were a revelation. Before Elonia, I'd thought of magic as, well, magic. Something outside of the laws of nature. I might have been wrong.

Nature as I knew it was governed by four forces, three of which played nicely with one another. The evil step-mother in this happy fairytale family was gravity. Unifying all four had become the Holy Grail of physics—one which might never be found.

The book before me hinted at a missing ingredient. A fifth force. A ripple of sheer giddiness rushed through me. No wonder Q always looked so smug when he played tricks on the crew of the Enterprise. This fifth force was magic, and it could affect any medium on an elemental level. Did this idea spring forth from a pseudo-scientist's imagination, or was it in any way quantifiable?

A new force could be a game changer. If what I read was true, nothing was as I thought, yet everything was as it should be.

If I could crack the math, do experiments, the results could be unfathomably important. Not just as a contribution to science in general, but as a contribution to Elonia. I'd never be a fighter. That was clear. But proper research could open up new options for Nieve and the king, including non-lethal options, to help keep the Shades' conquering ambitions in check.

Engrossed in my new discoveries, I nearly missed the valet's knock on my door. The king was getting impatient.

On my arrival in the dining room, he still sat at the table, this time with a phone in his hand. If this weren't a magical kingdom, and if he weren't a magical king, I'd swear by the chirps and grunts coming from his cell he was busy catapulting birds into pigs.

"I'm back." I slumped into a chair opposite him.

He didn't look up.

My throat closed around a golf ball in my throat. I got it. My long absence had been another sign of disrespect, even though it had been an accident. "I'm sorry. I got lost in one of the books Nieve left for me to read."

Without making a sound, the king placed the device on a newspaper spread out on the otherwise empty table. His calculated movements exuded every bit the control I'd expect from a man of power. A shudder ran from my neck to my tailbone. The air thickened, forcing me to take fast, shallow breaths.

He raised himself to his full six-foot-and-a-bit height and appraised me through narrowed eyes. It was one of those looks that made men cower and women rip off their clothes.

I cowered, if only to avoid the latter scenario. One day I'd have to seriously analyze my predilection for guys in leather.

"Where's your jacket?" he asked.

"Upstairs." I willed my voice to be louder. "It doesn't fit."

"Marge is our best seamstress."

I met his stare, somewhat distracted by the flicker of light reflected off his flawless face. Each twitch of his eyes and every shift of his head carried a meaning I didn't understand but was desperate to decipher.

*Stop gawking.*

My cheeks warmed. "What, you want me to show you?"

A curt nod.

Wobbly legs and butterflies made my march upstairs another slow one, and I lacked motivation to hurry back down. What was it about this man I found so captivating? I returned to the dining room, jacket swinging from my hand.

The king sat on the corner of the table, his cell phone replaced by the rolled newspaper he repeatedly thwacked against his open palm. "Put it on."

My nerves jingled like tennis balls in my gut. Did he mean here? No way. I slipped out the door, took off the T-shirt, and crammed my fleshy parts into the leather.

Behind me, the paper tube whacked his hand with more urgency.

"Hold your horses. Nearly done." My fingers moved like stumpy icicles. I dropped the slider twice before I zipped up the jacket as far as I could. "See?"

I re-entered, arms apart to grant prime view of the Eighties leotard effect I had going.

The king's hand clamped shut around the free end of the paper. "It fits beautifully. I mean it, um—" His gaze darted over my uniform. "It fits like a glove. As it should."

"If I'd wanted to wear a glove over my boobs, I would have."

His chin lifted. "The uniform's tailored for optimum maneuverability. Get used to it."

Since any of the responses that came to mind would have made my situation worse, I zipped it.

He rose and squeezed past me, his elbow brushing across my arm. "Now, come."

Without enthusiasm, I followed him through the kitchen, out a back door, into a yard.

At least the view was pleasant. The king's broad shoulders swayed with each step, long arms swinging by his sides. Beneath the bottom stitching of his jacket, a black belt hugged a narrow waist, with a holster for his sword. An impossibly tight butt crowned over muscular, long legs. Women all over the world would give their prized possessions for a guy like this.

I dug my nails into my palms. Women other than me. Women who liked being belittled. Or maybe, women like Nieve.

We passed a stable, where a young woman pulled a young man behind a pile of hay bales. Maybe they were hiding from the king or looking for a place to make out. That, or Nieve's spy was doing her work.

On the opposite side of the yard, a wide, one-story building hid the base of the majestic mountains. Inside, mounds of red sand and pebbles covered the floor. Each time I freed one foot from a sinkhole, the other one sank deeper. On one wall, rusty tools and horseshoes hung in a neat line, and behind me, a small window gave a view of a winding trail.

"When you fight Shades…" The king snapped his fingers to catch my attention. "Expect the ground to be lumpy with holes, or worse. That's how Shades like to use their magic. Destroying the ground so you lose your footing."

"Yeah, I found that out."

He held out a hand for Fallon. His taut features convinced me not to argue. I handed him the holster and dagger, and he hung both behind the door next to his longsword.

Then he pointed at the floor again. "Shades have a connection to the Earth, its stones, the dirt under your feet. Every Shade, warrior or not, can fling rocks at you with a wiggle of his finger. That's the thing about Shades. They hand out the secrets to magic like candy, without regard for the dangers that come with their powers. The more experienced among them can rip the bricks from a house or tunnel deep into the Earth to trap you."

"Uh huh." I shivered. "So how does their magic work? Do they give off an electrical field that somehow affects the molecules or electrons in rocks?"

His brows shot up.

"What?" I set my feet wider apart to avoid the appearance I cared about his reactions. "I'm curious. So what?"

"No, no, curiosity's a good thing. When I first met you, you didn't strike me as a…"

"Human being with a brain?" Despite my sharp tongue, the sudden shift in his opinion of me bolstered my self-esteem like a pat on the back. Maybe he wasn't the jerk I thought.

"In my experience, girls don't usually show interest in science."

"I'm not a typical girl." I crossed my arms. "For one, I'm a woman."

"That you are." He broke into a smile that opened up his face.

Liquid softness flowed into my chest, and I couldn't help but beam back at him. "Okay then."

"Why don't we start over? Hi. I'm Tristan." He took my hand.

Startled by the potency of his touch, my eyelids fluttered. "Not *my lord*? Or *your majesty*?"

"Just Tristan."

I shook his hand. "Lea. Nice to meet you."

My breathing stopped, and so did the world. His fingers lingered, long enough to let my imagination leap weeks ahead into a future with him that would never happen.

I sucked in air and withdrew my hand. He was a king. Not the kind of man who'd skive off work for a day to spend it playing games with me or do any of the other things normal people did.

He angled his body away from me and gave a half cough. "Let's continue the lesson. The Shades can wield their magic under a shield, away from Kindred knowledge, by calling up the shadows."

"Can we do that, too?"

His features sharpened. "Definitely not. Elonian magic allows you to manipulate the air and the light, but we do not use our abilities as a weapon, the way they do. When the Old Ones gifted the Touched with powers—"

"The Touched?"

"Us, the Elonians and the Shades." He shook his head. "Anyway, the Old Ones gave us our powers to help us as a society, not to equip us for war."

Clearly this dude hadn't left his castle in a while to get a whiff of reality.

"Did anyone tell the Shades? Because they don't seem to be

following the program." If my words alone didn't make my position known, my sarcastic undertone got the point across.

Tristan gave one of those face shrugs, where the eyebrows mirrored the motion of his shoulders. "The Shades learned their particular brand of magic in their pursuit of ever greater power. Since their violent acts were limited to only a few instances at first, we didn't worry and let them be. That changed the first time they killed an Elonian. We expected the Old Ones to return to strike them down, but they didn't. We were on our own. The Shades grew bolder, which taught us to fight."

"But I can use magic to defend myself, right? Make myself invisible."

"We'll cover that later, I promise. It's easier for me to check on your progress before you can make yourself invisible."

I chuckled. "Makes sense."

He fell into a casual fighting stance. "Let's begin with the basics of combat. Rule number one—we do not use magic to cause harm. That's not to say Elonians must remain victims." He looked me up and down. "You're short. Untrained. Unprepared. If I didn't believe in the prophecy, I'd say you'd make a lousy candidate for beating any Shade. So I expect your rapt attention and full commitment. Is that clear?"

I clenched my fists and my jaw. *Play nice.* Only then did I notice that twitch of his eyelids, that twinkle in his gaze. "You're baiting me."

"Is it working?"

"Not really." I shuffled my right leg to loosen the sand, and bent over as if to pick something off the ground. Instead, I hooked my hands behind his knees and rammed my head, full whack, into his stomach. He flopped to the ground, right onto his ass. My sore arms burned like lava flowed through my veins, but it had been totally worth it.

He feigned getting up and swiped my feet from under me. *Frak, that hurt.*

"Sneaky." He got off the floor. "But fruitless. You've gained no advantage."

"I don't know about that." I dusted off my pants. As he'd predicted, my new clothes didn't restrict my movement. "I expected to land on my back today. Did you?"

He grinned. "Enjoy your success. It won't happen—"

I kicked him in the chest. At least that's where I aimed my foot. In the end, the kick-box maneuver ended up below his belt.

Tristan grunted and clutched his prized possession.

I winced. "I'm so, so sorry. I was aiming higher, honest."

He waved me off, still clearly unable to speak.

Had I just earned myself a good decapitation? There had to be a law against kicking the king in the balls.

His head hung low, his breathing was loud.

Maybe a pat on the back would undo my faux-pas?

In one swift motion, he caught my ankle and swung my leg up toward my head.

I lost my balance and fell.

"Hey." My neck warmed, as did the tips of my ears.

"Let's get serious." He circled me, a mighty lion teasing his prey, every step, every roll of the head carefully choreographed. "A fight is not about how to score the next point. It's about planning your next three or four steps. For example, how would you react if I did this?" He snapped up his arm.

I hopped to the side and angled up my leg as a countermove.

He intercepted my knee. Held it. The tip of his tongue flicked out to moisten his lips, and I followed its progress like I would a charmed snake. Quite possibly, I forgot to breathe.

Before he noticed my misguided focus, I returned my attention on his arms to check for micro-movements advertising his next step. Yet unbidden, my gaze flitted to his face. Sought out his dimple.

Enough.

Leading with the edge of my hand, I put all my effort into beating the attractiveness right out of him.

OVER THE WEEKS, training took over my life. On the rare occasions that I spoke to Mom and Dad, I was distracted. They in turn didn't conceal their disapproval of my life choices, and even though it was my lies that had fed their opinion, the tone in their voice still hurt.

Nieve was away a lot, and when I saw her, she dodged any conversation that went beyond a hello. Sometimes I got the feeling she deliberately avoided looking at me. Was she disappointed with my progress? Angry I spent so much time with Tristan?

It wasn't like he and I were skipping through the tall grass holding hands, or sitting by a pool, sipping margaritas. In fact, he put me through my paces from morning to noon. After a while, my pants fitted me better, the zipper of my jacket went up further now, and the only reason I still became breathless during my lessons was that Tristan judged my level of exhaustion by the number of words I spoke per minute, or by how hard I laughed at his jokes.

The afternoons were reserved for studying, even though my ass typically ached too much to sit on my desk chair, and my arms were too sore for me to turn the page. But the wonders I'd witnessed here—levitation and flying, invisibility, focusing the sun's power into hot spots that set trees on fire only with the power of one's mind and a few choice words—slowly connected to the idea of this fifth force, although the correct mathematical approach still defied me. How could this force be accessed? Would it be the sound of the words spoken that affected the air around me, or would it be the shape of my mouth?

Today might be the day I'd find out more. Because today, I got my first flying lesson.

Tristan was already waiting in the training grounds, the sandy space where I'd done all of my falling, dropping, hopping, running into walls, and unintended somersaults so far.

"Ready?" he asked in that voice that still left me weak-kneed.

"I guess. Where's my Nimbus 2000?" I made a point of searching the walls.

"Your what?"

I placed my hands at my hips and shook my head. "You watch Kindred TV, play their apps, study their machines, but you still have many holes in your knowledge of the world I come from."

"That must be disappointing for you, since you've already taught me so much." He pressed his palm against his chest. "Before you, I'd never heard of belfies and lolcats."

"And wasn't yours a dark, joyless existence?" I grinned. "Imagine the wondrous life you'll lead once you've completed your education."

He spun me around and gently shoved me toward the exit. "How about we deal with your education first?"

We left the outbuilding and walked side-by-side past the stables, toward a field of grass that had been set out like an obstacle course. Large trees with perfectly round, triangular and zigzag shapes described an outer circle. At the center, from a large wooden beam, six tires hung from ropes like Newton's cradle. From another crossbeam further away dangled metal rods at various intervals.

"Looks like a great day for my first flying lesson." I breathed in deep.

"As long as you don't expect to be flying today." He laughed heartily. "You don't learn magic in a day."

"I know." The sulk in my voice bothered me, but I should have known flying wasn't going to be that easy.

On the other side of the field, two people sat on chairs and stared in our direction.

"Who are Statler and Waldorf over there?" I gave a subtle nod toward them.

"They're members of my Council," Tristan said. "You can't blame them for being curious and wanting to judge your progress for themselves."

"Why pick day one of flight training? Last Thursday, I almost got you into a headlock. They'd have got their money's worth then."

"I wouldn't allow them near the training area, so this is their first chance to catch a glimpse of the lost Elonian." His benign smile was tinged with something else. Melancholy, or regret, maybe. "Don't pay attention to them."

"Right." I forced my gaze back to the stubbly beard he was rocking, despite the fact that it grew in a darker color than his dazzling blond hair.

"Do you know how to invoke magic?" He, for one, didn't waste another glance at our audience.

"I think so." I hadn't memorized the passage from my book but read it often enough to recall the gist of it. "You speak the right words at the right speed at the right pitch."

"Yes, but you don't merely speak the words. Without intent, words are empty. *You* are the missing ingredient." He slammed his fist against his hand repeatedly. "*You* give them power. *You* pour your imagination and your will into them."

His passion for magic filled me with a feeling that came dangerously close to the belief that I, little old me from Seattle, WA could do this. Wield magic. Take flight. Become invisible.

"The speed with which you say the words decides the force of the magic you create." His gaze swept across the large field, past the obstacles, and back to me. "Most important is your pitch, though. You are the master of light and air. Your will is their command."

"Okay."

"Remember the incantation to form an air cushion?"

"Rigio atmos din pheria subes." I peered at the ground. Since air was transparent, how did I know if I succeeded?

"Correct. Now listen to the correct pronunciation."

He garbled a few sounds that bore little resemblance to the words of the incantation. "Now you try."

I made a gargling noise deep in my throat. "I'd say that's a good imitation of what you just said."

He took a deep breath. "Funny."

Nieve hadn't been half as patient with me that first day so many weeks ago. I'd hoped we'd grow closer, maybe even become friends, but she kept her distance. Every night I went to bed feeling exhausted and alone. The only people I spoke to were Tristan and a few of the servants.

My improvements had been miraculous, but I knew it wasn't enough. Tristan didn't say it, but every hour we spent training was an hour wasted. If the Shade army was assembling, shouldn't he be preparing the troops? Maybe I truly was their last hope, and he simply couldn't face the fact that his precious prophecy was a pile of hooey.

"Rrreekjo," Tristan said.

Slowed up, his strange sound did resemble the first word of the incantation.

"Reekjo." I beamed.

"No. Rrreekjo."

"Rreekjo." Something nudged my ankle. "Look, something's happening."

Whatever the blurry something by my foot had been, it dissipated quickly.

I glanced up at Tristan, who was rubbing his forehead.

"That shouldn't have worked," he whispered.

"You're an okay teacher, but you probably didn't know I'm an excellent student." I pointed my thumb at my chest, but my joke didn't receive the howl of laughter I'd hoped for. "Kidding. You explained it well."

"Thanks. I think." He dropped his hand and nodded. "Okay, on to the second word."

That morning I didn't build my first cushion. At best, I made the air dizzy, but in reality, I spent hours standing in a field contorting my mouth into shapes it wasn't designed for, imitating Tristan's noises that didn't seem natural, while two people watched from afar.

At noon, having covered only the first three words, we entered the dining room, where Nieve already sat. A deep frown shaded her face.

"Are you okay?" I asked.

"What have you found?" Tristan, the charmer, blurted.

She opened a notebook in front of her, filled with pages and pages of handwriting. "I'm not going to bore you with the details of my investigation, but Regan's the traitor."

Tristan grabbed the back of his chair, and then pulled it slowly out from under the table. "Regan? Are you sure?"

Nieve lifted her eyebrows.

He nodded and slumped into the chair. "Sorry. How do you know?"

Nieve tapped at a page. "I got a list of everyone who regularly went for long rides. Once I'd narrowed it down to a few names, I waited by the stables and then followed them unseen. A few days ago—"

"You've been flying invisible for days?" Tristan placed his hand on her arm. "Are you okay? You must be exhausted."

"I'm good." She slipped her arm from his gentle grasp and gave a tired smile. "Anyway, I watched Regan meet with two Shades several times. Once I got close enough to overhear a few words. She's been sending the Shade king updates about Lea's progress. Everything you told the Council, Galleo will know as well."

"Why is she doing this? What does she have to gain?"

Nieve eyed me with caution. "I've spoken to a few people who remember Regan from the days of the Mad Queen and even before. I've since come to the conclusion that she isn't trying to harm Elonia. Her issue is with Lea."

"She doesn't even know me." I stomped up to the table and sat on the chair between Nieve and Tristan. "Does she want to sell me to them or something?"

"I don't know if there's money involved." Nieve finally looked at me for a fleeting second before turning her gaze away again. "It's a question of power. She's afraid that Lea is going to steal the throne."

"What would I do with a throne?" I rolled a fist and silently cursed myself. "Okay, got it now. But the question remains. Why would I, and how? I trip less than I did when I first got here, but I don't think I can challenge Tristan to a fight yet. And I also don't want to."

"Regan thinks—"

"Nieve." Tristan's expression shuttered. "Don't."

"Lea has a right to know this." Nieve bore his intense gaze without flinching.

"I'm with Nieve." I raised my finger. "Either I'm part of this Team Elonia thing the three of us have going, or I'm not."

Tristan slumped against the back of his chair and briefly gestured at Nieve. "Fine."

"Tristan used to be the royal champion to the queen." Nieve studied her notes as if reading off them. "The Queen used to govern with kindness and strength and was a formidable warrior in her day. Always leading the charge into battle. Then she fell pregnant, and everything changed. Her behavior became erratic. She'd walk around barely dressed, speaking to people who weren't there, and not recognizing those that were."

"I don't think I like where this is going," I whispered, my neck suddenly stiff and cold.

"Tristan, the Council, everyone tried to do what they could to keep the country together, but we were in the middle of a war with the Shades. The Council united and deposed her."

"That queen, she was my mother?" I rubbed my stiff fingers against each other, kneaded them to get warmth back inside them.

"Yes."

"Tristan took her throne?" I flung my gaze from Nieve to the king.

He sat rigidly in his seat, his face as still as the rest of him.

"He was loyal to your mother." Nieve's soft voice tiptoed into my consciousness. "You can see it in the way he rules."

"And this Regan, she thinks I have a claim to the throne because I'm the lost Elonian, the previous queen's daughter?"

"You *do* have a claim to the throne," Tristan whispered. "According to our own laws, all you have to do is say the word, and it's yours."

"And you'd give it up?"

He scoffed. "If I believed for a moment that you could lead our country into war, make the hard decisions, I would abdicate. I believe in our laws."

Weirdly, his words didn't hurt me. His posture had shrunk, his eyes had lost their sparkle. This man didn't want to be the king any more than I wanted to be queen.

"I wish I could lead your country and make hard decisions." I leaned forward to catch his gaze. "I wish I could take on this burden, but we both know that's crazy. And our training has proven by now that I'm not like my mother at all."

He gave a weak smile. "Thanks."

The delicious aroma of something sweet wafted in from the kitchen. One after the other, eager valets served up large bowls overflowing with vegetables, meat, and salad. They shot furtive glances at me. Nieve shot less furtive glances back at them, and they soon scurried away.

"Plum-baked duck," Nieve said, and her look encouraged me to help myself.

The side-effect of all that exercise I'd been doing was an increased appetite, which Tristan had weirdly enabled. Sometimes I'd catch him staring at me in the middle of a meal, probably amazed at the amount of food I could put away.

"Anyway, what if I did take the crown?" I turned back to Nieve. "I mean, Regan doesn't know I'd suck at it. So why is this so important to her?"

"Regan thinks she has power now." Tristan moved a gravy-covered potato from one side of his plate to the other. "Maybe she thinks I'm weak."

Nieve made a sound.

"You have something to say?" Tristan slowly leveled his gaze at her. "Spit it out."

"She doesn't think you're weak." Nieve's hands shook, yet she raised her eyes to meet his stare. "You are weak."

Neither of them spoke for a few seconds. Many times over the past few weeks, I'd forgotten he was the king, but I'd never dared say anything this cruel to him. Had she lost her mind?"

"You and I should go outside." His voice had become dangerously husky. "I'll show you how weak I am."

Her sad face lightened as a smile broke. "I don't mean like

that. As a ruler, you've become weak. Being king was never your idea, and you make it clear every day that you don't want to be here. You've passed powers to the Council that aren't theirs. Taxes, housing, education. Only the army is still yours to command, but for how long?"

"I'm doing the best I can."

"No, Tris, you're not." Nieve was now the one to touch his arm. "The country needs you. Lea and I, we need you. You're stuck in this position, but don't make it harder than it needs to be."

He studied her hand with so much fondness it hurt my heart. This was a sucky time to be jealous, but that closeness between them meant something. Who the hell was I anyway? A brat from Seattle, who'd been doing her best to screw up her future. Hardly a woman to make kings swoon.

Tristan slammed his fist on the table, and I started.

"Slice it." His raised voice made the background mumble in the kitchen fall silent. "You're right. I should have been stronger."

This situation wasn't about my crushed feelings or me at all. Tristan was at a crossroads. We had no time for his self-pity. They'd found the traitor. Score for Team Elonia.

I glanced up from my food and swallowed. "I think being a king is like being a parent. You aren't born a father. You become one."

"Are you patronizing me?" He straightened his spine with sudden intensity.

"She's pep-talking you." Nieve chuckled and withdrew her hand from his arm.

"That's right, buckaroo. Saddle up and swing that lasso." I twirled my fork in the air. "That's what you told me when I couldn't make that roundhouse kick, remember?"

Nieve buried her face in her palm. "He said that?"

"Every cringe-worthy word." I nodded. "Anyway, you know who the traitor is. Deal with her with strength, and no one is going to come after you again."

"Maybe one day, when you're older, you might change your mind about being queen." A smile crept onto his lips.

I immediately waved him off. "Keep the throne, *my lord*, because I don't want it. But speaking of the queen, my mother. Do you think I could—"

Shouts from the Hall interrupted me.

The door banged open, and a man stormed into the room with heavy steps. His face distorted as if he suffered great pain.

"It's happening," he yelled. He glanced at the three of us in turn before collapsing to his knees. "We're doomed."

With Nieve's help, the man with the pudgy face slouched into a chair. His jacket hung open revealing a wooly vest straight from the not-so-sexy seventies.

"Hans?" The king slapped the man twice in the face. "Hans, can you hear me?"

"My lord." Hans puffed some more. "I bring grave news from across the mountains."

I glanced at Nieve. She didn't react to the man's distress. I assumed his news didn't concern me, so I heaped more meat onto my plate. The food didn't disappoint. A king's life might be a lonely life, the proverb said, but heck, royalty sure ate better than the rest of us.

Tristan filled a tumbler with water from a pitcher. He handed the glass to Hans and straddled his chair. "Tell me what's going on."

"We're doomed, my lord." Hans glided the outside of the tumbler along his forehead.

I shot Nieve a questioning look. "Is this guy for real?"

She shrugged. "Hans is our top spy. He can infiltrate deep behind Shade lines and nobody suspects his true allegiance." She didn't hide the tinge of resentment in her tone. "He sits in a tavern, and Shades just open up."

"It's more likely the alcohol doing it," I said in my most reassuring tone.

Tristan whipped his head around and fixed me in his gaze.

"It's true." I swallowed my vegetables. "The ethanol induces a state of euphoria, loosening the tongue and lowering inhibitions." I moved my fork through the air again. "Some governments have tried to develop truth drugs, but alcohol is still the most reliable, and is obviously easier to obtain."

Before I had time to utter a further intelligent thought, Hans let out another suffering breath.

"Pull yourself together, man." Tristan's voice sharpened to a blade's edge.

"Of course, my lord. Of course." Hans wiped his leather sleeve over his face and unwound his spine. "It's hopeless, but I will not let it be said that I failed to discharge my duty."

"The country appreciates your service." Tristan tapped his knuckles against the top of his chair. "Now, why are we doomed?"

"The Shades are celebrating. The Divide is going to fall."

To my right, Nieve lifted her head and squinted. "The Shades are always celebrating."

"Not like this. I've prodded and poked my sources, checked and double-checked. The whispers from the Shade underground confirm it. They've found the vessel."

"Interesting." Nieve shoveled another forkful of food into her mouth. Despite her lackadaisical tone, her eyes had widened a fraction.

"You know about the vessel?" Tristan shot her a sharp look.

She shrugged, but the change in her expression brought a lump to my throat. Something important was going on, but once again, I was in the dark.

"What vessel?" I asked.

"According to the prophecy, the vessel is what the Shades will use to bring down the Divide." Tristan took a deep breath then lowered his voice. "We'd hoped you and Nieve would find it first."

Despite my best efforts to deny the reality of my situation, Hans's news focused the stakes. Maybe we were already too late.

"Where's the vessel now?" the king asked.

Hans patted his own cheek. "I tried, my lord. But the Shades... You know how suspicious they've become."

"Indeed." Tristan rubbed his chin between thumb and index finger. He rose to his feet and clapped a palm on Hans's shoulder. "You've done well. Go and recover. I trust you will not discuss this matter with anyone outside this room."

"You can rely on me, my lord." Mr. Drama Queen staggered out the room, mumbling to himself.

Tristan rejoined us at the table. "Someone will have to go and speak to Markus."

"I'll send Dachsoon," Nieve said.

"You go." Tristan's voice didn't lack power now. "Dachsoon is Regan's nephew, so we can't be certain of his loyalty. Besides, doesn't Markus prefer dealing with you anyway?"

She grimaced. "Yes."

"There you go. I'll finish things with Regan, do double-time boot camp with our new recruit here..." He pointed at me. "By the time you're back, we'll know our next step."

"What do you mean by double-time boot camp?" I pointedly stretched out my back with a suffering look. "Because I've been working my ass off already."

Tristan smiled the sweetest of smiles. "You ain't seen nothing yet, buckaroo."

Resistance seemed futile. Now I knew how Captain Picard felt. I hung my head and waited for Nieve to finish her meal.

# CHAPTER FIFTEEN



*"Don't consider death the end. Look on it as change. And change is a good thing, right?"*

I stood on top of the mountain, calf deep in snow. Torren always smelled off to me, as if the darkness that clung to every stone and grass helm was borne out of clay and brimstone. A bitterness that scratched the far back of my throat.

My dark brown Pegasus, a breed of horse comfortable in the air, stood by my side, its skin twitching from the cold. I patted its long, feather-soft fur to keep it calm, but mindful not to disturb its delicate, magical wings. If they got damaged, I doubted I had enough energy to carry me home alone. Below me, a vigorously farmed field extended up to a line of trees, then nothing. Down there, the sun didn't shine. If I ran out of magic here, I was as good as dead.

Deprived of visual cues, I asked the air to carry the sounds of my surroundings to me.

The bleat of a goat, the rustle of a scarce plant in the wind. No sign of the telltale crunch of a boot sinking in the snow. Not even a breath.

I was alone.

I'd left home more than a month ago, but it felt like two years. Tristan would take care of Lea, of that I was certain. He would train her like he'd trained me. But he was an uncompromising mentor. He needed to be, because cutting corners meant death.

My entire life I'd put more stock in the oracles than technology. I was willing to believe the prophecy—the stakes, the vessel—all of it, but I couldn't accept that Lea was going to die. I had not saved her only to lose her down the way.

First things first, though. This mission was my one priority. We needed to know what the Shades knew, and for that, I had to speak to Markus. No other contact of mine had such a far-reaching network of spies in Galleo's court.

I placed one foot into the stirrups and swung myself onto the horse. It reared up a fraction and readied itself. I dug my heels into the animal's flanks. Two cautious shuffles, then the stallion stepped into nothing, trusting the wind under its command to carry our combined weight.

With the mountains behind me, we flew head-on into the darkness, where I could no longer call on my invisibility if needed. I steered my mount toward a cluster of trees.

The silence deepened the feeling of solitude, but I was used to my own company. My struggle to the top had left me with few friends and even fewer lovers along the way. I envied Lea's carefree upbringing, without the confines of duty. Yet despite my burdens, I loved Elonia with a fiercer passion than any man I'd met. The haze over the valley, the tranquility of the lake in the royal gardens, they deserved my loyalty. And Tristan—I would give my life for him without hesitation.

No other force on this planet could make me undertake a mission to see a man I hated.

"...without the coins I'd have..."

The wind carried the voices of two people into my ears. Since flying was no longer safe, I directed my horse into a heavily wooded area and landed. Soft whispers into my stallion's ears calmed him. My spell, spun from the moon's rays, was too weak to conceal him, but it helped him blend in with the environment. Now on foot, I headed north.

Tightening the defenses around my luster, I kept the wind at the ready. Without sunlight to aid my visibility, the air remained my only crutch out here. And due to my waning energy, it proved a pathetic crutch at best.

I snuck through the trees, searching for the voices' owners.

"Halt." A man stepped in front of me. His tunic and helmet were similar to my disguise, but the indentation in the metal on his head pegged him at a higher level than my uniform. *Slice it.*

"Who are you?" He raised his sword.

The oxygen in my lungs solidified and sank into my midsection.

I saluted. "I was sent by Cassius, third Senator, to meet with the rebel leader."

The last time I frequented this realm, Cassius was a Senator, but the Shade government was nothing if not unstable. If the king didn't slay his staff on a whim, the senators usually did it themselves in a bid to gain more power.

"The rebel leader?" The man rubbed the furrow between his eyebrows. "I wasn't informed of this."

"It's a message of the highest importance." Despite the giant fist massaging my stomach into a liquid froth, my voice kept the steady pitch of authority. Any hesitation would spell my death. "I cannot divulge details, you understand. Let's say it involves the upcoming triumph."

The man's features softened. "I see. Well, if you could show me your porta-pass, you'll be on your way."

"Of course." I pretended to rifle through my pockets for the written authorization. At the same time, I called upon the wind for a diversion.

The branch of a large tree behind me shook and splintered.

I let my gaze dart between the soldier in front of me and the creaking wood. "How secure is this position?"

"It's secure." Neither his tone nor his face held conviction.

"My mission cannot be compromised." I ran my finger over my jugular. "Or heads will roll."

The branch shook again. A loud crack, and it dropped to the ground, causing the earth to tremble.

"Go," the guard shouted. "Go. I have to investigate this."

I saluted with cold fingers and slipped past him, ensuring the wind kept him distracted for another few minutes.

Despite the low temperatures, sweat collected in my tunic. Tempting as it was to use the air to propel me at greater speed, I wouldn't squander my precious reserves. Instead, I kept my gait and pace even in case he should glance back at me.

The Shade underground was an odd organization. Not numerous enough to topple Galleo, yet too powerful to ignore. It was kept in virtual exile. I'd met with its leader, Markus, on more than one occasion. A dangerous man. Also an attractive man. On my last visit, he'd left an impression. A two-inch scar on my thigh in the shape of an N. I'd disarmed him before he finished his initial.

Without any attempt at deception, I marched toward his mansion. His people would have observed and followed me as soon as I entered his territory. The only question was whether I'd been recognized as me, or whether my disguise still held. Either way, they would not harm me.

Two men stood by the gate, helmets drawn deep over their eyes. "Wait." The one on the right raised a hand.

Another two Shades came up from behind, took my weapon

without wasting words on me, and accompanied me into a chamber. The room was adorned with velvet and grapes, and statues of naked men and women. On a large pillow, the length and width of two sofas, sat a bare-chested Markus, surrounded by scantily clad "business associates." His skin, a flawless light brown, always carried a satin sheen.

One of my Shade guides applied pressure to my shoulders to force me onto my knees. I complied without complaint.

"I knew you'd come back to me." Markus clapped his hands and beamed. "On the eve of the Shades' greatest triumph, you've left the self-righteous Sparks to join me on my throne."

"Oh, Markus. How well you know me." No variation in my pitch would betray my nerves.

He threw his head back and laughed out loud. "Are you rejecting me again?"

"If there were any chance of you becoming king I might change my mind. Besides, you don't want the Divide to fall any more than I do."

Markus stretched, his smooth, well-defined torso on proud display. With a wave he dismissed his friends and beckoned for me to join him. Revulsion roiled my stomach with each humiliating knee slide. I hated physical contact with anyone, especially with psychopaths like him, but at the same time, I didn't want to anger him. Of all the Shades I'd encountered over the years, Markus was by far the most dangerous.

Of course I'd known what to expect even before I set off from home. Markus would try to charm me, seduce me, and turn on me like a snake the second I showed any weakness.

When my knees touched his legs, he lifted the helmet off my head and undid the knot so my hair cascaded over my shoulders. Without shedding a single garment, I felt utterly and completely naked. He weaved his fingers through my hair, sending ripples of unwelcome heat along my skull. Yet I suppressed the shudder that threatened to follow. I would not give my enemy the satisfaction of knowing my dislike of him was laced with the tiniest seed of attraction.

"So, my Angel," he said. "What can I do for you?"

I gulped a dry swallow. "I need information if I'm to have any chance of preventing the fall of the Divide. Rumor has it the Shades have the vessel. Is that true?"

*Old Ones, help me.* My voice hadn't held steady. His knowing gaze trailed past my shoulders and circled my small breasts.

"Is that true?" I asked again, more forcefully this time. Whatever happened, I would not betray my thumping heart.

He peered up. "Why should I give you this information for free?"

"Because we have the same goal. If I foil Galleo's plans, you will benefit without dealing a single blow yourself."

His features flickered in the light, switching from angelic to demonic on the whim of the tall candles that marked the corners of the room.

He took my hands between his. "That isn't true, my Angel. No, I don't wish the Divide to fall. Gaining power over my fellow Torrens will be easier without the complication of the Kindred world. Yet I derive no benefit from the status quo either." His fingers squeezed maybe a tad too hard.

I bit the inside of my cheek, resisting the urge to free myself.

He leaned in. "Your entire existence is at stake. Your people's lives. I'd say you're the one at a disadvantage."

"What are you after?"

"In addition to your body?"

No slicing way. I cast my features in hardened steel.

He dropped my hands. "Oh, how you wound me." Then he replaced the playful glint in his blue eyes with a look of cunning. "I will tell you everything I know. In return, you will grant me one kiss."

No wonder he preferred talking to me over dealing with Dachsoon. I couldn't imagine Markus making a deal like that with him. I glanced at the complex tapestries covering the wall. Not surprisingly, they depicted scenes of an explicit nature. Markus didn't just flaunt his sexual appetites; he used them as a weapon to unnerve his guests.

"What do you say?" he asked again.

My skin tightened over flexed muscles, sensitive to the room's stifling heat. How much trouble would I be in if I punched him in the face? On a scale from one to ten, too much, that was sure. I had no choice. "You have my word."

He leaned in.

"*After* you tell me," I said.

He laughed. "You know my lust for you comes from a place of genuine devotion, my Angel, don't you?"

Of course I knew the place of his lust, and it was situated far south. "I hope the information is worth my sacrifice."

"I think so. I can confirm the rumors are true. Galleo has let his people know that his son, the crown prince, has it. He says that means his triumph is near."

My chest tightened. *So it is as we feared.* "Is it a chalice?"

"I don't know." A vibe of frustration came through in his voice. "The king keeps its nature confidential."

"Why hasn't the crown prince performed the ritual to unleash the vessel's power?"

He leaned back on his arms. "The crown prince and the king had a disagreement. Maybe the crown prince wants the power to himself. Others say the king's announcement was premature, because the crown prince had the vessel but lost it. Who knows?"

Markus stared at me, as if searching for a tell in my face.

I bit my bottom lip. No way would I give him my insights. "Where is the crown prince?"

"Mingling among the Kindreds, believe it or not, in a place called Seattle."

I'd expected that answer. If the crown prince was making a play for his father's throne, he might want to dangle Lea in front of Galleo's nose, too. Good thing I got to her in time.

"It's not much." I rose to my feet.

Markus followed suit. Despite being an inch shorter than me, he seemed taller. "It's all the information I have. You're not backing out of our deal, are you?"

If only I could. "Not at all."

I stared at his well-proportioned face. Maybe it wouldn't be so bad.

Markus gripped my shoulders and kissed me. His tongue prodded against my lips, trying to part them. I pressed them together with all my might, but he managed to pry them open. A spark zinged from my throat down my spine before I could suppress it, while my insides did a three sixty. He dug his fingers into my flesh, and I yelped. My mouth opened further, and he blew raw magic into me. A black veil fell over my eyes that seeped into my skin as his Shade power filled me, dark and oily, clogging my organs, my lungs, my blood.

I freed myself from his embrace and sucked in air to soothe the bubbling fluids in my stomach.

"You'll be okay in a second." He stroked my cheek. "These powers are temporary, but they should see you safely home."

Slowly, I released my fists.

"Thanks. I think." My voice was rough and bumpy.

Markus laughed. "Anytime, my Angel. Anytime."

Then I was dismissed. I stumbled out of his chamber, needing my hand to support myself along the corridor.

Outside, the wind recognized the fresh power in my belly

and yanked me back into reality. I hadn't asked for his help. My Elonian gifts were plenty, but Markus had to have his own way. He'd always known how to push my buttons. I shivered, revulsion striking my stomach, and walked on wobbly legs into the woods.

One hand on the solid trunk of a tree, I took a deep breath. The feel of Markus's hands, his Shade stink, clung to me like mud. At least I'd received the intelligence I'd come for. The rest I would hide away in my mind as simply another memory never to resurface.

Drawing on my new supply of magic, I sensed the earth around me. At a bolt, the history of every stone, every plant, and every tree in my vicinity unfolded itself before my mind's eye. So this was what the Shades felt, what they saw. My nerves pulsed under the influx of information, even though part of me balked at it. I was an Elonian. The Old Ones hadn't designed these powers for me. I closed my eyes. It didn't matter. For however long, these powers were mine.

I concentrated on my surroundings. My brain had no trouble deciphering the guards' positions from the vibrations under my feet. But to find my stallion, I had to consult my memory. Earth magic couldn't detect the spell I'd placed on my horse. For the first time I understood the effect Elonian magic had on the Shades. Our magic showed their limits, reminded them they were not omnipotent. No wonder they hated us.

I bypassed the Shade's military line and headed back to my horse. Too many things whirled through my mind. As a warrior, I wasn't responsible for making sense of what I'd learned from Markus. That was Tristan's job. Although maybe we'd better forget about training Lea. My chest tightened. The prophecy had guided me toward that one destiny all my life. A destiny with her fighting by my side. But she was too green, and we were out of time. Since the Shade crown prince already had the vessel, I'd have to go to Seattle and confront him alone.

I swung myself into the saddle and galloped through the air toward home. We still had time to turn events to our favor if we acted swiftly. I scrunched my face against the biting wind. Something told me it wouldn't be so easy to convince Tristan of my new plan.

# CHAPTER SIXTEEN



*"I don't know what kind of pill could possibly make you this dumb, but kudos to the inventor."*

In the outbuilding belonging to the castle, Tristan smoothed a sand mound with his feet. After six months of practicing with him, I'd expected to grow accustomed to his leather-clad legs and his graceful, powerful moves. But no. Too bad for me.

After Tristan had detained Regan, all hell had broken out. I'd only caught rumors, because to him, Council affairs were sacred, but rumors were all I needed to piece everything together. He was using her betrayal to claw back power. From the Councilors' looks, I assumed they somehow blamed me for the end of their cushy life.

In the afternoons, I hid in my room, studying and avoiding them. The mornings, however, had become my favorite time of the day. My training was coming along, not least because I enjoyed hanging out with him.

"Again, from the top. This time put your heart into it." Tristan's voice was all rock, even though that vanilla ice cream tone he did so well would have enticed me to work even harder.

"Slave driver," I mumbled, loud enough for him to hear.

He squeezed his eyes shut, an expression I'd come to read as *give me strength*. "Your reaction times have improved, although your other skills remain choppy. Without agility, you can't use your dagger to full effect. So I want to see another scissor assault."

I kicked up my legs—right then left—and landed right, left, in quick succession, as I'd done at least a million times today.

"Good. You've got it." He slammed his fist into the palm of his hand. "Between you and Nieve, the Shades will tumble like bowling pins."

My insides gave a jig, as they did each time he mentioned fighting the Shades. "Watch out. Only yesterday you praised my invisibility shield. I'm worried all these compliments will make your head explode. Or mine."

"Let's go for a ride." He hooked his fingers into his belt. "Step up."

I whispered the incantation and focused. In my mind, the mass of air in front of me condensed into a solid platform. Once I poured energy into my mental image, it became reality. Using outstretched arms for balance, I climbed on top. Flashbacks to a surfing lesson fired in my brain. Staying upright on a cushion of air had proven less difficult than surfing the ocean waves.

Tristan took a deep breath and expanded his already broad chest. "Do you remember the three pillars of air magic?"

He was testing my ability to concentrate without falling on my face. "Magic is a sacred gift. With it, we may command the air to convey people, magic, and words."

"Good. What is it *not* to be used for?"

"For self-serving purposes, like cooling down pea soup or picking up a dropped book." Two lessons I'd learned through error. Tristan sure could shout a lot.

"That's right. For what other purpose shouldn't you use

air magic?"

I glanced at the sand beneath my air cushion. "To bash you over the head?"

He rubbed the back of his skull and grimaced. "Precisely. For the last time, our laws prevent the misuse of wind and air under the penalty of life imprisonment, no matter the circumstances. Are we clear?"

"Clear."

"Good. I'd hate having to throw our brightest hope of salvation into my dungeon."

*Hope of salvation. Way to downplay his expectations.*

"You ready?" he asked.

The energy that spilled from me into my air cushion vibrated like crazy. "Race you?"

He smirked and climbed into the air. "By all means. You go first."

I whizzed off, robbing him of his chance to launch into flight before me. He was sneaky like that.

I zoomed toward the open door, into the yard, and up, up, up into the sky. Over the outbuilding. Down the other side.

The ground rushed by too fast to pick out the rocks that lined the path or the flowers that covered the valley. I didn't hear or see Tristan following me, but I sensed him. My body tracked his movements as if we were linked like a row of foosball figures.

A large oak about five hundred yards out marked the end of the path. To loop around it, I shifted my weight onto my back foot, leaning into the turn. My stomach lurched from the abrupt change of direction, accompanied by a pleasant prickle across my abs. I laughed for the sheer joy of flying.

The king came at me, the sun reflecting off his platinum hair. The expression on his face warned me. Advertised a cunning maneuver.

I reacted too late.

He sliced in front of me, missing me by an inch and upsetting the thin sheet supporting me.

I wobbled. My heart sputtered like an old engine, and I called on the wind to catch me. As soon as the solid air stabilized beneath my soles, I accelerated.

Not fast enough.

Tristan came from behind and careered past me, a wicked laugh straggling in his wake. He was gone before I could shove him.

Drawing power from the sun, I stepped up my pursuit. Within milliseconds I'd broken through my comfort zone, and by the time I reached the castle, I approached the speed of a space shuttle.

Ten feet ahead of me, Tristan rocketed up and over the roof.

I missiled up behind him.

He zoomed into the yard.

I trailed by inches.

He bulleted through the open door.

We were level.

He conjured a cushion of air between him and the wall.

I forgot.

Instead, I slammed into the wall and ricocheted back onto my ass. The burn spread from my face down my neck and spitfired into my lower back. "Shit. Oh frak, that hurt."

Over the past months, I'd discovered many things the painful way. By far the coolest was that magic quickly healed most aches and complaints. Unfortunately, when you were in pain, even *quickly* felt like forever.

Tristan snorted another of his all too rare laughs and rushed over to help me up. He dusted me off and lifted my chin with his fingertips. "Not bad. You almost had me."

He stood close enough for me to count every whisker on his

stubbled chin. His chest, working hard from the exercise, lifted in step with my own. As if to test my flimsy defenses, he scorched me with a killer smile.

A feral desire clawed at my skin, teasing the animal inside. If I made a move, would he reciprocate?

I gave myself a stern talking to. Those thoughts could get me into big time Tristan trouble.

I shook off his touch. "What do you mean, almost had you?" A slight crack in my voice. Easily explainable as post-race jitters. "We were level at the end. Strictly speaking, by whacking into the wall, I was ahead of you."

"I'll settle for a draw. Otherwise you'll whine all the way through lunch again."

Right on cue, my stomach grumbled. "You'd think I should have lost weight, but I swear I've gained at least five pounds since I got here."

His gaze traced my curves up and down. "All in the right places."

My insides contracted in a flawless Kegel exercise. Jeez, this guy was going to be my undoing.

He picked up his longsword from the nail on the wall and passed me Fallon. "Come on. Let's see what's on the menu."

I shot him a cautious smile. Once again, his charm had made me forget the reason for our training, at least for a while. I buckled the holster around my waist and marched toward the door. Tristan rested against the doorframe, watching me.

I slowed. "What?"

He reached for my wrists. Holding them gently yet with determination, he lowered his head.

My breathing stopped for a giddy second, before kicking off again at twice the speed. I rocked up onto my toes, hungry for the contact.

He held me close enough to taste his breath, too far to

connect. His teasing distance turned my core into goo. *Almost* wasn't enough, not close enough to still my desire. Every inch of me needed to feel his body. What did this man see in me? He had reasons to train me, sure, but the patience he'd shown me, his will for me to succeed, and his concern for my wellbeing—they'd come from a different place than mere duty. He'd taken the time to get to know me, as I'd come to know his strength and his generosity, his steadfastness and his wit.

His gaze swept over my brow, circled around and lingered on my mouth. The want in his eyes was everything I'd hoped for. Everything I'd convinced myself I'd never see nor deserved. He licked his lips, sending a jab of need to my core. Nostrils flared, he drew in air as if to soak in my scent.

"Perfect." A soft wisp of a word with the impact of a drum roll.

At last, he brushed my mouth with his. His lips rested for a precious second; warm, soft, light. A fleeting graze. No more.

It was enough to rupture my sanity.

The next kiss stuck. I'd learned my lesson. This time, I fed off his lips, tasted him with greedy desire, while holding on to him for dear life.

He let me. I couldn't read his mind, but neither did I need to. It was all there in the way he grasped me. His large hands gave support when my knees threatened to buckle. His warm breath proved the perfect antidote to the shivers racing down my spine.

When he finally let me go, his smile was the most relaxed I'd ever seen on his face. It suited him.

"Are you sure about this?" I asked, breathless.

He chuckled and kissed my cheek. "I should be asking you this. I don't want you to feel like I'm taking advantage of you."

I tutted, even though my insides did a happy dance. "As if you could."

"How about we take the afternoon off and hang out?"

"Can a king just hang out?"

He stroked my hair. "As it turns out, a king can do what he likes. Who knew, eh?"

A LOUD BANG woke me from a pleasant dream. I sat up with a start, somehow managing to hold on to the covers. Ohmygod. I stared at the alarm clock, which wasn't in its usual place.

The exaggerated cough from the doorway slammed me into reality. Leather trousers, too big for me, draped over a chair. A plush carpet instead of hardwood floor. Crap. I'd fallen asleep in Tristan's bed. I rubbed my eyes, and the blurry figure at the door turned into Nieve.

Next to me, Tristan lifted his head, his hair even more disheveled than my own. "Don't you knock anymore?" His sleepy voice held a tinge of annoyance.

We'd spent the afternoon and evening talking and kissing, no more, but from where Nieve stood, the situation had to look five times worse. Her scowl snapped between me and Tristan, but mostly rested on me.

A sickening wave of guilt surged. She'd put her life on the line for me, and I'd paid her back by making out with the man she cared about.

Yet the words of apology crumbled in my mouth.

Her frown intensified, her gaze devoid of light. She spun on her heels and marched out of the room.

Tristan cast a glance ceiling-ward, shrugged, and reached for his pants. "Let's go see what she found out."

"Okay." My voice came out as a squeak.

His bare back on proud display, he followed Nieve out, grabbing his jacket on the way.

After locating my clothes, I stepped into my pants with slow deliberation, zipped my jacket with precision. When I was out of clothes and out of excuses, I plodded after them.

It was too late to deny my encounter with Tristan, but maybe I could convince Nieve my indiscretion didn't mean anything.

Except it did. To me, it did.

Her voice sounded from downstairs. "Let's go, Lea. You should hear this, too."

I entered the dining room where Tristan and Nieve sat on opposite sides of the wood table, conversing at a low whisper over a pot of steaming black tea.

Nieve looked up. "Sit. We don't have much time."

I sagged into a chair.

"I met with Markus."

Tristan placed his cup onto its saucer. "Did you two kiss and make up?"

Despite his light tone, his earlier exuberance had disappeared. He was back to his serious self.

"Oh, like you two have?" Nieve struck him with a bruising glare. "To answer your question, yes, in Markus's twisted mind we probably did. Anyway, the Shade crown prince is in the Kindred realm and he probably has The Vessel of Orrin. But father and son may not be on speaking terms, and assuming only the king knows the ritual to destroying the Divide, we still have time. But we need to act fast."

"What's your plan?" Tristan asked.

"I want to return to Seattle and find the crown prince. Take the vessel off him if he still has it. At least, get him to tell me where it is."

The king sent me a furtive glance and lowered his head. "Both of you?"

"I don't know." She squinted at me. "She can't possibly be

ready yet."

My heart beat in my ears. She was right. I still needed another year or two.

"She is ready." Tristan inhaled and tapped the tabletop. "Or close enough. Guess we can't stall the inevitable, can we?"

This was crazy. Nieve had grown up like this. She probably had her first fight when she was still in diapers. What was I going to do, other than give her one more thing to worry about?

"You knew we'd leave sooner or later." Nieve replaced her tone's sharp edge with a more soothing lilt.

"I thought there'd be more time." Tristan fidgeted with his cup, rotated the handle from left to right. "Never mind. Let's get the two of you on your way."

My ribcage tightened. Why did they never listen? I was a newb at the whole fighting thing. Even Wesley Crusher, with all his promise, wasn't dropped off to face the entire Romulan race by himself. "What about the rest of my training?"

"We've covered the basics of combat, air magic, and light magic," Tristan said. "Your luster is also under control. It doesn't begin to scratch the multitude of things a warrior should know, but you'll have a fighting chance. Playtime's over."

He was all business, no emotion. A chill zinged through my veins and cracked my heart. It was as if our intimacy was a book he'd returned to the library.

Did he blame me for his indiscretion? For betraying Nieve?

"Come." Nieve rose and patted my shoulder.

"The cure," I said quickly. "My father's cure. You promised."

"I will send someone to take care of it." Tristan's voice held firm. "You don't have to worry about him."

"We must leave now." Nieve pulled me up from my chair. "I bet you'll be glad to get home."

Her false cheerfulness threatened to shatter my composure. I followed her out, up the stairs, into my room.

"Do you need help packing?" She walked up to my desk and ran her finger across the spines of the now well-thumbed books. "The seamstress has set aside a new set of clothes for you. I'd recommend wearing them even in the Kindred realm."

"Um, I guess."

"You're upset about Tristan, aren't you? My brother can be abrupt sometimes. Don't take it personally. He's the king. It's his prerogative."

*Brother?* The world around me went into free fall. I plunked a steadying hand against the wall. Yet everything made sense. The intimacy between them, so deep and yet devoid of romance. Emotions, without the longing glances.

"Does he—" Deep, soothing breath. "Tristan does that a lot? You know, being with women?"

She cast me a knowing glance. "No, but girlfriends don't usually feature in his life. The crown and his people must come first. Do you understand what I'm saying?"

"Yeah. I didn't… Doesn't matter."

She tapped the books by her side. "Take them with you, if you wish. I'll meet you downstairs in ten minutes."

I nodded, cocooned in a weird sort of trance. My feet carried me across the room, my hands stowed my clothes and the books in my large bag, but my brain had switched off. I wilted onto the edge of my bed and dropped my chin in my palms.

I bit into the heel of my hand, letting the pain distract me from the pit in my core. How had I arrived here, at this point? Had Tristan turned my head so much I no longer thought straight? Since he and magic took over my life, reason and logic had shifted down my list of priorities. But magic was too wriggly a comfort blanket, always threatening to glide out of my grasp. Like mental soap.

In Tristan, I'd found someone who didn't switch off at the mention of the word "atom." He'd enjoyed arguing with me, had endured my lessons on all things science fiction and science fact. His interest hadn't been an act. I was sure of it. In return, I'd come to crush hard on that multi-layered guy with his thick, blond hair that dropped into his handsome face and covered his sky-blue eyes whenever a chuckle escaped him. Now, just like that, I was dismissed.

Maybe I should have seen this coming. What had I thought was going to happen between him and me? Unicorns and rainbows? My parents had made it clear my lack of foresight was going to be an obstacle. After all, the future didn't just come to those who planned for it. Frak it. Why didn't I ever use my brain to plan ahead?

I grabbed my bag and rushed downstairs, overcome by the urge to leave Elonia and Tristan's castle.

Voices drifted through the corridor, and I slowed.

"You hurt her feelings," Nieve said.

"This wasn't something I wanted to happen. It just did." Tristan sounded uncertain.

"What, she accidentally fell into your bed?"

"Nothing happened between us, not the way you think. I'm saying I had no choice. She's so…I mean. Hell, she's special."

"You're old enough to know you two have no future. You'd do well to remember the prophecy. More than that, you're the king. The *king*, Tristan."

"And you'd do well to remember *that*. Don't use that tone with me."

Nieve fell silent.

I stomped on the carpeted floor to announce my presence.

"I'm ready. Let's go." I forced strength into my words.

"Fine." Nieve lifted a shoulder. "I'll be outside." With a flick of her head and a glower at Tristan, she left.

*Subtle.* Now he'd give me the *it's-not-you* speech.

"I—" His mouth twisted.

He couldn't even let me down with a tried-and-tested script to aid him. Maybe it was up to me to be the bigger woman.

I lifted a brow. "Yeah, don't worry. I get it. You're the king. Thanks for the training."

"Lea. I—"

I gave a quick wave, aware that my jovial grin stopped at my mouth. "Make sure my father's okay, or I'll come back and kick your ass."

Concealing balled hands in the sleeves of my jacket, I followed Nieve into the Great Hall. Tristan had been a distraction. Nothing more. We weren't even compatible. After he kicked Regan out of Elonia, he'd quickly become used to issuing orders. I needed a life mate, not a barking corporal.

News of our departure had already spread around the castle.

"Good luck." Draben, the chef's youngest son, handed me a bouquet of flowers. His round blue eyes stared up, too young to understand the stakes, yet full of trust I'd handle whatever life threw at me.

If only I shared his confidence, but by now, the stakes had become clear even to me. These wonderful, ordinary people lived in fear of another war. Without a scrap of magic to call on, their lives were in the hands of their warriors. And possibly in Nieve's and mine.

I crouched and kissed Draben's cheek. Frak, he alone was worth risking my life for. The jumble of gratitude, love, and elation overwhelmed me, and the defenses I'd built to safeguard myself against worship-induced arrogance came crashing down. For a few minutes, I was handing out smiles and handshakes like a desperate politician.

"Lea." Nieve's suffering voice prodded my ego back into place.

I followed her out of the swarm of people, which wasn't an easy task. Hands slapped my back, brushed over my hair, and once or twice, I was pulled against a woman's bosom in a bear hug.

"We need to go." Nieve's tone grew more urgent.

I wasn't as highly trained as her, and doubts about my future still plagued me. But for the first time, my usual negative thoughts called in sick. Who was to say I couldn't be a warrior? Heroes didn't all wear capes and masks. With Nieve by my side, I felt strong.

We were Cagney and Lacey, or Thelma and Louise. Except with leather.

Besides, all we were going to do was find a vessel. Hardly the kind of quest that required a tactical team and a bunch of assault rifles.

We left the Great Hall among waves and goodbyes and trekked the long, winding path into the woods.

"Why do you let Tristan speak to you like that? As if you're a servant?" I asked, once the adrenaline had subsided.

"Because I *am* his servant. Well, his subject, but the difference is hair-thin."

"He's your brother. Family should come first." Simply saying those words out loud gave me a pang of longing for Mom and Dad. Our relationship had deteriorated as my lies had grown harder to spin. The weird time jumps and lags hadn't helped communication. When their disappointment became impossible to ignore, my calls to them all but stopped. Maybe now that I was going back to a shared timeline with them, we'd be able to heal the rift. Once Tristan came through on his promise to help my dad, the burden on my parents would lift. Without the stress, we'd find our way to each other again.

Nieve scoffed. "Family doesn't come first for us." A slight hesitation, then more quietly, "Never for us."

"How old is he anyway?"

"Thirty-four."

"And you?"

"Twenty-nine."

I brushed my hand over the soft fern lining the route. This place blossomed with life, light, and lusciousness. Steeped in a pleasant heat without humidity. I could see why the Elonians would do everything in their power to protect their home.

I bit my lip. "Tell me more about the prophecy. What did you find out?"

Her step didn't falter on the pliant ground but her gait grew stiff. "What about the prophecy?"

"You and Tristan seem to believe in it, and since this vessel is such a big deal, I want to understand why your faith is so strong."

"Why wouldn't we believe it?" She circled a dead tree and ducked a leafy branch. "It's called a prophecy for a reason."

I quickened my steps to catch up. "What exactly does it say about me?"

"It's not my place to tell." Nieve pointed at an ordinary oak. "This is the Tree of All Journeys, our Gate. It was imbued with magical properties at the birth of the Divide."

Elonians and their secrets. First they wouldn't let me get close to my bio-mother, then Tristan hid books in the library to stop me from learning the magic I wasn't yet allowed to use.

"The prophecy is the reason I'm here." I halted and planted my soles onto the gnarly roots. "Dammit, Nieve. I have a right to know."

She took a deep breath and kicked a stone at her feet. It whirred through the air, bounced off the trunk of another tree, and vanished in a bush. "It says…"

"It says what?"

She stood, her eyes wide, almost crazy. "The prophecy says you're going to die."

A loud *pop*, and the Gate opened.

# CHAPTER SEVENTEEN



*"Are you certain your aggression isn't misplaced frustration at your own inadequacies? No? My bad."*

Lea and I stopped in an alley, a good twenty yards from where the Gate had deposited us, surrounded by trashcans and grime. At least it was daytime, maybe noon, judging by the position of the sun.

Lea hadn't spoken since I'd told her the truth. For weeks I'd been carrying this terrible secret. Weeks of avoiding her, of formulating and discarding explanations, excuses, reasons. Maybe I'd hoped Tristan would have told her in my absence.

I waved at Lea. "Your luster."

"What?" Her eyes darted wildly before she extinguished her life light and cast the incantation to hide her dagger.

I tried a kind smile, which quickly died on my lips. Too many times I'd tried to come up with words of comfort, or with an apology that would make a difference. Nothing was going to soften the blow, except maybe time. The one commodity we didn't have.

"Does Tristan know?" She gave a deep chuckle. "Strike that. Of course he knew."

I held on to my elbows and shuffled. Whatever questions she had, I'd answer them. I owed her that at least.

"What about you?" She raised her chin toward me. "Are you going to die?"

"Not according to the prophecy."

"Well, that's something."

"If I'd known—"

She vehemently shook her head. "You saved me from the Shades. If you hadn't found me, I might be dead now."

Lea showed more grace than I would have.

She drew a long breath through her nose and slowly released it. "Okay, fine. It's a stupid prophecy. Even with the time shift between the realms, the arrow of time is intact. You can't know what's going to happen. It's not possible."

I opened my mouth, then stopped myself. If she still had hope, I wasn't going to pull it out from under her.

"You disagree?" She crossed her arms. "You truly believe I'm going to die?"

"Honestly, I don't know. I've always had faith in the oracles and their powers to tell the future. Their prophecies are sacred." I shifted onto my back foot. "But I can't imagine a situation in which I'd allow you to die. Not as long as I'm still alive."

Lea let out a whistle and laughed. "Wow. You lot are full of surprises."

"I'm going to visit an old friend of mine who lives here in Seattle. Not only might he know where we can find the crown prince, but he knows the prophecy better than I. Maybe he can tell me something new."

"Can I come?"

"It's better if I go alone. You know how to use the Inter…net?"

"Of course."

I nodded. "Good. Go home and research this vessel while I'm

out. It is my understanding the Internet contains a lot of information. Information is what we need."

Together we exited the Gate onto a busy street. Seattle wasn't a place of just one thing. Green spaces, old buildings and new high-rises co-existed in a flimsy peace, as did people of all colors, religions and fashion senses. No one had ever taken issue with the way I dressed, and even Shades with their unusual outfits blended in with the help of magic.

Lea swung her bag over one shoulder. "Is it safe to go home?"

I shrugged. "I don't see why it wouldn't be. The Shades never tracked you to your home, or they wouldn't have needed to follow you by car. During the day and with your luster under control, there is not much to identify you as the lost Elonian."

"The leather?" She gestured along the length of her body.

I nodded my head at a group of men and women with brightly colored hair and overlong coats, who were taking advantage of the rare sun as they sat on a set of stairs not far from us.

"Okay then." Lea pointed to her right. "I'll get a cab. I have my wallet right…" She patted first her waist then her butt. "…here."

It was obvious why she captivated the king. With curves, a wide-eyed innocence and quick wits, his guy hormones would be in quite a froth. But the last thing Lea needed was distractions. What the slice had Tristan been thinking?

"I mean it." She flicked her fingers in an away motion. "Go, but don't be long."

Her tone was breezy and cold. But now that there were no more secrets between us, we had a chance to fuse into a team. I hadn't seen her fight, but, assuming Tristan hadn't spoken from his view behind rose-tinted glasses, she at least wouldn't get in my way. If she followed my lead, didn't act rashly, we might find the vessel before either of us had to die. Before *she* had to die.

I nodded my goodbye for fear my voice would reveal more than I was willing to admit, and headed south.

My destination was the less affluent side of town. I didn't know street names that could guide the way, but I was accustomed to using landmarks for orientation. The most prominent of which in Seattle was the Space Needle.

After an hour's walk, I was getting close. The greasy window of a small shop and its dilapidated sign announcing, without conviction, the sale of fresh produce were hard to forget.

I passed a group of young men in low-rise jeans. They'd tied bandanas around their heads like makeshift bandages. Whether they were the walking stereotype of a gang or aspired to appear like one, I couldn't say. Without being subtle about it, they trailed me through the neighborhood, whispering loudly among themselves about the *hotness* of my leather outfit.

For now they kept their distance, which suited me fine. I had little time for a confrontation with adolescent wannabes.

After shooting a warning glare at my tough-looking entourage, I stepped through the raised gate of an auto shop. Inside, three cars, one elevated on a platform, filled the space. Oil and grease fumes bit into my nose. I breathed through my mouth. When the clanking of metal on metal drowned out my greetings, I ventured deeper into the hall.

"Excuse me." I waved to catch the attention of a man in gray and blue overalls. "Any idea where I can find Gerrit?"

He switched off his welding torch and placed a gloved hand behind his ear.

"Gerrit?" I shouted for simplicity.

The man pointed at a door in the back of the shop.

I nodded and made my way to the frosted glass partition. Although I didn't expect a trap, I opened the door with caution.

A man in a shiny suit stood with his broad back toward me. He was immersed in a file he held in one hand. His other hand was wrapped around a steaming cup. Paper, dirty rags, and gadgets covered a small desk in the center of the room.

"Gerrit?" I said.

The man didn't react.

I closed the door, walked up to him, and tapped him on the shoulder. He flinched, spilling a brown liquid over the white pages in his hand.

"Nieve." His frown changed into a smile. He chucked the folder on his desk and hugged me with one arm.

Under his physical closeness, my body stiffened. His cologne seemed geared toward overpowering the smell of grease, a mission at which it succeeded. He released me and removed plugs from his ears.

"It's so good to see you. How's life? How are you? How's the king?" His words tumbled out like they'd waited in line overnight.

Carried away by his enthusiasm, I beamed at him. "Let's see. I'm well. The king hasn't changed much. Or at all. Life's..." My grin faded. "Life could be better. I hate to barge in here and get straight to the point, but—"

"Hey, whatever you need."

I gave a curt nod. "I need to find the Shade crown prince."

Gerrit lifted a single eyebrow. It was a noticeable tell, and I had to stop myself from drawing attention to it. Once upon a time, he'd never have allowed his face to betray his thoughts. A preference for coffee and chaos weren't the only Kindred traits he'd picked up since he left the king's employ.

He gestured at a stack of paper, under which I found a three-legged stool. I placed the pile onto the ground and took a seat.

Gerrit planted himself on a padded chair on the other side of his desk. "I've only met the crown prince once or twice. At the end of the war, when I was working for your brother." He squeezed his lips together, no doubt reliving painful memories. "I should have been with them, you know."

I scooted the stool closer to the desk and patted his hand. I knew exactly what he was talking about. While Gerrit discussed peace terms with the Shade king and the crown prince, another two of the king's sons had led a raiding party into Gerrit's village. No one knew for sure if they chose the location because Tristan's closest friend called it his home, or if the village was a random pick, but I didn't believe in coincidence.

The male guards were killed outright. The Shades rounded up the women, including Gerrit's wife and their daughter Belinda, for soldierly fun, locked them in their houses, and burnt the entire village to the ground. Not a soul survived.

I was one of the first to arrive on the scene, the first to witness the result of the Shades' massacre. The acrid smell of blood, mingled with the smoke of burnt bodies, still haunted my dreams.

Gerrit's negotiation gave us the peace we'd longed for, but he'd paid a high price. Far too high.

Tristan had offered him a new life on Hawaii, in the South of France or at any of the other sunny destinations the Gate connected to, but Gerrit had punished himself by relocating to Seattle.

I lowered my voice. "If you'd been there, you'd be dead now, too."

"Don't be fooled by the living shell you see before you. I died that day."

I gave him a moment to collect himself. "The crown prince has entered the Kindred realm. He's found The Vessel of Orrin. I'm not sure if he still has it, but he did, which is why I need to locate him. You're the only person I know who's met him."

"The vessel." Gerrit rubbed his earlobe between his fingers.

*"Lest the Divide be broke and fade into the water of The Vessel of Orrin,"* he mumbled, quoting from the prophecy. The edge of one hand swiped over a document as if to flatten it. The pressure he applied caused the desk to creak. "So the day you've been preparing for is near?"

"We're sure of it."

His shoulders wilted. Gerrit was my brother's age, yet a decade in the Kindred realm had added many wrinkles. His once full head of hair sported a bald spot in its center, and beneath his wide chest bulged the early stages of a food belly. But it was the stricken expression on his face that aged him the most.

He twisted his hands. "I have no idea where the crown prince could be."

"Would it help if I told you he and his father have fallen out?"

He double-clucked his tongue. "I'm not surprised. He didn't turn out anything like the old man, although the Shade king sure tried. Oh, he's committed plenty of atrocities, no doubt. That's what war demands of you. But graded on his family's curve, he's a ball of fluff."

"If he has the vessel, maybe he won't—"

"He's still a Shade. If there's one thing the past has taught us, it's this. Never trust a Shade." His scowl tolerated no opposition.

"I don't."

"Good."

Maybe coming here was a mistake. A knot lodged itself in my throat, and I tried unsuccessfully to swallow it. Dragging out this conversation had awoken Gerrit's ghosts, and who knew how long it would take him to lay them to rest again. But he was my one lead, the one hope I had of finding the crown prince and ultimately The Vessel of Orrin. "Can you tell me anything about him? Name, preferences, looks?"

He bore my persistence with a graceful calm. "I don't know

his name. The minions addressed him as *my lord* and his father addressed him as *son*. Mind you, the king has fifteen sons. He probably can't remember all their names."

The heat from the workshop took its toll and sweat rolled along the nape of my neck. I mopped at it with one of the rags Gerrit had lying around while I filed away his words. "Anything else?"

"He has dark hair, but could have dyed it. And height?" He examined my figure through squinted eyes. "I'd say he's about as tall as you."

"Great, I've narrowed it down to about thirty percent of the population."

A hint of a smile drifted over his face. "Wait. I'm not done. When I last saw him, he had a bright-red Z-shaped scar above his collarbone. And he always wears Derinda's symbol around his neck. All Shades do, of course, but his is made of solid silver. The detail on the medallion is exquisite. It's overlaid with an iridescent coating and shimmers with the colors of a blue and white butterfly when the light hits it."

I put on a brave face. He tried to be helpful. It was hardly his fault he fell short of my overly high expectations.

He placed his hand palm-up before him on his desk. "Why don't you catch yourself a Shade and ask them? If the crown prince is at odds with the king, the king's men will keep tabs on him. Count on it. Once you know where to find him, Derinda's symbol will help narrow down your options. It's all I have for you."

I swallowed my disillusionment and put on a grateful face. "Thank you. I appreciate your help." I got to my feet.

"If the prophecy is coming true…" He rubbed his arm. "Have you found her?"

"Yeah. Her name's Lea."

"Is she up to the challenge?"

On the basis of our one and only training session, I doubted she was up to preparing a fruit salad. The king had had a mere six months to train her, and drastic improvement was improbable. "She has the spirit of a warrior," I said.

Gerrit closed his eyes. "*On that day, two children shall unite their powers and battle to preserve the Divide. Yet all shall be lost in the fawn's death.*"

"That was a new one for me." I gave a low chuckle. "No one had told me that the young woman I was supposed to find is to meet her death so soon."

"Don't kid yourself. None of this is your doing." Gerrit leaned back in his chair, the fabric of his suit rustling with the motion. "Imagine what the Shades will do to this world. Take power and twist the Kindreds to their purpose. Then use the Kindreds' overwhelming numbers to subjugate the Elonians." His voice shook. "It's our day of reckoning."

"But Lea is innocent."

"Does she know about the prophecy?"

My muscles tautened, and my voice came out rough. "Yes, I told her. Tristan doesn't know about that. You know what he's like. Lose one and save many, or save one and lose all. To him, it's a no-brainer, even if we have to sacrifice Lea."

"You could, of course, save all and lose none."

"You don't think Lea's death is certain? But the prophecy...."

He leaned forward with his folded hands on his desk. "*On that day, two children shall unite their powers and battle to preserve the Divide. Yet all shall be lost in the fawn's death.* The fawn's death. The Divide's fall. Who says both these things occur on the same day?"

His words knocked the breath from my lungs. "I just assumed."

He raised a finger. "Never assume. What's more, it could simply be a warning. All will be lost if the fawn dies. *If.*"

His speculation made my head whirl. He couldn't be right. For months, I'd torn the wording apart every which way and never come up with that conclusion. But he'd had years to ponder its meaning. If it meant Lea was going to live, I'd take it.

I shot him an uncertain smile. "I've got to get back to her. We don't have a lot of time."

"Not so fast. It's not every day I get to hug a pretty lady." Gerrit rambled out from behind his desk and captured me in a tight squeeze.

My muscles hardened, but instead of rolling out of his embrace, I forced myself to soak his scent into my memory. He released me, and I turned and walked out, gaze fixed ahead. Goodbyes made me uneasy.

Outside, I veered left. On cue, the group of troublemakers roused themselves from the curb to follow me.

As lovely as it was seeing Gerrit again, my visit had wasted valuable time. Had I really believed finding the crown prince would be simple? Time pressed against my chest, suffocating my options. His idea wasn't a bad one. Catching a Shade shouldn't be too difficult. Maybe the Shade from the alley. With the right incentive, he might share with me what he knew. After all, he'd shown little to no loyalty to the Shade king.

"Hey mama," a voice behind me shouted. "Wait up."

I spun around, fixed my face into a stern glower, and cracked my neck. The leader of the pack of teenagers dropped his cocky smile like the wrong end of a branding iron.

I assume that, in the end, it was the hanbo I brandished that sent them packing.

I allowed myself a smile. Who said I didn't know how to have fun?

# CHAPTER EIGHTEEN

*LEA*

*"They say every day is a gift. But don't you ever feel the urge to ask for directions to the 'returns' department?"*

Nieve walked off to meet with her friend, leaving me behind to find my way home. I strolled down the street, grateful to be back in Seattle. Healthy, clean air and pretty flowers were great for vacations, but without the licorice smell of gas, the lulling hum of engines, and the privacy city life afforded, relaxation didn't come easy to me.

Everywhere I looked, the urban transformation continued, as evidenced by construction sites with giant cranes, building a new, better, and even less recognizable Seattle. Years ago, while I'd been away, an Internet mega-outlet had swooped in and created a town within the city, complete with domes and skyscrapers and the reek of ambition. Seattle was still my home, of course, but Elonia had left a mark on me, too. My routine of training and study had provided comfort in the midst of a crazy situation. Here, I had no routine to fall back on. Suddenly, my home had become this weird, unfamiliar place.

What would my parents make of my new understanding of the world? Or the Kindred population at large? Would panic spread if I rose into the air? Not too long ago, I'd been one of the crowd, willfully cocooned in preconceived notions, my greatest concern whether to have a salad or a burger for dinner. That had been six months ago. Six months? I checked my cell's display. According to Washington time, I'd been gone just over five months. Close enough.

What was proper etiquette when the apocalypse lurked around the corner? Stand on a soapbox and preach? Panic-buy bottled water and canned spaghetti? I placed my palm on my stomach to calm my insides. Despite the confidence I'd projected for Nieve's benefit, I was so far out of my depth, solid land was a distant memory. If only I could tell my parents to get to safety. Even if I could, where the hell was *safety*?

"You all right there, kid?" a gruff voice asked.

"Yeah, thanks." My reply was automatic, absent-minded.

"Cuz ya looking pale about the gills."

I glanced around. What the hell? To my right and left, people bustled along the sidewalk, chatting, laughing, or avoiding eye contact. Not a soul had stopped to speak to me.

"Down here."

I lowered my gaze. A dark stone gargoyle in a gray coat and a hat leaned against a cement planter, a cigarette tucked between spiky teeth. Black wings extended on its back.

"There ya go," the voice said. "Knew ya could see me, kid. Took me long enough to find ya. Now how's about we dust outta here?"

The creature would have been carved by hand, with oversized ears that were unnaturally pointed. Over the decades, the weather had pitted its exterior like the surface of the moon. And yet, words seemed to come from its direction.

I blinked, but the image didn't change. What the heck had I eaten for breakfast? "Excuse me?"

"Scram. Anyone sees ya jawing to one like me, well, they gonna think ya gone loco."

Maybe I had. Rubbing my eyes, I twirled and checked the area for the real owner of the voice. A ventriloquist with a gargoyle-shaped case, maybe. A telltale wink or a smile somewhere in the crowd. Nothing.

"Look at me, kid. C'mon. I don't bite."

I refused to be like one of those drifters who hung out on park benches and talked to themselves. Crouching to pretend-tie my bootlaces, I unzipped my bag and stuffed the gargoyle inside, discarding its cigarette in the process.

"Hey, careful." The voice sounded muffled through the bag.

I clutched the heavy bag tight to my chest. "Quiet, I'm taking you home. Whatever you are."

Plastering on a nothing-to-see-here face, I made my way toward Westlake Station and hailed a cab.

"We there yet?" the creature asked when the car peeled off the curb. "I gotta use the john."

"Shush," I whispered, which earned me an odd look from the driver. I clawed my hands into the bag's faux-leather exterior and didn't let go until my driveway came into view.

Once I'd paid and exited the cab, I raced inside as if the hounds of hell snapped at my heels. I dropped the bag on my sofa and retreated into a corner of the living room. From there I glared at it. What was I supposed to do with a speaking gargoyle?

Sure, this wasn't the strangest thing that had happened in my life. It didn't even top the list of strange things that had happened this month, but it sure qualified as one in a long line of issues for which my future therapist would charge double.

The zipper moved, and the gargoyle peeked its stone head out. His gray fedora hat perched on a grotesque, yet oddly adorable face with bulging eyes, while his pointy ears projected through its wide brim.

"Good, we're alone. Now, where's the john?" he asked.

Hundreds of the little buggers could be found around the city, monsters crouched high on churches or other old buildings, but never had one talked to me.

I pointed to the hall. "Second door on the left."

"Thanks, kid. 'ppreciated." He hopped out of the bag and dropped from the sofa onto the ground with a loud *thunk*. Then he waddled off, his coat dragging along the floor. In a previous life, it might have been a children's raincoat, but it had since been shortened to about half-length.

I took a deep breath. My parents owned the house and paid the bills, but unfortunately, they'd refused to pay for a cleaner. Tristan should have sent a few servants, because the air in my house smelled staler than the bread I'd probably left in my fridge. I opened the windows and inhaled again. Better. In the kitchen, I filled the coffee machine with water and enough coffee grounds to make my hair even curlier. I wanted it strong enough to burn its way through the mug, strong enough to jolt me out of this bizarre dream.

Three minutes later, the gargoyle returned.

Flapping his wings, he lifted himself onto the kitchen table and sat, crossing his stumpy legs in front. "How ya doing there, kid?"

How could he even lift his mass off the ground? *Physics, people.* I'd seen its laws abused over the last few months, but now magic was just plain mocking me. I opened my mouth, blew out the beginning of a consonant, and closed it again. If I talked to a gargoyle and nobody heard it, would I still be crazy?

"I'm good," I eventually said. "Who are you?"

"Kirk." The gargoyle slapped his chest then his waist,

extracted a phone and finally a packet of cigarettes and a lighter from his pocket.

"Don't even think of lighting up in here." I raised a warning finger.

"Kid, I'm gonna give you so much info, you'll wanna marry me. But you ain't my wife yet, so don't start nagging."

"Fine." After rummaging through the recycle bin, I picked up an empty green bean can and placed it in front of the gargoyle. "Use this."

"Neat. Now, where's the hooch?" Kirk pivoted his heavy stone neck until he faced a bottle of bourbon I kept for emergencies. He pointed with a stubby, claw-like hand. "Don't be stingy."

I forced my lips together and fetched the bottle from the cabinet. Then I pressed a glass against the pad in the ice dispenser to fill it up, and poured the bourbon. "What's this information you have for me?"

"First things first. You're the one, ain't ya? The Spark the Shades are all in a tizzy 'bout?"

"You know about the Shades?" I handed him the glass.

He took a long swig and lit his cigarette. "I know 'em all right. Know you, too."

The smoke ring hit me right on the nose.

I scrunched my face. "Me?"

"Sure. Ya don't have no luster no more, but ya did. Hard to miss. Learned ourselves a bit of magic now, eh? Good for you, kid." His voice rasped, and he coughed.

Having vocal cords made of stone would do that, I supposed. But if he gobbed in my kitchen, I'd chuck him straight out the window. My hospitality only stretched so far.

"Hang on." I rubbed my face. "Only Shades call Elonians Sparks. Are you a Shade?"

"What's wrong with ya, kid? Use ya peepers." He creakily shook his head. "I'm a gargoyle."

It was the most syllables anyone had ever used to say *duh*.

"So, *Kirk*. What is it you want?"

"Help ya save the Divide, of course."

"Why? What's it to you?"

He gulped more bourbon and flicked ash from his cigarette into the empty can. "My kind are made of stone, and the Shades control stone. For millennia, they's kept us as slaves. Long as we're in this world and they're not, we're A-okay. But if the Divide falls, we're back to being their goons. And I ain't nobody's goon."

"I see." I repositioned a chair and sat. "What type of information can you give me?"

"Whatever ya need."

"Have you ever heard of The Vessel of Orrin?"

Kirk stubbed out his cigarette. "No. But I sure can tell ya about Orrin."

"Great. What is it?"

"Not what. Who. Orrin's one of the Old Ones, the beings that roamed the globe before any of ya took ya first breath. He was the big cheese of the Old Ones. The boss, ya know."

"What happened?"

"Back when you was still all one race of humans, a bunch of ya went and got yourselves some faith, a belief in gods and stuff, and you forgot about the Old Ones. Fired Orrin all up, it did. He and his woman cast a spell, creating a wall to keep out magic from the god followers. They made a whole new realm."

"I assume the Elonians and Torrens were the non god followers?"

"Right. Later, before the Old Ones left the new world for good, they shared their powers with their children. Some got air and light magic, the others got darkness and earth.

Depending on who their sponsor was. Orrin gifted the Sparks, and his wife Derinda helped the Shades. The Old Ones have different skills, ya see. Even the great Orrin had his limitations."

"Where are the Old Ones now?"

"Dunno. No one's seen 'em in years." Kirk lit another cigarette. He inhaled and exhaled, watching the smoke unfurl.

I sputtered and fanned myself then opened the window wider. "You don't know what The Vessel of Orrin is or how to find it?"

"Not a clue."

A rattle coming from the stairwell started me. It was followed by the creak that sounded each time I opened the main door. I held up my hand, silencing Kirk. Nobody knew I was back in town, and the Shades weren't supposed to have found my home. But what if they had? My heart thumping low in my chest, I rose and slid my dagger from its sheath.

The door slammed shut. Footsteps ricocheted against the wooden floor. Nieve walked in.

I loosened my grip on Fallon and breathed out. "Don't sneak up on me. Nearly gave me a heart attack."

For once she wore her platinum hair loose, allowing it to fall straight over her shoulders. The style suited her better than the tight ponytail she preferred, although she would probably argue it was less practical. At the sight of Fallon, she smiled. Then her gaze flitted to Kirk and her features tightened. Even her lips disappeared into a pale pink line.

She slid her hanbo out of its holster.

"Step aside from the traitor, Lea." Her voice echoed with authority.

I furrowed my brows and swiveled my head. Kirk dropped his cigarette onto my tablecloth and went airborne.

The stench of burning plastic drilled into my nostrils.

"Crap." I sheathed Fallon and poured the rest of my coffee over the glowing ash.

Nieve swiped her stick at the gargoyle.

Kirk took refuge behind me, hovering like a dark and dumpy hummingbird. His hiss would have done a rabid cat proud.

"Calm down." I extended my arms to keep the two of them apart. "What's he done?"

She jabbed her hanbo at him, close by my ear. Luckily, she missed both. "It's a gargoyle."

"So?"

"Gargoyles work for Shades." Keeping her hanbo aloft, she tracked Kirk with absolute focus.

"What? Not Kirk. He wants to help." Kirk's alcohol-laden breath crept over my skin, like an itch I couldn't scratch.

"Don't be naïve." Nieve glued her gaze to the gargoyle. "Come on, we need to leave. The Shades are probably already on their way."

Kirk flapped his wings wildly. "No, they're not."

I swatted him away.

Was Nieve right? Was I too trusting for my own good? I glimpsed over my shoulder at the flying stone monster. If he worked for the Shades, why hadn't he followed me home rather than speak to me on the open street? There had to be a million easier ways to spy on me.

"Unless gargoyles can talk to Shades telepathically, he hasn't told anyone about me." I soaked up the coffee spill with a sponge. "So simmer down. Both of you."

Nieve lowered her stick but not her vigilance.

I bobbed my head. "Kirk, you too. Sit. Please?"

Reluctantly, both did as I asked. Kirk landed on my table and fumbled for another cigarette, ignoring my disapproving glare. Nieve sat on the chair opposite him.

I poured her a cup of coffee and buffer-zoned myself

between the two, in case the ruckus started anew.

"There," I said into the fragile peace. "Isn't this pleasant?"

Both scowled. At least I assumed Kirk scowled. With him, it was difficult to tell.

"Great." I fake beamed at the two. "Let's clear the air. Kirk, are you a Shade spy?"

He flung his lighter on the table. "I'm nobody's spy. I'm a free gargoyle."

"No such thing." Nieve's tone hadn't mellowed.

Kirk hissed again, exposing his sharp teeth.

I placed a hand on his thick shoulder. "Please."

"The First Prince himself set me free. I ain't serving no one no more."

"So the Shades can no longer compel you to do their bidding?" I asked.

"Yeah. Others ain't so lucky, though. It's why I wanna help." He pointed his glare at Nieve.

I tapped the table to draw his attention back to me. "So how did you know the Shades were looking for me?"

"I said I'm free. Not deaf. I hear things. Shades are looking for ya all over."

Nieve clicked her tongue. "I've never heard of a free gargoyle."

"There's a bunch of us. We can be useful."

"We can't trust him." Nieve's voice had lost its certainty, but she wasn't yet ready to discard her old worldviews.

When the powers-that-be handed out an unreasonable belief in useless traditions, old gripes, and duty, she'd been first in line. Then she asked for seconds. Good thing she had me now.

"Seems to me we're in no position to decline anyone's help." I fixed her with a stare. "If you'd listened carefully, you'd know Kirk has info we need. He told us he knows the Shade crown prince."

# CHAPTER NINETEEN

*NIEVE*

*"War isn't about who's right and who's wrong. It's about me kicking your bony butt all the way into the afterworld."*

Could it be this easy? Had the gargoyle prattled away without realizing he'd given us a vital clue? Lea acted as if she had little doubt. More likely, he was attempting to lead us into a trap. Maybe I could use his treachery to my advantage. Gerrit had suggested snatching a Shade, and this would be the perfect opportunity.

"All right." I opened my arms to appear mollified. "I'm listening, gargoyle. Where's the Shade crown prince?"

The gargoyle tilted his head back and blew rings of smoke into the air. "I ain't no snitch. The Prince is on the level. He was the one that freed me."

As if the combined stench of coffee and cigarette smoke weren't enough to put up with, the creature grated on my nerves. But since I wanted him to tell me about the prince, I'd have to postpone my plan to throttle him until after our conversation.

"I admire your loyalty." Lea brushed a crumb off the table. "But the thing is, the prince has The Vessel of Orrin. He might be keeping it safe from the other Shades, in which case no foul, right? We want to help him." She swiped her hands along the tablecloth and leaned in toward the gargoyle. "But what if he's planning to destroy the Divide with it? What's going to happen to your fellow gargoyles?"

*Nicely done, Lea.*

The gargoyle made a *cluck-cluck* sound and bobbed his head. "So, if he ain't planning no trouble, ya won't take a poke at him?"

She nodded earnestly. "I give you my word he'll not be harmed."

"What about that one?" The gargoyle jabbed his cigarette in my direction before stubbing it out in a green bean can.

"Don't worry about Nieve. We don't hurt people unless they deserve to be hurt. Right?" Lea sent me an indecipherable glance.

"Right." In my opinion, all Shades deserved to be hurt, so I saw no reason to contradict her.

"I'll tell ya what I know then." He lifted a chipped stone claw. "But don't cross me." His voice was part cough, part threat.

"We won't." Lea raised four fingers, while her other hand crossed her heart.

The childish gesture seemed to appease him.

"All right. He's about her size." He lifted his chin in my direction. "Dark brown hair, and's always suited up. Last time I saw him was by the waterfront. Said he got a job somewhere, all legit. All Kindred-like."

"Where does he live?"

"Some'ere on Western Avenue, he said. Gets home 'round six or seven."

"His name?" Lea asked.

"No clue. We's call him My Prince or My Lord."

"Of course you do." I stared at the ticking clock at the wall, for once willing time to move faster.

Lea waved off my comment and sloped forward. "If we have more questions, where can we find you?"

"I hang out at the W Hotel on Fourth. Or hey, if ya leave the hooch, I'll stay right here and you can call me."

She rose from her chair and moved the bottle closer to him. "Why not? You've earned it."

I stood and zipped up my jacket. Outside the open window, the sun cast long shadows onto the overgrown lawn. It was twenty to five. Plenty of time to set up our trap for the Shades. Most likely, they'd arrive with the onset of dusk.

The gargoyle tapped his finger against the bottle. "Help, please?"

At least he was polite. I unscrewed the cap for him and lifted the bottle to pour him a drink, but he stopped me with a shake of his head.

"I'm good." The gargoyle took flight, grabbed the bottle between two stubby hands, and poured himself a generous helping before placing the bottle back on the table.

"Hold on, I've got an idea." Lea shoved her hand deep into her pocket and withdrew a strip of gum, some fluff, and her phone, which she held up in the air. "I'm going to take pictures of men that fit your description and text them to you. You let us know which one is the crown prince. Okay?"

He ran his heavy finger over the rim of his glass before giving a determined nod. "I can do that." He cited a number, which Lea typed into her phone. "But don't tell the prince it was me that sent ya."

"We promise." She elbowed me.

"We'll keep your secret." What I didn't say was that, even if the gargoyle's story were true, my plans for the crown prince didn't involve talking.

Lea clamped my sleeve between her fingers and dragged me out. "Be good!"

Outside, I cleared my nose passages of any remaining smoke stench and glanced up the street. "Here's the plan. When the Shades arrive, we single out one of them. You distract, I snatch. Understood?"

"What *are* you talking about?"

"You know, once the gargoyle alerts the Shades. If he hasn't already."

Lea frowned and glanced back at her house. "You still believe Kirk's working with the Shades? But he's helping us."

"Seriously?" My teeth scraped against each other. Slice it, that girl still had so much to learn. "I suppose it's not entirely your fault. When it comes to our history with the Shades and the gargoyles, you lack the relevant background. So let me condense it for you. He's a gargoyle. Gargoyles work for the Shades."

"Don't patronize me." Her eyes narrowed.

I took a measured breath through my nose. "Lea. I know what I'm talking about."

"So am I. In any case, my plan is going to work." She touched her stuffed pocket. "And if it makes you feel better, we can scout the neighborhood when we come back."

"Why are you indulging him?"

"I'm not. I'm following the only lead we have. What if he's speaking the truth? We can't afford to ignore it." She'd never sounded more certain or more forceful.

Her simple argument struck a chord. I was used to calling the shots, but was I merely the foot soldier in this prophecy? Lea hadn't shown signs of being a great warrior, even though Tristan had witnessed her unusual skill when it came to magic. Either way, she had to bring something to this relationship. My years on the battlefield hadn't required subtlety or finesse from me. I usually pointed my hanbo and took aim.

Lea had this ability to look at things from different angles.

Maybe my aversion to gargoyles had closed me off from even considering Kirk might have given us a useful clue.

I took a more relaxed stance. "The gargoyle's description of the prince *does* match the one I got from my source."

"Great. So are we agreed?"

Maybe my people's faith in Lea wasn't misplaced. I'd been so focused on her mediocre combat abilities, I forgot cunning and strategy were also vital parts of a warrior's arsenal.

"Okay." I rolled my shoulders. "We'll try your way first."

She opened the doors to her orange Ford with a beep. My steps faltered. From her point of view, driving to our destination made sense, but to be honest, I'd rather rub my eyes with a broken bottle than get in. As her mentor and teacher, I couldn't chicken out, though. Somehow, I had to match her stoic resolve.

I took my seat next to her and fastened the seatbelt.

She turned on the engine and reversed out of her driveway. While she hummed along to a song on the radio, I anchored myself by looking at the large billboards and flashy neon signs that zoomed past us.

Once or twice, my hand sought the grab handle over the door. I was no stranger to speed, but Lea's bordered on suicidal. More troublesome, the other drivers matched her driving style, weaving in and out of lanes as if Galleo himself was after them.

Soon the sea peeked through the buildings. A dark cloud, streaked with pink, hung low over the deep blue water. Up the road from a red-bricked, ivy-covered building, Lea spotted a space outside a nail salon. She pulled in with a flourish, cutting off another driver who'd spied the same space. He hooted, gestured, and drove on.

I clutched the door handle, my knuckles pale.

Lea grinned. "You think that's bad. You should see how they drive in Germany."

"I'll take your word for it."

Once my feet were back on asphalt, I got my bearings. The air was salty fresh, as if the grime and dirt on which this city was built had been soaked, washed, and dried with an ocean-scented dryer sheet. So close to downtown Seattle, I'd anticipated more bustle. Instead, the area exuded a peaceful charm. Leafy trees brightened the street with their fall colors, and the tall buildings flanking us boasted large, open windows and flake-free paint jobs. After a few minutes' walk, Lea pointed at a bench tucked away in an alcove, situated next to a set of stairs. Long-leaved shrubs framed the bench on three sides.

"Is this it?" I asked.

"Yeah. There's a popular restaurant up there." She jutted her chin at the stairs. "Best pork chops in town." She sat and brandished a flat, purple phone. "As good a place to start as any other, right?"

The sun still held twilight at bay. Rubbing my arms, I scanned the area one more time and took the spot next to Lea. If the crown prince had landed himself a Kindred job, he'd most likely follow Kindred custom and return home between five and seven o'clock. I'd give Lea's plan an hour or two, then I'd spur the horses and get ourselves to safety.

The bench overlooked a T-junction, with Western Avenue extending to the left and right, and another street rolling out ahead of us. Strategically, a good choice.

We picked the most likely candidates from the passers-by, and Lea clicked away on her phone's camera, sending each photo to the gargoyle. Within the first half hour alone, we'd spotted six guys who fit the description. Just as I'd thought, Kirk didn't reply.

I rolled back my head and let the breeze brush over my face. "I told you, you can't trust a gargoyle."

"I don't think it's that." Lea, stubborn as always, pursed her mouth. "He has stubby fingers, and texting can't be easy. I bet he'll let us know when we hit the jackpot."

I chose not to press her further. Some mistakes she had to make on her own. Soon, the traffic of people thinned and the number of positive sightings dropped.

Lea nudged me in the ribs. "If none of these men turn out to be the prince, think we should open a dating website? Some of our *models* look rather tasty."

I laughed. "From your tone, you might be your own best customer."

"Don't worry. I don't mind sharing."

A soft heat engulfed my heart. Maybe if I'd had sisters, girl talk would have been an everyday occurrence. Neither the warriors in my units nor my brother had ever spoken this casually about men. I glanced at Lea from the corners of my eyes, willing her to teach me how to act like a girl.

She took another picture. Her chin whipped up. "Hey. Be right back."

She forced the phone into my hand, leaped up from her seat, and raced off.

I stared at the contraption in my hand. Guess I was taking over. Even though I doubted it was worth my effort, I forwarded the most recent pictures to Kirk.

Lea stopped running and walked with fake casualness toward a stranger. From my angle, I couldn't make out his features, but going by his straight posture and tilted head, he was happy to see her. They chatted for a while before she hooked her arm into his and they made their way over. The light from a street lamp struck them, and I got a better look.

He had green eyes. Not a gray-green or brown-green but the color of the sea on a hazy day. I forced my gaze away, at his extended arm.

"Nieve. I want you to meet Kieran." Lea rolled up to her toes, maybe to cover her shortness relative to me and her friend. She failed. "Kieran, this is Nieve."

"Nice to meet you, Nieve." Kieran's voice carried the self-assurance of a man of power. It hooked itself around my consciousness like the teeth of a lion closing around its prey.

I handed Lea her phone and placed my hand in his. His long fingers folded around mine, topped off with a gentle squeeze but with enough kick to spike my pulse.

"It is," I said. "Nice to meet you, I mean." I retracted my arm.

I could perform twenty roundhouse kicks in half a minute without losing my bearings, could balance on the tallest rooftops, but a nice set of eyes wiped away every ounce of grace. My klutziness was doubly silly because I knew, beyond a sliver of doubt, he wouldn't be interested in me anyway. Kindreds that looked like him, dressed like him, and carried themselves like him preferred women in designer clothes with little dogs in their purses.

"What brings you two ladies to my neighborhood?" His mouth relaxed into a comfortable smile.

Lea sent a searching glance my way. I shrugged, still too aware of the knot in my tongue to attempt an explanation.

"We were going to hook up with a friend." She shifted her weight, admitting defeat in the height challenge. "He didn't show."

"What lowlife would bail on you two?"

A tingle crept into my cheeks. I fiddled with my hair, let it fall into my face to hide the blush. What was wrong with me?

"Flatterer." Lea leaned into him. "By the way, I'm sorry about not calling back. Is your father feeling better?"

"Unfortunately, yes." He waved a hand. "Don't mind me. Let's say my relationship with him hasn't improved."

"Sorry to hear that." She patted his arm.

I squinted at her. With her easy manner and sultry looks,

men would line up to be with her. Her life must have been one of parties and dates, whereas mine had been a life of duty. That wasn't her fault, of course.

A wide grin flitted over Kieran's face, sending my insides into a frenzy. "So, Nieve. Are you from Seattle?"

With my butt glued to the bench, I crossed my arms over my breasts. "No. I'm here on vacation."

He looked around with an exaggerated lift of his eyebrows. "You spend your vacation in Seattle and not on the beach?"

I cleared my throat to prepare for the blatant lie. "I'm not one for sun worship."

"I see." He jerked his head in Lea's direction. "How do you know each other?"

"Work." Her lie came without hesitation.

"Oh, you're a translator, too?" he asked me.

"Something like that, yes."

"Interesting attire for translators." His stare intensified, his left eyelid flickered.

Despite the chill, sweat collected at the nape of my neck. "I, uh…"

I'd maneuvered myself into a defensive position. To get out of it, I had to take control, get in questions of my own. If only my extensive weapons training had covered telling lies.

"Where do you live?" he asked.

I rubbed my arms against the rising cold. "Florida."

"That would explain it."

"Explain what?"

"The tan. And why you don't vacation on the beach."

I lifted my chin, glad for the reprieve. "That's right. It's hot in Florida."

My head drooped again. *It's hot in Florida.* At home, I enjoyed an excellent reputation as a proud, fierce warrior. Why was I behaving like a complete idiot?

"Hang on." His head angled to the side. "How can you know Lea from work and live in Florida at the same time?"

In an instant, my heartbeat doubled. He'd confused me with all his questions. "I, uh…"

Lea placed her hand on his arm to catch his attention. "It's a national company. Nieve works out of our Florida branch." Not a second too soon. "We'd better get going, though. It was nice seeing you."

"Yes, it was my pleasure." He shot me an exaggerated wink. "You do have the nicest friends."

I bit my lip.

Lea jingled her car keys. "Nieve?"

A seagull cried above our heads. I looked up with a start. Nightfall had crept up on me. Usually the transition from dusk to night manifested in a deep shiver down my back.

I wrapped my arms around me, my senses on high alert. "Yeah, we should go."

"Sure I can't talk you into a glass of wine at The Fly first?" Kieran said. "It's too early to go home. Nieve is on vacation, after all."

"Okay." The word bulleted out my mouth.

"Are you sure?" Lea shot me a huge smirk. "Not worried about our house guest?"

I raised my shoulders in an embarrassed shrug. The gargoyle had escaped my mind, but what harm would a couple more minutes do?

"Just one drink." I avoided her gaze.

Kieran steered us back in the direction we'd come, turned left, then up a set of stairs. His chat helped take my mind off the cold seeping through my jacket.

He talked about the beauty of Seattle, how on a clear day you could see Mount Rainier on the horizon. "I know it's hard to believe, but there's no correlation between the mountain's name and the weather."

We came upon a car-heavy road. Kieran stepped onto the pedestrian crossing, and the cars stopped.

"And it's not that rainy at all anyway." He herded us across the road. A tour guide par excellence. "Sure, Seattle's not as sunny as Florida, but I hope you'll soon discover its unique charms." His voice slid into my ear and down to my belly.

I mm-hmmed my agreement.

We turned left, leaving the noise of the engines behind. Sleek, white buildings on both sides of the sloping street reached high up to the heavens. The neon sign of The Fly flickered in the distance.

Despite my best attempt to remain indifferent, a shiver tickled the inside of my stomach. I'd visited taverns with the men serving under me before. Alcohol went a long way to dulling your memories and fostered an atmosphere of trust and collegiality, but I was unaccustomed to Kindred bars. This was where people relaxed, where they made friends, maybe even found life partners.

"They have great food, great cocktails, and decent music." Kieran placed a hand on my arm. "Only the best for our visitor, right?"

Snippets of another man's conversation drifted into my ear. "…comes here a lot. He's always…" The stranger stopped mid-sentence as if something had him startled. "That's them."

I whipped my head around.

Shades.

# CHAPTER TWENTY



*"I understand the concept of maturity. Just not as it applies to me."*

I followed Nieve's gaze down the sloped street, and everything around us fell quiet. We'd stopped by a small alley between a dark-bricked building and a tall wooden fence. Cars that were parked at an angle lined the two-lane road on both sides. Behind a tree, the emergency lighting of a small boutique cast green light on the ground. All of this I noticed, even though my sight fixed on the spot about thirty yards downhill, where six helmeted men in brown leather uniforms converged.

They, too, halted their conversation.

The pulse in my neck thumped wildly. My hand hovered over my dagger. The last time I'd encountered Shades I'd witnessed what they could do. I had no appetite for an encore.

One of them lifted his arms. Dark fog rose up past my knees and closed around my head.

"Come on. Let's go." I nudged Nieve's side.

My nose and throat clogged with the taste of something acidic. The same phenomenon had surrounded Kieran and me outside the *Orchard Lounge*. Hard to forget this scent, like the whiff of old parking garage and burnt tires.

"No, let's not." The firmness of Nieve's voice had a comforting effect. "Let's capture one of them instead."

"There's six of them and only two of us."

"Maybe, but they weren't expecting us, so they won't be elite warriors. Simple scouts, I'm guessing. Besides, escape isn't always an option. You can fly, but have you ever tried to stay in the air while Shades fling bricks and stones at you?"

"No." I kept my rattling heart in check, forced my breaths not to run away from me.

She was the one with experience. If she said running wasn't an option, I wasn't going to question her judgement. But even though I couln't leave, Kieran should.

With projected calm, I pushed him out of the way. "You should leave, or at least stay out of sight," I whispered. "This is no office party gone wrong."

Not that we couldn't do with his fighting skills, but he was unarmed, and the Shades looked ready to eat us for dinner.

He retreated to inside the alley. "Okay."

"Come on, Lea." Nieve drew her hanbo and walked toward the center of the fog.

The Shades communicated without words, using military hand signals like the members of *Stargate One*. They, too, knew the gameplay, carried years of experience on their shoulders.

The only one who didn't belong was I.

The phone in my pocket vibrated, but a tuneless song from further uphill snatched my attention first. Three men in suits had their arms wrapped around each other's shoulders as they marched toward us in step. A drop of hope halted the sick rumble in my gut. Two of the guys appeared burly enough to do serious damage if they decided to come to our aid.

The fog had caught up to us now, and they headed into The

Fly without sparing us a glance. For a brief moment, a thumping bass spilled into the street. The door closed behind them, leaving us alone again.

Was I accepting Nieve's role as leader too easily? Her idea to take on the Shades made sense up to the point when it didn't. We could have tried to lose them in the crowd inside the club. Utilized our energy to reach the car, after which the Shades would have had a hard time following us, no matter what they tossed at us.

I extracted my phone to call the police. The Shades might be magical warriors, but cops had guns. Not just that, they also had cars and eyes and cameras—all things the Shades would probably want to avoid.

Gruff noises sounded nearby. The clunk of weapons. The shuffle of boots on asphalt. Crap. Nieve was already in the middle of a fight.

The picture that opened when I unlocked my phone carried a caption. *"That's him,"* Kirk had written.

My fingers flew to my mouth, and I stepped back. Kieran?

My head swiveled. "You're the crown prince."

Kieran flattened himself against the wall, lips squeezed tight. "Sorry."

"You set us up." I glowered.

"Lea." Nieve's voice pulsated with urgency. "Come on."

Her foggy outline kicked and whirled her hanbo, holding the Shades at bay.

"You should help your friend," Kieran whispered. "I'm not going to stop you."

My gaze darted between him, Nieve, and my phone. On second thought, cops would complicate the situation. I pocketed my cell and hurried toward Nieve, whose hanbo whirled through the air faster than my eyes could track.

Two of her attackers peeled away from the fight and charged

up the hill to intercept me. One was significantly older than his partner, but I wouldn't mistake age with arthritis and lethargy. The younger man's most noticeable feature was one long bushy brow crossing his forehead. I traipsed toward danger, my feet sluggish, my vision dulled.

After months of backbreaking training, my memory should have spat out instructions like a computer, but so far, it only showed the loading circle.

The younger Shade rushed at me like a hazy blob and tripped me.

On my way to the ground, I swiped his legs from under him and rolled to my feet. A reflex move, and the first sign I was no longer a helpless damsel. I lifted my arm, almost surprised to find my dagger on the other end. Now if I only recalled what to do with it.

The older Shade, a superior smile on his lips, casually approached me.

I jabbed Fallon at him.

He gracefully stepped aside, but I almost got him.

Then again, this wasn't training camp, and *almost* no longer cut it.

Fallon weighed down my arm, unwieldy like a lump of clay.

"Why don't you just be on your way?" I shifted my grip. "We won't tell anyone. There's no reason for any of us to get hurt."

Unibrow looped around me. "But where's the fun in that, little Spark?" He twirled his knife in the air and caught it by the hilt, with the blade sticking out on his pinkie side.

He swiped at me. I ducked, and a trail of air swished by my cheek. Close one.

With the pointy ends of their knives aimed at me, the two Shades hustled me between two cars.

Why had Tristan never trained me for real? Pitched me against others, given me a taste of a proper fight? Maybe my hand wouldn't be shaking that much now, and maybe the tight squeeze acting on my bladder wouldn't be half as distracting.

Up close, the Shades' weapons looked long and sharp. These weren't training knives, but knives that cut and sliced and killed.

My cautious steps jerked me backward along the length of a Mustang. I sashayed past the mirror, dagger clutched in my fist. If I tripped, the fight would be over.

The old Shade, his face wizened with hard lines, jerked forward.

I propelled off one of the cars and rammed past him, with my dagger aimed at his leg. My blade carved only the air in front of him.

If I'd kept Fallon's trajectory straight, the way Tristan had taught me, my opponent would be in serious trouble now. Another *almost*.

Unibrow once again forced me into the gap between the two vehicles. A strategically devastating move for me. The old man joined his partner, his face set into a stiff leather mask.

They closed the distance between us. Their cold, cold eyes glinted in the sparse light. My back hit something solid. A wall. The end of the line. Only my wildly moving dagger prevented them from overpowering me.

"Nieve?" I didn't dare take my gaze off the Shades. "Nieve!" I called again, louder this time.

"Air cushion." Her voice sounded pressed.

My arm was tiring. Its rapid movements kept me alive, but brought no advantage. I blinked to clear my sight and gage my situation. My attackers hovered too close for me to construct an air cushion and ride it to safety. But magic wasn't just for flying. I whispered the incantation to summon the wind, and my power well sparked. The atmosphere rallied not beneath me but in front of my chest, between me and my attackers.

With the power of the wind on my side, I dropped my arm and massaged my cramped shoulder.

A shadow whirled past my attackers and knocked them over. Kieran had joined the fight—on my side. He stared at me, waiting for my reactin.

I smiled, which in turn elicited a relieved grin from him.

"Help Nieve." I jutted my head. "As much as I appreciate your support, she has double the trouble."

"If you're sure you can handle this…"

*Sure* wasn't the word I'd use to describe my state of mind, but for now, I was safe. "Go, help her," I shouted.

He nodded and ran off.

"That was the crown prince," Unibrow mumbled as he helped his buddy to his feet.

"No." I grinned. "That was my friend."

If Kieran was a prince, he wasn't too spoiled to fight. Suddenly the tide had turned in our favor.

The Shades pounded my air wall, but not even their knives cut through the shield. For now, my stopgap measure gave me time to think of a plan.

*Keep moving. Deflect with small movements. Control your breathing.* Tristan's voice flowed into me like a fresh stream of confidence.

I shut out the world and breathed into my center, regulating the adrenaline dump. In a flash, my senses sharpened. My grip on Fallon tightened.

The dagger responded. A circuit of power closed between us, pumping a sizzle of energy back and forth. A loud *pop*, and Fallon's length and width increased. Its straight blade caught the light from a far-away streetlamp—like an Elonian's luster. The weapon I'd grown irrationally fond of was reborn as a sword.

*A fraking sword.*

Now that my hand had stopped trembling, I slid my

fingers along its steel and tried a few mock slashes in the air. Fallon's balance had changed, but the weight remained manageable.

The two Shades leaped back.

I chuckled, because I hadn't taken aim. In fact, for a second I'd blanked out their entire existence.

The Shades ogled Fallon through squinted eyes. Gone was their initial air of superiority.

Fallon's metamorphosis was indeed impressive, but I'd known we were going to win from the moment Kieran had joined the fight.

The fog allowed a limited view, but both he and Nieve held their three remaining attackers at bay. Kieran had found a knife, presumably from the felled Shade that lay as a dark heap on the ground.

"Fight, Spark!" The old Shade hammered against my shield, which flickered but held firm.

"In a minute!" I shouted and wrapped both hands around the hilt of my sword.

Where was my personal cheerleader when I needed one? Fine. What did I know? I knew I was no longer a clueless chick who'd trip over her own two feet on her way to the toilet. I knew the prophecy had got a few things right, so why not the part about me being a fearless hero? And I knew that a tangible power circulated inside my veins. The fifth force.

To paraphrase the Jedi knights, may the fifth force be with me through this fight.

I breathed deep until my diaphragm expanded then zeroed in on my wind wall. The atmosphere's minute shifts lay bare in front of me. Here and there, molecules rose as bubbles, popped and rebuilt, giving me a clear picture of where to cram in more air. Layer by layer, its density thickened until my shield was as solid as steel.

The Shades circled to my sides, prodded the tightening barrier.

"Anything?" the old guy shouted.

"It's not working," the other replied.

With their noses wrinkled and brows furrowed, they returned to their attack positions in my line of sight. Guess they'd never participated in a fight where one person had checked out.

That's when I shoved the entire mass of air into their stupid faces.

The force flung them up and away. Trusting in my destiny, I went on the offensive.

The old Shade wobbled. I heaved the sword onto his arm and drew blood at my first attempt. Extending Fallon's motion, I caught the other one's shoulder.

Unibrow cried out in pain and stumbled against a post, whereupon both men retreated a few yards.

"What, I finally drop my shields and you chicken out?" I tilted my head. "How disappointing."

I dashed forward and let Fallon's energy guide my arm to seek and pierce any gaps in their defenses. Swept along by my sword's enthusiasm, I parried and pushed, crissed and crossed, and swiped and swung at my enemies. My lungs worked overtime, but God help me, the rush was exhilarating.

The two men outdid me in size and strength, but with Fallon's help, I equaled their combined skill. On the glass half empty side, we'd reached a stalemate. I needed an edge, something to tip the scales in my favor.

Gliding on an air cushion wouldn't increase my agility, and without the powerful rays of the sun, invisibility was also off the table. I'd exhausted all the tricks Tristan had taught me. Then again, his lessons had covered only the authorized uses of magic, and desperate times called for illegal measures.

I whirled to the side and blew power onto my free hand. A dense sphere of energy formed, as solid as a squash ball. I took aim and hurled it into Unibrow's open mouth.

He coughed.

Score one for Lea! I squeezed more force into it, inflated it, willed it to grow.

My opponent wheezed as if water clogged his lungs, and his throat gurgled. Both hands clawed at his neck. He was in serious trouble, and it was my magic that had caused his distress.

I immediately withdrew my power, commanded the ball to return to me—it refused. The man's eyes bulged from his sockets, growing unnaturally large.

I stepped back, stared at his frozen figure. God, no.

His skin went ashen, and he dropped his knife. Dark blood flowed from his mouth and ears. With a terrifying rumble, the earth opened and swallowed him as if he'd never existed.

But he had.

I gaped at my hand, the instrument of my kill. What on this Earth had given me the right to take a man's life? Had magic pumped up my ego so much I believed I was above the law? Above fraking morality?

"How did you do that?" The gray-haired man sounded as sickened as I felt.

"I didn't mean to," I whispered.

The man's lip curled up as he lifted his chin. "You're going to pay for that."

I almost chuckled. He was right. This was the stuff of which nightmares were born, the kind that would haunt you into your grave. Worst of all, this fight hadn't even been my idea. The Shades were the ones who'd come after me in the first place. Because of them I had no job, no life, no nothing. Now, they'd made me a killer.

"You want to know how I did this?" I lifted the tip of my

sword. "Magic, with a capital M. You want to see what else I can do?"

The Shade's features twisted, but he didn't run away. Instead, he heaved his knife into the air and rushed at me.

Why was he sticking around? Hadn't I proven to him that I was a cold-blooded monster? I stepped back, almost tripping over a dip in the sidewalk.

His knife sliced through my leather jacket into my collarbone.

My eyes burned, and the pain brought back the shakes, the doubts, while he angled his body for another strike.

I leaped out of his way and slammed a passing gust of wind into his chest.

"Shit." He struck the pavement with a dry thud.

The fog thinned, bringing into focus all the little scratches and cuts I'd inflicted on him. If I wanted to see my family again, I'd have to do the unthinkable and kill him.

"Lea!" Kieran called my name.

"What?" I shouted back as I patted my own wound. Slick wetness seeped through my jacket. "I'm a little busy here."

"Nieve's in trouble."

Crap. Fallon's length did a good job of keeping my opponent in his spot, so I glanced down the street. Nieve's left hand gripped her hanbo, her right arm pressed against her waist. She performed a sluggish half-turn and led her attack with her stick, but her move lacked power.

A Shade darted around her and jabbed his blade into her stomach.

With a cry of pain, she lowered her hanbo, leaving her flank unguarded.

Nieve was a true hero. She was fast, unpredictable... invincible. A sickening cold washed over me. One miscalculation would have been enough to change her fortune.

Her opponent took his chance and lunged.

"Look out," I shouted.

A kick into my abs sent me tumbling back. I windmilled my arms, caught my balance.

The old man followed up with a thrust of his knife. His arm swung wide by a fraction too much, opening up his side.

I aimed a quick air ball to mess up his equilibrium.

He bowed to the side by no more than an inch, but enough for me to slip Fallon into his stomach. One smooth stroke, and he fell to the ground, blood streaming from his wound. With my sword poised over his prone body, I became aware of the shaking. Not just my hand was affected, but my entire arm trembled. Maybe I didn't have to do this. He'd be dead soon enough either way.

"Lea," Kieran shouted again, and my attention snapped to Nieve.

Her legs buckled, and she sank onto her knees, which took the full brunt of the impact.

Kieran fought close to where she sat, his suit torn and dirty. His opponent, a giant of a man, didn't allow him a moment's pause.

My friend needed me, which meant that, one way or another, I wasn't done. I rallied myself and took wobbly steps toward her.

Nieve swayed and toppled over, her stick abandoned by her side.

"Hang on," I mumbled and blasted her attacker with a ball of air.

This wasn't how this was supposed to go. I was the one who was meant to die, not Nieve. She had to find the vessel. Fight and save Elonia. Save everyone.

The Shade stood over her, cracking a smile at my friend's suffering.

"Don't hurt her!" I yelled.

He glanced up. His brows narrowed. Then he changed the grip of his knife and bent over toward Nieve.

"I'm right behind you," Kieran shouted.

I got there first and hurled myself at the last Shade. The force of my impact was enough to take us both down. My chin struck his nose and he cried out.

Fallon was too long to skewer him from my current position, so I leaped up and got back into a fighting stance.

The Shade got to his feet, blood dripping from a gash on his nose. Another deep cut gaped in the area of his kidneys. Nieve was the one who was down, but she'd taken a huge chunk out of him already.

"Are you okay, Nieve?" My gaze remained fixed on my target.

"I'm good." Her voice sounded as weightless as a breath. "Just give me...a minute."

Kieran built himself up by my side. "You should take her home. I'll deal with him."

Kieran and I could fight him together. We'd probably win, too, but one false move, a single slip of attention, and our opponent would have a chance to finish Nieve.

"I can't carry her," I said. "But I can cover you." No point mentioning the throbbing in my shoulder or the rapid energy drain making my muscles tremble. "He's already injured anyway."

"Why are you helping them, my lord?" The Shade pivoted back a step. A vein in his neck bulged.

"The question is, why are *you* fighting them?" Kieran handed Nieve her hanbo and swept her into his arms. "Don't give your life for a madman who doesn't give a rat's ass about you."

"Go." My voice held, not betraying my fatigue. "Get her to a hospital."

"No. Help Lea." But Nieve's voice was too weak to change anyone's mind.

"Be careful." Kieran gave a curt nod and hurried off.

Weirdly, his belief that I could take care of this loose end lifted my spirits. The Shade was injured, and I had Fallon.

I smiled. "Let's finish this."

A blur darted through my peripheral vision. I whirled my head around and lifted my sword. But a sudden burn in my stomach stole my breath before my blade even made contact.

I stared at the grinning Shade in front—who hadn't moved a muscle—down at the knife stuck between my ribs, then to my side, at the man who'd put it there.

"Gotcha." The old Shade, left face swollen and his leather soaked in blood, glared at me.

My flesh pulsed under the onslaught of pain, and I sucked in air. Why had I not killed him? Tristan had instilled ruthlessness in me. Empathy or guilt, emotions had no place in battle. What mattered was that the other side lost. I took a lopsided step toward the enemy, but tumbled to my knees. Fallon dropped to the ground, no longer a sword.

The Shade crouched before me. "Where's that magic with a capital M now?"

Blood poured from my stomach, dragging my body's warmth with it. The chill spreading in my veins soothed the wound and dulled my mind.

I glanced over my shoulder, but Kieran and Nieve had already disappeared. Good. At least my friends were safe. At least...

My head exploded with pain, and I drowned in a black silence.

# CHAPTER TWENTY-ONE

*NIEVE*

*"It's not as if I don't understand your pain. Seriously, I do. I just don't care."*

A persistent knock inside my skull woke me from a dreamless sleep. My lids slid open, revealing my surroundings frame by frame. A white ceiling with recessed lamps, black furniture, a king-size bed, and a soft, cotton blanket. Not my room. I closed my eyes.

*Lea.*

I sat up. Pain zinged in my head, but my cry didn't make it past my parched throat. I had no choice but to lay back down.

Not only was I injured, I, royal champion, had lost a fight. Worse, so much worse, I'd left Lea behind to fight alone. She was supposed to be my protégé. I, her mentor. A staggered breath worked its way into my weak lungs. She'd fought bravely. A far cry from a real warrior, but in the end, she'd been the one left standing.

I rubbed sleep from my eyes. Light shone onto a blue chair in the corner of the room, yet it didn't reach me. Despite its distance, I could feel its energizing power. Outside, the muffled horn of a car sounded, starting me.

There'd been a knife. A Shade had snuck up to Lea while she'd covered our retreat, shielding us—me—from danger. While we were fleeing like cowards, she'd stood firm until…

She'd been stabbed.

The Old Ones, have mercy. No! I slung my arm over my eyes, unwilling to face reality. Was she even alive?

The door opened and a man walked in. Not just a man. Lea's friend Kieran. He placed a tray with a glass and a jug of water on the black nightstand next to me.

"Good. You're awake." Mindful not to sit on my legs, he eased himself onto the edge of the bed and touched my forehead with his hand.

Kieran had carried me away from the fight. Away from certain death. A flush spread through my body and into my cheeks. I'd thought I was dying, yet how safe I'd felt with my head against his chest. His clean, inviting scent. His whispers of comfort.

Where had my whispers of comfort been when Lea needed them? I'd recruited her, encouraged her, and then abandoned her in the middle of her first fight.

"Is Lea okay?" I touched his arm, my voice more than a little needy. "Tell me she's okay."

"I don't know." Kieran poured a glass of water, placed a straw in it, and guided it to my mouth. "Here, drink."

I sucked in the cool liquid, and the thump in my head lessened almost immediately. "How can you not know?"

"Lea doesn't know where I live, but I've texted her." He returned the glass to the tray, his motion rocking the mattress. "She'll get here when she can, I'm sure."

His back had been turned while he'd carried me away, so he hadn't seen what I'd seen.

"Can you try calling her?" I asked. "I think she got hurt."

He let out a small sigh. "I promise I'll find out what happened to her. For now you should rest."

He got up and tugged his T-shirt straight. The fabric strained across his chest and hips. His arms were muscular rather than lean, probably useful both on a battlefield and off.

My gaze dropped to my own arms, covered in inch-long cuts sustained during my fight. Paper cuts compared to my abdominal injury, which sent searing pulses through my nervous system. Worse than the pain was the bottomless weakness that clung to my body.

Kieran's green eyes gazed into mine. "I'll check on you later."

"Thanks." I hoped those eyes would feature in my dreams. Instead, I dreamed of her…

*Twenty Shades surrounded Lea and me. Before I landed my first swing, my hanbo slipped through my fingers and dropped to the ground. I bent to pick it up, but each time, my hand passed through it, as if it was a mirage. Lea, armed with only a spoon, used her body to shield me against the Shades' slashing swords. I shouted at her to get to safety, pleaded with her to leave. She laughed at me as, one by one, the Shades advanced and skewered her torso. When she lay motionless and bleeding at my feet, the Shades shrugged and walked off. They didn't spare me a single glance.*

I awoke sweat-soaked and weary.

Kieran perched next to me, pressing something cool against my forehead. "Bad dream?"

"Yes," I croaked.

He removed the cloth from my head and held a glass of water in front of my face.

I sucked the straw until I slurped air bubbles. "Lea?"

"Nothing yet." He smiled and placed the glass back on the nightstand. He refilled it. "More?"

"No, thank you."

He folded his hands in his lap as if unsure what to do with them. "Feeling better?"

I inventoried my body. The pressure in my skull had diminished, but my stomach still stung. I held a hand against the wound. Good, it was dressed. Which was more than I could say for the rest of me.

I slapped around for my leather uniform. Found my bra. Panties. "Where are the rest of my clothes?"

"I had to take them off to tend to the wound," Kieran said, eyes twinkling. "I didn't look."

I shifted up along the mattress to sit but lacked the strength. What warrior wimped out from a little knife wound? Disgusted with myself, I stopped struggling.

Kieran picked up a spare pillow from the corner chair and fluffed it. He leaned over and propped me up against him. The usual panic that set in at the first sign of forced closeness stayed away. If anything, I found myself tilting toward him. His chest hovered over my face, and I soaked in his scent. A sweet grassy aroma bathed my senses, chasing tiny shivers across my skin.

A pendant on a chain dropped out of his collar. I squinted.

And my world tumbled.

Depicted on its surface was Derinda's butterfly, the mark of the Shades.

The man tweaking the corner of my pillow was an enemy, close enough to kill me—and close enough to be killed.

"There you go." His contented look dissolved into a frown. "What's wrong?"

Light from the bedside lamp bounced off his amulet in the colors of the rainbow. Kieran had dark hair. Was about my height. A white line peeked out from his T-shirt.

I pulled at his collar, where a faded scar sat on his neck.

"What the hell?" He swatted my hand away.

Every detail matched Gerrit's description. Kieran was the crown prince.

Not only had I abandoned Lea to her fate, I'd delivered myself into the hands of the Shades. What the slicing hell was wrong with me? How could I have misread the situation? Why hadn't I been more cautious?

"You're him." My tone was controlled, even though my body itched to put distance between us.

Kieran straightened, his gaze fixed on my face. "You finally recognize me?"

"Your pendant gave you away. You're the crown prince."

What a skilled liar he was. His father would be proud.

His hand touched the iridescent metal disk. "Oh, that. I thought you remembered me from the alley."

He was the stranger from the alley? The first Shade I'd ever considered a real person, a man with a past, with emotions? A fellow warrior?

"That was you?" I drew a line in the air with my hand. "Why did you talk to me that day? You'd been following Lea and then you let her go."

"I'd heard rumors of the prophecy and was curious about her. When I sensed other Torrens nearby, I called up the fog to suppress her luster. To keep her safe. Then I saw you. I've always wanted to meet the woman behind the myth."

I frowned, and my head was sore enough for even the creases on my forehead to hurt. "You didn't speak highly of your father, the king."

"If he were your father, would you?" He twisted on his heels and turned his back toward me. "He's not a good man, or a good king for that matter. Back then, I hadn't yet worked out his plan, of course, but I knew it involved Lea. I wanted to learn who she was. What was it that made her so important?"

"You befriended her?"

He raised one shoulder in a partial shrug. "Yeah."

He'd taken advantage of her trusting nature. "You could have warned her about the danger she was in."

"At first, I wasn't aware of any danger. Not until two scouts attacked her. They got the shock of a lifetime when they realized I was there, too." He laughed. "Word came down that my father didn't appreciate my interference. You have to understand, I have a complicated relationship with my father. Not even I would be safe from him if he thought I betrayed him."

"Do you know his plans?"

Kieran turned back to meet my stare. "I'm still piecing things together, but I know that none of what he wants will be possible without Lea."

If I hadn't led her to Elonia to be trained, if we'd instead locked her up for her own safety, we could have foiled his machinations before they could take effect—and she'd have been fine. The prophecy hadn't mentioned that part.

"You still should have warned her. She thought you were her friend." My voice broke.

"If I could turn back the clock, I wouldn't hesitate to tell her the truth." He paced across the room, raking his hands through his hair, then fell against the wall. "I'm trying to find out if she's safe. But I can't..." His voice became muffled.

I pressed my fingers into my palms. But once again, I blacked out.

# CHAPTER TWENTY-TWO



*"Be positive, I always say. Not to cheer people up, but to remind them of my blood type in case I get into an accident."*

Something sharp poked me in the ribs. I sniffed the air. Wine or port. Dry air. An old cellar, maybe?

Mist hung before my opening eyes, and it took a few seconds before my vision cleared. I was in a room, too large to be underground, yet without windows. Around me, a brown type of sand held together the dark-red bricks of four unadorned walls. I lifted my head off the cold stone floor and used my sleeve to wipe away the blur. A sudden pain pierced my left side, and I groaned.

In front of me, a heavyset man sat on a throne overlaid in embroidered red velvet. Trunk-like calves poked out of his brown skirt, and Roman-style sandals tied around a pair of large feet. Around his neck, a round medallion dangled from a chain.

"You're awake." The man's goatee-covered chin wiggled even after he'd finished talking.

I heaved myself into a seated position and only now noticed

the two men by my side. They too wore leather outfits. Their hands curled around long, pointy lances.

I was alive. I sent a quick prayer to whoever listened that Nieve and Kieran were also safe.

One of the guards handed me a glass.

"Drink." The man on the throne saluted me with his own glass containing a blood-red liquid.

"Is this water?" I took a careful sip and grimaced. "It's bitter."

"That would be the maidenhair tree extract and a few select herbs. As useful as they are, delicacies they are not." He chuckled.

I swallowed the horrible concoction in five large gulps. The guy by my side took the glass off me and carried it to a table at the far wall. I gently prodded my stomach. My wounds itched, a sign they were knitting themselves back together. *Hallelujah for magic.*

Throne Man leaned back and draped an arm over his armrest. "I was afraid you'd been killed."

"I guess I was lucky." I briefly closed my eyes at the painful reminder of the knife in my ribs, but discovered it hurt less if I didn't use my muscles or, well, breathe. "Thank you for saving me. Who are you?"

His chest spasmed from a single heave of laughter. "My dear, don't you know? I'm Galleo, ruler of Torren."

His words sent my heart into a fiery freefall straight into the center of my stomach. "Seriously? But you want me dead."

"Dead?" He smirked. The dimple in his chin deepened, and his eyes lit up. "How about you get to know me yourself? What would you like to ask?"

"Where to start." From Nieve's tales, I'd imagined a hulking ogre of a brute, but he reminded me of my uncle Bob, a friendly, sympathetic man with an unnatural love of patent leather shoes.

Galleo gestured for me to begin.

"Is it true you want to destroy the Divide?" I shifted into a more comfortable position. If he was game to answer all my questions, well, we'd be here a while.

"The destruction of the Divide isn't my goal as such. It's a wonderful example of the Old One's powers and deserves to be preserved. But occasionally, we have no choice and must destroy a great monument to make space for other things."

So far, so reasonable. "The destruction is a means to an end?"

"Quite." His fingers stroked the length of his goatee. "You have to understand. When the Old Ones gave us the gift of magic, they never meant to divide us into two races. They called us the Touched—not the Torrens and the Elonians—and magic was supposed to be our chance to create a better world. A small group of the Touched, those who later called themselves the Elonians, had the notion magic needed to be controlled. We disagreed. Imagine a world where everyone knew just of what they're capable? Where magic wasn't even a secret from the Kindreds?"

I folded my hands in my lap and ordered my thoughts. If magic had been freely available, my dad could have been cured months ago. Cancer would be eradicated.

The Uncle-Bob lookalike wasn't at all as I'd imagined him. I fixed him with my gaze. "Why do the Elonians refuse to share their knowledge?"

"If no one but the army under your control can wield magic, the Crown need not fear challenges from powerful subjects. What the Elonian king doesn't get is that controlling magic is a way of controlling people."

Galleo had a point. "I was told magic is too dangerous to be disseminated to the masses."

"Poppycock." He swished a fist through the air. "I choose to have faith in people. Yet many layers of Elonian society will never learn to wield any magic at all, even though wielding magic is no more dangerous than knives and axes and guns."

I wanted to find fault with his logic, wanted to hate him the way Nieve hated him, but his opinion in this respect coincided with my own. "Guns don't kill people. People kill people," I whispered.

"Exactly. And denying your subjects their right to exercise the gifts we were granted is cruel. We waged war with the Elonians to reunite the Touched and liberate those kept in the dark. Free the oppressed. Sadly we lost. This failure cost me dearly in the political arena, but I'm not giving up my mission."

I shook my head. This is where he lost the high ground. "I can't deny the force of your arguments, but war cannot be the right path."

His face twisted, and he dropped his gaze. "I dislike violence. But I want better for my people. For all people. Luckily, I've since learned of another path. Total reunification without the bloodshed."

My spine snapped straight. "With the Elonians?"

"And the Kindreds. Think of the advantages. Kindreds don't share our aptitude, but there's nothing preventing them from performing simple spells. Let magic do the dishes, iron their clothes." He raised a finger. "You know, with support from one forward-thinking Elonian who permitted us access to the Gate, my scouts have been able to establish contact with a handful of Kindred leaders. Yes, I believe they'll be receptive to my ideas. And finally, confronted with overwhelming odds, the Elonian king will have no choice but to accept magic must not be hidden away in large vaults. Sadly, without the Gate to facilitate, the Divide must go."

"Won't destroying the Divide also destroy your home?"

"I didn't say my way is without sacrifices. But we can always build new homes. A new future. Together, as one people."

Going up against the Shades, I'd resorted to means Tristan would have called illegal. If I hadn't ignored his rules, I'd be dead now.

On the other hand, Galleo had been the one who'd sent the Shades after me in the first place.

"And of course, you'd be in charge." I infused my accusation with all the loyalty for my friends I could muster.

Galleo laughed. "That's the plan."

I slid closer. "So, how does this *plan* work?"

He placed his fist under his chin, and his gaze lost focus. "Derinda, one of the Old Ones, shared a spell with me. Once I invoke it, the realms will reunite, and we, the Touched, will finally return to our original home."

"What makes you so certain you'll be the new leader?"

"That's part of my deal with Derinda. Her condition was she would take possession of you."

"Uh, what?" I took a sudden breath.

The conversation had taken a sharp turn into the bizarre. Despite his amiable tone, my heart thumped in my chest. This was where he'd drop the other shoe.

"Why me?" I pointed at myself. "I mean, I'm nothing special. Seriously. Nothing special."

He clicked his tongue, a funny sort of half chuckle that emphasized the laughter lines around his eyes. "I wondered this myself. As far as I could tell, she doesn't like you." His words crawled down my back like icy fingers.

"Whoa, hang on. That's crazy. I don't even know her."

"In any event, that was her demand."

My flustered mind scrambled for a way out. "But if she's already told you the spell, there's no need."

"Your handover is an integral part of the ritual I have to perform. You shouldn't take it personally."

"Not personal? Well, that's certainly a big phew off my

mind." My gaze darted to the blank walls of the large hall. No help was coming, of that I was sure. Yet the door stood open, inviting me to make a break for it. How far would I get? The two guards by my side were impassive on the outside, but their stiff postures indicated a keenness of mind I didn't want to test.

"If we're all ready." The king rubbed his palms together. "Let's not keep Derinda waiting."

Four hands grabbed my shoulders and yanked me upright. The sudden motion split my healing wound like a coconut.

"Don't!" I yelled. "Oh God. Don't hurt me." My entire network of nerves sizzled with pain. "I can help you find another way." I sought his gaze. "Just don't kill me. Please."

The guards ignored my cries and hauled me backward. My feet slapped the smooth floor for grip, finding none. The Shades stopped in front of a wooden wheel the size of a truck.

I thrashed my head, kicked out, tried to catch their flesh between my teeth. Whatever this contraption was, I didn't want to be near it. How had I ended up in this situation? What did this woman want from me, and why did this man, this monster, do her bidding?

The guards lifted me and tied my wrists and ankles to the wheel.

"Please don't do this!" My cheeks stung with wetness, and I blinked through the tears.

The men walked to a console straight from the history books, made of gears and bolts in tarnished metal. One of the guards rotated a lever, and the wheel lifted with a haunting creak. He actuated another lever and tilted me into a near horizontal position, facing the ground. Gravity tore on my shoulder blades, nudging the bones loose from my sockets. I clamped my jaw shut through the pain and concentrated on a single spot on the ground to call on the air's support.

Nothing. Not even a refreshing draft came to my rescue.

The king approached with a smug saunter. "Now, now. Play nice. Your death will benefit so many."

I craned my throbbing head to glare at him. "You can't kill me. You said yourself, you're saving me for Derinda." My whispered words didn't hide my fear.

Galleo leaned to his side to look at me the right way up. "Derinda resides in the afterworld. There is only one way for you to meet her. I hate to end the life of someone so young, but you understand why this sacrifice is necessary, don't you?"

My veins iced over, and the cold spidered into my bones. "If you wanted me dead, why did you tell your goons to take me alive?"

"The ritual requires your blood. With skilled manipulation, we will milk enough life force out of you. The herbal blood thinners you drank should already be taking effect."

My stomach twirled with revulsion at my own stupidity. "Tristan and Nieve are going to come for me. They'll avenge me." My words faded quickly in the vast room. Even I heard the lie in their wake.

Nieve and Tristan had no idea where I was.

Galleo slid a long serrated knife from his holster. "Open her jacket."

"No." I twisted against my constraints. The ties dug into my flesh with each futile muscle contraction, but would not loosen.

One of the guards yanked open my zipper. The fear-tinged aroma of sweat furled up my nose, clawing its way into my delicate guts. With my bra and bare midriff on display, I hung limply from the wheel, helpless. My arms grew more tired by the second, and the pull on my shoulders intensified.

Galleo considered my exposed skin clinically. "Ready the containers."

The guards arranged large bowls underneath me in a tight

formation. With lightning speed, Galleo punctured my midsection in five or six deep gashes.

"Please, no," I yelled as loudly as my meek voice allowed as a new wave of agony pulsed through me, scattering through my limbs, my fingers, my toes. Then I screamed my panic and terror into the ether. Screamed from the deepest pit of my stomach. Screamed because I was going to die.

"Please stop." The tears flowed, and with them, all attempts at bravery. My mind clung to an image of my mom, to her warm smile as if it had the power to save me, to stop the pain, to make everything okay.

"I'll do anything," I pleaded while hot blood dripped like molten lava from my wounds, casting the world in a washed out red. "I don't want to die. Please." My voice faded to a whimper.

The king leaned in. "Tell Derinda we're even."

He added more cuts, in the crook of my arm, through my leather pants into my legs and groin.

My quiet sobs closed my throat, and my sight tapered into two small cones of light. The bowls filled with the blood dripping from my body. The drops splashed into the bowls, like rain pelting a metal roof.

Then came the silence.

# CHAPTER TWENTY-THREE



*"You should value each day as if it's your last, because the day you
meet me, it will be."*

My eyes opened to a room lit by artificial light. The
windows— There were no windows. Was I in a
cell? Yet the comfortable bed, the nightstand, even
the chair in the corner were the same as they'd been before.
Kieran's room.

Kieran, dressed in loose jeans and a white T-shirt, peeled off
from a dark spot inside the room and walked toward me.

For reasons only known to him, the Shade crown prince had
saved me. Had he told his father he'd captured me by now? The
prince didn't have nice things to say about his own flesh and
blood, but if he wasn't going to hand me over, what use was I
to him?

I smoothed the blanket to regain my nerves. He was unlikely
to reveal his plans to a hysterical woman. "Am I your prisoner?"

"No."

"Then why am I here, in this cell?"

He shrugged. "This is no cell."

Now he treated me like I was stupid, but I didn't mind being underestimated. Usually, that was an advantage. "How long have I been here?"

"It's been a week since the fight."

"Where's Lea?" I clutched my blanket. "Did you sell her out? Is that why she's not here?"

"I would never sell her out. We were friends." He stood with his knees bumping against my mattress. "Would you believe I even tried to warn her she was in danger once? We'd met up and I tried to tell her everything, about the scouts that had attacked us, about magic and the war, but getting that woman's attention is impossible. She can talk for Torren, that's for sure."

How much time had the two spent before Lea came to Elonia?

"Then I got called away," he said. "I discovered later that my father had me followed hoping I'd see her again. That's how they found her."

"What happened?"

"My brothers texted me that my father was very sick. He's a bastard, but..." He waved off. "When I got home to check on him, he refused to receive me. Turns out, his apparent illness had been a ruse to get me out of the way. For weeks, I'd thought he'd got his wish and captured Lea, because of me, but I later heard she was all right." He shot me a curious glance. "She was with you."

His words stung. Yes, she should have been all right with me.

"You should have left me to die and protected Lea instead." I rubbed my face. "I'd underestimated my opponents. They were no ordinary scouts."

"No, I think the Torren presence received an upgrade after Lea continued to elude my father's forces." He shook his head. "I think the group that attacked us were actually looking for me that night. My fault."

"There's a lot of blame to go around." I stroked my blanket, feeling wistful. "Except for Lea. She never asked to be in this situation, yet did what was asked of her. It was my duty to keep her safe, and my right to give my life for hers."

"That may be so." A weak smile appeared on his lips, transforming his face into something so beautiful it made my chest hurt. "Despite everything, I'm glad you're well."

A ripple of heat warmed my cheeks, and I scrunched a blanket corner with my hand. "Why?"

"Maybe because the idea of the Spark's champion owing her life to the Torren crown prince tickled me?" His tone was light, he even sounded amused.

I licked my suddenly dry lips. "They say if you save someone, you become responsible for their life."

He sat on the mattress, separated from my bare legs only by a blanket. "There are worse fates I could face."

"Have you been able to reach Lea?" My cheeks quivered. "Please tell me your father didn't abduct her."

He coughed out a bitter laugh. "Things are worse than you think."

I tensed my muscles. Worse than Lea being abducted?

"She's dead." His jaw tightened. "That I know for sure."

Even though I'd been expecting the words, I didn't want him to speak them. For a few long seconds, the world shook before my eyes. The pain that ran through me was a physical one, traveling from my skin deep into my organs, skewering my liver and kidneys, slicing my lungs and my heart.

I'd watched Lea being stabbed, but I'd been hurt too. Why was I alive? This wasn't right. It couldn't be real. Kieran had to be wrong.

"I'm sorry. So sorry." He slung his arms around his torso, his long fingers rolled into pale fists.

Was he grieving for Lea? Did Shades mourn? He had no

right to feel regret. She'd been *my* responsibility. If anyone was going to mourn her, it would be me, and me alone.

I rubbed the ridges of the cuts on my arm. "How...?" *Go on, Nieve. Say it.* "I mean, are you sure she's...?"

"Dead?" His pitch was low, yet the word shrilled through the air with the power of a siren.

If she'd been kidnapped, I'd run to get her back. If she'd been hurt, I'd nurse her better. But Kieran kept using the word *dead.*

*Dead, dead, dead.* It was just a word. Four letters. Not real.

"Once I had you stowed away, I went back, but couldn't find her," he said. "Next, I went to see my father, but wasn't allowed near him. Turns out, I've disappointed him one too many times and he's disowned me. But my brothers gave me the story blow by blow. That night, the soldiers dragged her away, still bleeding, to present her to my father. He killed her."

"How do you know they're not lying to you?" I grabbed his arm. "She could still be alive."

"She's not. I know, because the world has changed."

A churning nausea crept through my insides. "What do you mean, changed?"

"The Divide is gone."

A chill iced over my wounds, drowning out the pain. No way.

I let go of his arm and sat as straight as my injury allowed. "What? How?"

Sure, I'd been told Galleo wanted to get rid of the Divide, but I'd never given any thought to what that might mean.

"This formerly Kindred world..." He raised his arms. "...is now ruled by my father. And all the Torrens and all the Elonians now live here as well."

"No." My stomach plunged, splashing up a wave of bile. I placed both hands next to me on the mattress for balance as everything I knew tumbled criss-cross inside my brain.

"Worse, this isn't the Kindred world you remember either," he said. "It's been remade. New buildings appeared—windowless, of course—and others vanished. The educational system, the government, everything's different." He leaned forward and placed his head in his hands. "It's still happening now, out there. The world is in flux, and every day pushes it further and further away from the life we knew."

Kieran's words made no sense. None of it did. Even assuming the Divide did fall, it would take the Shade forces years, decades even, to defeat the Kindreds. "Kindreds aren't known for backing down without a fight, and neither are Elonians. How are we not at war?"

"There was no time." He tilted his head to gaze back at me. "There's magic at play, a greater and more terrible magic than I've ever known. How my father discovered it... Anyway, this new magic is re-wiring people's brains. The Kindreds were overwhelmed immediately. They accepted the new world order, and a new history, without a shot being fired and without any alarm being raised. As far as they're concerned, my father has always ruled them, and magic has always been real."

"And my people?" I swallowed, reluctant to hear the truth.

"If they were confused at first, many Sparks have now followed suit. They took to the changes faster even than Torrens. A few pockets of resistance remain, mainly former warriors, but my brothers are on it. With me out of the way and the position of crown prince up for grabs, they're outdoing each other trying to impress daddy dearest. They've issued house arrests, filled up the Kindred prisons with Sparks, and even imposed a curfew. Anyone caught outside after nine is fair game to their patrols."

What was I going to do now? How could I make up for my failure to protect Lea now that she was gone? Now that the Divide had fallen?

I placed two fingers against my temple and pressed small circles into my skin trying to force it all to come together. "How is all that possible? And what does any of this have to do with Lea?"

"I'm told her death facilitated the fall of the Divide." Kieran scrubbed both palms over his face then over his hair. "My father must have planned all this, but I gotta admit, I never saw it coming. I knew of his cruelty, having been both witness and victim over the years, but this... If I'd known..."

I stifled the urge to lean over and touch his hand, calm his distress, or seek comfort myself. "If your father commands the power to do all the things you described, you wouldn't have been able to stop him anyway."

"That's just it. I think he had help. Powerful help."

"The Old Ones?" I reached for the water on the nightstand, my hands shaking so much it took several attempts to align the straw with my mouth.

"It makes sense." Kieran placed a hand on the far side of my legs to support himself as he faced me. "They made the Divide, and they have the magic necessary to bring it down. I met this man in the supermarket this morning, brimming with political opinions. He says the Kindreds started to rely on Torren magic for military support in the early seventeenth century. From there, Torrens extended their influence into the government. History has been completely rewritten. No human being—Kindred or Touched—could do that."

Lea had died for nothing. My mission had failed. Maybe Tristan should have spotted my weakness earlier. He was the one who'd trained me. How could he not have known I wasn't going to get things done? If he'd paid attention, he'd taken my place, kicked Shade butt, and then the world wouldn't be in this mess.

"I don't even know what to say." My voice crackled. "Is this the end? What about you and me? Will we forget the old world?"

"Possibly, over the next few weeks and months. So many things have already been rewritten. The Torren-Spark war?" He snapped his fingers. "To most Sparks, it never happened. The Space Needle?" He snapped again. "Never built."

"But Lea, still gone," I said in a quiet voice. Total destruction of everything I cared about. "Slice it. You know, the stupid prophecy saw this coming, but its text was too vague for me to recognize the implications. What good is a warning if you don't understand it?" I punched the mattress with my clenched fist. "It didn't even take an army and epic battle, just a skirmish between a handful of Shades, a rookie, and a careless Elonian warrior to bring about the end. How is that fair?"

"It's not."

I curled my hands around the corners of the crisp white blanket, a fire burning in my gut. "How is that fair to Lea? To us? To the rest of the world? How the slicing fuck is that fair?"

He watched me take a few breaths and then shot me a strained half-smile. "It's everything my father dreamed of. A united people, with free magic available to anyone. As long as you're on his side, that is."

"You mentioned pockets of resistance. Does that include the Elonian king?" My chest tightened as I held my breath.

The whites of Kieran's eyes showed little red lines. "Yes. He's in hiding."

Thank the Old Ones. My lungs expelled the air with one quick thrust. At least Tristan was alive. I had to find him. He'd have answers.

Kieran rotated his neck as if to release tension. "Are you hungry?"

"No."

"Okay then." He got up to grab a first aid bag from the navy blue armchair. "Let's change the dressing."

"What?" In the flow of conversation, I'd forgotten he was a Shade, but now, the prospect of Shade fingers against my naked skin filled me with alarm. Rightly so. So why was my flesh practically humming for his touch?

He returned and raised his eyebrows. "The dressing?"

Fine. No big deal. Fighting his people and rescuing me weren't the actions of the typical Shade predator, but he'd done both and earned himself a few provisional trust points. I slid aside my blanket to expose my bra and stomach.

He sat next to me and unzipped the bag before pressing a bandage into my palm. "Hold that."

His touch warmed my skin, made it tingle and sizzle. Our hands lingered as if they had a mind of their own. His fingers were those of a warrior. Strong. Calloused. Capable of doing a great deal of damage, but put to good use now.

He broke contact and placed the bag on the nightstand. My fingers, no less rough than his, curled around the dressing.

"Here we go." He lifted the corners of the red-stained gauze my abs to peel off the bandage. "Tell me when it hurts."

Blood had crusted the fabric to my skin, causing him to pull harder. The bandage came loose with a soft ripping sound. My face distorted, and he winced in sympathy.

This should be me, looking after Lea, making sure she was healing. But Galleo had killed her, and it was his son of all people who was patching me up. How had I ended up in this upside down scenario?

I inhaled a deep breath that turned into a jagged sob, quickly covered by a cough.

"Y'okay?" Kieran asked.

"The gash," I said with a rusty voice. "It will leave a scar."

"I'll see what I can do."

"Where did you learn to tend wounds?" My gaze traced the tiredness around his eyes, didn't miss the hitch in his breath at my question.

"Battlefield." His tone was sad, solemn.

I nodded once for solidarity. Just as I'd suspected that day in the alley. Like me, he would have seen action, witnessed his men fall. Like me, he'd be reluctant to talk about his experiences.

His attention, his care, lured me into a sense of comfort, and I lacked the strength to fight it. I hadn't seen the new world yet, but Kieran's description had scared me to my bones. Worse, I'd have to face the future without Lea. Alone.

Yet here was this man, cleaning my wound, even though we should be enemies. He lifted the new dressing from my hand and, rather than applying it straight away, he ran his thumb over my waist to brush aside a stray piece of gauze. Heat whipped through my veins, cajoled my pulse into a sprint. His unhurried touch came to a stop on my lower ribs, inches from my injury.

A harsh intake of air was my only objection. He was teasing me, yet I needed his touch. What did I care that he was a slicing Shade? How could I extinguish the small flame burning for him when my body needed its warmth so badly?

His gaze swept up along my torso, lingered on my breasts. His eyes moved higher, past my lips, until our gazes met.

My core trembled under his attention, and I squeezed my pelvis to relieve the pressure.

With a twitch of his lips, he broke eye contact and shifted his concentration back to my wound. As he leaned in to inspect the gash, his breath deposited a tiny puff of air on my ribs—a caress without a touch. I bathed my lungs in his clean, calming scent, held it in my belly, loathe to let go.

My ribcage trembled enough to give away the turmoil of emotions inside me, but Kieran appeared focused on my injury. After a quiet sigh, he straightened his back and finally unwrapped the new dressing. Once the square piece of fabric covered my wound, he gently pressed down the sticky corners.

"There we go. That should do nicely." He sounded satisfied.

How come I felt anything but? I needed to feel whole again. Needed something to fill the void. How could he not see that?

He zipped up his first aid bag and pitched it across the room. It landed square on the armchair. "I know you're not hungry, but you should eat something. It'll help you heal."

"Maybe later."

He stood and headed to the door. "Rest now."

Then he was gone.

Now I really was alone. Cold. Lost in a strange world without a compass and no prophecy to show me my way.

For a while, I listened to the sound of his footsteps as he puttered about in the apartment. What would Lea make of my sorry state? I'd let her down. Worse. I'd led her straight to her own slaughter.

A thick stew of bleak misery seeped into me. My blanket weighed me down, on top of an already heavy mass that sat at the top of my stomach, squeezing until I got woozy. Lea had urged me to run from the Shades, but I'd thought I could defeat them. Thought I could kidnap and question one of them. Thought I could protect her.

How could I have been so wrong?

But I'd seen her whizz through the air, bend the wind in ways I'd never even contemplated. Despite breaking Elonian laws with her offensive use of magic, she'd made me proud. Her strikes had been confident, her attacks balanced. And in the end, *she* had saved *me*.

In one blow, all my memories and unfulfilled wishes merged into one desperate anguish. The sobs came in little hitches, wracking my chest, getting louder. I wrapped my arms around my face and wept.

Lea's survival had been my responsibility.

I was meant to be her partner. Her friend.

In the end, I was her killer.

# CHAPTER TWENTY-FOUR



*"Take my advice. I have no use for it."*

I wandered in total nothingness. A cold sea of pitch black that made the spookiest cave seem like a funfair. I rubbed my hands together to combat the chill. A whiff of home-baked bread, far off in the unknown distance, tickled my nostrils, but not even the homiest scent of them all managed to calm me. Without visual markers or sounds to guide me, I was lost. As if I were a photon inside a perfect vacuum, time and space did not exist.

The unwavering knowledge that I was dead filled my head. I knew it with a level of certainty at which the scientist in me usually balked. The memory of Galleo slicing me was still fresh, but at least the pain had ended. And somehow, my dagger was by my side. All things considered, my situation could be worse. Brimstone and hellfire worse.

Except, there was nothing left for me to fight. What good was my weapon in death? A long, bone-rattling shiver ran though me. I wasn't yet ready for my final resting place. My life was unfinished. I was too young to die.

The things I wanted to achieve, the friends I'd hoped to

make, none of this would come to pass. Just one more time, I wanted to tell my parents I loved them. Just one more time, I wanted to hear Tristan whisper the word '*perfect.*'

Out of the black, a tall figure emerged. A man with a white curly beard and a food-loving belly. He didn't look like the Grim Reaper—certainly not like the old one Dean had killed in Supernatural, and not like the new, female one either. And yet this man carried an air of finality with him.

With each approaching step, he whirled up a cloud of dense white fog, which quickly vanished into the black nothing.

"Hello, Lea." His voice had a gentle, slightly amused ring. "My name is Orrin. I've been looking forward to meeting you."

He knew my name. Okay. Normally I'd have thought that was a good sign, but Galleo had known my name, and that didn't work out too well for me in the end.

"Are you dead, too?" I asked.

"No. Neither are you. At least not completely."

Until now I'd assumed death was a binary state—either you were or you weren't. But maybe I was like Schrödinger's cat: alive and dead at the same time, until someone opened the box to find out for certain.

The man's long robe shimmered like sunlight on water, suggesting a form of light source nearby. Yet beyond his shape, only the blacker-than-night darkness filled the void.

Without a warning word, he gathered me in his arms and buried my face in his chest. "You've gotten so big."

*Ever hear of personal space, Mister?*

I nearly gave voice to my feelings, but this guy could be dangerous. Aggravating him wouldn't be smart. If, on the other hand, he was on the level, we were basically two peas sharing a very, very dark pod. Better still, he had the lay of the land, and this seemed like a place where insider knowledge could come in handy.

"Hang on." I wiggled out of his embrace. "You're *the* Orrin? The Old One?"

"That I am."

Not prepared to trust his jovial demeanor, I retreated a few inches. After all, Galleo hadn't come across as a total psycho until he started cutting me.

Orrin dropped his hands. "I'm sure you have questions, but we should get going."

"Do I have questions? Let me see. Do babies poop? Damn straight, I have questions."

He held a hand against his belly and laughed. "Ah, you're delightful."

I admit, that tickled me. Not many people thought of me that way. A rambler, maybe. Amusing, if I was on form. Never delightful.

I shifted on my feet. "How come you know my name?"

"I see, you have your mother's talent of getting straight to the point."

"You know my mother?"

Orrin combed his beard with his fingers. "Oh yes. I was smitten with Anna the second I saw her." He sighed as if recalling the flavor of a delicious cake. "You have her eyes, you know. A beautiful woman, strong and independent, but with such a kind heart. At least before she…"

"Before she went nuts?"

"My relationship with her was a mistake. I should have known that, once she was with child, your powers would seep into her." He lowered his head. "The Elonian constitution isn't equipped to cope with the powers of an Old One."

Was he implying…

"When the pregnancy drove her out of her mind, I was afraid I'd lose you both. After your birth, I took you to the

Kindred world." Once again, he briefly gathered me against his side. "I knew you'd be safer among Kindreds than in Elonia."

"You're my father?" My breath stopped while I stared at him, willing him to say both *yes* and *no*.

"Of course. Sorry, didn't I say?"

*No, you fucking didn't.* I filled my glare with all the words that somehow didn't make it out of my mouth. My arms shook, my lips quivered, but no sound. *Shout, dammit. Just do something.*

"In any case, I couldn't be happier with the way you turned out." Going by his chest-beating tone, he actually believed he'd contributed to my upbringing.

"My adoptive parents are great." My dig at him elicited no reaction. I pressed my fingers against my temple. What was the use of being petty right now? Nothing I said or did would make a lick of difference. I stared into the tight blackness around us. "Where are we?"

"This is Balor, the afterworld. Or rather, the in-between world. This is where the dead go before they move on." The humor fled his eyes. "It's not a safe place for you."

"Why?" I studied the darkness. "There's nothing here."

"Just because you can't see the danger doesn't mean it doesn't exist." He glanced over his shoulder, as if checking for eavesdroppers. "My wife is looking for you, and you don't want her to find you."

"Your wife." According to Galleo, she was the reason I was here. "Derinda. Were you married to her when you and my mother...you know?"

"Yes." Orrin smacked his lips, making his beard quiver. "We've both done things we aren't proud of."

Understatement much? "So she traded my life for the Divide because you cheated on her?"

He listened for something and patted my arm. "Let me take

you back to the Kindred realm, and if we have time, I'll answer your questions."

He turned and wandered off, his robe rustling with his steps. Not like I had a choice. I followed him, even though my gait was stiff. Yet I wasn't in pain. I touched the spot where the knives had pierced my skin. My jacket sported several large gashes, but underneath, the wounds had healed.

Before us, a door appeared in a shimmer of magic. It slid open, like the doors on the Enterprise, and we stepped through.

The sudden brightness hit me between the eyes like an arrow. I blinked, and the world fell into focus.

# CHAPTER TWENTY-FIVE



*"They say death is forever. Consider this your head start."*

Staring at the wall opposite my bed, alone and confined to the bed in Kieran's apartment, I savored the scent of the T-shirt he'd loaned me. His detergent reminded me of meadows and forests. Reminded me of him.

He'd made it easy to forget he was a Shade. The cruelty I'd come to associate with my enemy's eyes simply wasn't inside him. Something had gentled him. Quite a feat considering his father's personality.

If he made for an unlikely Shade, he bore all the hallmarks of his gender. Wheedling information out of him was like splitting a hair with an axe. He refused to discuss his political ambitions, the nature of his fallout with his father, or why he'd saved me. Nevertheless, his skills as a healer were admirable.

As for me, I made an excellent patient. Not once did I complain about his meticulous care. Every six hours on the dot, he changed my dressing. Every five hours and fifty minutes, my skin tingled. When the moment came, Kieran would awkwardly announce the time and perch on the edge of my bed. His strong hands would brush over my skin, bolder each time. Neither of us would point out my injury no longer needed such dedicated attention.

I checked the digital clock on my nightstand. Still three hours to go. I bit my lip, hard enough for the pain to drive away my mounting affection. My feelings for the enemy confused the heck out of me and, twist and turn it, he was still a Shade.

The real torture took place between his visits, when Lea's face appeared in the shadows of the room, in the shape of my blanket, or in the nook of the armchair. Those painful reminders weren't necessary—I was well aware of the blame I carried—but I'd accepted them as part of my punishment.

The furniture in my room didn't offer much in terms of distraction either, making the enormous wall-mounted television a startling indulgence.

I took the remote and turned on the device.

Regan, former Councilor and traitor, appeared on the screen, her luster on full glow. "The recent attacks against Torrens and Kindreds spread terror among ordinary citizens. I shall not stand for it. *We* shall not stand for it. So I encourage my fellow Elonians to open their lives, their bank statements, even their journals to the authorities. Prove to the world you have nothing to hide. As for the terrorists, they will betray themselves by clinging to their secrets." She sent a penetrating look into the cameras. "Let us work with the president to ring in a new era of trust, in which we are all safe. Long live President Galleo."

Her being the figurehead of Galleo's Elonian followers made sense. Once a traitor, always a traitor. However, it was just as possible that she simply couldn't remember her previous position as Tristan's Councilor.

Even though I hadn't yet ventured outside, the TV screen had shown me too many confusing images to wrap my head around. What was clear from all of them was that Elonians were third-class citizens. Special laws had been introduced to keep ordinary people, aka Shades, safe and happy. Now the few rights the rest of us still enjoyed were being chipped away by Galleo, with support from the likes of Regan.

Back in the war, the battle lines were clear. I knew who was on my side. Not anymore. An Elonian had turned traitor, and a Shade had saved my life. What a topsy-turvy place this world had become.

"How's my patient today?" Kieran's question tore me from my musings.

I muted the TV. "Better, thank you."

For once, my voice didn't betray my heartbeat's sudden acceleration.

He slumped into his armchair. I'd come to read him well over the past days. Each time he was about to mention Lea's name or raise other subjects outside his comfort zone, he narrowed his eyes and squeezed his lips into a thin line.

My midsection contracted before he'd uttered his first word.

"I have news," he said.

I shifted into a more comfortable position before gesturing. "Go on."

He interlaced his hands behind his head. "Although my father continues to refuse to talk to me, I still have contacts inside his administration." He rubbed his nose. "They're going to issue an arrest warrant for your king. Well, former king."

My heart went into a tailspin. "What? Why?"

"Terrorist activities. They say he's responsible for an explosion that killed twenty people; twelve Kindreds, eight Torrens."

I balled both hands into tight fists. "He'd never be so careless or callous as to risk injuring innocent people. That's not him."

Kieran raised an eyebrow. "Just to make sure we're on the

same page. In your view, the Kindreds are the innocents, and the Torrens had it coming, right?"

I breathed through my nose, not caring that my nostrils flared. "I didn't say that."

"Anyway, I agree with you. Planting explosives doesn't seem his style. But my father isn't generous with the truth even on his better days."

Play time was over. I had to find Tristan, warn him and protect him. Whether I'd be welcome was another matter. Lea was dead, and all Tristan might consider me good for was looking after his plants.

"Do the Kindreds swallow your father's lies?" I asked.

"Why wouldn't they?" Kieran's lips turned into a grim line. "Their memories tell them that the world has always been like this."

"I see Galleo's getting plenty of help from Elonians." I jutted a finger at the screen where Regan was still spouting her lies. "And if there's one thing besides violence the president excels at, it's propaganda. Otherwise your father wouldn't have been voted into office twelve times."

Kieran's lips formed a thin but crooked line.

"What?" I asked. "Whatever you have to say, just say it."

His strong jaw relaxed. "Why do you think my father's been elected twelve times?"

I frowned, trawling through my brain. "I must have heard it on the news."

"No. That's a new memory."

"It can't be." I sat up with a start, stressing my almost-healed wound. "I'd be able to tell if I'd been affected. Wouldn't I?"

He stared at a point above my head and suddenly threw back his shoulders. "How about a game of Kravatch? You know it?"

I pressed my tongue against the roof of my mouth to stop me from yelling. It would do no good. Kieran was the guy who'd put the 'I' in 'privacy.' Each time I dug deeper, he clammed up tighter than a gargoyle in a mudslide. Maybe a casual game or two would relax him. In a relaxed state, he'd be more likely to do me a favor. His informants could have information about Tristan's whereabouts or any underground movements I might become involved in, and if so, I needed to know.

I nodded and shared a brief smile. "Fine. You deal."

# CHAPTER TWENTY-SIX



*LEA*

*"The worst thing about reality is there's no background music to tell you how you should feel."*

I shielded my eyes against the brightness, but the outlines before me wouldn't sharpen. The sun, out in full force, shone on a generously sized street of white houses with mid-range cars parked in their driveways.

A typical suburban scene except for one major difference. The picture before me was one giant double exposure, and my mind had difficulty separating the superposed image from the original.

Orrin waited for me to catch up then swept aside his arms in a panoramic gesture. "Before you is the world without the Divide."

My throat closed and trapped my breath in my windpipe.

"The Divide is really gone?" Typical. I'd failed before I'd even had a chance to make a difference. I placed a hand on my queasy stomach and dropped my head. "Derinda caused this as a favor to Galleo in return for my life—or rather, my death."

Orrin's face crumpled and his mouth moved, but no words came. He didn't need to speak them. They already echoed in my head together with the disappointment of all those who'd put their faith in me. I'd failed. But then, I'd told them from the start I was the wrong woman for the job. Why hadn't Nieve listened? Not that the blame game made any difference now. I was dead and done.

I blinked to clear my vision, rubbed my eyes. Nothing worked. "Why can't I see right? Everything is wrong. The houses have no windows. I mean, I can make out the window frames in faint lines, but they're walled up."

"You see the world as it is. You can make out the past in thin outlines. The rest is a world molded by the Torrens, and they have little use for windows. They perform magic at home, and for that they prefer darkness."

"Isn't it confusing for the people who live here? I'm getting all dizzy from the double vision."

"Only you and I see both worlds at once, others don't."

He might as well be speaking Klingon because none of this made sense. "What exactly happened after I died?"

"When you died, the Divide fell, and every tree and stone in Elonia and Torren released their magic. Magic in its purest form, you understand, not the neat trickle we once bestowed upon the Touched. Pure magic is more powerful than anything the Torrens or Elonians can even imagine, and it is wild and untamed. If it's not bound in the form of objects, it searches for a task, and Derinda gave it one. To change the very fabric of reality in accordance with Galleo's specifications. Kindreds, Torrens and Elonians alike are experiencing new memories and rewritten history."

I rubbed my forehead, my mind a jumbled Rubik's Cube. The only frame of reference I had were the magic books I read on the subject of the fifth force. "I get that magic affects physical objects and energy, but changing the synapses in your brain to form new memories and erase the old seems exceptional. How is it possible?"

"In the end, the synapses in your brain are matter, too, just like mountains and leaves and snow."

He did have a point. "Derinda was supposed to get me as part of her bargain with Galleo. Won't she be mad at you for spoiling her plans?"

Lips drawn into a thin, crooked curve, he averted his face. "Derinda crossed a line. She acted in petulance and pettiness over my affair. Since she cannot seriously hurt me, she wants to take it out on you. Even if it means destroying everything."

"Won't she find another way?"

"She might try, but now I am forewarned. I shall remind her of our sacred pact. When my kind left your world, we agreed: no more interference in Touched or Kindred lives." His gaze drilled into me, giving weight to his words. "Magic or not, humans would have to make their own choices. You, daughter of mine, might carry my blood, but you are also human. I will do everything I can to make sure she leaves you in peace from now on, but we can't underestimate her."

A gentle breeze lifted the ends of my hair and carried them across my face. I brushed them aside and checked my surroundings. Nieve had warned of the Shade threat, spoke of the Shades' desire to control the Kindred world, but a complete rewriting of history?

I inhaled a bellyful of oxygen, working hard to get my emotions in check. "Is there no way to get the old world back? Lock up the magic again?"

"There are always ways." He flinched as if startled by a loud bang.

I craned my neck, but didn't spot anything to account for his jolt. "What's wrong?"

"I'll take you home now." He shook his head, tugged on his beard. "I must handle Derinda before she sees us together."

He waved his hand, and the landscape around us changed from suburban to city though we hadn't taken a single step.

Faded outlines separated the Seattle skyline from the bright sky. Not a silhouette I was likely to forget, yet startlingly different. A new world had taken shape. Between small homes and stores with names I'd never come across, high-rises without glass or windows stretched into the sky like giant concrete boxes. The double vision disoriented me, roiling my stomach.

Orrin grabbed my shoulders and turned me to face him. "This is where I must leave you."

I clutched his sleeve. "You can't. I still have questions."

Like, where should I go? How did I fit into this world? The nature of the changes Orrin had mentioned wasn't yet known to me, but I didn't want to find out. I wanted to go back to before the Shades found us. Before Galleo sliced and killed me.

Orrin stroked my hair and gathered me tight. "I wish we had more time. Be safe, daughter of mine."

He disappeared before his last words rang out.

I huffed and glanced around. A few months ago, I'd come to Seattle a stranger hoping to reconnect with her old home. I'd spent days driving through the city, re-familiarizing myself with its layout. There was comfort in familiarity, but right now, I found nothing to latch on to.

I rushed through the foreign-looking streets toward Pike Place Market, the traditional home to buskers, noisy market vendors, and salmon-slinging fishmongers. Yet changes lurked behind every corner.

The cranes that once towered over the city were gone, and with them the construction noise. They'd left behind a silence that didn't just stem from a lack of sounds, but from the wrong kind of sounds. Gone were the happy whispers of couples and cheerful screams of children, the muted conversation of shoppers and the shouts of exuberant friends running into each other. Only the silhouetted mountains in the west, the slender sea marked with the wakes of ferries and sailboats, and the faintest outline of the Space Needle reminded me of the place I knew. I wallowed in the sea-fresh smell infused with a chocolaty sweetness and the scent of ripe fruit, and welcomed all odors like old friends.

A primal longing for a hug or a kind word rose inside me. Everything I once had had dissolved into air. My job? Gone. My parents? Upset with me. My career as a hero and savior? Short-lived. Maybe I'd even lost my life, because Orrin never did get around to explaining whether I was dead. Had Nieve made it, at least? She'd been badly hurt but was responsive when Kieran took her to safety. What about Tristan? Was he still king even if Elonia no longer existed?

Questions came easy, but answers I had none. Crap.

Okay. Deep breath. What did I know? The Divide was kaput. Going by the unsmiling, hunched men and women in the streets, extremely kaput. Meanwhile, I was trapped in this nightmare world without a way out. I loosened my jacket's zip to free my lungs.

A shift in the atmosphere, more a feeling than a visual phenomenon, drew my attention to the Athenian Inn that was part of Pike Place Market for as long as anyone remembered. Its outlines faded into translucence. In its spot, a vegetable stall sprang forth in a cloud of gray smoke. A woman prizing her goods stood next to it, glaring at visitors.

I shut my eyes and opened them, but the Inn remained semi-transparent, its watered-down image surrounding the woman's stall. Nobody noticed the change. Nobody raised an eyebrow. People walked through the Inn's formerly solid walls without bumping into them. My body tensed. That was what Orrin had tried to explain. The new reality was still forming right before my eyes, and the humans were clueless. Soon I'd be the only one left who knew how the world should be.

A figure bumped into me. The man didn't apologize, but at least the incident confirmed I was still alive, not doomed to haunt this place for eternity. Bolstered by that knowledge, I set one foot in front of the other, inching my way toward the market center. Maybe I'd spot a familiar face, like a friend from school or a former neighbor. I searched for solid eye contact in the sea of people without finding a familiar gaze. The path around the stalls led me straight into the faint outlines of a trash can, but the object caused me no pain. It wasn't real. Not anymore.

My vision blurred, but I wasn't going to fall apart now. Not yet. Not ever. I had my life. I had Fallon. Time to see what else I had left.

Six armed men and women in brown leather uniforms and steel helmets wandered in pairs through the stalls without taking note of the goods on display. They exhibited neither aggression nor anger, yet all the same, people gave them a wide berth.

There was a time when I'd have given Shades the benefit of the doubt. Nieve's stories had sounded so clinical, Tristan's warnings exaggerated. Now I knew better. Shades were evil.

Fallon prodded my senses with an electric charge, urging me to challenge them to a fight, one that I would win. As if I was going to fall for its false confidence again. The last time I'd been sure of victory, I died. Instead, I ducked between two stalls and observed the Shade patrol's path through the crowd. The leader's gaze darted, ever watchful, from left to right. He glanced at me and stopped in his tracks.

My leather clothes were a dead giveaway.

The Shade signaled to his friends and then not-so-sneakily

pointed at me. Even the traders turned to look at me. My heart collapsed in my chest.

"Stop her," the Shades' leader shouted.

Two market traders left their stalls and circled in my direction. Seriously? What the hell had I ever done to them? They whispered something into the air then wafted their hands.

A gust of wind knocked me off center, and I stumbled.

Frak, since when could Kindreds wield magic? I caught myself and reeled through my options.

Flee.

Fight.

Or pee myself.

I chose a tactical retreat. Bending the sun's beams around me, I made myself invisible and called on the wind to carry me high.

Suspended on a cushion of air, I hovered over the scene below me. The Shade patrol spread out, shouting commands, but soon their shoulders sank and their movements became less urgent. They regrouped, whispered with each other, and finally detained the two men who'd failed to catch me. The men pleaded with the Shades, but the brown-suits ignored their cries, cuffed them, and escorted them away.

I crossed my arms and shook my head. The Kindreds had simply followed orders. It wasn't their fault I escaped.

Where next? I craved a hideout more than anything, somewhere safe to order my thoughts. If Nieve had survived the fight, she might have holed up at my place. There was even a good chance she and Tristan were already working on a plan to reclaim our future.

Even though the dual nature of reality continued to unsettle me, at least the nausea I'd experienced since I first stepped out of the darkness had subsided. I flew high in the sky, scouting the city while taking note of the differences. Each change slammed my heart against my ribcage, while each familiar feature triggered a mental high five.

When I was well out of sight of Pike Place Market, I landed and dropped my invisibility. Maybe it was a mistake to walk around so openly in my leather gear, but if people dared speak about the world, if they even hinted at anything Elonian, I needed to know.

The reality of the new world rammed home once more as soon as I entered my street. The windowless houses stood in neat lines, the driveways were well looked-after, but the soul of the place had changed beyond recognition. Where were the rock tunes drifting from Mr. Trueman's window, or Mr. and Mrs. Alexander's cat that always sat on the fence watching over its neighbors?

I stood in front of the house that used to be my home. Ran my hand over the unfamiliar Chrysler parked in my driveway. Finally the proof. The Divide was gone, and with it my world.

My house belonged to a stranger, my car may never have been built. How many other changes would this world spring on me?

With ice cold fingers, I trawled my pocket for my cell and dialed my dad's number. *"Kein Anruf unter dieser Nummer,"* a robotic female voice said. The number wasn't connected.

I put my parents' names into the only search engine my cell found. Could I be this lucky? According to the DESY website, they still worked in Hamburg. I dialed the number it gave, and the reassuring *Meep* told me my call had gone through.

"Hello." A deep, distracted voice.

"Dad?" I tightened my grip, afraid I might drop the phone. "Oh God, it's good to hear your voice. It's me. Lea."

A pause. "Lea who?"

"Your daughter? Light of your life?" I swallowed. "C'mon, Dad. Quit kidding around."

*Meep. Meep.* He'd disconnected the call.

I pushed the phone into my pocket. My fake memories rolled out my fake past like a foul carpet, draining the blood from my limbs. I shivered against the rising cold. Growing up in an orphanage, loved by no one. After a stint in rehab, I obtained my GED and started work as a customer service rep.

As surely as I knew these events to be false, they came wrapped in the air of truth. This couldn't be right. My dad, my mum, they'd been the one steady thing, the ones who… Oh God. They were gone. My lungs tightened into a ball, turning my breaths into a wheeze. Was Dad doing okay? If Tristan's friend had administered the cure before I died, he should be fine. If not…

I should have insisted on the cure from the start, before I'd taken my first step into the training area. Too wrapped up in the wonder of Elonia, I'd pushed my parents aside and neglected my duties as a daughter. Maybe that was why Dad didn't know me now. Why they hadn't adopted me. Because I didn't deserve their love.

I wheeled around and ran. At the end of the street, I slowed and stumbled to a tree. It couldn't be true. Why did Orrin bring me back here if I wasn't wanted by anyone? I leaned against the trunk and banged the back of my skull against it.

Finally, my brittle self-restraint collapsed and I slid onto the ground, while the rough bark tore at my jacket. I hugged my knees and placed my head on top of them, swaying from side to side. My parents had been the focal points in my life. They'd guided and supported me through even my craziest ideas. If this world didn't remember me—the real me who was once loved—where would I go? What would I do? I had no one. Nothing.

I was alone in a place that played by rules I didn't understand.

Nieve, Tristan. Assuming I found them, could I somehow retrieve their memories?

"You're Lea, aren't you?" a voice asked.

I glanced up at a small boy, enveloped head to toe by a bright luster. It was Draben, the chef's son from the castle. Immediately, I leaped up. Hadn't his parents taught him how to conceal his life light?

I dragged him behind the tree to make sure he'd be less noticeable to any passing Shades. "You remember me."

Huge, brown eyes stared at me from his somber face. He gulped then lifted his chin. "Yes."

Thank God. If this boy remembered me, there might be others like him. Maybe even Nieve.

"My father said you would save us." His chubby pointed finger might as well have been a blade. "But you didn't."

I slumped my shoulders. "I tried to prevent the world from changing. I did."

He shrugged like a man ten times his age. To him, I was simply one in a long line of disappointments life sporadically threw his way. "'s okay. Mom and Dad no longer remember you. They don't remember anything." He glanced around. "I want to go back to the castle, but they say *this* is our home."

My vision tunneled into a red spot. If a Shade passed now, I'd beat him to within an inch of his life. Maybe more. What had Derinda and Galleo done to these innocent Elonians and Kindreds? How could they trifle with people's lives? My accusations fanned the roaring fire in my core. I breathed in the heat, let it fester inside me, claw deep into my flesh. From now on, this fire would be my guide. The one thing no one and nothing could take away from me.

I set my jaw and touched the boy's arm. "If there's any way to change back the world, I will. But first, you need to tell me where the king is. Tristan, the Elonian king."

He squinted. "He's not our king anymore."

My hold tightened. "But do you know where he is?"

The boy looked first at my hand then past the tree. "There's my mom. I have to go."

"Wait."

But he'd already escaped my grip and sprinted away.

No matter how fueled I was to keep my promise to right the world, it rang hollow in my ears. I was no one's savior. That was clear. But I was scrappy, determined, and, more importantly, I was pissed-off big time. My best chance lay in finding Tristan, and with luck, Nieve.

Yet I had no idea where to start. I cast another glance at my former house. I couldn't stay here. With metaphorical quicksand under my feet, I wandered off, away from my one link to my parents and the "good old time" before the Divide fell.

# CHAPTER TWENTY-SEVEN



*"I'll fight the Shades until my dying breath. Or preferably, until their dying breaths."*

Kieran glided the armchair over to my bed and dealt the cards. I picked up three hearts, two high spades. The rest dispensable. A decent start.

It had been nearly two and a half weeks since that fateful night. The night I lost Lea. The night when I'd met Kieran who, as reserved as he was, had shown me true affection.

The old me didn't have any use for it. When Tristan became king, he stopped being my brother. The last time we hugged— Well, he might have patted me when the oracles handed me my certificate and I became his royal champion.

Kieran wasn't like that. As long as we didn't talk about his family or the Torren-Elonian war, he was quick with a joke when my thoughts revolved around Lea; quick to offer a drink or a sandwich when boredom struck; and quick to regale me with Shade myths and legends when the reality of the new world encroached on the sanctity of this room. Because in this apartment, the change never happened. Within these four walls, only the two of us existed.

"I remember playing this with my brothers when I was younger." He fanned out his cards. "That was when we still got along."

"What were you like when you were little?"

He laid down the seven of clubs. "Climbing trees. Play fighting with swords made of sticks. Swimming in the lake." He peered over his cards. "Isn't that what all boys do? Even in Elonia?"

Point well made. I shot him a teasing glance. "Girls, too."

"I can imagine you scaling trees." He leaned forward, so close I saw the dark flecks that occasionally graced his green irises. "I bet you were good at climbing. Probably still are."

"Yeah, I bested a boy or two in my day." I outbid his seven with a queen.

When I glanced at him, his face had lost its sparkle. He stared at my queen, but his focus had wandered.

"Kieran?" I waved to catch his attention.

With a sharp intake of air he drew his focus back on the game.

"It's yours." He chin-pointed at the stack.

I picked up the pile and opened the next round with the eight of spades. "What's on your mind?"

"I was thinking about my brothers. We were always competitive. I had to climb the highest, run the fastest. I usually won because their mothers would stop them."

"But not your mother?"

"No. She wasn't around." His voice had dropped a few notes. "I never met her."

"I'm sorry." No point pushing my luck on this difficult topic. He'd only shut down. "How does your father get on with your brothers?"

"They worship him despite everything he's done. I used to ride with him into battle or when he met with Sparks. There was a time when I thought the accusations against him were Spark propaganda. Lies. A few years ago, I discovered the truth about the orders he'd given to my brothers, about the atrocities they've committed in his name. How can a man burn..." He swallowed hard and placed his hand in front of his mouth.

I didn't rush him. At one time, I'd have blamed Kieran for his father's sins, but his tone of voice, his lost gaze, they told me beyond a doubt that he hadn't known.

"At that time, I distanced myself from him." Kieran looked into my eyes. "Don't get me wrong. I share many of his beliefs. Like for instance, magic was a gift from the Old Ones for all the Touched, not for a select few. The Spark elite shouldn't keep that knowledge from the guy trying to put food on his family's table."

"In an ideal world, I'd agree with you, but without controls, magic is easily abused. Wouldn't the world be better if your father had never been allowed near magic? If everyone knew how to attack someone with the power of the wind, what's to stop them?"

"Reason. Kindness. Morality. The same thing that stops them from picking up a sword and decapitating their neighbors. You know your argument doesn't stand up."

I huffed. "What other beliefs do you share with your father? The war?"

"I prefer diplomacy. Torrens and Elonians have a shared history. We must have common values that we can build on. But my father says our differences are too great, and war is the only way to peace."

"Do you agree with him?" My throat twisted into a tight knot.

Kieran tilted his head, a challenge in his frown. "What do you think?"

I met his expectant stare, but when I opened my mouth, no

sound came. With each heartbeat, the knot in my throat grew. I'd seen too much carnage committed by Shades to abandon my entire belief system, and Kieran deserved better than a lie.

He dropped his cards and stood. "Thank you very much."

"I want to believe you." I put my cards aside and shot him a pleading gaze. "Doesn't that count for something?"

With a heavy gait he stalked to the end of the room and chuckled grimly. "In the old world, I still had hope that the fates of Torren and Elonia would once again intertwine. Once it was my turn to lead my people, I'd put their wellbeing before my own." His voice rippled through me like a haunting melody. "But power leads to loneliness, which in turn makes you bitter. That realization sets me aside from my family, and maybe even from my people."

"You're not alone, though." The words slipped out.

He spun around, his arms hugging his torso. "Aren't I? Are *you* going to keep me from falling into the abyss? You don't even think I'm a good man."

Maybe he was, but he was also the son of Lea's murderer. Brother of the men that had killed Gerrit's family, including my one childhood friend. Kieran himself had been on the battlefield, cutting down people that had been under my command. In the end, he was a Torren and I was an Elonian. The fall of the Divide hadn't changed our genes nor had it altered my memories of the war.

At least not yet.

I picked up my cards again to avoid his gaze.

Kieran returned to his chair. "Is it my turn?"

"Yes." Unable to contain my discomfort, I shifted in my seat. "Get ready for the beating of a lifetime."

"We'll see about that." He opened with the ace of spades.

Our first-ever frank conversation had pushed Kieran and me apart. It had shown us how opposite we were. Still, we played nice, stayed cordial, probably because we weren't ready yet to give up our cocoon. The world out there was too strange and too cold for either of us.

After a snack, it was time to change the dressing on my wound. In reality, the injury was nothing more than a crusted-over spot. My excuses for staying with him were running thin.

"There you go." Kieran smoothed the edges of my bandage, as if afraid the glue would fail. Unaware that my skin would forever remember his every touch.

"It'll hold." My breath came in little rasps. "It's as good as healed."

A shadow flitted over his features.

"Hey, the absence of injuries and pain is meant to be a good thing." I reached for his hand, but stopped before I made contact.

"No, it is." He stood, back to being a man trapped in his own world. "I take it you want to leave now?"

"Want isn't the word I'd use."

"You're going to, though, aren't you?"

"I have to." I sought his gaze in vein. "I've tried calling the king, but his number is disconnected. The only way I'm going to find him is by getting out there myself."

"Why do you need to find him anyway?" Kieran rubbed the back of his neck. "I know you were born to fulfill the prophecy, but that's over now. The Divide is gone."

I lifted the blanket and walked over to the sofa, aware of Kieran's gaze on my bare legs.

"You have a gift for condensing complex information into tiny parcels of insults, don't you?" I inspected the jeans, T-shirt, and jacket Kieran had procured in my size.

"No, I meant, say you find your king. What then? Will you join his resistance?"

A sharp ache ran through my heart, and I balled my hands

around the rough denim. A resistance to Shade rule would put me firmly back on the opposite side of Kieran.

"I have no choice." I slipped into the pants and zipped them up. "Even without the prophecy, I'm still the royal champion."

He stepped toward me and gripped my shoulders. "Except, the king is no longer the king."

The bright light of realization flashed behind my eyes, and I snapped my spine straight. His point was valid. I'd sworn loyalty to the Elonian crown. Without a king, there was no crown and no royal champion. So in a way, a very real way, I was absolved of my duty. Unfettered by royal protocol. Released from destiny.

A grin spread over my face. "I'm a nobody."

Kieran let out a low laugh. "Being a nobody makes you happy?"

"More than happy." I grabbed his head between my hands and pulled him close. "Ecstatic."

His brows lifted, the corners of his lips twitched. Raw heat gave his sea green eyes a darker, jungle-like sheen.

What was I thinking? Had I nearly kissed a Shade? I yanked back my hands as if stung by a bee. "I didn't mean…"

In a flash, Kieran gathered me in his arms and pressed his mouth to mine, squishing my lips against my teeth. I opened my mouth, maybe to protest, when a rocket lit in my stomach, exploding into a jumble of desire and longing and *Oh-My-Sweetness*es. I tasted the hunger on his tongue and licked it into me, determined not to waste a precious drop.

A heavenly pressure bubbled up inside, spiking my adrenaline into dizzying exhilaration. For weeks, I'd waited to feel his heat. Our unspoken experiences had forged a bond between us, while our spoken ones had created understanding. Now that I lay in his arms and he in mine, why would I ever let go? Whatever happened, our twosome was safe, and warm, and so slicing perfect.

A gasp followed a moan. His or mine, I wasn't sure. He drove his hips against my waist, rubbed his excitement along my groin. I scratched at his shoulders, crowded his mouth with my lips, ran my hands over his chest. His muscles, his erection, hard as granite. I tore at his shirt buttons, eager to brush myself against his naked flesh. If I could get closer to him, I could fuse us together. No one and nothing could yank us apart.

"Don't leave," he whispered.

I breathed in his light, ginger scent, gave myself to its reassuring familiarity. His hair tickled, and I grabbed a handful, forcing his head deeper into my neck.

"Stay." He trailed urgent kisses along my cheek to my ear then bit my earlobe. "Can you do that for me? Can you forget *what* we are and simply enjoy *who* we are?"

His words cut through my fuzzy mind, yanking me out of my madness. *What* I was determined *who* I was. Under my brother's guidance, I'd become my duty, a warrior prepared to give my life for our beliefs and our values.

I slapped away Kieran's touch and stepped back, holding my fingers to my mouth. "Bad idea," I mumbled. "Bad, bad idea."

"Why?" His chest was trembling, like my own. His lips swollen and deep red. "Why is this a bad idea? We work. We make sense."

I satisfied an itch on my shoulder with my fingers, giving me the perfect opportunity to cover my still perky nipples with my arm. "You're a Shade."

"What does that even matter anymore?" His tone matched the hurt in his eyes. "Under my father's rule, we're all fucked in the same way."

I retreated into a corner of the room, where the air didn't carry his scent. The world outside was a dangerous mess, Lea was dead, and here I was, getting my thrills by kissing the enemy.

"I'm sorry," I whispered. "I'm not... Everything's—"

"Screwed up?"

"I'm sorry."

"You mentioned that." He lifted his hands in a what-the-hell gesture then dropped them to his sides. "Why am I even surprised? You're right. Go. Find your king."

"You don't understand. He's all I have left now."

"Is he?" He turned and walked out the room, slamming the door behind him.

"Kieran," I called out, as if I had a way to fix things between us.

He didn't return.

I pressed my shaking fist against my chest. Probably for the best. Given who we were, no other outcome was in our stars. Plus, no awkward farewells. I crossed to the sofa and donned the top. Even though the label claimed it was my size, it didn't sit right. Too loose. I rubbed my stinging eyes. Who even cared?

I put on the red jacket Kieran had bought for me and left the room. Walk out. Don't look back. Why make the break harder than it had to be? Despite strict laws prohibiting Elonians from owning weapons, I strapped on my holster and the hanbo, placing a cloaking spell over them before I left.

Outside, I took my first breath of new air. It smelled every bit as foul and rotten as the old, like old chips and petroleum. I glanced up, searching for the Space Needle to guide me. Although Kieran had warned me that it had never been built, its absence from the skyline chilled me to the core. Seattle looked as naked as I felt.

I headed south. Gerrit would be my best shot at finding my brother. They'd been tight as twins once. With Tristan in the Kindred world, they surely would have reconnected.

Deprived of my usual landmark, I stumbled from one street corner to the next, desperate to find a place I recognized. Streets, shops, buildings, all different. The hours passed, darkness fell, and still I wandered through Seattle. Surprising how little the nights frightened me now that the days held the same terror.

Maybe it wouldn't be so bad if I didn't find my brother. He'd spent his life preparing me for this one fight, and I'd let him down. He'd entrusted Lea to my care, and I got her killed. He'd probably lost his faith in me as the royal champion, too.

One hour till the nine o'clock curfew. If I went back, maybe Kieran would let me stay one more night. Or two, or three.

A dark structure loomed ahead of me, its outline oddly familiar. I took a deep, measured breath and walked up the sloping street. This was the spot where I'd lost Lea. This was where she'd taken a stand to protect me. This was where I'd abandoned her.

I ground my teeth. Regrets never changed anything. She had merely fulfilled the prophecy. The oracles had never expected me to save her. I tried to change the vague text to fit my purposes, thought I could keep Lea alive, but I couldn't fight destiny.

Running my hand over the coarse bricks, I glanced into the alley that ran between the building and a tall fence. Right on this street, I'd ruined everyone's life because I hadn't been fast enough to evade the jab of a knife—a move I'd performed thousands of times before.

A resonant clank sounded from the alley, like vibrating metal sheets. I squinted into the darkness. Probably a cat knocking over a trashcan. But what if I was wrong? I only had Kieran's word that Lea was dead. What if she was still here, crouching in the darkness? Hurt. Alone. Waiting?

I rushed down the empty path and stopped before a brown

wooden door. Locked. Frantic, I threw my body against the wooden slats. It didn't budge.

I stood still, listened for noises other than my beating heart. "Lea? Is that you?" No reply. I set my jaw. "Lea?"

Not a peep.

The energy that had propelled me down the alley drained from my body. I recognized my symptoms. Survivor's guilt. Many of my men and women had suffered similar illusions during the war. Back then, I'd considered myself immune, but like them, I was only mortal. Shoulders heavy, I turned.

And came face to face with a Shade.

His knife was drawn, his eyes narrowed.

"What do you want?" I tried not to sound scared. My Kindred disguise should offer me protection. "Curfew's still half an hour away."

The Shade showed a row of uneven teeth. "I know you, Spark. You're the royal champion."

My eyes widened. In a world where memories had become precious, it was my luck that this Shade should remember who I was.

My gaze darted side to side, looking for a way out. The hanbo still sat in its holster on my back.

I faked left and hurled myself to my right. Soared past an empty cardboard box, where I gripped a large rock, and then rolled onto my feet.

The Shade wasn't fooled. He'd covered the same distance, landed inches away. When had they gotten so good? With a spiteful smirk, he reached back to swing his knife.

A large rock slammed into his back, knocking him off balance. My pulse vibrated in my veins as I leaped out of the way, his blade missing me by a leaf's breadth. Who else was here? Had Kieran followed me?

A figure zoomed past me, a dagger in one hand. With a

whoosh of air, its steel pierced the Shade's belly. A brief gurgle, and he disappeared into the ground.

I glanced up at my savior.

Lea stood over me, hands on hips, a twinkle in her eyes. "Miss me?"

# CHAPTER TWENTY-EIGHT



*"I can be spontaneous. Just say when."*

I brushed a lock of hair out of my face and beamed at Nieve. My heart swelled, while my cheek muscles yanked my mouth into an almost painful grin. Instead of her customary leather, she wore a pair of jeans, a loose-fitting T-shirt, and a tailored red jacket. The girl-next-door look softened the sharp edge of her tightly pulled-back hair.

I checked the length of the alley to ensure we were alone then ripped out a handful of grass growing from a crack in the cement to wipe the blood off Fallon. Another kill.

Nieve still hadn't said a word. What if she didn't remember me? What if the magic had affected her already?

I sheathed my dagger and raised my hands so as not to alarm her. "I don't know if you—"

"It's you?" She lunged and threw her arms around me. "You're alive."

"Right back at ya." Her joy was like caffeine to my system, and I drank it up in one heady slurp.

She stepped back and surveyed me, from my head down to

279

my boots. Her mouth moved, but the expected smile didn't come out. Instead, she averted her gaze. "I thought I'd lost you."

"Yeah, for a while I thought I'd lost myself." Balor's total darkness had been the stuff of nightmares. "Guess it wasn't my time."

For two nights and days I'd flown around evading Shade patrols, getting used to the double vision still plaguing me. If a morbid curiosity hadn't drawn me to the spot where I'd been stabbed, I never would have found Nieve.

So a big woot for morbid curiosity!

Her gaze roved over my green jacket and black denims. "Are you hurt?"

"All healed. No biggie." I sounded confident, but my casual smile slid straight off my face.

As much as I liked her touchy feely display of happiness, the nerd in me would have loved a few heartfelt words. Even Loki greeted Thor with an, 'It's good to have you back,' before he ambled off to destroy Jotunheim. Was that too much to ask for?

She licked her lips. "Then where were you? Kieran said his father had killed you."

My pulse skipped a beat. "You know he's the crown prince?"

"Yeah, I know." She placed a hand against her lower ribs. "He helped me heal and, um, it came up."

I scrunched my face. What happened to her endless soliloquies about never trusting those bastards? Clearly, Miss I-Hate-All-Shades still had the ability to surprise me.

"I'm glad Kieran got you to safety." I smiled. "And yes, Galleo did kill me. Do you have a safe place where we can go to discuss it? It's a story worth hearing."

"I haven't found my brother yet, so how about Kieran's?"

"You trust him? I mean he's cute, sure, but he's also a Shade and—"

"He's not your typical Shade." She angled her body away from me, like a bird about to take flight. "He's been good to me."

"I see." My voice remained breezy, even though her words weren't those I'd expected. Who was this soft creature wearing Nieve's face? The baggy clothes didn't hide her protruding bones, but her weight loss wasn't the only change. She'd lost her kick-ass edge. The sharp cut in her voice. Compared to her, Mother Theresa would look like a ninja.

She glanced toward the street. "Curfew is about to set in."

"Is there something going on between you and Kieran?"

"What makes you think that?"

"You playing house with a Shade was my first clue." I ran my hand through my hair. "Wow. This definitely isn't Kansas anymore."

"We weren't playing house. He healed me, then we went our separate ways. That's it."

Her tone was too defensive. Their relationship wasn't as over as she made it sound, I'd bet my last bacon sandwich on it.

We had no time for her vagueness and excuses. Fingers clawed around my waist, I looked into her big blue eyes. "Did you at least weasel information out of him on what he knew about Galleo's plan? Like, how it was going to play out? How the effects can be reversed?"

She lowered her head. "We didn't talk about that."

"What, the subject of the brand new world hasn't come up between sips of morning tea?" A not-so-subtle bite had worked itself into my voice.

She took a half-step back. "It's complicated."

"Tell that to Facebook," I mumbled, but didn't press the subject. Both of us had taken a hit. Besides, she was all I had left in this world. "Never mind. You haven't found Tristan yet?"

"I left Kieran's to go looking for him." Despite the darkness crowding into our little alley, Nieve's face burned a noticeable pink. "Kieran says the president has accused Tristan of killing innocents."

"The president?"

"President Galleo." She glanced around as if expecting more Shades to jump out at us.

"Well, lucky for us I do know where to find your brother. Thanks to Kirk."

"How did you locate the gargoyle?"

I waved my hand. "I followed the booze. Now let's head out. We need Tristan for my plan."

Finding a gray gargoyle in a city of gray concrete had taken a while, but someone who liked alcohol with such devotion wouldn't hang around churches. After checking out a few bars and hotels, I finally tracked him down at a small establishment not far from here.

"Should we even bother?" Nieve asked. "The old world is gone."

"Temporarily gone." I lifted my arm, my hand clenched in a fist. "The change is still going on. Nothing's settled yet. And as long as you and I still remember the old ways, we'll fight. That's what you taught me. Right?"

"I guess."

What the frak? Why wasn't Nieve as fired up as I was? The Shades had ruined our lives, taken everything from us.

"I know things look bleak." Squeezing my face into a facade of, what I hoped to be, grim determination, I stepped close to her, close enough for my cold breath to cling to her jacket. "But whatever we have to do to reinstate the Divide, we'll do. Okay?"

She bit her lip and glanced past my shoulder.

My words hadn't been intended to stump her. Under the circumstances, I'd even go as far as to declare my attempt at a rousing speech deserving of at least a *Hell, yeah*, and a high five.

I nudged her shoulder. "You and I were given a job by the king, and last I checked, you're still the royal champion."

She wrapped her arms around her torso. Her trembling lips drew into a thin line, and she closed her eyes. "Yes, I am."

# CHAPTER TWENTY-NINE

*NIEVE*

*"Oscar Wilde said, 'The truth is rarely pure and never simple.' Let me add that it's also hardly ever true."*

"I was hoping for more enthusiasm." Lea grabbed my arm. "Nieve, I need you."

"I hated thinking you'd died. I never wanted to let you down." My glance zipped from the dark-bricked building to the tall wooden fence, too aware of the fear in my voice. "But I didn't hate thinking I was done fighting. I'm so slicing tired. All my life, I've been expected to protect our kingdom. Now the kingdom is gone. That's terrible, but..."

"But so is that sense of responsibility?"

I glanced up. She understood. How was that even possible?

"Yes." I nodded. "I'm free."

"Are you?" Lea gestured around the darkness. "How can you be free in this world? Did you know that people's memories are changing? Probably even yours?"

I flicked my tongue against the roof of my mouth. Maybe forgetting my failure, Kieran's kiss, and the feelings he'd breathed into me wouldn't be too bad. "Yes."

"My parents don't remember me. I have no one in this

world." She exhaled sharply. "Except you. And if you forget me too..."

Even after my abysmal failure, she still needed me. Maybe this was my chance to atone. If I supported her now, no matter how hopeless our situation, she would forgive me.

"You're right." I smiled, even though the strength she was looking for in me had gone into hiding. "And I'll never forget you. I promise."

She stared at me with narrowed eyes. "Good. Make sure you remember your accomplishments, too. Even the war, the people you grieved for. If you forget, what did they die for?"

Slice it, she was right. "Okay, I'm on board. What do you want us to do?"

"How about we go get Tristan on board, too?" She set off down the alley back to the street. "Come, let's get off the streets. The Shades have a nasty habit of showing up where you don't want them to. And with normal Kindreds now having rudimentary magic at their disposal, the world is too damn dangerous. Let's fly."

Would she never learn? "Flying will eat our reserves too quickly."

"Not flying will get us into trouble with the Shades." Without regard to who saw us, she lifted high into the sky.

"Fine." I gathered the wind by my side and joined her. "You really think we can do this? Get the old world back?"

"We will." She nearly sounded confident.

Without the Space Needle, I had no idea where we were, even from fifteen feet in the air. After a few minutes, the concentration of tall buildings thinned, replaced by small, cookie-cutter boxes.

Lea looked at me sideways. "Why do you look like you're going to puke?"

Because I was about to come face to face with the man I'd

disappointed. "I'm worried. If the gargoyle knows where the leader of the resistance is hiding, the Shades may, too."

Lea descended onto a wide, deserted road and placed one hand on her waist, waiting for me to set down beside her. "You still don't trust Kirk? He never sold us out, you know. Isn't that proof enough that he's on our side?"

"Possibly. It just doesn't feel right to trust a gargoyle." I brushed off my jacket. "That reminds me. When we see my brother, could you not tell him about Kieran and me?"

"I thought there was no Kieran and you."

"There isn't." I straightened my ponytail, if only to hide how uncomfortable this conversation made me. "I want to make sure that that's exactly what you tell my brother."

"Won't he think it odd if I say, 'hey Tristan, great to see you. Before you ask, there's nothing going on between Nieve and Kieran'?"

I bit my lip. "You're right. Maybe we shouldn't mention Kieran at all."

"Then where should we say you've been for the past few weeks?"

I noticed the twitch of her lips and took a deep breath. "You're making fun of me, aren't you?"

"Who, me?" She gestured down the road. "Come on. We'll do the rest by foot. Because calluses seem to make you happy."

I rolled my eyes and walked by her side. My earlier doubt about Kirk's loyalty was a speck compared to my real fear. How was I going to justify my botched mission to Tristan? Decades of training, and it had all been a complete waste of his time.

He'd no doubt give me the dressing down of a lifetime, and I'd bear it because it was my duty. And because it was well deserved.

# CHAPTER THIRTY



*"Maybe there is intelligent life left on this planet, but is it me, or does it seem like it's only visiting?"*

I squinted up at the tall, whitewashed building. Was such a flashy mansion the best hideout for Tristan and his underground movement? Then again, not too long ago, he'd been a king. In a way, this was a serious downsize.

The mere thought of him made my heart beat to the rhythm of *Staying Alive*. I held back my tapping foot and listened for sounds from inside. The sun was out in force, but its warmth didn't penetrate the nervous chill in my bones. Next to me, Nieve stood as still as a toy soldier.

The last time I'd seen Tristan, I was a naive, science-obsessed girl. A different person than the Xena-like warrior I'd become almost overnight. The warrior I *had* to become. I'd given Draben my word that I would undo this horror show. And one way or another, my father would call me his daughter again.

Nieve's commitment might still be shaky, but that only meant it was up to me to make up for the difference. Together, we could get this done.

Question was, would Tristan like the new, less fluffy me?

Trudging steps approached from inside, and the heavy door creaked open. A plump man raised bushy eyebrows, which fell deep when he spied Nieve. His brows leveled and he gave a curt nod. "Nieve."

As far as greetings went, it was tepid. He clearly knew her by sight. You'd have thought he'd be glad she was alive, but I was already wise to the fact that, unlike me, the Elonians weren't generous with their feelings. For all I knew, his lackluster words were an outpouring of emotions for which he'd flog himself later.

"Dachsoon." Nieve's voice carried little more joy than his, making his name sound like *dachshund*.

So, this was the traitor's nephew Tristan had mentioned. Tristan hadn't trusted him enough to meet with this Markus guy and had sent Nieve instead, but now he and Dachshund were palling around? Even in this world beggars couldn't be choosers.

Dachshund stepped aside and pointed toward a long, straight corridor with hospital-white walls. "Tristan's in the back."

In profile, his nose appeared long and thin, making the nickname even more appropriate.

I set off in the direction he'd indicated, trusting Nieve to follow. The wooden floor gleamed under the light from bright chandeliers. White doors lined our path on both sides, labeled with the names of what I assumed were their occupants. A brawny, broad-shouldered man in faded denim jeans and a crisp white shirt blocked our entrance to the room at the end.

He widened his stance. "What is your business?"

The sounds of quiet conversation behind him fell silent.

If his question was a challenge, I wasn't prepared to accept it. I shifted to my left to let Nieve do the talking, Elonian to

Elonian, but she still lingered by the entrance, whispering with Dachsoon. Going by her face, they exchanged heated words.

I turned back to the Hulk and tried to look around him. The thought of being so near Tristan messed with my body something fierce. Somewhere in that room, he sat on a sofa maybe, drinking his customary cup of tea, knee-deep in plans of intrigue. Unaware that the prospect of my seeing him again was turning my knees to molten wax.

At least I hoped he was in there. All I saw from my spot were potted plants on a small wooden table and, next to it, a large stereo.

"I said, what is your business?" The man pushed out his chest until it seemed to fill the entire doorframe.

Nieve came up from behind and placed a hand on his arm. "Gerrit. She's with me."

Her voice was tender and quiet, almost a whisper.

"And who are you?" the guard asked. He blinked as if seeing her for the first time. "Nieve? You're alive?"

She smiled and held out her arms. "Surprise."

His expression softened, and he pulled her into a bear hug.

Something heavy toppled onto the floor in the back of the room. Voices began talking over each other and steps approached. Tristan shot through the doorway like a muzzle flash.

"Nieve?" He shoved Gerrit aside and yanked his sister to his chest. His expression broadened into an open smile, joy radiating from his glistening eyes down to his twitching lips. "Thank the Old Ones you're all right." He held her close and rocked her in his arms.

All this time I'd dreamed of my reunion with Tristan, without realizing what being separated from him had meant to Nieve. This was all I wanted for myself, too. Didn't everyone deserve someone to love them? A pressure rose from deep inside my chest, and I cleared my throat.

Tristan's head swiveled. His eyes widened. "Lea?"

I managed a lopsided grin. "In the flesh."

He extended one arm and gathered me close too, and the three of us huddled in a group hug. He'd exchanged his leathers for normal clothes—blue jeans, a shirt—but the scent of his woodsy cologne hadn't changed. Something touched the crown of my head. An accidental brush with his chin, or a deliberate kiss?

The hollow in my chest filled with the overwhelming sense that everything was going to work out. We were safe.

But this was the worst time for my crush to get a second wind. Outside his embrace, the world held as much warmth as an industrial-size freezer. Unless I was ready to accept this as a fait accompli, I'd better get my act together.

I shook off his touch and stepped back. "We have to talk."

Nieve took her cue and wriggled free from his arms. Yet his hand held on to her wrist.

"Of course." His voice sounded less gravel, more dirt road, but it still poked all the right places in me. "Follow me."

He hustled us back the way we came, leaving his friends to puzzle over what was going on. Dachshund passed us on the way, carrying a tray of tiny sandwiches. I snatched one for myself, meeting his glower with a killer stare of my own. Hell, I'd died for the Elonians. The least they owed me was food. To prevent Dachshund from retrieving it, I gulped my snack down in two bites. Then I winked at him, drinking in his thunderous glare.

Tristan sidled up to me, his left arm draped around Nieve's shoulders. "In here."

We entered a long, narrow room with oversized oil paintings of battle scenes on one side and a curved velvety sofa with gilded arms on the other. It was like stepping into the past. The door at the far end opened into a bedroom/home office, no less sumptuously furnished, with a four-poster bed in the back, and a massive, dark wood desk and filing cabinet on my left.

Tristan might no longer be the Elonians' monarch, but he'd sure picked himself a crib fit for a king.

He gave Nieve one more squeeze, then rolled three chairs into a triangle. "I don't even know where to begin. Too many questions." He tapped two fingers against his temple. "What happened? When the world changed, I feared you were dead."

Nieve placed her elbows onto her lap and dropped her head into her palms. "We... After..."

I'd hoped being reunited with her brother would rouse the old Nieve from under her layers of insecurities, but once again she hesitated.

I took a be-patient-with-the-recently-wounded breath. "We were looking for the Shade crown prince when a bunch of Shades attacked us. Is *bunch* the right collective noun for Shades?" I pushed the stray question away with a wave. "Anyway, let's say the odds were stacked, and we lost. I was brought before the Shade king, and then he killed me."

"What? He killed you?" Tristan blinked a few times. "Are you making a bad joke?"

"How dare you?" I pressed my palm against my heart. "My jokes are always of the highest quality. So, no, I really died. I ran into Orrin, of the Old Ones fame. He told me that Galleo had conspired with Derinda, Orrin's wife, to destroy the Divide. In return, she wanted me dead, because Orrin had made my biological mother, your former queen, pregnant with me, and somehow killing me was a way to get back at him."

Nieve and Tristan's mouths hung open, and for the first few seconds, I took a modicum of enjoyment from their surprise. But patience wasn't a skill I'd mastered yet.

"Isn't anyone going to say anything?" I asked.

"You're Orrin's daughter?" Nieve's voice wobbled.

"That's what he told me."

"Interesting." Tristan said confidently.

"I know. He also indicated there's a way to undo this mess."

"Okay. Fine. Let's start from the beginning." Tristan's tone was precise, and he kept his features largely constrained. Only a sporadic twitch affected his eyelids, although I didn't know him well enough yet to know what that meant. "How did the Shades find you?"

"Bad luck. They too had been looking for the prince, and it was a matter of right place, wrong time."

Nieve leaned forward, practically tipping the chair over. "If Orrin is your father, were you Orrin's vessel?"

"So the fall of the Divide can be reversed." Tristan tapped his knuckles against the arm of his chair. "Did Orrin tell you how?"

"Okay." I pointed at Nieve. "Yes, I'm the vessel." Then my finger shot to Tristan. "No, Orrin didn't."

Tristan lowered his lids. "We need to find out soon. More of my people are forgetting the old world. I'm not sure who I can trust anymore. Those who fought by my side during the war suddenly change into Shade collaborators or High School teachers or accountants."

"You mean like Gerrit?" Nieve's voice was hollow. "He's your best friend, and it took him a bit to place me. We spoke only a few days ago and he was, you know, Gerrit. Now?"

"He's one example." Tristan clicked his tongue. "I can't be sure that I haven't been affected yet. Or either of you."

I killed the bitter laugh rising in my throat. Orrin's vague words and my own double-memory suggested that I might not be affected by the changes at all, which made the situation so much worse for me. I'd have to see my friends forget first their history, and ultimately me. And then I would be truly alone.

"I remember what a pain you can be, so my recollection's intact for now." I grinned.

He shot me a glance so naughty my heart lurched.

"Charming." He rolled his chair closer to his sister and reached out. "Were you hurt in battle?"

"I was hurt, but I'm okay now." She withdrew her hand and held her fingers to her mouth to cover a hearty yawn. "Just tired."

He rubbed his right thigh. "I'm a bad host. Do you want food? A shower? Anything?"

"Food, please," I said. The finger sandwich from earlier hadn't as much satisfied my appetite as reminded my stomach it was hungry.

Nieve linked her hands behind the chair and stretched her shoulders. "Do you have a spare bed? I'm beat."

I was tempted to roll my eyes. Nieve BF, that is Before the Fall, would have pushed for action, not pushed for sleep. We had a limited amount of time before she and everyone else would forget.

Tristan activated the intercom and asked the bodiless voice that answered to prepare food.

"Come on," he said to Nieve. Then he shot me a wicked wink. "As for you, don't run away."

They left the room. I leaned back in my chair, only superficially registering the tall yucca next to the filing cabinet. How odd that, in this crazy world, someone had taken the time to place plants into windowless room.

Maybe getting sleep wasn't a bad idea. It had been a while since I had a good night. I'd broken into a car one night, and Kirk had found an empty house for me after that, where I'd exchanged my leather uniform for something less conspicuous, but always the fear of discovery had hung over me.

Nieve's world had been destroyed just like mine. Her home

was gone. Her army, the prophecy, her entire purpose had disappeared. When *my* world had collapsed the first time and I had to relocate to Elonia, she'd been patient—in her own way. More than once her face had told me she wanted to beat sense and manners into me, but she'd done her best. I owed her the same, at least until she rediscovered her old mojo.

Could I do it, though? Shoulder the burden for the two of us when I myself was so new at this?

A cough from my left tore me out of my thoughts. Dachshund walked into the room, past our group of chairs, and placed a tray next to a stack of folders on the desk. More snack-sized sandwiches, a whole platter of peanut butter goodness just for me. A point for him.

He planted his tush on the desk and crossed his arms. "You're the one. The one from the prophecy?"

Unsure what he was getting at, I put my expression into neutral. "Guess so."

"You two did a great job not saving the Divide. Truly memorable performance."

I shrugged. "Can't recall you helping out. Where were you when the fight went down?"

"I wasn't part of the prophecy."

I wanted to bury my face in my hands, or better yet, bury my fist in his face, but I wouldn't give him the satisfaction. "Lucky for us, huh."

He tilted forward, bringing his head closer to mine. Even his breath reminded me of a dog. "If I'd known you two girls wouldn't get it done, I would have done it myself. And done a better job of it."

I averted my face, fanning away his smell. "Sure you would."

"Enough." Tristan's voice echoed against the walls.

Both Dachshund and I flinched.

Tristan stormed into the room, past the filing cabinet and the plant, and built himself up in front of my chair, facing Dachshund. "You didn't even believe the threat was real at one time."

Dachshund stood, head bowed.

*Good little doggie.*

His fingers fidgeted with the belt loops of his jeans. "But—"

"You're angry, Dachsoon. I get that. We all are. But it's not Lea's fault. She's not a warrior. You want to blame someone, blame me. I gave the orders."

"Yes, sir. I mean, no, sir. I would never blame you." Dachshund circled Tristan then darted off before his leader scolded him more.

Tristan slapped his chest and beamed at me. "I still got it."

"Aww, the boy who would be king." I picked up a sandwich. Did Dachshund have time to spit in it?

"I *am* king."

"Not unless we succeed in undoing the destruction." My rumbling stomach overruled my doubts, and I gulped down the food.

"*If* we can, that is." He grabbed a sandwich off the tray and sat back in his chair. "I'd almost given up hope before you two showed up."

"For the record, I fought well. We nearly beat them."

"As I said, our expectations of you were unrealistic."

A heavy weight dropped down my stomach.

"It's not my fault." I hung my head.

His words, which were surely meant to reassure me, spoke only of disappointment.

"Hey." He tilted his head to catch my attention. "If nothing changes, the Fall will erase the Elonians' recollections soon enough. Nobody will care what you did or didn't do. Until then, let's enjoy the memories we have. Agreed?" He took a large bite and chewed through his smirk. "My favorite one is that of a particular incident that involved a lot of kissing."

Heat crawled along my neck into my cheeks and ears. Yet I hadn't forgotten his dismissive attitude after our special night.

"You hot, me bothered, buddy." I spoke in an early morning voice, as if rough from lack of use.

He placed the remnants of his sandwich on the desk and rolled closer to slip his knees between my legs. "Poor Lea. Has the Fall already messed with your head?"

His fingers touched my temple, soft as a snowflake, while his thumb caressed my cheek.

The urge to suck in a deep breath overcame me, but I held back, afraid that any movement would break the contact. "Oh, the details are still clear in my mind, thank you very much."

"Maybe you could refresh my memory then? I believe it started something like this." He slung my arms around his neck and traced his hands along the lines of my body.

I should have stopped him. Stopped the desire in his eyes. Stopped the slight parting of his mouth. Yet I'd lost the power to speak or move of my own accord. Still like a puppet, I allowed him to hook his hands behind my knees and slide me onto his lap. All the way until I pressed hard against his erection.

He trailed his fingers to my lower back and licked his lips, his gaze fixed on my mouth.

The wild throbbing in my crotch played havoc with my brain. My legs clamped tight around his waist.

He lavished my lips with a tenderness that took me by surprise. Just as gently, he glided his tongue in, sharing with me the subtle flavor of his peanutty snack. The kiss woke a thirst in me, and I drank deep from his mouth, breathed him into my lungs until his passion warmed my blood.

A kiss like his had to mean something.

"Why did you treat me so coldly when you sent me away?" I held his head between my hands, seeking his gaze.

"Despite my better judgement, I'd fallen for you. Then you had to leave, and I didn't know if I'd seen you again. The prophecy—"

"Was a bunch of hooey."

He smiled. "You did die."

"But all's not lost yet." I forced another kiss from him.

Supporting my thighs with his hands, he rose from the chair.

I didn't let go, wouldn't even let him catch a glimpse of the room's layout. Treading cautiously, he bumped into the corner of the desk, and my teeth scraped against his bottom lip. A low grunt of pain escaped his throat, greedily devoured by me. His legs collided with the bed and he sat, without a molecule of air coming between us.

He said he'd fallen for me. For the geeky, uncoordinated mess I'd feared would die a virgin. I was twenty-four, for crying out loud. It was time.

Our kiss deepened, interrupted only when I impatiently tore off his shirt. His shoulder carried the same mark Nieve and I had. I shoved him onto his back. Okay. This guy wasn't a college dude trying it on. Frak, this was a real man. Guess I'd better woman up. Starting with his lips, I alternately sucked and licked a path along his neck to his shoulders. His hard plate of chest muscles lifted and fell in rapid succession, twitching whenever I hit a sensitive spot.

His groan spurred me to explore him further, and I teased and nibbled my way down his long body, while my fingers fumbled with his button and zipper.

After some trial and error, I got it open. Eager to keep him excited, I pushed my hand in and grabbed his pulsing penis.

He touched my wrist. "Not so fast. It's not a race."

I snapped back my arm. "I'm sorry. Didn't I...do it right?"

The crook of his finger guided my gaze back to him. "Have you never done this before?"

*Oh my God.* I couldn't be more humiliated if he announced my virginity in the local newspaper. Right next to a big fat photo of my tomato-red face. But he didn't understand. In college, I'd glued my nose to my textbooks, and men didn't even enter my peripheral vision.

I scrambled off him and, teetering at the edge of the bed, rummaged for something cool to say, anything to overplay my embarrassment.

"What's wrong?" He sat up and wrapped his arms around me.

I shook him off. "Nothing."

He tightened his embrace. "Talk to me. It's okay if you haven't done this before." He kissed my ear, his breath driving a smidgen of confidence back into me. "I was just surprised."

"I didn't hurt you?"

"Believe me. Nothing you did could be described as painful."

His chuckle loosened my tense muscles better than any massage. I twisted toward him.

"So." I cupped his cheek, my thumb running over his stubble. "Does that mean you want to try again?"

He leaned in. "I want to do more than try."

He lay back onto the bed, holding me close, and rolled on top of me.

I took his face between my hands, checking his eyes for judgment. All I saw was passion, and something much, much gentler. I didn't dare guess what emotions were running through him. For now, being with him was enough.

I coaxed his mouth closer. He took the cue.

His kiss blew through me like a solar flare, scorching any thought, any worry, out of its way. This was how I'd dreamed it would feel. My skin vibrated from his touch as he stroked my waist, my sides, the curves of my breast. Every touch enough to drive me out of my mind. My lungs pumped hard, each fall of my ribs widening the distance between us, each breath-in a blessed relief.

He let his mouth follow in his fingers' trail, plucking and teasing the skin around my belly button.

"Come here." He lifted me with one arm and took off my T-shirt with the other.

The fabric of my bra barely affected the sensation of his mouth closing around my breast. He flicked his tongue, and a heavenly rumble darted from my core.

"Are you okay to carry on?" he whispered.

I nodded, my almost tears spilling out as laughter. "Definitely."

He flicked again. My eyes rolled under my lids, my back arched.

I'd always figured I'd be more hands-on in this situation, but Tristan took charge. He shifted, arranging a pillow under my head, and reached into a drawer next to the bed to retrieve a condom. My breath stopped as he found the clasp of my bra and undid it.

"You've done this before." I laughed, but the thought left a better taste in my mouth.

"Not as often as you think, and never with this amount of interest, I promise you." He dragged his fingers to my breast, cupping, feeling, preparing it for another assault with his wicked tongue. "Don't for a moment think you're competing with anyone."

"Okay." My voice trembled. Keeping my wits about me was getting tougher by the second.

"No one comes to close to you." He firmly closed his mouth around my lips and slipped one hand into my underwear.

My head fell back, and I whispered his name.

I awoke in a spooning position, with Tristan's hand on my breast and his nose against my neck. Wow. For one night, he'd made me feel like a queen, caring only about my pleasure. I cat-stretched, pressing my butt into his hard body. He stroked my side, my hip, then thigh, while his lips traced warm kisses across my shoulders.

When his fingers sought the spot between my legs, I laughed and shook him off. If I gave in to him now, we'd never make it out of bed.

I slid out from under the blanket and grabbed my bra from the floor.

Tristan's hair brushed down my spine until his face pressed against the sheet. He let out a frustrated growl. "We have a little time, don't we?"

I stuck my right arm through the hole and glanced over my shoulder. "Not long enough for what you have planned."

"If that's what you're worried about, I can be quick."

I sat and slipped my legs into my jeans. "As tempting as that sounds, I don't think we can afford to waste time. You said yourself, every hour, the Divide's fall wipes out more of your memory. One night's rest was probably more than we could afford anyway."

"Rest? You call what we did rest?" He poked his head past my waist, gently bit my midsection, and reached for his shirt. "So when did you grow all sensible?"

"Let's say I found the apocalypse a sobering event." Once I had my boots on my feet, I stood. "I did have one question. Before the Divide fell, did you send someone to cure my father?"

"I gave the order, but shit went wrong before he left the

castle." He rose when I got off the bed, and pressed himself against my back. His arms encircled me. "I'm sorry."

What was I going to do? Demand he held up his end of the bargain now, in the middle of Armageddon? Besides, I shouldn't have left it so late to begin with.

"If Galleo made magic free to be used by everyone, is cancer even still an issue in this world?" I turned and focused on Tristan's ocean-blue eyes.

"Don't buy the propaganda. Galleo shares only part of his magic. He's not the benefactor he appears to be." Tristan stroked my cheek. "In other words, yes, cancer and Alzheimer's and other diseases are still an issue among the Kindreds. And sadly, the changes that are going on affect only the memory, not the body, so if your father was sick before the Fall, he is still sick now. I'm sorry."

"That's okay. It's not your fault." I wiggled free from his embrace. "Where's the bathroom? I need to pee."

He gave an exasperated raise of his eyebrows and pointed at a door in the corner of the room. "Take your time. I'll use another one."

I nodded and slipped into the bathroom. As much as I needed the affection of another person, last night didn't change what needed to be done.

Orrin hadn't given me a time frame, but from what Tristan had told me, the Fall was already taking a toll on his friends and warriors. From everything I'd observed over the days, I surmised that past exposure to magic gave them protection, at least for now. After all, humans had succumbed first, followed by ordinary Elonians. If Tristan had permitted everyone to use magic freely, like Galleo had, the resistance might count more members.

Using my finger, I spread toothpaste around my mouth. In a weird way, I could still feel Tristan inside me now. He'd given me everything I asked and more. I'd felt warm, safe, and loved. How crazy to be feeling so happy and downright miserable at the same time.

When I reappeared from the bathroom, washed and somewhat cleaner, Nieve had returned, like me dressed in yesterday's clothes. She shot me a questioning glance and I nodded. Her mouth twisted into a shallow grin.

We followed Tristan, who spoke on his cell phone, into a small room, stuffed to the corners with large displays and shiny electronics emitting a monotonous beep. Three monitors showed split screens of the building and what I assumed were its surroundings. On another, a sine wave traveled with unerring determination. Call me a geek, but I wanted to don my lab coat, get out my pencil, and start measuring stuff.

"Not an option." He held a hand over the phone and mouthed "Mayson." "No. Both Nieve and Lea will stay." He rolled his eyes. "I've told Dachsoon, and I'm telling you. They will not influence my decisions." Pause. "Fine. No, that won't happen. You have my word."

Tristan hadn't learned his lesson. He was still the leader of the resistance, so why was he justifying his actions before others?

Tristan snapped his phone shut and gestured for us to sit on the chairs. "Back to business. We need to figure out how to undo the Fall. Anyone have an idea on where to start?"

"Maybe." I avoided his gaze, if only to make sure I didn't smile inanely at him. "Galleo planned for the Divide to fall. So he will know how to put it back up. Right?"

"I loathe to burst your bubble," Tristan said, "but the president is untouchable. I've been told by those who've already succumbed to the Fall that he's heavily guarded."

Tristan's last failed attempt to kill Galleo formed clear in my mind. Dear God, I remembered it as if it had happened. I leaped up off my seat. The history of my part in the Elonians' resistance sprung into life in my head, in multicolor brightness and full-surround sound, without destroying the knowledge that the same events had never happened. The two versions hovered side by side, linked but separate at the same time.

*Jeez, talk about brain fry.*

"What's wrong?" Nieve stood by my side, one hand on my shoulder. Her light squeeze reassured me.

"I'm okay." I shot her a grateful smile and sat again. "I just had an idea. A guy like the king, or president, doesn't come without his enemies. If we connect with a bunch of Shades who have their own beef—"

"Work with the Shades?" Tristan swiped his hand through the air. "Never."

"Listen before you make up your mind." I punched my palm with a balled fist, formulating the beginnings of a plan while I spoke. "We need an army. More muscle than the twenty or so people that live with you. If we combine forces with disgruntled Shades—"

"I said no." His features hardened. "Nieve? Make her understand."

Nieve shifted in her seat, keeping her gaze glued to her lap. "I don't know. She's making sense to me."

"Are you serious? This is madness. Shades can't be trusted. They'd sooner rat us out than work with us. You know that. Or have you forgotten already?" He tilted his head. "Have you?"

"No, but our way hasn't brought us luck exactly, has it?" She lifted her head. "We should follow Lea's lead on this. She's earned the right to call the shots for once."

My way was the right way. I knew it in my core. "Can you not trust me?"

"I did," he bellowed. "But you failed. It was my mistake to

leave Elonia's fate to you two, but it's not a mistake I'll make again. This time, we'll do it my way."

I shot to my feet. "Hang on. We had a setback. Whether we've failed or not hasn't been decided yet."

"I will not make peace with any Shade." He cleared his throat. "And I command you to stop even suggesting such foolishness."

"Your final word?" I asked, intoning my words into a challenge.

"Yes."

Desperate times required fresh ideas, yet Tristan either had no clear perception of our reality, or he lacked the necessary vision. Where was that warmth he'd shown last night? I thought he'd valued me and what I brought to this team. Had I simply been a bed warmer for the night?

Nieve's bottom lip quivered, but she made no sound. Merely glanced at me with puppy dog eyes.

I nodded at her, and she rose.

At least she had my back. If my plan succeeded, we might not need Tristan anyway.

I rushed toward the door and peered over my shoulder. "Play your mind games with the Shade government for all I care. Continue living in your small, small world and see how you like your future. Nieve and I can do this without you."

He shot to his feet, his eyes wide. "What are you saying?"

"I'm saying I finally understand why there was no prophecy about a dark-haired one, a blonde, and the blonde's pigheaded brother."

# CHAPTER THIRTY-ONE



*"No need for panic. As long as we haven't set off any alarms. Oh, in that case, panic."*

Lea stormed past me, her face flushed. At her current speed, she'd show up within seconds on the monitors that showed the road outside my brother's mansion.

I shot a questioning look at Tristan, who had never looked less royal to me.

His face weary, he waved a hand. "Go with her."

I nodded. At least he didn't make me choose between the two.

Staying with him would have meant familiarity. He'd give orders, and I'd follow. Lea, on the other hand, signified everything crazy about my life. What had begun as stubbornness had developed into full-on determination. She had a plan, and she was going to follow it. Damn the rest of us.

I caught up with her outside on the street. For a few minutes, we walked in silence back the way that brought us here.

When the mansion was out of sight, she slowed her pace. "Who does he think he is?"

"The king?"

"Is that true, though? On the one hand, Tristan gives orders like a king. But did you hear him on the phone? Someone called Mayson is calling the shots."

"A Councilor." I tightened my ponytail before planting my hands inside my jacket pockets. "You know, Tristan's a skilled and seasoned warrior, with a strategic mind that comes along once in a generation."

"You mentioned that before." Lea gave a rock a good kick with her solid boot, whereupon it landed about twenty feet ahead of us. "So why is he playing the minion to a Councilor? Why can't he use his brain and realize that our plan is a good one, given the situation?"

"Tristan's world collapsed, just like mine and yours. He feels lost, and when you're not sure of your place, there is comfort in taking orders." The irony of my words didn't escape me. "As for your plan, joining the Shades to overthrow the Shades is one of the oddest ideas in the history of ideas."

Lea continued to push the rock forward with the inside of her right foot. "At least you're with me."

"Of course I am." I shook off my doubts and hesitation, determined to play the role of a good sidekick. "What now?"

"We need specifics on Galleo's security detail. More than Kieran has given us. I assume the president lives at the White House?"

"What white house?"

"You know, *the* White House?" Lea looked at me as if I'd lost my mind.

"I can't tell if you're joking or citing from one of your science fantasy shows. Galleo lives in the Old Stockade right here in the capital, where he spends most of his days." I pointed vaguely to my left, even though I had no idea where we were in terms of geography.

Could it be that Lea's memory was already impaired?

"Of course." She rubbed her forehead then smiled. "Either way, we need inside knowledge. According to Kirk, gargoyles' memories are immune to the Fall."

"Or we could try—and I can't believe I'm even suggesting it—but maybe the Shade Underground has information on the president's security. Markus used to boast of having contacts deep inside Galleo's inner circle."

"Can we trust him?"

"Not in the least. The only genuine thing about him is his dislike of the president."

"What can I say?" Lea shrugged. "Sometimes Luke Skywalker needs to work with Darth Vader. For the common good, you know."

"Who?"

She gave the rock another deft kick and then peered up. "Sorry. I mean we can't always pick our bowling partners. Occasionally we need to deal with the devil."

"Markus is closer to being like your devil than you know." I chuckled. "He didn't want the Divide to fall, although I'm not so certain of his agenda beyond that."

She sent a wistful look at the field that had swallowed her rock. "How do we find this Markus?"

"This new world is still one giant maze to me. Maybe the gargoyle would have an idea."

"Good idea." She fished out her cell phone and placed her finger on the screen to call the number "Kirk? It's me. Any idea how to get in touch with the Shade Underground?" She chewed her bottom lip. "I know the place. ... Yes, we'll be careful. Oh, the leader's name. Is it still Markus?"

It took a special personality to oppose Galleo, and Markus had this undefinable quality in spades. The thought he might no longer lead the Underground therefore hadn't even occurred to me.

Lea angled her phone's bottom half closer to her mouth. "Thanks, Kirk."

If she truly had the gargoyles on her side, there was hope for humanity yet.

Relying on her knowledge of the area, I hardly paid attention to where we were going. A train took us part of the way, the rest we walked. The people we encountered in and out of town carried sour expressions on their faces. Shade rule had beaten the happiness out of them, and their whispers and sideways glances brought back my paranoia. Would anyone recognize us as Elonian? Would anyone rat us out? Once we'd left the city behind, buildings popped up with less and less frequency, an out-in-the-sticks feel I found attractive. It would be nice to live out here, without being bothered by the Fall or the Divide or a stupid prophecy.

"The Fall of the Divide, my death—none of this is your fault." Lea slid her hands deep into the pockets. "Our defeat was a matter of bad timing and limited information. We did the best with what we had. No one can ask more of us. No one!" Her voice zinged with passion. "Especially not Tristan."

She had a knack for reading my emotions. Unfortunately, she also had a habit of calling me out on them.

I inhaled deeply, catching scents of wet grass, open farmland, and a touch of mulched leaves. In the near distance, the sky turned from off-white into a dark, bluish grey.

"My head knows that this mess isn't our doing. But in here..." I tapped my heart. "It's a different matter. It'll take a minute for me to get my bearing again. To find my place post-prophecy."

"I get that." She peered up at me. "There's something else bothering you, isn't there?"

Gusts of wind tore at our hair. My ponytail kept mine under control, but Lea's face occasionally disappeared behind unruly strands of her locks.

"Yeah." I gave an ambiguous laugh. "It's Kieran. He's got to be up to something, right?"

"I'm finally onboard with the whole Death-to-all-Shades mantra you had going on, but Kieran has saved both our lives." She scooped her hair back behind her ears, where it refused to stay. "The greatest mystery, though, is why he befriended me."

"He says it was curiosity at first. He later tried to tell you about Elonia and Torren, and about the danger you were in, but it didn't work out."

"The pirate speech?" Lea giggled. "I've been wondering what that was about. Oh boy, you should have heard it. *Change is good, Lea. Pirates have adventures.*" She did a bad impression of Kieran's voice. "If that was his attempt to ease me into the whole 'magic exists' chapter of my life, he sucked at it."

"He kissed me." Despite the cool breeze, heat rushed into my face. "Why would he do that, seeing how we're supposed to be enemies?"

"He likes you. I figured that out the moment you two met." She stared up at a large mesh-wire fence that encircled a large building. "Kieran or Markus, if we're going to work with Shades, we must learn to get along. If we cling to old rules of hatred and distrust, we'll only get the same failures. It doesn't take Einstein to work that out."

"I can assure you." I chuckled bleakly. "Elonians working with Shades is a brand new concept."

"Good, that's what we need. Soon, the Fall will take all memories. Once that happens, there will be no one left to fight. We're the last-chance train."

I dropped my head against the onset of rain. "I like your confidence and take-charge attitude. It's comforting."

"Oh, that's not confidence. I'm pissed, I'm hurt, and I'm sad."

Her drive had been evident even during our first training session. What no one suspected was that Lea's stubbornness was greater than death. If anyone was going to return Elonia to me, it was she.

Lea chin-pointed at the large building we were approaching. "This must be the place."

Splitting the shallow valley ahead of us in two, a narrow stream ran past the old farmhouse. A selection of cars and pickup trucks parked out front and between a handful of outbuildings. The fence was eight feet tall, with rolls of barbed wire set on top.

Lea forged ahead without hesitation. Before I'd spied a doorbell, the heavy steel gate opened automatically. Shades in their traditional uniforms patrolled the yard, but let us pass without incident. Clearly, Markus knew we were here.

At the main entrance to the brick house, a Shade gestured for us to enter. A long scar crossed his cheek, as if I needed a reminder of the danger we'd placed ourselves in. Just as I counted off the hundredth reason why I didn't look forward to seeing Markus again, he appeared.

Lea sucked in a breath and glanced at me. I nodded, to indicate that the man, so casually dressed in jeans and a half buttoned shirt, was indeed the leader of the Shade Underground.

What a figure he struck. Rumor had it his ancestors had come from all four corners of the world. His big blue eyes could hark back to the European continent, and whether the warm tone of his skin indicated long-ago African, South American or Asian origins was anyone's guess, but in terms of personality, he was one-hundred percent Shade.

"Angel." He approached me with quick steps and pulled me tight against his chest, forcing my nose against his neck.

A shudder rolled down my spine. Not long ago, he'd blown dark powers into me with a kiss. What did he have in store for me today?

He released me and focused his attention on Lea. "I see you've brought a friend. I can't say I haven't dreamed of this moment."

"If you can get your mind out of the gutter for a second," I said, "I'll introduce you. This is Lea."

"Ah. The famous Lea. First, a point of order. Two Elonians walking around without their luster on show. I'd be remiss if I didn't report you to the government."

"Nieve never mentioned you were such a riot." Lea's smile was polite. "But we're on the clock."

"Oooh, look at mini-Nieve. She's a tough one, isn't she?" He winked at me. "Of course, my dear. If you'd like to follow me."

He led us into the bedroom. *So far, so predictable.*

The room offered enough space for my elite team of warriors to perform their morning *kakei* ritual, in which swords were broken, repaired, and thrown. Despite the sparse furniture, the sumptuous Markus feel sat in every detail, from the gold penholder on a narrow cabinet to the huge fireplace, in which a crackling fire sprung to life as he walked past. The fibers of the plush carpet parted like the Red Sea before his bare feet. Since his Shade tricks rarely impressed me, they were most likely designed to awe Lea.

I shook my head at her so that she'd keep any surprise to herself. He didn't need encouragement.

Subtle lighting from concealed lamps in the corners of the room focused my gaze at where I assumed a window had existed in the building's previous incarnation. In this life, the spot was covered by a painting of Angelic creatures in compromising positions.

"So, Angel. About that plan of yours to find the other chosen

Spark and prevent the Divide's destruction." He dropped into a chaise longue, draped his arms along the backrest, and crossed his legs. "How's that going?"

He pointed toward his bed, motioning us to take a seat.

My steps faltered and the room spun. The ground twisted beneath my boots, immobilizing me. Yet these things happened only in my head. In reality, Lea sat at the edge of the bed, her eyebrows arched. She probably expected me to provide context that would satisfy her curiosity about our host, but how could I? Markus defied explanation.

One way or another, she needed help dealing with him and his machinations.

On woozy legs, I approached her, but didn't take a seat. I was lucky Markus didn't possess the gift of reading other people's thoughts. If he'd caught on to my minor panic attack, he'd have had me sprawled on the mattress minutes ago, fawning over me with pretend sympathy.

"How about for once we spare ourselves the games and get right to it?" Not a flutter in my voice, not a creak. The control over my emotions, absent since the Shades' knives first sliced into me, was flowing back into my spine. "We need your help, but there will be no power play, no manipulation, no tricks. If that's not good enough for you, we'll leave and look for support elsewhere."

"My, my. So forceful." His fingers brushed over his hairless torso under a suddenly entirely unbuttoned shirt. "Makes a guy go all gooey."

Before I fired my next salvo, Lea shifted and coughed.

"I hate to interrupt..." She wiggled her hand between him and me. "...*this*, but how about you drop the act?" She glared at his bared chest. "And button up, for heaven's sake, at least while you have company. What the hell's wrong with you?"

His arm dropped to his lap, and he gaped at Lea.

My neck tensed, went icy cold. We were surrounded by enemies, and the building had no windows. Worse, at least twenty guards stood between us and the nearest ray of sunlight. This wasn't the right moment for her infamous lack of tact.

Markus's eyes narrowed, then he tipped his head and let rip a deep roar of laughter.

I smiled, didn't dare breathe, waiting for his call to have his bodyguards skewer us like barbecued pork.

It didn't come.

His shoulders heaved, and he lifted his sleeve to dry his eyes.

Lea, meanwhile, tapped the back of her wrist, the universal sign for *get a move on*.

"No offense, Angel." Markus spewed between fits of breathy coughs. "I think I've fallen in love with your friend here."

"I'm sure she's thrilled by your attention." Yet I had no idea if his interest in Lea would help or hinder our cause.

A woman in a wrapped kimono-style dress entered the room and approached him, but not without shooting eye-daggers at us. She leaned over Markus to whisper in his ear, allowing her dress to fall open at the top. Like most Touched, she wasn't better endowed than me, but she'd cupped her goods in a red lace bra which she put on proud display.

Markus, however, had no patience for her lovely presents, his focus entirely on us. He flicked his arm at her to leave and rose. "We have another visitor. If I'd known there was going to be a party, I'd have dressed for the occasion."

The woman arranged her deep V-neck collar and left the room, head held high.

"So you don't get dressed unless there's a party?" Lea asked.

Markus smirked. "Your interest in my personal habits is flattering. Once the festivities are over, how about we discuss me in more private surroundings?"

Lea's lips twitched into the general shape of a smile, but it was fleeting enough not to boost his ego.

Steps from the corridor sounded, and Kieran entered.

"Markus." He walked up to our host, his gait confident.

My heart wiggled in my chest, urging me to run toward him, yet I stood still as lamppost. Had he been following me? If so, should I be thrilled or annoyed?

Markus got to his feet and clasped Kieran's outstretched hand between his palms like a practiced politician. "My lord, what an honor. What brings you to my humble refuge?"

The heavy beat of wings trailed Kieran, and the gargoyle flew in, making a beeline for Lea. That explained it. The gargoyle had led Kieran to us.

"How ya doing, kid?" The small creature waved. "Glad you're not dead."

"Lea?" Kieran's face went slack, and he gasped for air. "Is that you?"

She rose, pushed her hands into her pockets and raised her shoulders. "In the flesh."

In three quick strides he'd circled around Markus and hugged her to his chest.

She stiffened, but didn't shove him off.

When he released her, he gave her a puzzled look. "I don't understand. My brothers told me you were dead. What happened?"

"I was. It's complicated." She narrowed her eyes. "Before we say anything else, there is one thing I need to know from you. How are you involved in your father's affairs?"

His gaze darkened, a look I'd seen on him before.

"Simple question," she said.

"And here's one answer for you. I'm not involved." He folded his arms in front of his chest. "I thought Nieve would have told you."

"She did. Just wanted to hear it from you."

Markus pointed from Kieran to Lea. "I take it you know my beloved?"

"Yes, we've met." Kieran's voice held a tinge of impatience. "Your beloved?"

"Unless you've already laid claim to her, my lord? I don't want to tread on anyone's tootsies."

Kieran sputtered a throaty laugh and glanced at me. "My personal interest lies elsewhere."

Markus followed his gaze and nodded his understanding.

If I'd known being considered an ordinary woman rather than a warrior would make me feel like a juicy steak, I'd never have wished for it. Now that the moment had arrived, I was overcome by the desire to whack both men over the head with my hanbo. But Markus was still a dangerous beast, and I wouldn't give Kieran the satisfaction of seeing me lose my temper.

"By all means, lay claim to Lea." Kieran bowed to the other Shade. "That's a show I don't want to miss. I've seen her kick ass, and I have thought in the past that yours would benefit from that particular treatment, Markus. No offense."

Markus raised his arms. "None taken."

"Now, I believe there's a reason the two most famous Sparks have come to seek your counsel, and I for one am dying to hear it." Kieran rocked back and forth on his heels, waiting with obvious interest.

Lea sat back on the edge of Markus's bed. "I guess I have to trust them, don't I?"

"That was your plan," I whispered loudly. "Trusting Shades. Remember?"

"Yeah." She blew a lock out of her face. "Fine. I can do that."

Kirk took a seat on Lea's lap, took off his ridiculous hat, and dabbed a pointed ear between her breasts, which were squished inside her dark green jacket.

"What the frak are you doing?" she squealed.

He peered up with one eye. "It's gargoyle tradition. A sign of respect."

She leaned back on her hands and robbed him of the opportunity to honor her more. "As I was about to say, my thinking is Kieran's father, the former Shade king, current President of the United States, and continuous pain in my neck, must know how to undo the Fall."

"What makes you think that?" Markus gestured for Kieran to sit on the chair his personal attendant had provided.

Lea made a thoughtful face. "He strikes me as a person who'd have a backup plan. He couldn't know for sure Derinda would hold up her end of the bargain."

"Derinda?" Kieran leaned forward on his chair. "What does she have to do with this?"

"Oh, that." Lea fidgeted with the bed sheets. "Derinda told Galleo how to make the Divide fall and made him ruler."

"In exchange for?" he asked.

"Me." She pointed at herself. "It's a long story."

"No, I get it." Kieran's mouth twitched. "Shit. The whole thing was about your blood, wasn't it? In the original spell, it was Derinda's and Orrin's blood contributions in perfect equilibrium that set up the Divide." He tugged on his chin. "In reverse, the Divide fell because *Orrin's* blood was spilled through Lea's veins, causing an imbalance. The Divide collapsed."

"You knew about Orrin being Lea's father?" I rubbed my temples with my fingertips.

"I've recently found out." Kieran flexed his arms. "But let's get back to the discussion about reinstating the Divide." He swiveled in his seat to face Lea. "You could be right about my father. Every plan of his has an out."

"Good." Her face brightened. "I say, let's go bag the guy and ask him."

"Smart thinkin', kid." The gargoyle fluttered its wings and landed back on Lea's legs. "Knew ya were the one. Didn't I tell ya?" His gaze swiveled to Kieran.

"You did mention it." He hid a grin behind his hand. "Repeatedly."

"Just a second." Markus raised a finger. "Where do you intend to *bag* him? His office in the city is too protected, with dozens of guards. That leaves his commute home and the Old Stockade."

"Remind me." Lea glanced at me. "The Old Stockade is where he lives, right?"

I frowned. "Well, yes."

She patted the gargoyle's head. "The king won't be expecting an attack right inside the Death Star. From his point of view, Shades wouldn't dare challenge him, and the Elonians don't have the numbers or the *cojones* to pose any real danger. Especially not in a place I assume has no windows and no access to natural light. We'll launch the attack during the day to even the odds."

Seemingly captivated by her madcap plan, Kirk nodded at her every word.

"I have prided myself of forming the unofficial opposition to Galleo, but I've never attacked him outright." Markus smoothed the fabric of his slacks and settled deeper into his seat. "Assuming any of what you say is possible, I don't know why you'd need me."

Lea raised her eyebrows like a woman about to repeat herself for the tenth time. "Manpower."

"If it's manpower you need, I'm more than happy to chip in."

Kieran stirred. "I, too, have a handful of people loyal to me. But even if we take out the protection detail, my father is powerful in his own right."

"You and Markus together might match his powers. Plus, Nieve and I will be the little daytime surprise, all amped up on solar energy."

"You make it sound so easy." Markus's voice was rough.

Quite possibly I'd caught my first glimpse of the real him, without the layers of seduction and the mind games that covered his persona.

"It won't be. It's dangerous, probably foolhardy, most likely fatal." Lea's jawline tautened. A small dimple appeared above her nose. "But we've run out of options. I don't know how often I can say this. If you're happy with this world, I'm asking the wrong people. But if you want the old ways back, as imperfect as they were, we must strike before all memories have been overwritten. We must strike tomorrow, not three weeks down the line."

"Still…" Markus bit his lip.

"I've thought this through." She gave us all a grim look. "But if anyone has a better idea, please, tell me." She leaned back further onto her forearms and stared at the ceiling. "Otherwise, that's the plan, guys."

Her words sank deep into my consciousness, bringing with them sickening unease. I'd hoped for a mind-bogglingly fiendish scheme that would guarantee success and, *snap*, we'd be back in the world-that-should-be.

But this? By the Old Ones, it was barely a plan.

"I know you're said to be this great hero, but this is madness." Markus stood and jammed his fists into his pockets. "Then again, a hero's madness might just do it. Okay. I'll give you my men on one condition."

There was the Markus I knew. "What?" I asked.

He anchored his gaze on me. "If the Divide is reinstated, I want permanent, unfettered access to the Gate."

"You're making such demands now?" Heat settled on my cheeks, in my neck. Access to the Gate meant power. Too much power. "I cannot make such a promise on behalf of the king."

"I believe you can. A little fairy told me that you and the king are close."

I didn't respond to Kieran's questioning look. "Tristan is never going to agree."

"That's why I want you to swear this to me not in his name, but in the name of the Elonian Crown." Markus crossed his arms. "Just in case that king of yours tries to escape your promise by abdicating. I also want your personal assurance you will fight for my share of the Gate. To the death, if necessary."

Slice it, this was a bad, bad idea. Handing over the keys to the Gate would be treason. My stomach rebounded, and I swallowed hard. "Why do you want the Gate so badly anyway?"

"Let that be my concern."

Lea shrugged. "I say go for it."

I closed my eyes. Tristan would have me for breakfast if I conceded to Markus's terms. Then again, any chance of the plan succeeding depended on Markus's participation. "Agreed."

"Then let's strap one on. It's time to jam." He spun on his heels and hurried out of the room.

Lea shook her head, amused. "I get why you and I would have to strap one on, but he isn't coming out too well in that, is he?"

"He may have been talking about a weapon." I sounded doubtful, even to myself.

Kirk rearranged his hat, flapped his wings, and lifted himself off Lea's lap. "My kind have been the Shades' puppets for too long. You gotta let me help."

"Gladly." Lea rubbed his head. "Thank you, my friend."

"It's a bold plan." Kieran's words tiptoed across the room as if afraid to be overheard.

"It's a Hail Mary, before everybody's brain is too fried to think of a better plan. Either you're in or you're not, and you have to decide right now." Lea exhaled loudly. "I promise you, we'll try not to harm him."

"That's not the issue." He stretched out his legs and averted his head. "Believe me."

"She's right." I crossed the distance to his chair and laid my hand on his shoulder. "This isn't a world I want to live in, and it's not a world I can be happy in. We have to try."

"What about your king?" His mouth and jaw were sharp like an eagle's. Only his eyes held the kindness I craved, the kindness that stole my breath and sometimes made me forget centuries of hatred. "Where does *Tristan* stand on all this?"

By the way he'd mangled my brother's name, Kieran might be jealous. Maybe Lea was right, and he did like me.

I crouched by his side. "Tristan has declined his help, mainly because it would mean working with Shades."

"You don't mind all of a sudden? Working with Shades?" His fingers sought a strand of my hair and tucked it behind my ear, sending shivers of need down my spine.

"Let's say my horizons have broadened over the past couple of weeks." I inclined my head toward Lea and was glad to see her shoot me an almost imperceptible nod.

Kieran brushed his knuckles over my cheek for a moment then withdrew and stood. "In that case, I'll make a few calls."

# CHAPTER THIRTY-TWO



*"Twice now I've escaped you. Either you're getting careless, or I'm just that good."*

The gurgling stream split the moon's reflection into a thousand slivers of light, shimmying and dancing on the water like tiny twinkling fairies. Despite the brisk breeze, the birches lining the banks clung to their leaves as if letting go meant losing themselves.

Fallon's weight tired my hand, yet, for once, holding my dagger didn't settle my nerves. Tomorrow, we would attack the Shade king.

Strike that.

We'd attack the frigging President of the United States. Not a sentence I ever thought I'd say and mean. A few months ago, I was a geeky girl with a decent but uneventful future ahead of me, whose few accomplishments included a great degree and a soccer participation medal from my kindergarten days.

Then, for a fleeting moment, it looked like I'd won the lottery. I'd become a magic-wielding superstar, got a bunch of new friends, and even landed a guy who set my core on fire.

Most of all, I'd had a purpose. I was one of the chosen ones, with indefinable strength and ability to overcome any odds.

I wanted it all back—the certainty, the future, every little crumb of my broken dream.

The clear air didn't clear my head nor did the serene surroundings calm my spirit. This wasn't going to be a mere fight. We were planning a full-blown, first-come-first-die battle.

I tightened my fist around Fallon's cool, silvery handle, thumb and index finger pressed against the curved cross-guard. Unfortunately, the smooth metal gave me no reassurance. Its magical energy was gone. If its power didn't return in time, the Shades would be facing plain little ol' me. Hardly a prospect to make them faint with fear.

"It's cold." Kieran crunched across the graveled driveway. His words left white clouds in the air. "You should come inside."

"Is it always like this before a fight?"

"Nausea, headache, and vertigo? Yep. It's what they call the joy of war."

"Fantastic. Nieve's asleep?"

"Yes. I have no idea how she does it."

"She used to be the most hard-core person I ever met." I sheathed my dagger. "I worry about her."

"You shouldn't." He positioned himself next to me, his side resting against the wall of Markus's farmhouse, and looked out into the darkness. "She's misplaced her confidence. Happens to the best of us after a setback. But her skills and determination are still with her, just buried under a heap of grief. You're not the only one who's had to give up her innocence."

"She's also losing her memory." I stared at my palm, which still carried the impressions Fallon's handle had left in my skin. "Or I my sanity, but I'm certain Seattle isn't supposed to be the capital of the United States. Still, there it sits in my brain, this fake history of our fake capital I'd fake learned in fake college, right alongside the correct but obsolete information of how Washington had become the seat of our government."

"That's the advantage, or curse, of you being an Old One's offspring." Kieran scooted closer, providing a measure of warmth. "Nieve's memory lapses started a few days ago, even before you came back. I don't think she's aware."

"Maybe her ignorance is a blessing. My brain plays host to a number of contradictory memories, and even though I can distinguish real from false, I'm freaked to all hell."

Drawing my fists into my sleeves to protect them against the cold, I turned to face Kieran, not least to better catch his body heat before it dissipated into the night. "Tell me if it's getting too personal, but what exactly is going on between you and her?"

"Damned if I know. She's hung up on the whole Torren-Spark animosity."

"Yeah, her loyalties are all messed up. You're on our side, which is more than I can say for her brother."

His head jerked up. "I didn't know she had a brother."

I gave him a sideways look. Elonians and their secrets. When would they learn?

Whatever Nieve's reason, I wasn't going to betray her confidence. Kieran was an okay dude, but Nieve was my girl. Chicks before dicks. That was the unwritten law.

"I'm glad we're all working together, though. It's reassuring somehow." My wistful tone startled me back into determination. "What's the deal with Markus, by the way?"

"Markus is an odd beast. He doesn't break promises unless he can wiggle his way out on account of a technicality. He's like a lawyer that way. Ambitious, too, with his own plans for our people. The reason my father hasn't killed him is because of his popularity. At least before the Fall. Who knows how much support he still commands in this new world."

I rolled my shoulders, loosening the muscles. "What's his goal? Clearly he wants to reinstate the Divide, but then what?"

"Not a clue. He says he wants to steer our people in a different direction, but I don't see him as a true leader."

"If your father died while you're the crown prince, would Markus throw his weight behind you?"

"I doubt it. And for the record, I'm only the crown prince because my father hasn't yet decided which of my brothers is the best replacement." Kieran scratched his neck before folding his hands under his arms. "Maybe he fears that as soon as he announces his official heir, his life will be at risk. That comes from raising your kids to be piranhas."

"You once told me your father wanted a military career for you." I laughed without humor. "Good joke."

"I thought so at the time." He patted my shoulder. "Come on, it's cold. Only a couple of hours until sunrise. You should try to get some sleep."

"I will. Good night." I nodded him goodbye and turned my gaze back to the stream.

When I mentioned earlier that Derinda had played a role in the Fall, Kieran had turned as white as a hospital wall. Did he know something about his father's ritual he hadn't shared with the rest of us? Something that could affect our success? Or was he merely concerned about standing up to his father for once?

Kieran wasn't the only question mark in this operation. Over the few hours I'd spent with Markus, I'd gained little insight into what made him tick. His innuendos and mind games were a cheap facade, of that I was sure, but the man beneath remained a mystery.

No, my trusted allies would not give me the peace of mind I needed to get any sleep.

After ingesting several gallons of coffee, I sat in Markus's kitchen, staring at our map one last time. The prison cell that was to hold our royal guest had been reinforced with magic from Kieran's and Nieve's respective boxes of magic tricks.

Since I was a big picture kind of gal, I'd left the finer details of our strategy up to the men. Markus would leave the bulk of his forces at the farmhouse, but still managed to rally thirty men and women for the assault, Kieran another twenty. On paper, taking care of the king's forty guards should be a cinch.

By rights, Tristan should have joined us. His disappointment in our failure to prevent the Fall was yesterday's news. Any king worth his salt should have been able to look ahead and recognize the value of my plan. Had my biological mother set a bad example to his former royal champion? Whatever it was that stopped him from greatness, at least Nieve was ready to step up. No one wanted a quiet life more than her, and yet she was here, prepared to risk her life—while trying her best not to swoon over Kieran.

Markus, for his part, had amped up his efforts to seduce me. His compliments and insinuations had an effect on me, no doubt, but probably not in the way in which he intended. If pushed, I'd admit to finding him cute, but also insecure, spoiled, and petulant.

The phone on the table vibrated. That could mean only one thing. Turning slow motion into a new sport, I accepted the call.

"Hey, kid." Kirk's scratchy voice rattled through the speaker. "'s that you?"

"It's me."

"Right. Hold on to ya hat, doll, 'cos the wackiness is about to begin. King's just gone off to give a speech at some rally. That means it's time to prep. Meet me outside the back gate, 'kay?"

"Thanks. We'll be there in twenty." I hung up and placed the phone in my lap to hide my shaking hands. My mouth was too dry to give orders to the faces staring my way.

Markus rose and turned to his followers that had joined us in the kitchen. "You heard her. Saddle up, guys."

A manic five minutes later, everyone spilled into the vans we were using for transport. Markus's vehicle took the lead. Nieve and I hitched a ride with Kieran.

The drive to the Old Stockade nearly killed me. The coffee, my nerves, the shaking car, all contributed to an almost unbearable pressure against my bladder. How come James Bond never obsessed about bathroom breaks? If I were a real hero, I'd be focused on the plan, running through the variables in my mind until I glowed with self-belief.

Yet the lump swelling at the top of my lungs wasn't as much a sign of confidence as of abject terror.

Nieve had cozied up to Kieran and spared me only an occasional *buck-up* smile. Kieran, for his part, patted her hand, her knee, her arm; basically wiggling about like a nervous hummingbird. Those were the two warriors I was counting on to have my back.

What could possibly go wrong?

The vans stopped a quarter of a mile away from the remotely situated estate and parked behind trees and bushes to avoid arousing suspicion. I slid open the door a fraction and Kirk flew in, landing on my lap. His earthen scent mingled with the stink of nicotine, yet despite that, he'd fit right in with the assortment of stuffed toys in my bedroom.

"Hang on." I called Markus's cell and put our conversation on loudspeaker. "Okay. What have you found out, Kirk?"

"There's four men on the balcony at the back, another four at the front." Kirk leaned his solid head against my chest again.

All this "honoring" was beginning to carry the stench of sexual harassment.

He ran through the guards' precise locations in quick succession. When he'd finished, he glanced up, probably seeking approval. I figured using my breasts as a pillow was reward enough.

"My men are ready," Markus said from the other end of the line. "We'll leave as soon as you hang up."

"Good luck," I whispered.

"To us all." He ended the call.

This was happening. Now would be the perfect time to call my parents and angle for their support, the words that promised that everything would work out.

Thanks to Galleo, that wasn't going to happen.

I pushed Kirk off me and ripped open the van door. "Let's go."

Kieran got out first, his eyes ringed by dark lines. Out of all of us, he was taking the greatest risk.

"See you soon," he whispered and wandered off to brief the rest of his men.

"What about me?" Kirk waddled after me.

I crouched down to near-eye level. "You get started on the electrics. You're our secret ace."

He nodded as if his importance in our plan was too obvious to require further explanation.

I gifted him with what I feared might be my only smile of the day and turned to Nieve. "Are you ready, too?"

"As I'll ever be. I mean, we're due some luck, right?"

If only luck worked that way.

The Old Stockade impressed in terms of both size and architecture. Even though its name suggested a building made from wood, the reality was the opposite. Roman-style beams supported a second floor much larger than the first, and the rooftop balcony overlooked lush grounds. Nieve and I positioned ourselves by the rear gate. Our plan was to infiltrate the Old Stockade while the president was out, and incapacitate the guards. On his return, we'd pick off his personal protection detail one by one, without anyone calling for help.

Kirk was in charge of cutting through the power lines to stop any electronic alarm system that might be in place.

I gnawed on the hem of my sleeve and avoided the expectant glances from Kieran's men who were whispering spells and working on the stone columns anchoring the metal gate. How had I ended up in charge? Nieve was the royal champion, Markus the leader of the Underground, and Kieran the crown prince. And I? I was Newbie McGrenhorn, a nobody plucked from obscurity with only failure on my résumé. Was it too late to pack my stuff and mosey on home?

A blast rang out from the other side of the Old Stockade, and a cloud of ash billowed up high above the estate. Shade magic wasn't subtle, yet Markus had reassured me that, after the initial assault, his men would have everything back in place. We didn't want to alert the king when he got home.

Kieran brushed his hand over Nieve's shoulder and signaled his men to do their part. One of them, I forgot his name, raised his arms. Multiple threads of gray tendrils spread from his fingers. The ribbons wrapped around the rocks and yanked, collapsing the columns, and with them, the gate. Skillfully done, with a minimum of noise. For now, we wanted the king's guards to focus on the front of the property, where Markus's forces outnumbered them.

Kieran raised a fist and advanced, and his men and women followed. Within seconds, they'd disappeared among the dense bushes and shrubbery surrounding the building. Once the estate was secured and returned to its original state, Kieran's men would hide nearby, ready to take care of Galleo's security detail and to cut off any escape.

Nieve and I stayed behind for now.

The flaps of heavy wings announced Kirk's arrival.

"Hey, kid," he said, ignoring Nieve. "Electrics are outta action. So's the phones. The guards Galleo left behind are putting up a fight but Markus is in control. It'll be over in a jiff." His voice boomed with pride as if victory was assured and all down to him. The only thing missing was for him to finish his speech with an evil *mwa-ha-ha-ha*.

"I guess that's our cue." I slapped Nieve's shoulder. "Come on then. I hear meeting the president's quite the honor."

We drew our weapons and sneaked through the undergrowth toward the building, with Kirk scouting the area ahead. Although our Shade allies were busy subduing the guards, one or two of the president's men might have been overlooked and were now—

A blur charged from my left, too fast for me to react. My dagger went flying, while I nearly lost my balance.

But Nieve was ready.

The Shade attacker gave a pained gasp before I even registered her hanbo's lightning-fast blow to the neck. Her follow-up kick threw him onto the ground.

I picked up my dagger.

Nieve twirled her stick and plunged its end into the fallen guard. His leather tunic was no protection against the pointy end of the hanbo, and he melted into the Earth.

Kieran had been right. Nieve just needed to fight one or two bad guys to regain her confidence.

"Excellent reflexes," I whispered.

"I couldn't let you die again, could I?" She gave a broad smile. "Thanks. Ready?"

She touched her fist to her heart. "Always."

After I'd tasked Kirk with patrolling the grounds, Nieve and I tiptoed into the building, up the stairs, where we let ourselves into the king's private quarter, a space with more gold and sparkle than Buckingham Palace. Here, we positioned ourselves on opposite sides of the room.

I squatted under a heavy wooden desk in complete darkness, in effect, a high-suspense version of the games of hide and seek I used to play with my father. Except this was no game, and we certainly weren't in my childhood home.

Any minute now the king would walk into the spacious room. How long would it take him to detect my breathing, or hear my thumping heart? I gave myself a mental kick. Focusing on my inevitable demise wasn't the best way to stay positive.

My line of sight into the main of the room was cut off, but I knew the positions of the other three. Nieve crouched in an alcove while Markus hid all the way over in the adjoining bedroom. Kieran, camped out on the sofa, would involve his father in meaningless chitchat, and Markus would sneak up from behind and trap the king with a body cuff.

Of course, Nieve and Kieran had been warriors long enough to know plan A never worked out, so we'd wisely prepared plans B and C.

A sound from the corridor caught my ear.

"I can hear something," I whispered.

"Shush." Kieran warned.

Footsteps approached the door. More than one person.

My mind feverishly rummaged for the scenario involving multiple targets. There wasn't one. Kieran would have to improvise.

The door opened and someone stepped inside.

"Kieran," a deep, pleasant voice said. "How did you get in here?"

"Your security is lax. I just walked in. How are you, father?"

"Fromer, Salander, leave me and your brother alone."

Kieran's brothers were another factor we hadn't included in

our calculations. Still, we had the upper hand in terms of numbers.

"He's a traitor," Fromer or Salander said.

"We'll see." Galleo's voice still held the smooth lilt I remembered from the day he killed me. "He is here now. Maybe he's ready to rejoin us. Go."

"As you wish," the same brother mumbled. The footsteps faded and the door closed.

"To answer your question, I'm doing well," the king said. "I'd be doing better if a certain son of mine was standing by my side during the changeover."

"You know how I feel," Kieran said.

"Yes, you've made that clear, but a father can hope, can't he?"

A *clink* drifted into my ears, followed by the sound of liquid pouring into a glass.

The king swallowed and clicked his tongue. "Now. If you're not here to join the cause, why did you come?"

Slow steps traversed the room. Kieran was supposed to distract him, but so far, he'd let his father do most of the talking. Hopefully Galleo's words didn't sway his resolve.

"I've been meaning to talk to you for a while, but my brothers shield you well." Kieran's tone remained firm. "I'm here because I want to talk to you about my mother."

"What's there to say?"

This wasn't supposed to be therapy for Kieran, but a quick kidnap. Had he not read the playbook at all?

Kieran took an audible breath. "You're working with her. How did you manage that?"

"What's that supposed to mean?" Galleo asked.

"I know how I was conceived. I know everything now. You..." Kieran's voice broke. "You sick bastard."

"Son." Galleo's voice had lost its certitude. He cleared his throat. "That thing between your mother and me is ancient history. She got something out of our deal, too. I've given her my word that you will be my legitimate successor despite your obvious distaste for my policies. Just don't tell your brothers. They already suspect you're my favorite."

Kieran had gone completely off-script. Why wasn't Galleo cuffed yet?

As if he'd read my mind, Markus charged into the room. "Now."

I scrambled from behind the desk, readying both the air and my dagger. Nieve was already behind Galleo, her hanbo pressed against his throat.

The old man, held stiffly in place by the metal cuff Markus had placed, screamed for his guards, his black chin beard shaking with the vibrations. No one came to his aid.

"You abused my mother." Kieran's eyes darted across his father's face. "There is something so twisted in you…"

"Son. You're not thinking clearly."

"You sent people to kill Lea, an innocent, while she was in my care, and placed a bounty on Nieve's head, even after you discovered how I felt about her." With his knife in his hand, Kieran approached his father. "You take advantage of our people; kill, torture and maim for pleasure. You're a monster."

"Where is this coming from?" the king shouted. "Someone has been feeding you lies."

"We got this, Kieran." I nudged him before addressing Galleo, my shoulders squared and my chin high. "Nice to see you again."

"I killed you." The old man jerked his head. "You can't be here."

"You think death is going to stop me? But where are my manners? This." I pointed at Nieve. "Is Nieve, the Spark champion."

"You betray your own flesh and blood?" He looked from Nieve to his son then spat at him. "We're family, son."

"Family?" Kieran's hand shook almost as badly as his mouth twitched.

"I tried to be patient with you." Galleo's face lost its smooth kindness as he bared his lips. "You want to kill me? Go ahead. You have a knife. What are you waiting for?"

Kieran stared at his blade.

"No one's killing anyone." I chuckled, but inched aside, out of Kieran's way.

"You can't do it, you whiney son of a bitch, can you?" Galleo laughed. "You have the talent and the power to take what you want. You could take the reign from me right now, son. But you hide from it, like a sniveling mama's boy."

"Yeah." Kieran lowered his knife an inch, then embedded it deep in the king's heart. "Are you happy now?"

My lungs stopped moving. What movie had I ended up in? Had someone changed the plan and forgot to tell me?

Galleo sagged toward his son, who caught his body before dropping it onto the carpet.

"What the hell just happened?" Markus knelt beside the limp body, feeling for a pulse on the old man's neck. "We needed to question him."

Nieve's face confirmed she was as much in the dark as me.

Every muscle in my body tensed while my eyes made efforts to convince my brain of what just occurred.

Kieran retrieved his knife from his father's corpse, mumbled something, and then ran his sleeve over his eyes.

Galleo melted through the beige carpet into the cold stone beneath.

With him went my last hope of seeing my parents again.

"What. Did. You. Do?" My voice rattled like a steam pipe seconds before bursting.

Kieran replaced the blade in his sheath, his movement slow and robotic.

Finally he met our accusing stares, his cheeks stained with tears. "He'll never hurt anyone ever again."

"He was our only chance." I ground my teeth and leaned forward. "I can't believe you did that."

I walked to one end of the room and smacked the wall with my fists. "Damn."

Another hug from my mother, another smile from my dad. What right did Kieran have to take these things from me? Take hope from me? I rushed back, ready to punch the tears off his face. At the last second, I sailed past him and kicked a chair instead.

Galleo's life meant nothing to me. The bastard had killed me, after all. But I needed what was in his brain. After the interrogation, Kieran could have killed him any which way he wanted. Hell, I'd have provided the weapons. Cheered him on. Baked him a fucking cake to thank him.

*After* the interrogation.

How was I going to get my family back now?

Kieran blew his nose, straightened his back.

Had I seriously considered that man a friend? A chill raised the hairs on my arms. Out of nowhere, sparks bright as fireworks flew over our heads. What the hell?

No. They didn't come out of *nowhere*.

They flowed out of *me*.

Energy jetted from my hand straight into Kieran's stomach. His body spun through the air into the far wall. I gaped. His head slammed against the ceiling, ramming his chin into his chest. With a dull moan, he dropped to the floor.

Nieve cried out and sprinted to his side.

He lay with his arms outstretched, no longer moving.

She sent me a scolding look. "Be careful. You have blood of the Old Ones in your veins."

Tristan had often commented on how easily I'd taken to magic, but this level of power had never been at my fingertips. Yet it was difficult to deny the glow that bathed my hand.

Kieran stirred. He lifted himself onto his arms then his knees and targeted me with an icy glare. "Don't try that again."

Why wasn't he crying anymore? Who gave him permission to even speak?

"You want to give me orders?" I flicked my wrist. "From boy prince to almighty king in sixty seconds, eh? Like father, like son." Once again, energy sizzled through the air, finding the quickest path to his body.

It swooped him up, his mouth and eyes rounded into big Os. It wasn't enough. Where was his apology? His admission that he'd wrecked my plan, destroyed my life?

Kieran turned his face toward me, his fingers dangling as if reaching for the floor.

"You want more?" I edged closer. "There's plenty left."

I wasn't tired in the least. This magic didn't come from the sun or from the darkness. It came from inside me. My body was alight with it.

"I don't want to hurt you," he whispered.

I stared at the traitor, my heart pounding in my ears. Was he mocking me? How could he possibly inflict more pain on me than he already had?

"You won't get the chance to hurt me again." I swished my hand, as if I'd been punishing people with my powers all my life.

Kieran's head smacked into the ceiling again, causing him to let out a roar of pain.

"Stop it," Nieve shouted. "Please."

Hovering six feet up, his gaze slowly focused. As fast as

lightning, a new wave of sparks surrounded him—but I hadn't sent them.

They sprayed from *his* hands, *his* skin, *his* eyes.

It couldn't be. Unless… I gulped as I put the pieces together. Galleo had worked with Kieran's mother—Derinda.

Why hadn't I paid better attention? Only last night he'd casually mentioned that Orrin's blood protected me from the Fall's changes. He'd known I was immune, because he was, too. Because, like me, he was the child of an Old One.

"Derinda, the woman who wants me dead, is your mother?" I asked. "And the man who actually killed me is your father. Oh my God. We trusted you!"

"It's not—" he shouted.

"Now your path to the throne is clear, and we idiots helped you." I lifted my arm, maybe to gesture, maybe to prepare another beam of magic.

"Stop it already." He hurled a jet of energy across the room.

I didn't have time to dodge the glittering bolt, and its force hit me in the chest, catapulting me back. I bounced off the wall and plummeted onto the carpet, my angled arms absorbing some of the impact.

"You want to play, pal?" I sat up, blood trickling from my mouth. "Let's play."

The whole room, every oxygen molecule above, and every rock below brimmed with the potential to be used by me.

"Is anyone going to tell me what the slice is going on?" Nieve moved toward Kieran, who was still suspended at the ceiling.

"He betrayed us." I brought the foundation up to trap her feet. This was between me and him. She'd only get in the way.

"Are you kidding?" she shouted.

Kieran lowered himself gracefully to the ground, where he took position behind her.

Coward. He knew I'd never hurt her.

"I'm with Nieve." Markus emerged from his hiding place and helped me up from the floor. "I want an explanation."

"We're caught between two Old Ones that don't share a single brain cell between them." Nieve's voice sounded unnaturally high. "Can you two stop now? We need to talk about what happened."

The tremble in her voice shook me back into reality. Despite everything he'd done. I didn't want to kill Kieran. Not yet. Maybe, once he'd crowned himself the new king, or president, then I'd take a new swing at him. Right now, I simply didn't have the stomach for it.

"Go." I pointed a finger to the door. "Before I do kill you."

He brandished his knife and grabbed Nieve's arm. "Come on."

"You don't need her." My heart leaped into my throat. "I told you. I'm letting you go."

Nieve's lips twitched, her skin paled. She looked utterly forlorn. Why wasn't she using her fancy fighting skills to tear herself free? Could the memory of the old knife wound still paralyze her how?

"Don't follow us." Kieran's words were pure threat, but his tone held fear.

With barely a nod at the ground, he freed Nieve's feet, and they inched backward out of the room.

His warning rooted me to the spot.

Damn. He knew I wouldn't put her life at risk.

Their footsteps faded.

I rubbed my forehead. Kieran hadn't held the knife to Nieve's throat. Had she left with him to protect herself or me from his powers? Or had the appetite for the fight deserted her?

The Old Stockade lay quiet. Markus slumped against a wall and gasped for air, his expression pained, as if the world had just backhanded him.

Me? I had little time for his drama. Once again my hesitation had come back to bite me in the ass. I should have ended Kieran when I'd had the chance. What good was nostalgia over a lost friendship if it cost me another one?

"What do we do now?" Markus asked.

"Now?" I slowly lifted my gaze to him. "Now we go home and find a way for me to kill that friend-napping son of a bitch."

# CHAPTER THIRTY-THREE



*"Why don't you leave her alone and start beating on someone half your size?"*

Kieran's men covered our retreat against a befuddled group of Markus's supporters. We took one of the vans and headed out of town. Kieran hardly paid attention to the wound on his head, which was seeping blood. Driving with his left arm, he let his right hang limply on his lap. The journey proceeded silently, while he constantly checked the rear-view mirror.

My heart raced at a gallop, second in speed only to my mind. Would he have used his knife on me if I hadn't left with him? Would he have hurt Lea?

Maybe those weren't the important questions. Why hadn't he told me Derinda was his mother? Of course he hadn't confided in me about anything during our time together. I'd thought he'd been secretive because he was a man, and men weren't forthcoming with their feelings, right? What a fool I'd been. All along he'd been scheming about how to use me to kill his father.

I threw him a sideways glance. What would he do if I tried to make a dash for it? Rumors about Old magic were all I had to go by, and if only a tenth of them were true, my skillset was worth nothing compared to his abilities.

We pulled into the parking lot of a motel, composed of four rectangular, parallel units, with another unit extending perpendicular to the others.

Kieran handed me a wad of money. "Get us a room, okay? I don't want to explain the blood to the attendant."

No warning not to run. Would he come after me, or did he simply trust me? I took the money and made my way to the attendant's building. I'd play along. For now.

The guy behind the screen barely looked up from his TV when I spoke to him.

I hurried back to Kieran. His face held a sickly pallor, but he voiced no complaints. We followed the graveled path, which gave the motel a clean look, past a grouping of exotic palm trees. Outside our room, Kieran leaned against the yellow wall and pressed his hand to his injured shoulder.

I unlocked the door. "You think it's dislocated?"

He walked in ahead of me and stood stiffly at the edge of the bed, sweat beading on his cheeks and nose. "Definitely."

The well-furnished room looked clean and homey. At another occasion, this place would make for a nice getaway.

"I can't say you don't deserve it." I crossed my arms, unsure what to do next.

He'd ruined everything—our chance at returning the world to its rightful path, and sure as hell any chance he had with me. His actions didn't make any sense.

He briefly closed his eyes. "Let me explain."

"We had one shot, Kieran." I hid my trembling lips. "One shot."

"I know you think that. Please, just hear me out." He kicked the nightstand to the right of the bed, and it bounced off the wall, rocking the empty vase on top of it. "It all started with a dream." He covered his face in his one functional hand and sank onto the bed.

"I'm listening." I lifted my chin and looked down at his sorry shape. "What dream?"

"The worst kind." His shoulders hitched as he let out a sob. "My mother, Derinda, sent it."

Had I made him cry? Accidentally said the wrong thing? Hang on. *He* was the bad guy here. I was the victim. So why was he sobbing?

He kept his face buried, but his sniffs told their story. Whatever was eating him, it had broken him.

Despite his betrayal and his secrecy, I sat on the bed and put my arms around him. His wide shoulders didn't hide his vulnerability. His muscular arms appeared incapable of doing harm. If I hadn't witnessed his actions with own eyes, I'd never believe him capable of killing his father and our hopes with one jab of his knife.

Gradually, his breathing became regular.

"My mother lives in Balor. I've never met her in person." Kieran straightened without shaking off my gentle embrace, his pale face reflecting the overhead lights. "Dreams are the only way she communicates with me."

"What did she show you?"

"My mother doesn't like Balor and was looking for solitude in Torren." Red-rimmed, his eyes met mine before drifting past me. "Old Ones like her and Orrin can only get out of Balor if they leave their powers behind, but she felt safe to do so. Torren used to be her home, and she didn't think she'd be in danger. She was wrong, because my father found out and set a trap."

I set my jaw, steeling myself for the rest of the story.

"My mother showed me how he forced himself on her while she begged for him to stop." Kieran took a long, shaking breath.

"Day after day he raped her until she became pregnant —with me."

I'd always thought Galleo a brute, but the depths of his depravity still stole my breath. How could any person do this to another?

I leaned closer and placed my cheek against his. "I'm so sorry."

"After I was born, my father had no more need for her. If he could harness my powers, mold me in his image, the world would be his for the taking. As for my mother, he dropped her in a remote cave, still bleeding. Threw her away like a piece of used underwear." He turned away, his jaw firm. "All the horrors I've witnessed on the battlefields were nothing compared to what my mother went through. I mean, she's my mother."

My heart turned heavy, weighed down by compassion and disgust. I placed a soft kiss onto his neck. As far as excuses for screw-ups went, his had won over my heart.

"Orrin found my mother, barely alive." Kieran wiped his eyes with his sleeve. "Instead of avenging or at least comforting her, he punished her for leaving Balor. She accepted anything he dished out. All she asked was that he'd help her get her son, allow her to raise me, but he refused. And when she wasn't ready to lay with him again, Orrin broke his own rules and sought relief among the Touched."

"He seduced our queen, Lea's birth mother."

"Yes. That, too, turned tragic when the queen fell pregnant and lost her sanity. Orrin should have known ordinary humans, even the Touched, cannot withstand the unbound powers of an Old One. Lea's growing life literally poisoned her mother's mind. Wherever that man goes, he leaves chaos and pain in his wake. He's every bit the monster my father is." A short pause. "Was."

He shook his head, his face gray with exhaustion and pain.

I swallowed the ache I felt on his behalf. "Now she wants to hurt Orrin by killing his only child."

"I didn't know about the arrangement with my father until Lea told me, I swear." His face was an open book now, and not a lie stood between us anymore.

"I believe you."

Kieran readjusted his position and winced. "She loves me, but she shouldn't have bargained with him to ensure my role as his successor. It's not what I want." His eyes glistened.

How much hatred did it take to assist the man who violated you? But if she indeed loved Kieran, why had she burdened him with nightmares that would never leave him? He deserved better than that, better than being dragged into his parents' power plays.

"Now you got revenge for her." My voice was emotionless, a stark contrast to the whirlwind of raging inside me.

"I didn't plan to." He shifted his position and immediately took a sharp breath. "I hadn't seen my father since my mother had shared her secret with me. Coming face-to-face with him was harder than anticipated. All my resentment, every ounce of my hatred flowed out of me, not only for what he'd done to my mother, but for his lies, for killing Lea, and for placing a bounty on your head, too."

"I didn't know he had."

"I didn't want to worry you." His smile melted the last of my frustration. "There I was, confronting my father, when an idea struck me. He'd brought about the Fall, but he wasn't the architect of the Divide's demise. No, that dubious honor belonged to my mother. I figured if I could convince her to help me restore the old world, we didn't need him anymore. So I killed him before he got the chance to hurt anyone I loved ever again."

"The problem is, Galleo has already done his worst. How sure are you that your mother is going to help you?"

"Why wouldn't she? She's my mother."

She was also a woman out for revenge.

Kieran sought my gaze. "You think I'm like him, don't you? Like father, like son?"

"No, I think your plan would have made for a great plan B." I placed a hand against his cheek. "But you're *not* like your father."

"If only I could believe that."

My heart pulsed for him, a sharp, physical pain I wished I didn't feel but couldn't deny.

"Stop it already. Self-pity isn't going to help." I shifted around to fully face him. "Let's deal with your shoulder first."

"Don't worry about it." He stared at the opposite wall. Almost motionless. A broken man.

How I longed to make him whole again. To take away his pain. But this didn't call for a soft approach.

"For Balor's sake. Pull yourself together." I punched the mattress. "You're hurt."

A ghost of a smile crossed his face. "You almost sound like you care."

"I can't kick your butt if you're helpless. Now tell me what I can do."

His gaze fell on his arm. "You need to set it."

"Shouldn't a healer do this?"

"I just killed the president. Going to ask my people for medical aid might be pushing my luck."

My gaze drifted across the room, looking for answers. "I don't know what to do."

"It's an anterior dislocation and shouldn't be difficult to correct. If you really want to help, that is." His last words were barely a whisper. "I'll guide you through it."

Slice it. Despite everything, I couldn't make myself hate him.

Maybe I'd have even acted in the same way if I'd been in his shoes.

Once we explained Kieran's plan to Lea, she'd come around. No one had even known if Galleo possessed the knowledge needed to restore the Divide. Derinda did for sure.

Kieran took a labored breath. "Okay, before you start, I need pain killers."

I crossed the room and rummaged through the bathroom cupboard under the sink. "We have a first aid box with bandages and plaster strips, but no drugs."

"Coffee will do then." He gestured to the narrow kitchen area. "There's a coffee maker over there."

I brewed the coffee and added cold water from the bathroom faucet so he could drink it.

"Now, make sure the upper portion of my arm remains still the entire time," he instructed. "Bend my elbow at ninety degrees to form an 'L' against my stomach. Then rotate the arm and shoulder outward, hold my wrist, and push. Slowly." He swigged half the coffee without taking a breath. "Once my elbow goes up behind my body, the shoulder should fall back in."

"That all?" I scratched my forehead. "How do you know all this? And don't say you picked it up on the battlefield."

"The Fall turned me into a doctor." He glanced up as if he was fully aware of how crazy that sounded. "I can access my fake medical knowledge without forgetting what's real."

"A doctor, huh?" I took the cup from his hand and placed it on the small stand next to the bed. "Okay, Doctor Kieran. Let's do this."

With my concentration dialed up to full, I performed each step the way he told me. His breathing sped up, but he made no sound beyond that.

My insides warmed. He relied on me to take care of him. For

weeks I'd wanted him to talk to me without his barriers in the way. Now that I got my wish, I was unable to overlook his actions. Until his mother reversed the ritual's effects, Kieran and I wouldn't have a future beyond the next few weeks.

Kieran's shoulder fell into the joint with a muffled plop. Task complete, I let go of his hand.

"Thank you." His tone held no hint of fatigue or pain or any of the other things he should have been feeling; only the force of his affection, which settled around my shoulders like a scarf.

"You're welcome." I gave myself a few seconds to skim his face and tore myself loose. "Anyway, I'll get the bandages. I wouldn't want to become an expendable hostage."

I had no intention of making life easy for him. Besides wrecking our plan, he'd also kidnapped me—after a fashion. Where I came from, we took this kind of conduct seriously.

"I didn't kidnap you." His whispered words slid into my ear, a gentle caress demanding to be taken seriously. "You came willingly."

"You had a knife." Aware of his attention on me, I bandaged his head with not a little roughness.

"Ouch." He laughed. "The knife was nowhere near your body. I made sure of it."

I reinforced the first bandage with a second one as a belated tremble shook my bones. In her anger, Lea could have taken him from me. Snuffed out his existence with the flick of her hand. *Slice it.* Despite the trouble he'd caused, I had feelings for the man. Feelings too strong to simply sweep aside.

"You'll need better care than what I can give you." I didn't meet his gaze, scared I might lose my cool. "Pain killers, more bandages. I can go to a pharmacy."

"No, what you can give me is enough, and magic will take care of the rest. My arm's already free of pain." To prove it, he waved. "Please. Stay."

He tugged on my top and pulled me onto the bed beside him. I didn't pull away. For a moment, we sat on the edge of the bed and watched the furniture.

My fingers traced up to his dressing again, checking my handiwork, and he flinched.

"Sorry," I said. "I know magic is working on your injuries, but is there anything I can do to make it hurt less?"

His mouth solidified into a mischievous grin. "I thought you'd never ask."

"I didn't mean that." I glanced down.

"No?" He pressed his hands against either side of my head, his fingers tousling my hair, and leaned toward me.

I wanted to backed away, should have backed away, but he was so close. And hurting. And so damn beautiful.

He quickly covered my mouth with his. An orchestra of electric sparks shot through my muscles, weakening each one in turn until I lay helplessly in his embrace. Never before had a loss of control been so quick and so absolute, yet my heart beat not from fear.

He rolled me onto my back and prowled my waist with his fingers, hitching up my top in the process.

"I'll prove to you I'm worthy of your trust," he whispered.

I believed every word.

He opened our kiss and slipped his tongue deep into my mouth, teasing, beckoning, taking command of my will. I gave it up freely, because I knew of no better caretaker.

As if he read my desire, he forged his way to my breast, slid his fingers under my bra.

I ran my thigh up along his hip. "I don't want to hurt you."

"That's never going to happen." He hovered his palm over my top. The fabric shimmered and vanished as if it had never existed.

I stared at my bra and my naked stomach. "What the slice?"

"Your sweater's over there." He pointed toward a chair at the far end of the room.

My top lay folded on its cushion.

"That's cheating." I grinned.

"Cheating's what evil Shades do, or hadn't you heard?" He cut off my response with another kiss.

One by one, he made our clothes disappear, until not an inch of fabric separated us.

He covered my naked flesh with his sculptured chest and abs. His muscles weren't the only feature of his anatomy pulsating with eagerness.

Heat welled up inside me, making my skin tingle. The feeling of loneliness that had stalked me since the Divide finally subsided. Kieran was my antidote. His smile filled the hole inside me, his kisses blew confidence back into me.

Using his teeth, he teased my neck, my shoulders, my breasts. Each time he brushed across one of my nipples, I let out a moan. Bolder now, he rolled his tongue around each sensitive tip, sucked, and rolled again without letup, without pause, and entirely without mercy.

"Kieran," I whispered.

"Mhm?"

I nudged him off me, brushing my palm against his flushed face. "I don't know if this is a good idea."

He buried his head in the pillow and grunted. After a few seconds, he looked up. "Why not?"

"The timing is bad, don't you see that?" I used the space between us to turn my back toward him. "We don't even know if I'll remember you in the morning."

"I'll never let you forget." He nibbled my earlobe. "Never, ever, ever." He wrapped his arms around my stomach. My body slackened in his embrace.

What did it matter if I remembered? I had my wits about me now, and every fiber inside my body wanted to be with him.

He slipped his right hand down my waist and ran circles around my navel, then he inched his fingers downward and teased the opening of my legs.

Without the jab of a sword or the cut of a knife, this Shade warrior had tamed the royal champion. Yet I was the one who felt like the winner.

I itched to trace the ridges banding his abs, but his tight embrace stopped me from turning back around. He cupped his hand around my neck, rotated my head, and lowered his mouth over mine. He licked my parted lips until our tongues connected, soft and demanding.

This time, when Kieran nudged my legs open, I gave in to the pulse throbbing through my core and complied. He slipped his fingers to the front, where he lavished me with long, insistent strokes. No words could justly describe the sensations he aroused. I arched my back, unable to cope with the building pressure, while the rest of me melted into his body.

I'd lain with men before, drunk from wine after a battle, but none of my experiences had been this intense. Kieran's movements were precise, captivating, devastating. But it wasn't his skill alone that enraptured me. No, it was his smell, his essence, his affection. He cared about me. How else could he make me feel this happy?

He touched his mouth to my ear and grazed its surface with the tip of his tongue while sliding two fingers inside me. I rocked my hips, trying to draw him into my depths. He chuckled, his warm breath sending a tremble down my nerves. When I reached back toward his waist, he squeezed his elbows and lock me in place.

His stubble scraped against my skin.

"Don't move." His voice a firm command in my ear. "Understand?"

I nodded, completely at his mercy. Immersing his fingers fully, he pushed in and out while my muscles clinched around him, begging for relief. His thumb worked my most tender spots, swirling, massaging, plucking, until every fiber inside me coiled taut.

Without his thumb missing a stroke, he entered me from behind. His first plunge filled me, his erection swelling as he drank in my gasp. He built a rhythm, one layer over another, without allowing stray thoughts to break the spell I was under. Not once did I feel the need to take control, enraptured as I was by his attention. He continued to drive into me, deeper and deeper, his breathing more ragged with each thrust.

Whether my memory would fail me tomorrow, next month or never, he and I would face the future together. The Old Ones willing, I'd never be alone again.

His movements quickened. My chest lifted and fell, fighting for oxygen. Each of his thrusts made my insides tighten around him as sparks popped across my head. Every sensation built into an exhilarating, mind-bending pressure, begging for relief.

"Nieve." Kieran breathed my name.

The vulnerability in his voice as he came apart, pulsing deep inside me, brought me to an eye-rolling climax.

# CHAPTER THIRTY-FOUR

*LEA*

*"Friendship—that serene moment between betrayals."*

Markus and I had returned to his farmhouse, empty-handed and confused. Nieve was gone, at the mercy of Kieran. How dangerous was he? Not too long ago, I'd assured her he liked her. That taught me to play match-maker.

Nieve had been my anchor since I'd returned from Balor. She'd given me strength even in her weakened state. I raked my hand through my hair. Except, I wasn't strong now—my confidence had collapsed the moment she was gone. Christ. If she saw me now, she'd give me a right talking to.

The walls of Markus's bedroom closed in, squeezing the sanity out of me. The Shade's gaze tracked me as I paced the length of the room.

"This is stupid." My voice squeaked as if my tongue had stepped on a doggy toy. "I can't just sit around and do nothing. It's been nearly twenty-four hours."

"You're not sitting." Markus was Mr. Calm himself. As usual, he'd draped himself over his chaise longue, dressed in slacks and a tight fit T-shirt molded around his muscles.

I came to a sudden stop and frowned at him, certain he'd just spoken. "What?"

"I said you're not sitting."

My frown deepened. "Why would I be sitting? What the hell are you talking about?"

He lifted his arms and chuckled. "Never mind. Go back to ignoring me."

I gave a grunt. "Any news?"

He overdid the eyebrow action, which gave him a startled appearance. "Oh yes, the tiny news fairy has whispered Nieve's whereabouts in my ear, but I enjoy watching you wear out my carpet, so I'm keeping the information to myself."

"I'm in no mood for sarcasm."

"So I noticed." He exhaled. "You'll know when I know. Here, why don't you sit and watch TV with me?" He patted the spot so close to his legs he might as well invite me to slink onto his lap. "Take the weight off."

I shot him a bruising glower. "What is it with you and sitting today?"

This time, his sigh stretched. Guess he was running out of patience. Well, tough luck.

"Your constant sighs are wearing on my nerves, pal." I rubbed my pounding temples.

"I was breathing, babe. I'm still allowed to breathe, right?"

"I guess." I shrugged. But hey. Why let him off the hook that easily? My impatience needed a target and he had a bullseye tattooed on his forehead. "But don't call me babe," I said.

"Lea, I swear, if you don't calm down, I'll find a way of knocking you out, Old powers or not. Now sit."

Maybe I was tightly wound. I unclenched my fists and snapped the TV on then sat a good two feet from Markus on the bed.

A blonde woman looked out of the screen with a serious

expression on her face. To her right were pictures of Galleo. "Yesterday, a battalion of sixty Elonians stormed the Old Stockade and killed the president. The terrorists' whereabouts are currently unknown. In the face of this crisis, the vice president turned down the presidentship and handed the full power of the office to the president's sons, Fromer and Salander. Ten minutes ago, they released a statement vowing to bring the criminals to justice."

"Great," I scoffed. "No doubt, their militia will be using innocent Elonians as punching bags, pretending to search for their father's killer."

I got to my feet and resumed my useless pacing. Waiting for Markus's scouts to return was driving me insane.

There had been a time, not long ago, when the concept of magic had turned me into a wide-eyed Harry Potter. Now, somehow, I'd discovered extra powers over which I had no control, and I hated them all. My old spells had been plenty.

"I have an idea." I stopped pacing and glanced at Markus. "Nieve found me initially simply by calling on the wind. Why can't I use the same technique to locate her?"

"Do you know how?"

"In theory." I picked up Fallon from the nightstand. "Guess we'll find out."

"Okay." Markus sat up and gave me a thumbs-up. "But be careful. I want you to come back to me in one piece."

I pretend-gagged over his weak flirtation and waved him *auf Wiedersehen*.

I hoped it was.

/

OUTSIDE, my only companions were a group of trees and the long, empty road. I closed my eyes and concentrated on Nieve's face, her voice, then whispered her name into the air. The sun hid behind clouds, but it provided sufficient energy for me to stand a chance of getting this done.

Forcing myself to focus, I sent my message in little gusts. The technique had a limited range, but maybe my Old powers gave me a little extra juice.

After an hour, I hadn't caught any sign of my friend. Dammit. I slumped against a tree to give my legs a rest. My forehead was slick with sweat, maybe a sign that my magic energy was nearing its limit. But I'd never been a quitter. As long as a single trickle of magic remained in me, I'd keep going.

"Nieve," I whispered again.

Silence. Either the wind was working against me, or Kieran wasn't saying her name. Why would he? If she was dead, he'd have no reason to. I gave a frustrated grunt and doubled my efforts.

*"Nieve."*

I straightened my spine and got to my feet. *Bingo*. It had just been her name, but I didn't need more. The air rearranged itself into a solid corridor and guided me. All I had to do was follow its path.

I lifted high and flew along the route the wind carved out, even as the rain started. A few drops of water weren't going to slow me down. I might not be as adept at using my Old magic as Kieran was, but he'd regret the moment he took my friend from me.

Shielding my vision against the wind, I landed near a collection of bungalows. A damp sheen coated the walls of the motel, and raindrops clattered across the patio to form large, muddy puddles.

The air parted and led me to room 202. This was where he'd taken her? A motel room? Nothing good ever happened in motel rooms. Just look at Bates Motel.

I held my ear against the door, tempted to blow it off and run in guns blazing. But Kieran's powers were a big unknown, and I had yet to get a handle on my own.

Inside, everything was silent. I gulped down a knot, trying hard to block the many gruesome scenes of what might await me on the other side. We'd given him our trust, and in return, he'd stolen everything from me. My hope of reuniting with my parents. Any hope of reversing the Fall. And worst of all, Nieve. I closed my hand around the handle and concentrated on the spell.

The lock snapped back, and I quietly turned the handle.

Kieran leaped up in a flash, naked as the day his bitch of a momma dropped him into this world.

"Lea." He covered his privates with the blanket. "What are you doing here?"

White-blond hair popped up from the pillow.

"Lea?" Nieve sat up, her chest bare. "This isn't what it looks like."

My heart hammered twice then stopped. Why wasn't she lying wounded in a corner? Better yet, why wasn't he?

"Oh God, please tell me you didn't." I inched back out the room. Of all the horrid things I'd pictured, this scene hadn't even featured. "No way."

I reached for the doorframe to steady myself. Was this for real? Nieve was my friend. Why would she do this to me? Her feelings for the Shade hadn't been a secret, but his betrayal should have poured cold water over them. Instead...

"Look, I'm sorry." Kieran held up his hands. "We can fix things. It's going to be fine."

Sorry wouldn't make up for blowing up my plan. Sorry wouldn't erase his deceit. Sorry wouldn't right this nightmare of a world.

But my mind was too frazzled to tell him. I shuffled back

into the rain, tripped, recovered. Heavy drops assaulted my skull, dripped off my nose and into my eyes.

Then I wheeled around and ran. How had Kieran won Nieve over to his side? Had he promised to make her queen? Vowed to create a utopia according to their imagination? I engaged my magic, yet it took a few attempts before I'd composed an air cushion that would hold me. The wind could carry me to Timbuktu, for all I cared, but somehow, it led me back to Markus's farmhouse.

Nieve more than anyone knew what the success of my plan had meant. My father was still sick, without a cure in sight. But all the signs had been there. I simply refused to see. She and Tristan had made and broken promises and kept secrets from the start. I set down from my flight behind the mesh-wire fence and took deep breaths. The scent of moist earth hung in the air. My stomach gurgled, and my breakfast spewed out of my mouth, landing in a disgusting heap between my feet.

When I had nothing more to bring up, I pulled myself straight. The trees around me wobbled, as if I looked at them through one of those distorting funfair mirrors. I sagged against a trunk and gazed into space. Up high, a single bird whistled a cheerful song, but its calls went unanswered.

Like my feathered comrade, I was going to be trapped in this stupid world alone. If I couldn't trust my friends, what did I have left? Where could I go?

*Turn around. Bridge out ahead.* The end of the fucking road.

Maybe not quite. One person hadn't let me down. Yet.

# CHAPTER THIRTY-FIVE



*"Never underestimate Shades. What they lack in cunning, they make up for in cruelty."*

I slipped into my jeans while raw, searing pain ripped through my chest. *Stupid, stupid, stupid.* In Lea's eyes, I'd slept with the man who'd betrayed us. I might as well have set fire to her guinea pig.

"What will she be thinking?" My shrill voice bordered on hysteria. "Slice it. What was I thinking?"

The minute Kieran's arms had encircled me and his warm, full lips caressed my skin, my common sense had skipped town.

"Calm yourself. Please." Kieran buttoned up his pants and pulled on his shirt from the day before. "She'll come round."

"You heard her." I found support in a wall and leaned, just for a moment. "Did it sound like she was about to forgive me?"

"Lea needs time and an explanation."

"It's not going to be that easy. To her mind, you effectively killed her parents." And, by association, so had I.

"That's ridiculous. Besides, we have a new plan, remember?" The green of his eyes darkened. He stuffed his foot into his boot and yanked his laces tight.

"You talked to your mother in your dream last night, and she said she wouldn't help." I ran my hand over my hair, giving it a pull to let the pain knock sense into me. "She wants her baby boy to rule the world, whether he wants to or not."

"Once my mother understands what makes me happy, she'll change her mind."

No, she wouldn't. Derinda was a manipulative mother who knew his son would do anything to not disappoint her. Including taking the presidentship? If she worked on him some more, most definitely. But that was a problem for another day, assuming my memory survived that long.

I rushed to the door and grabbed the metal handle. "I still have to find Lea."

"I know, and I'm coming, too." He attacked his remaining boot with his other foot. "We both owe her an explanation."

"I have to do this alone, Kieran. I'm sorry." I stepped out of the motel room, and headed off without glancing back.

He didn't follow.

An hour later, and ignoring the hollow ache in my heart, I rushed into the well-lit lobby of my brother's mansion. My hanbo had quickly overwhelmed the lock, and no one had prevented me from entering. Animated voices jarred the air to my far left, but the community area wasn't where I was headed. I veered right. If memory served—and hadn't yet been compromised by the Fall—somewhere at the back of the building, I'd find my brother's quarters.

"Watch it." An open-mouthed Gerrit leaped out of my way, his back to the smooth wall. He stood on tiptoes and flattened his belly for that extra half-inch of space. His eyes sparked no recognition.

We'd lost Gerrit. I hurried past him without apology, struggling against the gaping hollow in my stomach. Was Tristan's memory still intact?

"Have you seen Lea?" I burst into Tristan's office.

"Lea?" He glanced up, his hair standing on end. A sign of too many late nights. "Why, what's wrong?"

He sat behind his desk, the desk lamp the only light in the room. I sat in the chair on the opposite side, aiming for calm, and told him the broad strokes of how our last plan had disintegrated.

"We have to do something." My voice was tight, but remained composed. "We must find Lea."

Tristan poured a cup of tea from a thermos and brushed a hair off his creased black-buttoned shirt. On his wrist, his indecipherable binary watch glowed like eyes watching me. "Do you know where she is?"

"Maybe." I encircled my neck with my hands and let their warmth flow into me. "Lea wanted us to work with the Shades. Markus is the only who's not let her down. I bet she's working on another plan with him now."

"Your last plan didn't pan out, and now you want me to work with the Shades anyway?"

"Yes." I swiveled in my chair and briefly closed my eyes to gather strength. "You can't be so stuck in your old habits that you fail to recognize a chance if it pokes you in the nose."

"Show respect."

I snorted. "You're no longer my king, so why don't you, for once, act like my brother? Support me."

"Do not push me." His expression flickered from anger to full-blown pain. "Each day I'm losing more of my friends to the Fall. Who knows how much of my own memory has already been affected. We have to shape our future, Nieve, not wallow in our past. And I need you on my side, not because you're my champion, but because you're my sister."

His words squeezed my heart until a gentle warmth bathed my body.

"And I need you." My voice hovered barely above a whisper. "*We* need you. Why won't you believe in us?"

He reclined in his chair and rubbed his stubble. "Neither of you has the experience I have. Stop wasting time and join the resistance. It's our only hope of survival."

Tears welled up, but I kept them under lockdown. "The resistance may be *your* hope, but Lea is mine. When I found her, I took responsibility for her life, and I will not abandon her. You owe her, too. She will come up with a new plan. I know it."

"Nieve. I command you—"

"Stop it." I banged my hand on his desk. "This isn't something you can command." I waved off, too tired to continue an endless argument. "You know what? Why don't you stay here and snuggle with your self-righteousness? This is pointless."

"Nieve!"

For once, his warning failed to break my resolve. "Goodbye, Tristan."

I stormed out. The biting wind hit me as soon as I left the mansion. I'd never gone up against Tristan, never disobeyed his commands, but Lea and I had an unbreakable connection. No one understood what we'd shared or what we'd endured. More than that, I believed she had a gift. Her simple plan had so very nearly born fruit.

Abandoning my duty as a royal champion stung, but when principles were all you have left, you might as well stand up for them.

# CHAPTER THIRTY-SIX



*"Mirror, mirror on the wall. Is it me, or am I looking screwed to you, too?"*

My clothes sagged from the rain, adding weight to the burden I already carried. Markus's farmhouse was brightly lit. The tales of our failure probably already flowed from room to room. Having no appetite for analysis and blame, I weaved through trucks and cars parked in the yard.

Nieve's betrayal had hit me like a Shakespeare play—tragic, but not real. If I blinked, she'd give her final bow. Make-believe at its finest. My chest tightened. She'd been my friend, for Christ's sake. The friend I'd always wanted. Beautiful. Smarter than me in most respects. What had gone wrong? A wave of pain ripped through my gut, making me double over. Hand on my thighs, I breathed. In. Out.

A patrolling Shade shot me a curious glance, and I straightened. Nothing to see here. Nothing but a nervous breakdown. I stumbled on through the outbuildings that dotted Markus's land, pressing my palm against my stomach. Was friendship supposed to hurt this much?

My steps slowed. A gust blew my wet curls into my face, but it had stopped raining a while ago. Betrayal or not, Nieve wouldn't remember me for long. Without her memories of our time together, my past would be erased as certainly as her own. Then I'd really be that little orphan girl that nobody wanted.

I changed course and lumbered back toward the line of trees by the stream.

The world didn't want to be fixed by me. It had sent every obstacle it could and made a return to the world I knew impossible.

Well, so what? I hadn't quit when Billy Jenkins had shoved me every day and stolen my lunch money when we were nine. No, I'd crept into the boy's room and taken his clothes, then took pictures as he snuck around, looking for his underpants. I hadn't given up when Tristan's sword slashes had bested me. Three weeks later, I'd spun his stupid weapon from his grip despite his superior skillset.

There was always a way.

I shoved my hands deep into my soggy pockets to keep them out of the chill. My new idea was so crazy, it might just work, but was I ready to pull it off? I damn well had to be ready. Galleo wasn't the only one who knew how the Divide could be restored. It was time to ask one of the original spellcasters: my biological father.

I picked a quiet spot away from the guards and sat on the wet ground, a tree my only shelter against the wind. Water soaked through my jeans, leaving my legs cold and almost numb. I slipped Fallon out of its sheath and slid a finger along its smooth length. Could I kill myself?

Orrin was my best bet. To see him, I needed to die. Then why did I hesitate? From an empirical point of view, he was the only play I had left.

Logic had often taken second place to my emotions in

recent days. Stripped of hero-hood by the fall of the Divide, then let down by those I cared most about, I'd forgotten who I was. Deep down, where I counted, I remained a physicist. Reason was my staple diet, and it was reason that told me to kill myself.

Distorted words drifted into my ear.

I'd know Nieve's voice anywhere. My mouth quivered, twisted slowly, but my joy faded. No, she didn't deserve my smile.

I tightened my grip around Fallon. Its energy prickled inside my veins, either hoping for combat or trying to stop me from doing what needed to be done.

"Lea? Are you out here?" Nieve shouted.

I shifted further around the tree so I wasn't found.

"Lea!" Nieve called again. "Tristan, since you insisted on following me here, make yourself useful."

My heart spun. Tristan had come, too?

No matter. I closed my eyes. Their presence couldn't prevent me from doing what I had to do.

Of course, if this didn't work, it was game over. My father was going to die for sure. Nieve and Tristan would lose their memories. At least I wouldn't be around to watch their decline.

"Lea?" Tristan sounded so close it made my heart surge.

*Focus.* I lifted Fallon.

"I don't think she's here," Tristan said.

His voice soothed the pain inside. He might not believe in me, but for one night, he'd given me the gift of happiness. Waking next to him, satisfied and content, had meant everything. This world might not give our story a second act, but there was one consolation. If the curtain fell on my relationship with him and on my future as a whole, I'd be the one to pull the lever.

On my terms.

My hand tightened around the hilt, and I plunged the blade deep into my chest.

⚔

THE FIRST SIGN I'd made it to Balor? The now familiar scent of freshly baked bread. Once again, I waded in a sea of black nothingness. It forced itself against my mind, my core, until I reached the one conclusion I knew to be true beyond all doubt. I was dead.

Again.

Sweat burned along my nape while the rest of my body went subarctic. What if Orrin didn't find me? What if he couldn't send me back? Clever questions I should have asked before I'd killed myself.

A noise broke me out of my thoughts. A scratch, like soccer cleats on a stone floor. Did other things beside Old Ones reside in the afterworld? Ghosts? Monsters? Wild animals?

A growl whirled around me, seeming to come from all sides.

Shit. I walked then ran without a plan or destination. Even though my soles slapped against a hard surface, the ground blended with the blackness. Without visual clues, I wasn't even sure I moved.

Another growl, followed by a roar. Adrenaline flooded my muscles like an overdose of speed. I fell into a wobbly-kneed fighting stance and reached for my weapon.

*Thank God.* Fallon had magically returned to its sheath, throbbing with power. It wanted to be drawn, wanted to tear apart the thing lurking in the dark.

Usually, inanimate objects didn't sway me, but right now, as I grabbed my weapon, its craving for violence struck me as an excellent idea.

A pair of glowing embers approached, set in a feline face that looked oddly human. I tightened my hand around Fallon's hilt. The bright orange and dark lines adorning the cat's sleek fur gave it an exquisite beauty.

Pretty or not, the creature's powerful muscles could do a whole load of damage.

Fallon vibrated, and its pulses urged me to make a short meal of the tiger before it made one of me. I took a step back and peered around. Where could I run? As it turned out, it was fraking impossible to hide in the dark.

"You're Lea," the tiger said in a melodious, female voice.

"I am. And you are?"

"They call me Derinda."

"Derinda." Her name fled my mouth like a gasp. *Show some spine, dammit.* "Heard a lot about you. Except for the bit about you being a tiger."

"I'm what I want to be. And you're my husband's bastard child."

I squared my shoulders. "Like you don't have your very own bastard child."

Her tail cracked the air like a whip. "Don't speak of my son that way."

At least she cared about him. Not that her motherly feelings helped *me* in any way.

"A bastard child is a bastard child." I laughed. "I don't make the rules."

"Shut your mouth." Her paws, the size of large saucers, padded toward me, forcing me to retreat further into the nothingness. "You know nothing about me."

"I know you've destroyed the world over a silly affair."

"An affair? You believe that's what this is all about?" Her pointy ears panned forward and back, giving her a thoughtful demeanor. "This is about justice against men who think they can destroy me. Galleo is dead. My husband might be too strong for me now, but your death should give him a taste of what's to come."

Normally, I was all for female empowerment, but my enthusiasm had quickly waned.

"Let's have some fun." In the darkness, only Derinda's bared, gleaming teeth shone bright. "To be sporting, I'll give you a twenty-second head start."

I glanced around. Where was I supposed to go?

The tigress flattened herself against the ground and placed her paws over her eyes. Clearly, our chat was over.

The oppressive darkness swallowed any hope I'd make it out alive. Yet I turned and ran. Blood pumped through my arteries, but my legs shook, weak and weedy, about to buckle under my weight.

All too soon, the pitter-patter of deadly claws followed.

I accessed the well that held my magic. Not long ago, I'd tapped into it to sling Kieran against a wall. Now, I was running on empty. The only buzz in my limbs came from Fallon, but my dagger's desire to kill wasn't going to defeat Derinda. She was an Old One, and she was close. Too close.

My feet pounded the ground. Was I moving? No wind to ruffle my hair, no corners, hills, or structures to orientate myself. A lunatic's giggle sounded out of the blackness. Derinda, enjoying the chase. She could probably already taste my flesh in her mouth.

All I tasted was bitterness. What had I done with my life? Twenty-four years with nothing to show for it. The world wouldn't feel my loss.

An orange shape soared from my left. I ducked. A striped twenty-thousand ton freight train slammed into my shoulder and toppled me to the floor.

The tiger twisted in the air and came at me from the other side.

I scrambled on all fours, a wave of sickness flooding my body. Crap, that's a big mouth. I leaped to the right, fell onto one knee, pushed myself up again. Behind me, the tiger's teeth cracked shut around empty air. *Snap.* Like a guillotine. My mind spat out one impassive command after another.

*Draw Fallon. Run. Weave. Swing dagger.*

My blade never even touched her fur.

Her teeth closed around my calf, her canines piercing deep into my flesh. An unending stream of pain shot up my leg, and I fell forward. With her jaws locked around my leg, she shook me like a doll.

Air gushed from my lungs, through my throat, forming a mind-shattering scream at the entrance of my mouth.

Derinda took off running and dragged me with her.

Up became down, left became right, and tumbling in between it all, the burning flame that was once my body. My arms couldn't protect my head, and my face scraped across the ground. Whatever the floor was made of, it tore strips off my skin. My teeth clanged against each other. Blood filled my mouth.

The tiger's lithe body lifted off the ground, soared upward, and spun. Her mouth opened, and I dropped to the ground.

"Stop it!" a man's voice shouted.

An unseen power flung Derinda further, and further, and further into the darkness, until her roar faded.

My mind collapsed under the torrent of pain rippling through my body, while my face burned among the ribbons of involuntary tears. Why couldn't I raise my head?

"Lea?" The lilt in my name was familiar. Feet approached, and a figure kneeled by my side. "Can you hear me?"

"Orrin?" My voice sounded rough, as if Derinda had dragged me by my throat. "Dad?"

"I'm here." He placed his hands on my back. "Hang on. You'll feel better in a minute."

A shock of cold replaced the heat, turning my blood into prickly icicles that pierced my flesh. Then a soothing sensation crept up my legs, my back, my shoulders, my head. I flexed my renewed muscles, found them working, and lifted my face.

"She-she..." I rolled onto my back and stared at his curly beard.

"It's all right." He leaned in and pressed me against his chest, wiping the salty trails off my cheeks. "You shouldn't have come back."

"I had to."

He kissed the top of my head. "Nothing is so important that you should risk your life."

A new kind of warmth curled around my heart. Not the stinging, oh-crap kind, but a heat that made me want to nestle in and give a contented sigh. However rotten he'd been to his wife, he did care about me. Yet as much as I longed for his love, I wouldn't allow myself to get sucked into his daddy routine.

My real father was the only father that counted.

I wiped my nose against the fabric of his oversized cloak and extricated myself from his embrace. "This *is* important. I tried to uncover a way to restore the Divide, but I failed."

His large hand stroked over my hair, flattening it against my ear. "I'd hoped you would think to ask the Shade king. Derinda seems to have given him all the answers." He glanced over his shoulder. "She'll come for you again. I used the element of surprise to beat her, but we might not be so lucky a second time."

I rubbed my calf. "Galleo's dead. I need your help."

"You know I can't perform magic in your realm." He clicked his tongue as if suppressing a curse. "My own rules forbid me from leaving Balor."

I jutted my chin. "Didn't bother you before."

"We've all paid a heavy price for my transgression." He crinkled his forehead in a deep frown.

"Can I perform the spell?" *Please say yes, please say yes.* "If you tell me how you and Derinda did it the first time around, maybe I can recreate it."

Orrin tilted back his head and took a long breath. "Very well. I shall teach you."

# CHAPTER THIRTY-SEVEN



*"I like you, but I'm telling you. When the apocalypse comes, I'll make sure you go before me."*

Why had Lea killed herself? Because of me? Because I'd slept with Kieran?

I'd planned to make it right. Somehow. Why didn't she just wait? I buried my head in my pillow. Had I missed the warning signs? Sure, she'd sounded devastated when she found us at the motel, but suicide? She'd been a fighter. I never even suspected she'd end her life.

I breathed in the fruity scent of the candles Markus had dotted around his farmhouse, from his bathroom to the guest room I'd holed up in. If I wanted to smell anything, it would be fish. Or rotting meat. Some horrendous stink would at least represent the world as it was. I clawed my hand into the pillow, kicking the mattress. Lea's death was my fault. My fault. A true friend wouldn't have allowed her to die a second time.

Alone.

Or at all.

Someone knocked on the door.

If I stayed quiet, surely they'd leave.

"Nieve?" Tristan's voice slid easily through the thick wood.

"Go away." I wiped my nose and pressed my face into the pillow. "I don't want to speak to you."

The door opened. "Markus has a new plan."

I looked up. My brother's shirt was untucked and half-open. His superior air had disappeared into the ether. He'd never been a convincing king, but now he was no king at all.

"A new plan to wrestle control from our presidents?" My tone dripped with cynicism. "Markus's plans never amount to anything."

Of course Tristan knew that. He'd followed the Shade's lead, meek as a mouse, humbled by his grief. As if his mind and heart had died with Lea.

"Fromer and Salander are on the war path," he said. "They've declared extraordinary measures against Elonians and Kindreds, and even some Shades. They're cleaning house, and we're going to be their first targets. We have to act."

My stomach flipped. I applauded his zeal, but what did it matter? What did anything matter now? "Life would be simpler if we just accepted our fate."

Tristan crossed the room and sat next to me on the bed. He stroked my hair, the way he'd done when I was a girl. "That's not how we're built, little one. We fight. It's all we have left."

I closed my eyes. "You're right. But I have to tell you, it freaks me out that Markus is so nice about working with us. Why isn't he blackmailing us or demanding our firstborns in return for his help?"

He patted my shoulder. "It's not about that anymore. We're standing on the brink of survival. Fromer and Salander will find us soon. We must be ready."

His hair had claimed dominance over his attempts to smooth it and stood at all angles. His blue eyes, red-rimmed and hollow, remained steady, his gaze fixed on me.

I sat up and gave a hesitant smile. "We'll be ready. We always are."

He gathered me to his chest. "That's my girl."

He pulled me to my feet and led me out of my sanctuary, back into the real world, which in the present case was Markus's luxurious conference room. Plush velvet and even suede made an appearance. If Lea were here, she'd make a smart aleck remark. I swallowed against the pain in my throat. Lea was no more.

If nothing else, it was worth beating Fromer and Salander's butts just for that.

Tristan, Markus, Kirk, and I assembled around the conference table. Tristan had put Gerrit, Dachsoon, and the twenty others he'd brought as reinforcement to Markus's compound to work sharpening weapons for the coming fight. Mayson and the remaining former Council had taken charge of the remaining Elonian resistance.

"The presidents are giving a speech this weekend," Markus said. "This is the perfect opportunity to strike at them."

A crash from outside jarred the negotiation. Kieran rushed in, followed by one of Markus's men.

"Forgive me, my lord. I couldn't stop him," the man whimpered.

"It's all right." Markus rose. "My lord." His frosty voice still held respect.

My breath froze in my mouth. Kieran hadn't changed.

I scoffed at my silly thought. Why would he have changed? Only a few days had passed since I last saw him. Several times I'd itched to visit his motel room, and several times I'd denied myself. However I defined my feelings for him, they didn't matter. Not anymore.

His eyes, sparkling pools of green, appraised me through his curtain of dark hair. My chest tightened. He shouldn't have come. His presence threatened the promise I'd made to Tristan to be strong to the end.

"Are you planning your next steps without me now?" His voice, which not long ago had whispered words that had driven me to ecstasy, hadn't lost its scintillating quality.

"Excuse me?" Markus squared his shoulders. "After you made a mockery of our last alliance, my lord, it would seem counterproductive to include you." He tilted his head. "No offense."

"I'm committed to rebuilding the Divide. I want to make it up to you. To all of you." He spotted Tristan. "I see you've found your king."

"Actually, this is my brother." Thank the Old Ones, my words revealed none of the turmoil inside.

Kieran blew the hair out of his eyes and observed me. Then he extended his arm to Tristan. "It's a pleasure to meet you."

Tristan, still unaware of my past with Kieran, hesitated, but shook his hand.

"How are you?" Kieran's focus flashed back to me.

I shrugged. Even this small movement proved difficult. My pulse raced. This was silly. I needed to be a warrior again, not a lovesick teenager stuck on a man who was no good for her.

Kieran's lips formed a thin line, and he jerked his head to the door. "Can I speak to you? In private?"

"I suppose." I shot Tristan a don't-follow-me look and left the room, my gait stilted and stiff.

Kieran trailed after me into the deserted corridor, which echoed our steps. Out of earshot of my brother, I turned my glare on Kieran. "Speak."

He peered over his shoulder. "Is Lea going to come rip my head off?"

By the Old Ones, he was oblivious. How was it possible the world didn't know about her death?

"She's gone." Two words. One tone. No emotion. "Dead."

"She's what?" He lifted his fist to his chest. "How? What happened?"

"She killed herself."

"What?" The color drained from his face. "By Balor. Why? Tell me this isn't my fault."

"It's *our* fault." I swallowed the guilt-ridden rock in my throat. "Why have you come here?"

He stared at me like I should know. "To be with you, of course."

His words tugged on my resolve to stay away from him, but our actions had brought death to my best friend. I needed to heal. Make it right even though Lea wasn't here to witness it.

I bit my lip. "I can't. Not yet. Maybe not ev—"

"Don't say it." He took my hand. "I'm still trying to convince my mother to tell me how to fix this mess, but..." He glanced down. "I'm beginning to think you were right. Either way, I don't know how much longer we have before the Fall takes your memories, but until that day, and every day after that, I want to be by your side. I'm not letting you go, Nieve."

How could such beautiful words cause such pain? Despite his pleading look, all I could see was Lea running from the motel room. Plunging a dagger into her chest. "I need more time."

"She's back." Kirk's baritone boomed through the building.

I frowned at him. "What?"

"Lea," he shrieked. "She's alive!"

# CHAPTER THIRTY-EIGHT



*"Always give one hundred percent. Unless you're donating blood."*

I walked into the farmhouse and waved my hand at its gaping occupants. "Howdy."

"Lea!" Markus shouted.

Before I could count to two, he rushed to my side. Kirk sidled up to my left. Together they squeezed me, elbowing each other in the process.

*Gee. Guess they missed me.*

Nieve ran into the main corridor with Kieran at her heels. The last time I'd seen them I wanted to smash both of their faces into the ground.

She stopped a few feet in front of me, dark circles under her bloodshot eyes. "I'm so glad you're back. I'm so, so sorry."

I peeled Kirk and Markus off me and gave Nieve a quick hug. "I know."

She scowled. "I thought I'd lost you."

"*We* thought we'd lost you." Tristan stood behind his sister, looking like a lost lamb. "Why did you kill yourself?"

I lowered my gaze. "I needed to speak with Orrin."

"We buried your body." Kirk happily fluttered between us and squeezed my arm. "Is this a new one?"

"Ouch." I swatted him away. "It's my old one. I think. I don't know how this resurrection thing works. For all I know I'm a zombie. No, Orrin and I had things to discuss, like the original spell that established the Divide."

"Seriously? Did he help you?" Tristan asked.

"I hope so." Although the proof would be in the pudding.

I'd been quick to assure Orrin I would be able to restore the Divide, but when would I learn to read the fine print first? What cruel acts was I prepared to commit in order to seize back the old world? Stupid question. What cruel acts wouldn't I commit?

If I did what I needed to do, I'd lose Nieve for sure. If I chickened out, her memory would fail her. Would we be friends in the new world? My stomach wobbled. Such thoughts were unhelpful.

I let my hand hover over Fallon's hilt, seeking reassurance, yet almost afraid to touch it. Maybe I was. Whatever the price, my decision was made. Orrin had urged me to act with haste, before the Fall's transformation was complete. Before I lost my nerve. And most definitely before anyone figured out my plan.

My vision tunneled onto Kieran, the man who was going to help me right the world. "I need to speak with you."

He jumped like a puppy receiving a treat.

"I'm really, really sorry." He made to hug me.

I crossed my arms to ward him off. His betrayal still stung too much for that kind of familiarity. "No need. I-I spoke with your mother. Can we go for a walk?"

"Um, yeah. Okay."

"Lea?" Nieve's voice shot through me. "Where are you going?"

"I'll be back in a minute." I waved her off and hurried to the door before I changed my mind.

Brushing her aside wasn't my intention. She, Tristan and Markus deserved an explanation. Their faces upon my return had fluttered with hope. I was alive. Again. But my new plan involved not hope but desperation. If they knew, they'd stop me from doing what needed to be done.

Kieran followed me out. At the end of the candlelit corridor, I pointed at a coat rack. "Better grab a jacket."

Outside, the air was heavy with moisture, releasing musty smells from our coats reminiscent of spider-infested attics. Low hanging clouds and distant thunder added to the grim atmosphere.

Two buckets I'd previously noticed by the nearest outbuilding would make handy containers. "Would you take one, please?"

Kieran grabbed a bucket. "Sure."

I fell into a fast walk, sure he'd keep up. We approached the outer perimeter of Markus's estate. The guard nodded and opened a gate for us.

"What was my mother like? I've never met her in person." Kieran's tone suggested more than curiosity. It held a profound longing for Derinda, an emotion that only made sense because he didn't know her.

"I know without a doubt that she loves you."

"Did she say that?" His step bounced, as if reinvigorated by my words. "I wanted her to tell me how to restore the Divide, but she's been refusing. She wants me to rule in my father's place. Guess she doesn't know me that well."

"Maybe she'd come around eventually." I took a deep breath. "Either way, we no longer need her."

Beyond the compound, the soft and slippery ground turned walking into an act of willpower. I bent to pick a tall, yellow flower and showed it to Kieran. "Gumweed. Put a few of these in your bucket."

He crouched and plucked one out the ground. "They're sticky."

"They need to be."

"I hope you know what you're doing."

So did I.

We walked in awkward silence, collecting flowers and listening to the rustling among the ankle-high grass. The rain unlocked a cornucopia of scents, from fresh, wet grass all the way to sugary, floral notes. Kieran's silence pressed on me more with each step.

Except for the birds circling above, we were alone. The time had come. I gestured at two rocks and took a seat. Out here, no buildings broke the wind's power, no trees to hold it back.

"What is your plan?" He pointed at the buckets. "I assume they have something to with it?"

"There are only two people who can restore the Divide. You and I." I got to my feet and placed a hand on his shoulder. "But the price we're asked to pay is high."

His posture sagged. "It's my fault plan A didn't work, but I'll do anything to make plan B a success."

"I'm glad," I said and took a strengthening breath. Then I plunged my blade into his kidney.

# CHAPTER THIRTY-NINE



*"I'm not bossy. I simply know what you should be doing and how you should do it."*

After combing Markus's house for Lea and Kieran, I took my search outside where a gruff guard who'd clearly not had his morning tea directed me through a back gate. Limp yellow flowers dotted the long, wet grass, and large flocks of swallows gathered in the sky. How could the world have changed so much, and in some respects, not changed at all? Plants still grew, birds still flew. I jammed my hands into my jeans pockets and strained against the wind whipping my hair across my face.

A short walk from the compound, Lea's and Kieran's figures came into view. One of them sat, slumped without a sign of life on a boulder.

"Kieran." His name scraped across my tongue, barely loud enough to be heard.

I pounded through the soft grass, swallowing the reflux of bile that stung my throat. Each time one foot took off, my stomach flung into my mouth, only to bottom hard when the other foot landed.

Kieran rose and stood tall, his hand pressed against his lower back. He swayed and took a balancing step.

But he wasn't dead. He wasn't dead. I briefly shut my eyes. He wasn't dead.

Lea fell to her knees, staring at Fallon. "I didn't know what else to do."

"You stabbed me." Kieran's voice sounded incredulous, his mouth locked in a terrible scowl.

A shiver down the length of my body spurred me across the last few yards. I threw myself at him, slinging my arms around his neck. He gasped and wobbled, but didn't fall.

"Are you hurt?" Without waiting for his reply, I twirled him and lifted the back of his coat so I could examine his wound. A dark bloodstain spread underneath his fingers and soaked through the fabric of his blue T-shirt. Not fatal. Thank the Old Ones.

I drew a noisy breath.

He wrapped his free arm around me. I buried my nose in his neck, anchoring myself to his scent. *I nearly lost him again.*

His lips brushed against my hair. "Shush. It's all right."

"No, it's not." I twisted from his hug. "Lea? What were you thinking?"

Lea kneeled on the ground, her blade discarded in the grass.

Why would she hurt him? He'd foiled our plan, but he wasn't a malicious person. If anyone had betrayed her, it was *me*. My heart skidded in my chest. Was she trying to get back at me by killing him?

I fixed her with my glare. "What happened to you? Since when do you stab your friends?"

She scrambled behind the rock Kieran had occupied a minute before. Shoulders heaving, she vomited and then cried until she'd exhausted herself.

Part of me wanted to go to her, soothe her with kind

reassurances. Instead, I steeled my heart. Kieran was the one who'd nearly died. She'd find no sympathy in my face.

Kieran's hand settled in the hollow of my waist. As he rolled me toward him for maximum contact, my body molded itself to his shape. Only my head remained cranked back to keep sight of Lea.

"Are you feeling better?" I asked, my tone softer now.

"Yeah." She sat back on her feet, her neck bowed like an old woman's.

"I know I messed up," Kieran said. "I shouldn't have killed my father before he gave us answers."

Lea clawed her hands into the yellowed grass. "That's not why."

"Then explain it," he said and rubbed his fingers across his forehead. "Because I'm drawing a blank."

She sniffled and wiped the sleeve of her oversized coat across her face. "Orrin told me how to restore the Divide, and it will take your blood."

"No." I stiffened in Kieran's embrace. "He's lying."

Kieran's shoulders sagged. "Why?"

"You and I carry Orrin's and Derinda's line." Lea pressed the heels of her hands into her eyes. "They performed a life force ritual, joining their blood in equal amounts to create the world of magic. When I died and my blood flowed, the magic that separated our worlds got out of whack."

That's why she tried to kill Kieran? She stabbed him on the deranged words of a stranger? "That makes no sense. Orrin and Derinda didn't die when they created the Divide. So why kill Kieran?"

"Blame his father. He was the one who bled me until I died, even though a few pints might have been enough to tear down the Divide. Kieran's life force has to equal mine. That's how the original spell worked."

I pressed closer against Kieran. This had to be a plot by Orrin to get back at Derinda. Even if it wasn't, the price was too high.

I shook my head, dizzy. "There must be another way."

Lea's mouth twisted into a withered smile. "Don't you think I gave it some thought? At the last second I changed my mind, but Fallon carried on moving. The damn thing has a mind of its own sometimes. Next thing I knew, there was blood." She gave a gargled burp. "'scuse me."

With her dark rings and hollow cheeks, she looked miserable. My heart lunged, but I wouldn't weaken. Not yet. She'd nearly taken Kieran from me.

"Hey." Kieran pried my hand off his hip and lifted it to his mouth. "It's okay."

Not even his warm lips unknotted my muscles or the boulder of dread, anger, and frustration stuck in my chest. Kieran had awoken emotions inside me I'd considered reserved for normal, softer people, people who hadn't been trained to fight and kill. People other than me. Through him, I'd come alive. I gazed into his emerald eyes, memorized every fleck of gray and gold. But the words I wanted to say refused to come.

He tightened his embrace. "Maybe you *should* kill me."

I shrunk back. "You're not serious."

"Deadly. Lea's died twice, and each time Orrin's brought her back. Maybe, if I died, I'd come back, too."

Why was everyone talking crazy all of a sudden?

Lea shook her head. "Orrin likes you about as much as moldy spores for breakfast, and I'm not sure your mother has the power to return you to life. You die, there's a good chance you're not coming back."

The wind picked up, and thick drops fell onto my head, mirroring the plummeting of my heart into my own personal hell. A possible life without Kieran.

He caressed my hair. "Just an idea."

Lea plucked a few blades of grass from the ground, rolled them between her hands and let a swirl of air carry them off. "Then we're back to where we started."

I stared back toward the compound. A figure moved across the field in our direction, hands tucked deep into pockets and head bowed to cut through the wind. I'd bet my last knife this was Tristan on his way to check Lea was still here.

Kieran straightened. "Hang on. This life force is blood, right? Did Orrin say I have to die, or is that just his preferred method?"

"He said the Divide was built by joining the life forces of him and Derinda in equal measures. He didn't specifically mention death." Lea glanced at him and her eyes widened. "Dammit. Why didn't I think of it? That might work."

"Well, it's an idea at least." Kieran blew into his fist as if to warm his hand. "If we can preserve my blood and keep it from clotting, prepare it in the same way as we do transfusions, then the life force would remain intact."

Lea bunched her lips. "How much blood do you think I lost the day I died? You know, the first time?"

"You're roughly hold eight to ten pints of blood in your body."

"That sounds a lot." She patted her hips. "Don't forget I lost weight over the last few weeks."

"Look who's joking again." He laughed. "You'd die after losing around four pints, so I would call four pints your life force. I'm taller and bigger than you, which means I'm carrying more blood inside me. That's good news. I'll have to rest between donations so my blood cells can be replaced, but it's doable." He hooked his arm around my neck and planted a kiss on my head. "I have my very own nurse to take care of me."

I closed my eyes and soaked in his scent for the umpteenth time. "Good. We have a plan, and no one has to die."

Lea's hair hung limp over her shoulders, her pale skin even whiter than usual. Her hands glided across the tips of the grass by her side. "One last-ditch effort then. The law of averages says we have to get it right at some point." She picked up Fallon.

"Don't do it." Tristan hurried past me and Kieran, fat drops pearling off his nose and chin. He fell onto his knees by Lea's side. "I'm sorry for how I acted. I know I was an ass. But please, don't kill yourself again. You're infuriating, opinionated, stubborn, but by the Old Ones, I love every infuriating, opinionated and—"

Lea scrunched her nose. "Stubborn?"

"...stubborn part of you." With his thumbs, he wiped the water from her face, and then he pressed her hand against his heart. "Please, stay with me."

My ice heart melted. If Tristan could ask for a do-over, she deserved one. Kieran was alive, that mattered most. We also had a plan. Just for a moment, the world wasn't so terrible a place.

I jerked my chin at my brother. "He's something, isn't he?"

Lea smiled and stroked his chin. "He's something all right."

Tristan's glance skipped from Lea to me and finally landed on Kieran. His tender expression darkened like the storm clouds overhead. "Why do you have your arms around my sister?"

THREE DAYS of bloodletting had taken their toll. I placed my hand on Kieran's forehead and frowned. If his temperature kept dropping like this, I'd put a stop to this madness.

Markus had given Kieran his own room at his farmhouse. I still didn't entirely trust his generosity, but we needed him as much as he needed us. Fromer and Salander had been slaughtering and pillaging their way through those who opposed them, and sooner or later, they'd take on Markus and his forces. For better or worse, we'd fight by his side.

Without windows, Kieran's bedroom air had gone stale, but it couldn't be helped. In an attempt to improve the situation, Markus had set his heater and air recycler to high. I nearly beat him over the head with my stick. Kieran was weak. One virus through the ventilation could kill him.

But by and large, people had been leaving us in peace.

I filled the glass on Kieran's nightstand with fresh water from the carafe, then stacked up the magazines Lea had given me to while away the time between his naps.

Kieran shivered, his pulse was racing again. The air was dense enough to cut through with a blunt knife, but if he was cold, I had little choice. I cranked the thermostat to the max and piled several blankets on top of him. One more day, I'd give him. After that I'd turn off the tap to his blood supply.

"Body heat is more effective." His voice cracked. "Join me in bed."

Was this a ploy to get me naked again? Because he had to save his strength, not waste it on sex.

"Trust me, I'm a doctor." He pulled the blanket up to his chin. "The human body is the perfect heat source."

I pushed aside the equipment Markus had procured to collect Kieran's blood. The long tube connecting the bag to Kieran's arm gleamed in a deep, solid red. No matter how much I loathed the tube and the whole setup, I wasn't stupid. We had this one shot, and we were taking it.

But that didn't mean I couldn't alleviate Kieran's suffering. Only one thing for it. I took off my boots, pants, and jacket, and cuddled up next to him. "Better not get any ideas, buster."

He clamped one hand around my buttocks and chuckled. "We'll see."

For the most part, he lacked the energy to follow our conversations, and his prolonged rest periods were more often than not interrupted by awful dreams. Yet he didn't complain. I pulled his head close. My good boy.

Tristan could learn a lesson or two from him. Somehow he'd assumed his confession of love would drive Lea back into his arms. Didn't he know her at all? For now, she was courteous, but remained distant. To really drive her message home, she spent her time with Markus or playing cards with Kirk and his gargoyle friends.

Tristan worked off his aggression with scathing remarks about my relationship with *"that Shade."*

Soon, he'd learn his lesson in humility. Like us, he was a cog. If he could put aside his ego and open his heart to new things, Lea would come back to him.

I picked up a book from the nightstand and opened it. "Where were we?"

Kieran nuzzled my neck, sending tingles down my spine. "Something about a united country?"

The last passage on the page I'd marked. "Got it. Right. 'Such was his dream for a united country.'"

The door slammed into the wall and Kirk fluttered into the room, followed by a red-faced Markus.

"They're comin'. The Shades are comin'." Kirk had trouble maintaining his position. "They're gonna storm the compound." He glanced around. "Where's Lea?"

I lowered the book, snatched up the blanket, and stared at the small gargoyle. He and his friends had become our spies among the Torren government, blending in with buildings, catching and relaying snippets of secret conversations.

Markus's eyes narrowed into black slits. "The gargoyle's

crazy. They wouldn't dare, not yet. I still have too many supporters among the Torrens and do business with the rest."

"No matter," Kirk said. "Fromer and Salander are telling everyone you were part of the assassination."

"How do they know?"

"They don't. They's made it up, but no one supports you anymore. The presidents are gettin' the militia ready now."

"My brothers would dare attack me?" Kieran's voice tore from his throat.

"They have no idea you're here." I patted his head. "Although I'm not sure if that knowledge would stop them or make them come running faster."

Kirk buzzed up and down, nearly bouncing off the walls. His gray coat billowing behind him, he zoomed out the room shouting, "The Shades are comin'."

Lea entered the room, followed by Tristan. "Please tell me this is one of Kirk's jokes."

Markus shook his head. "That's what I thought, but he seems sure."

"But we're not ready. Kieran?"

"We don't even have half of what we need." His expression twisted.

"Typical. It's like my whole life has become a Kobayashi Maru." She met our questioning stares with a sulky bottom lip. "Don't you people watch Star Trek? I'm saying events are designed for me to fail, whatever I do." She shook her head. "Remind me to get you guys translator microbes so I can stop explaining stuff."

"Try it anyway," I said. "Maybe we're closer than we think. You don't know exactly how much blood Galleo took from you that night."

Kieran and Lea exchanged a doubting glance.

"You're right." Lea smiled, although it was a sad smile. "What can it hurt?"

"Good. Then—" Tristan looked at me, and his face turned red. "Are you two naked?"

"You and I are going to have a talk." Lea tapped her index finger against his chest.

"About what?"

"First of all, about how Nieve and Kieran aren't your concern." Her voice was firm, as it tended to be. "But mostly about you. You, Tristan, are a king."

"Was a king." He lowered his gaze.

"No, you are. You have the heart of a king and your sense of duty, though a pain in the ass, marks you as a king, too. Look around you." She gestured across the room. "Markus is leader of the Underground, but he's not a soldier. Kieran is a warrior, but he's never led. You were a royal champion once, and you are a king now. So you are going to go out there, take charge of the situation, and buy Kieran and me the time we need to perform the ritual. Our safety, *my* safety, is in your hands."

I'd expected an outburst. Not the mellow smile that formed on his lips.

"Nothing is going to happen to you." He took her hand. "Anything else, dear?"

Lea grinned, although once again, her humor didn't seem genuine. "A good-luck kiss?"

He obliged, and I hid my face against Kieran's shoulder.

Tristan let go of Lea and clapped his hands. "Come on, Nieve. You heard the lady. We must organize our warriors, integrate them and Kieran's friends among Markus's ranks. I suspect the attack will occur at night. Still, if we strategize, our presence here might surprise our attackers, turning the tide in our favor. I have a few ideas about that."

I'd feared his blind trust in the prophecy and our succession of failures had robbed him of his talent, yet here was my brother, back in his full and calculating glory.

"I can't wait to hear them." I allowed myself a brief smile. "Now leave the room or I'll be forced to fight naked."

Tristan's smile faltered.

It was time he realized his little sister was all grown up.

# CHAPTER FORTY



*"Some people wrestle daily with their demons. I play poker with mine."*

Kieran and I opened the door to Markus's basement and turned on the lights. A short staircase descended into the large, musty space, which spread out to the right and left. Currently, the basement was used as a sort of pantry, filled with everything from rat poison to canned goods. The dampness crawled up my skin, seeking entry into my nose.

We picked a corner at the far end. While I laid out twelve bowls in a large circle, Kieran kneeled on the floor and smashed the plants we'd collected into a fragrant goo. His white, sweaty skin belied the determination with which he dedicated himself to the task.

"How will we know when your brothers get here?" I asked.

An ear-splitting sound boomed and the shelves surrounding us shook. I ducked.

"Never mind." I gave a short laugh that originated from a thumping heart rather than any sense of amusement. "Do you think this is going to work?"

"Honestly?" He shook his head and stared at the two bottles

of blood in his hands. "I don't think we have near enough, but Nieve is right. We must try as long as there's a chance."

I cleared my throat. "You're only saying that so I won't try to kill you again."

"What can I say? I like being alive." He spooned plant goo into the delicate china bowls.

"Are you worried about Nieve, Tristan, and the others?" I asked.

He exhaled loudly. "My level of concern for Tristan and Markus is lower than for Nieve." He got up off the floor and placed a hand against his back. "But in case she asks, I wasn't worried about her at all."

The thick mix stuck to the wooden spoon, causing me to scrunch my nose. "She lectured you about coddling her?"

"Yes. No point telling her how silly it is that the two people with the greatest powers are hiding in the basement while the others wade knife-deep in blood and gore."

"No offense, but you couldn't scare a puppy in your current condition." I pointed at the marked circle on the ground. "We have our hands full anyhow."

He stared wistfully at the staircase. "Yeah."

"Blood?" I held out my hand for the first bottle by his side.

He handed it to me and uncorked the second container. "Does this type of spell require any particular sequence of steps?"

"No clue." I shrugged. "Orrin was all about balance, equilibrium, yin and yang, and, you know, other synonyms. One life force must equal the other. The correct proportions of plants. Stuff like that. How about you start next to me and go along that way until we meet on the other side? Just make sure you spread your blood evenly."

I nearly gagged at the rotten meat smell of blood weighing down the air. The floral note added by the squeezed and mushed flowers made the atmosphere even more vomit-worthy. Maybe Nieve and Tristan had got the better deal after all.

Kieran stepped back to regard our arrangement and nodded his approval. "What now?"

"Now we take off our clothes and begin chanting." I kept my tone level and glanced at him with what I hoped was a look of innocence.

"Excuse me?"

"Your face!" I chuckled. "Only joking. We stand inside the circle and repeat the incantation, evenly, monotonously, without interruption. Orrin said it's best to go about it with my eyes shut to avoid getting distracted."

We stepped into the ring of bowls, and Kieran reached for my hands.

Physical contact hadn't been part of the instructions, but what the hell?

Now, where had I left my brave voice? "The crucial thing is the intent. You have to be able to picture the Divide as a physical entity, like a force field surrounding a snow globe. Got it?"

"Go ahead."

"On three." I counted us out, and we began the spell. "*Kalena morgana aventi gebana.*"

Or, 'Let our magic be bound.'

Right from the start, our voices flowed out of phase. Kieran galloped, and I tiptoed. My attempt to catch up ended with me overtaking him when he slowed his words. We found our sync zone in round three.

By round six, nothing had happened.

We continued even as the battle above us heated up. Furniture scraped or toppled, explosions shook the foundations. My mind played unhelpful pictures of Nieve getting stabbed.

Kieran squeezed my hand. He was right. I needed to focus.

We chanted the spell for the tenth time, our voices droning with the same pitch and speed.

Vibrations rattled my feet and shins, zooming through my body. *Whoa.* The whole floor shook, this time not from the commotion upstairs, but from pure, electrifying magic. The power built inside us, around us, charging through us like the fizz of a nuclear-powered sparkler.

Sweat pearled on my forehead, but I stuck with it, reveling in the exhaustion that followed each incantation.

After twelve loops of chanting, we stopped, just as Orrin had instructed.

"Did it work?" Kieran let go of my hands and glanced at the ground.

I wiped my face with my sleeve and took a raspy breath. The bowls stood untouched, mocking our pathetic attempt at producing big-time magic.

"I doubt it." I clenched my teeth against the rising frustration. "How are your memories?"

He tilted his head. "Still there, both old and new."

"Me too."

We'd come close. A reaction had indeed taken place; the tremors proved that. But in the end, we simply didn't have enough blood to match the amount I'd spilled the day I died. The ritual was incomplete.

"What now?" My gaze whipped to his face. "And before you offer to kill yourself, that's not an option. I'd rather take my chances up there."

I pointed at the source of the noise.

"Then that's what we should do." His jaw jutted back and forth then set. "Fight alongside our friends."

"Tristan, Nieve, and the gargoyles will be joining Markus's forces from the left. Your brothers won't be expecting them." I pressed a soothing hand against my forehead. "We might live to see another day."

My ability to lie had really improved over the last few months. But in reality, our life meters were low, and Princess Zelda was nowhere in sight.

"Come on." Kieran abandoned our setup and walked up the stairs. In his current state, not even his Old powers could turn our fortune.

I followed close on his heels. My fight to restore the Divide was a bust. All we had left was to fight for our survival.

The clanging and curtailed screams welcomed us like a scene from a gory movie. The activity inside the farmhouse was vicious. How did so many people fit in here anyway, let alone attack or defend themselves? Maybe Markus's farmhouse had become the manifestation of time and relative dimension in space.

Brandishing our weapons, Kieran and I slalomed through sword slashes and falling bodies. So much death, and I could have prevented it all. If I'd killed the old Shade that day outside The Fly. If I'd killed Kieran the way Orrin had told me. If…if…if…

Outside the farmhouse, the scene proved even more dire than inside. The freezing darkness was rife with the ringing of swords. The mesh-wire fences had been torn down, and hundreds of soldiers had descended on the brave men and women that fought on our side. They'd crammed themselves between cars and pickups, between wheelbarrows and other obstacles Tristan had placed to slow the opponent's advance.

Kieran disappeared in the fray without glancing back. The Fall had turned him into a doctor, but he was still a warrior at heart. He and Nieve could have had a great future.

I fell against a wall, staring at Fallon. My heart thudded in my ears, and my dagger sizzled with energy. My friends needed me. I should fight like them, kill like them.

"It didn't work?" Nieve asked, breathless. Gore covered her red jacket and jeans, her lovely hair matted with blood.

"No. As you can see, the building's still without windows." I avoided her eyes, but the guilt must have shown on my face. "Looks like Tristan was right all along. I'm a fraud. Not one of my ideas worked out."

Four yards in front of us, a man groaned and splashed into a million shards of pure white light then disappeared.

"Oh my God." A shudder zipped across my spine. "That was Dachsoon."

Nieve's gaze traveled past me to the now empty spot. "He was never a good swordsman, but I'd hoped he'd make it."

"Are you for real? He's another death I have on my conscience. This time it's someone I knew. God, look at me. My biological mother gave me the genes to fight. Orrin the genes to do magic. And I've failed at both."

"Stop beating yourself up. You did fine." Her gaze wandered over the faces of the men and women still fighting for their freedom, and of those seeking to deny it. "Ready to cover my back?"

Her hanbo flew up and met the attack of a Kindred soldier. The poor sod hadn't even been given a leather uniform to protect against the onslaught. The man dropped his sword and waved his hands at the ground, but his weak magic elicited only a rumble. Nieve plunged the tip of her hanbo into his ribs. Efficient as always. He gurgled and collapsed, blood staining his dark jacket.

"Are you coming?" She didn't wait for my answer and charged a Shade who'd cornered Gerrit.

Fallon urged me to join her, to make up the numbers, as if my dagger and I would make any difference to the outcome.

*Join the battle. Make up the numbers.* That was the solution. That was why the spell hadn't worked.

"Nieve!" I shouted. "I have it. I know what I did wrong."

She waved at me, although I wasn't sure she'd heard me. I turned on my heels and ran back into the house.

I ducked the swords, used Fallon once or twice to fend off an attack, but I didn't stop. How could I have been so dense? The pieces finally made that satisfying mental *click* as they fit together. Yin and yang in total balance.

Hadn't Orrin been repeating it over and over? The spell he'd given me wasn't about "matching" the life force Galleo had stolen from me with Kieran's. The Divide was gone. Kaput. What we should have been doing is start from a blank slate. Build a *new* Divide. And that required not just Kieran's but also my blood.

The basement door closed behind me, muffling the sounds of battle, as I ran down the stairs again. Time was short. Nieve had been doing well, her confidence fully restored, but I'd witnessed for myself how quickly luck could turn against us.

The ring of bowls lay undisturbed. I emptied half of them into a bucket before redistributing the remaining blood over the twelve containers. Donating two bottles' worth of blood while remaining conscious was outside my capability, but at no point had Orrin claimed that the ritual demanded anyone's death. After all, he and Derinda had survived the original spell.

I sliced my arm multiple times with my dagger and let my blood, my life force, mingle with Kieran's. By the time I reached bowl five, the flow slowed. I cut my other arm, and managed to fill another four bowls, but I was still three short. Worse, I was getting woozy.

My stomach, my legs, even my neck—where there was blood, I drained it. As long as I didn't hit any arteries, I'd be okay. Yet my knees were already trembling. My hand too weak to hold on to Fallon. Once the twelfth bowl had received my contribution, I closed my eyes and spoke the incantation again. And again.

And again.

With each repetition, the words flowed more quickly and evenly. The spell poured from my throat and mouth as if it had waited for the right set of lungs to give it breath.

A spasm seized me, and I fell to my knees, crying out from the pain on impact. The ceiling lights flickered. Pain quenched my breath as the magic words whirled around me like a tornado. My chest tightened then the magic burst from my body and into the white bowls. Lanced by blue jets of energy, the blood and plants bubbled and sputtered over the edges, forming three concentric circles around me.

This was it. This *had* to be it. I sat still, sucking heavy oxygen into lungs that were far too small. I'd thrown everything I had into this. Abandoned my friends in the fight of their lives for this one last try.

The voices and screams from upstairs grew louder, and the door crashed open.

*Nothing to see here. Just move on.*

Hesitant steps shuffled at the top of the stairs and then went away. In my current state, mounting any sort of defense to protect myself, to protect the ritual, wouldn't have been possible.

Tingles crawled up my spine into my brain when violent quakes shook me. My vision couldn't keep up, flashing into and out of reality. In the end, I could no longer track my environment. My pulse throbbed loud in my ears, my head felt close to splitting, and then everything went dark.

The ceiling lights had gone out.

Millions of needles pierced every millimeter of my skin. I cried out. Yelled. Yet just as suddenly, the pain disappeared.

I opened my eyes, cautious, not knowing what to expect.

Light struck me from behind, casting my kneeling form in a shadow. I turned around to check for the source. At the top of the wall, by the ceiling, long glass panes let in the rays of the moon.

I rolled onto the floor, staring at the windows. And then I cried. I cried from exhaustion, from relief, and from unbounded joy. For once, I hadn't failed. For once, I'd done well.

# CHAPTER FORTY-ONE



*"Some fights are worth the agony. And some joys are worth a fight."*

Swords and knives snapped around my ears, requiring every ounce of my concentration. The metallic smell of blood weighed on the atmosphere. Markus's men and women fought back-to-back with me. How far I'd come to trust them with my life.

Fromer and Salander had pitched around two hundred of their Shades and nearly two hundred Kindreds against a hundred on our side. The Kindreds moved sluggishly, which didn't mean they were less dangerous. Their swords cut and sliced just as deep as any Shade's.

Blades crossed and knives stabbed at every inch of Markus's compound. Inside and outside the farmhouse, around the outbuildings that had housed Markus's and Kieran's friends as well as our Elonians. So far, we'd been withstanding the assault, but would it be enough to survive?

I plunged my hanbo into another throat. Instead of melting into the ground or splintering into light, the Kindred corpse remained, easy to trip over, his face as forgettable as that of any warrior I'd killed today.

A battalion of oddly dressed gargoyles soared over our heads, occasionally rolling into a tight ball to bomb into the enemy's ranks. Some of Kirk's friends held up candles, so the Elonians among us would not fight blind. Tristan flew by their side in his Kindred clothes, shouting encouragement, relaying information, and swooping down if his help was needed. Soon, his reserves would weaken him.

A loud murmur behind me was the first sign that something was wrong. I didn't turn to check. A seasoned Shade warrior beleaguered me, slashing at me with a speed I myself could no longer muster. Sweat poured from his face, yet his lips pressed tight in stubborn courage. His skilled knife swishes demanded my concentration.

He peered over my shoulder. *Fool.* My hanbo slipped into his chest. He sputtered, fell, and dissolved into the earth.

I glanced up, prepared to take on my next opponent.

The two Kindreds nearest me stood on the spot, staring at the weapons in their hands. Who'd taught them they could rest mid-battle? This fight was about survival. I reached back to gather force and smacked my hanbo forward to—

Someone grabbed hold of me. "Hang on," said a voice so familiar I wanted to cry out.

I turned and gazed into Kieran's face. A thousand ripples of relief tore through my insides along with a thousand bubbles of pure joy. He was alive.

"Look." He pointed across the field, as the deadly clangs lessened, and one by one, Kindreds laid down their arms and ran away.

Elonians and Torrens fell into a deep, wary silence, weapons at the ready, but no more strikes fell. Fromer and Salander, both on horseback, whispered with each other and then one of them blew a whistle.

The battle was over.

I spun around to Kieran. His lips found mine, as he curled his hands around my face. I melted into his touch, blanking out the indistinct sounds around us. If anyone stabbed me now, I'd die happy. The relieved sighs from those around us barely entered my consciousness. Instead, I pressed myself against Kieran, incapable of getting enough of his taste, while my memories flooded back—my friend Belinda, Washington D.C., my parents' faces.

I encircled Kieran's waist with my arms and leaned back. "Is Lea okay?"

"She must be." He smiled. "Otherwise the ritual wouldn't have worked. How's your memory?"

"I think I'm back to normal. Although I remember some things both ways. Your father was the Torren king, but also the president."

"It's a bizarre feeling, isn't it?" He rubbed his nose against mine. "That's what it was like for me when the Fall tried to convince me I was a doctor."

I took his hands. "You do have the magic touch."

He chuckled. "Do you think we should find Lea?"

"I already found her." Markus walked toward us, a pale-faced Lea tucked under his arm.

She wobbled, and I rushed to her other side to prop her up. "Are you okay?"

"Yeah." Her voice buckled under her fatigue. "Just, you know..." She twirled her index finger by her temple. "Blood loss is a bitch."

"Blood loss?"

She waved me off. "I'll explain later."

"Look, Angel. Your brother's been busy." Markus nodded toward Tristan, who stood about fifty yards away by a swirling Gate. "As soon as he realized that reality had shifted back, he opened it and started sending people home."

Shades and Elonians rushed to the vortex, as if afraid a grave malady infected Kindred air.

"Kieran," a deep voice shouted across the battlefield. President Fromer sat on his horse, his face dark with fury.

No, not president. He was just plain old Fromer now.

"Hang on," Kieran said and faced his brother. "It's over. You lost."

The man who looked nothing like Kieran pulled back his horse, then leaned forward onto his thigh. "For now. As for you, you're a traitor and no longer welcome in Torren."

"Brave words." Kieran flicked his wrist, shooting a jet of sparks at the horse, which jerked around violently. "Off you go."

Fromer steadied his mount and reached for his sword, but Salander hurried toward him and took his arm. "Leave it."

Together they rode toward the Gate.

Tristan lifted the tip of his own sword yet let them pass without incident. We'd all had enough of killing for today.

Once the battlefield began to empty, Tristan made his way over, and his gaze came to rest on Lea. "You did well, Padawan. How are you?"

She blinked up, lips pressed together, her face as white as a glass of milk. "Just dandy."

A woman ran up to Markus and whispered into his ear. His expression became animated. "I need to go." He handed Lea to Tristan, then he turned to me. "Remember your word, Angel."

*Slice it.* I'd hoped he'd forgotten.

Tristan scowled. "Anything I should know?"

I fixed my gaze on the top of Lea's head, which served as a buffer zone between my brother and the news I'd have to give him. "I cut a deal with Markus to ensure his cooperation. I promised him shared access to the Gate."

"You what?" His volume rose.

"She did the right thing." Lea straightened, her eyes still

glazed. "It was the price we had to pay for victory, and with everything that's happened, I say we got away cheaply."

Tristan grumbled, but he tightened his grasp on her. "Fine."

"My lord." Markus bowed to Kieran and headed toward the Gate.

"I should thank you, too." Tristan slapped Kieran's shoulder. "You did come through in the end. I owe you."

"We had the same goal. Still, I must ask a favor." Kieran squeezed Nieve's shoulders. "You promised to release your sister from her oath once she completed this last mission for you. I would be grateful if you kept your word."

My brother lifted his chin, but his answer got cut off by a rocky song, sounding slightly tinny.

Lea slapped her pockets, located and extracted her phone. She glanced at the display. Life returned to her face. She held the phone to her ear. "Mom?"

# CHAPTER FORTY-TWO



*"Crap, that hurt. It's almost as if you take my attempt on your life personal."*

My grip tightened around my cell. "Mom, is that you?"

"Peanut. Are you all right?"

Oh God yes. I stepped out of Tristan's embrace, not wishing him to see my tears should they decide to fall.

"I'm good." My mouth trembled even as I reassured her. "Everything's good."

"I was so worried about you." Her tone was a mom's tone—half of it told me off while the other half made sure I knew she still loved me. "We both were. We haven't heard from you in ages."

"Dad? He's with you?" The iron band that had clasped my heart when my father had denied knowing me burst. I dropped to my knees, no longer able to support my body. "It's so great to hear your voice, Mom."

"What happened to us, Peanut? We used to be so close. You know you can tell me anything."

A chuckle almost tore loose from my mouth. "I'm fine." I ran my fingers through my hair, searching for an acceptable explanation for my absence. "Just really, really busy, that's all."

Despite everything I wanted to say to her, my ordeal, the truth about the universe, no adequate words formed. She wouldn't understand. Dear God, she wouldn't understand.

"We're coming over." My mom sounded determined. "As soon as we can. I'll get Dad to book a flight."

"You are?" The fog in my head cleared at once. My stomach finally settled.

Mom magic.

"Absolutely." Her voice shook. "You say you're fine, but you don't sound fine. A mother knows these things."

"I'd love to see you." Even my words flowed more easily now.

"We'll get right on that. I love you, okay? Don't forget that."

"I won't." My smile lasted even after my mother had hung up.

I rose and faced my friends. "Seems the world is back to what it should be."

"We'll give it a few days to see how things settle." Tristan's expression darkened. "Who knows what lasting effects the Fall has caused. Some Shades, and dare I say, Elonians, might choose to remain behind in this world, having got a taste of what their free use of magic can do here. That could cause trouble. I'll leave the Gate open for a few days, guarded of course, and try to get the word out, but—"

"I love seeing you taking charge, but can't you simply enjoy the win for a moment?" I placed my hand on his arm. "We saved the world."

"That we did." His gaze dropped to my hand, his expression pensive. "Nieve, your friend is right. You've done all I asked of you and more. I release you from your oath—on the understanding you will train our new royal champion."

"I can live with that." Nieve beamed first at him, then at

Kieran. "If you want, I can give you the name of someone who'd do the job well."

"I've made my choice." He pointed at me. "Lea's going to be my new chapion."

She blinked. "Are you sure? She'll be the first one to tell you that she's no warrior."

"Hey!" I stuck my tongue out at her. "Thanks to you, I'll be the second one to tell him. But yeah, I'm the worst possible choice."

"My mind is made up." He leaned in and placed both hands on my shoulders. "Warrior or not, you came through for us."

His blue eyes already held too much sway over me. I stared past him at the whirling Gate. "I don't know."

"Why do you insist on arguing all the time?" Tristan pressed his palm against his chest. "You're making me old before my time."

I made a face. "Fine, I'll be your royal champion, but only if you promise not to order me around again."

"I see we'll have to have another discussion about who's the king and who isn't." He winked. "But don't worry about your fighting skills. They will improve with Nieve's help."

This was really happening. Holy cow. Not too long ago Tristan had trouble trusting me. Now this? Maybe this world was even crazier than the last.

Despite my doubts, I projected a calm smile. "Has anyone seen Kirk?"

Kieran pointed behind him. "He's with his people, celebrating their victory. Yes, you heard right. *Their* victory."

"Well, they did help us and earned their freedom, don't you think?" I put force into my voice and glared at him until I was sure he understood.

He raised his hands. "I will see to it myself. Every gargoyle that wants to be free, will be free. I promise."

"Thank you."

Kieran ran his thumb along Nieve's cheek. "How about it? Want to show me those trees you were famous for climbing?"

A slow grin crept over my friend's face. "Are you going to try to beat my record?"

"Hmm, that sounds like a challenge."

She winked at me and walked off, arm in arm with Kieran. Maybe they would get their future after all. My two best friends. No one deserved happiness more than those two.

After their bodies melted through the Gate, I squinted at Tristan. "About this royal champion business. I have a few conditions. My father."

"Will be cured this week. You have my word."

"Good." I counted my conditions off on my fingers. "Next, I want to meet my birth mother. I know she's got problems, but I have a right to see her."

"Any other demands?" He slanted one eyebrow up.

"I have a list, don't worry. Next, I'll need to get Feynie back. He's my guinea pig. You're gonna love him."

He wrinkled his nose. "If you say so."

I widened my eyes in deliberate innocence. "I assume you offer medical?"

"Why don't we discuss terms later? For now, look at this as a new adventure." He placed the crook of his finger under my chin. "I know you like adventures."

"Mhm. You know what else I like? Leather. Please tell me you'll be swapping your denims for a pair of your old pants again?"

"Anything for my new royal champion." His gentle chuckle blew warmth onto my neck.

Part of me should be mad at Tristan for trying to control my future. But the twinkle in his otherwise serious expression, the twinkle that softened my insides like an ice pop under the

Arizona sun, the twinkle that only I saw, convinced me not to protest his decision.

I was ready to face my challenges. To do the work necessary to fulfill my potential.

Tristan was the cherry on top that made all the hardship worth my while.

I'd reached the last stop before Happy-Ever-After-Land. Now was the time to hop off the train. It's what any sane person with close ties to her family, and half an ounce of common sense, would do.

If only my head weren't tilting toward Tristan. If only my lips weren't parting in anticipation.

When his kiss swallowed my breath, I wasted no precious oxygen on gasping. I responded in kind, overcome by the desire I'd denied myself for so long.

Tristan gathered me close. The hardness of his body contrasted perfectly with his butter-soft lips.

This was what I'd been fighting for. This warmth. This affection. Blissful pleasure rode my veins like a rollercoaster, funneling into a delicious squeeze of my core.

Tristan pulled back and gazed at me, a glazed expression in his eyes. His mouth twitched, as if ready to speak. But any outpouring of emotions would spoil the moment just as surely as one of my usual, ill-timed quips.

"Shall we go?" I asked. "My lord?"

He smiled. An unfettered smile as if he hadn't just resumed his mantle as king of the Elonian people. "Let's."

We locked hands and stepped toward the vortex of the Gate.

*"Scientifically speaking, the odds are stacked against magical Happily Ever Afters. But given my particular circumstances, I'm rooting for magic."*

## LEA

Thank you for reading. If you enjoyed this book, I would appreciate it if you shared your opinion with your fellow readers by leaving a review.

Don't forget to check out Book 2 of the Champions of Elonia, HIDE AND SEEK. Go to www.carmen-fox.com/dac2 to discover more.

# ALSO BY
# CARMEN FOX

*The Silverton Chronicles*

Guarded

Bound

Trapped – Free download for newsletter subscribers

*The Wild Pack*

Moon Promise

*Champions of Elonia*

Divide and Conquer

Hide and Seek

*Also available*

Conversations with the Dead

A Knight's Quest

GUARDED

THE SILVERTON CHRONICLES


Ivy's neighbors have a secret. They aren't human. But Ivy has a secret, too. She knows. As long as everyone keeps quiet, she's happy working as a P.I. by day and chillaxing with her BFF Florian, a vampire, by night. When a routine pickup drops her in the middle of a murder, her two worlds collide. While Florian knows how to throw a punch, deep down he's a softie. His idea of scary? Running out of hair product. It's time Ivy faced facts. Even with a vampire on stand-by, one gal can only kick so many asses.

For help, she must put her faith in others. A human, who might just be the one. A demon, who will, for a price, open the doors to her heritage. And a werewolf, who wants to protect her from herself.

Torn between these men, Ivy must tread carefully, because one wants her heart, one wants her body, and one wants her dead.

MOON PROMISE

THE WILD PACK

All her life, Kensi has dreamed of being an alpha werewolf. The trouble is, she can't shift—and no one must know. Her plan B? Offering her talents as a private eye to the Wild Pack. If she can locate their missing werewolf, they're bound to support her claim to lead.

Stubborn and searing-hot Drake is assigned to be her guide. His constant push for dominance threatens the investigation from the start, yet far more dangerous are his mercury eyes. They watch her all the time, breaking down her defenses bit by bit. Unless she finds a way to control her growing feelings, he could uncover her secret before she even gets close to solving her case.

But when the missing girl turns up dead, Drake's story unravels...

# ABOUT
# CARMEN FOX

USA Today Bestselling Author Carmen Fox lives in the south of England with her beloved tea maker and a stuffed sheep called Fergus. She writes about smart women with sassitude and guys with an edge, and will chase that plot twist, no matter how elusive.

www.carmen-fox.com

facebook.com/authorcarmenfox

twitter.com/authorcarmenfox

goodreads.com/Carmen_Fox

# ABOUT
# CARMEN FOX

USA Today Bestselling Author Carmen Fox lives in the south of England with her beloved tea maker and a stuffed sheep called Fergus. She writes about smart women with sassitude and guys with an edge, and will chase that plot twist, no matter how elusive.

www.carmen-fox.com

facebook.com/authorcarmenfox

twitter.com/authorcarmenfox

goodreads.com/Carmen_Fox

# ACKNOWLEDGEMENTS

This book has quite a history. What you should take away from reading the acknowledgements is the amount of love and devotion that has gone into making it.

My first thanks go to the fantastic judges of RWA chapter contests who provided notes and repeatedly picked Divide and Conquer as a winner or finalist.

As always in my early days, Julie LaVoie was my first port of call, and she did an excellent job advising on, reviewing and improving every word. If I had any real power in the world, I'd make her re-join the world of writing. I miss you!

Finding a title for a book as crazy as this one wasn't an easy task. Paul Sadler and Carole Godley discussed different versions, and it was Carole who ultimately suggested Divide and Conquer. Thank you!

Many, many encouraging beta readers came to my aid when I needed advice and reassurance. Thank you Michelle, Kari, Mary, Renee, Kelli and many more. At this point I would also like to thank Mary Buckham (who has shaped so many aspects of my writing) and Anna J. Stewart, who both read this book and provided valuable feedback.

Cassie Knight first acquired Divide and Conquer for Champagne Books, where it was lovingly edited by Celia

Breslin. The final proofread was provided by Sharon Gibson, who quite simply rocks.

Once the rights reverted to me, I entrusted its second edit to the infinitely talented Dylan Quinn. As a friend she is kind, witty and tolerant. As an editor she is ruthless, thorough, and sarcastic—and also usually right. If you believe this book is too long, you have her to thank for it. Dylan, I couldn't do it without you!

The minute I came across Dandelion Cover Designs on Facebook, I fell in love with the formatting services, of which Divide and Conquer is just one fabulous example.

Getting a cover wasn't easy. I had a solid idea of what I wanted and how I wanted it. When my original designer dropped out of the project, the people at Deranged Doctor Design managed to fit me in. And boy, did they knock it out of the park. I love, love, love my covers. Thank you!

My warmest gratitude belongs to my readers, of course. This is my fifth full-length novel. If you didn't buy my books, well, I'd still write them, but I wouldn't be able to publish them. Hearing from you and reading your reviews is my greatest reward.

Finally, I want to thank my family for their love, and my mother in particular for her support. She is a talented, capable and generous woman who makes this world a better place for everyone who knows her. Danke!